The End of H

ETHERYA'S EARTH, BOC

By

REBECCA HEFNER

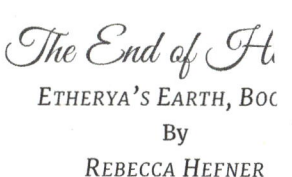

Copyright © 2018

RebeccaHefner.com

Julie,
Thank you for your support. Enjoy!

Rebecca Hefner

This book is a work of fiction. Names, characters, places and incidents are the product of the author's imagination and are used fictitiously. Any resemblance to actual events, locales or persons, living or dead, is coincidental.

Copyright © 2018 by Rebecca Hefner. All rights reserved, including the right to reproduce, distribute or transmit in any form or by any means.

Cover Design: Susan Olinsky Design
Editor: Megan McKeever, NY Book Editors
Proofreader: Bryony Leah, www.bryonyleah.com

To everyone who had a dream and was brave enough to pursue it...

Table of Contents

Title Page and Copyright
Dedication
Map of Etherya's Earth
Prologue
Chapter 1
Chapter 2
Chapter 3
Chapter 4
Chapter 5
Chapter 6
Chapter 7
Chapter 8
Chapter 9
Chapter 10
Chapter 11
Chapter 12
Chapter 13
Chapter 14
Chapter 15
Chapter 16
Chapter 17
Chapter 18
Chapter 19
Chapter 20
Chapter 21
Chapter 22
Chapter 23
Chapter 24
Chapter 25
Chapter 26
Chapter 27
Chapter 28
Chapter 29
Chapter 30
Chapter 31
Chapter 32
Chapter 33
Chapter 34
Chapter 35
Chapter 36
Chapter 37
Acknowledgments
About the Author

ETHERYA'S EARTH

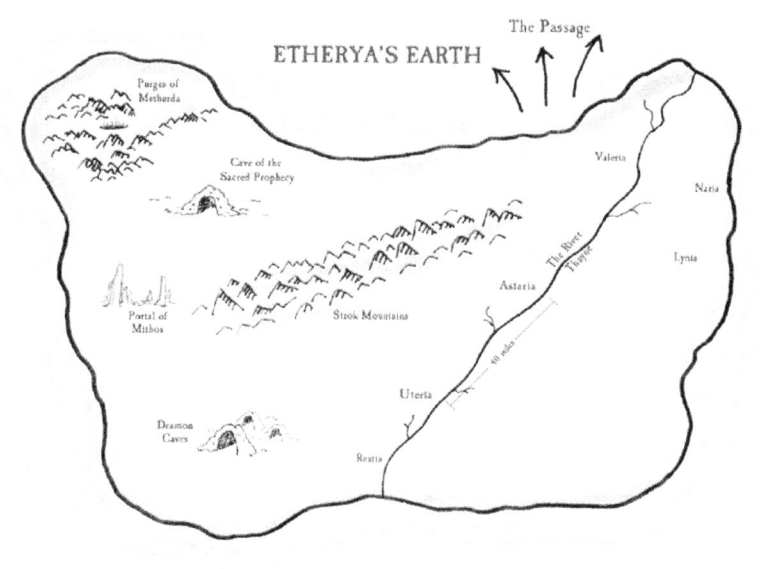

The Passage

Purges of Metherida

Cave of the Sacred Prophecy

Portal of Mithos

Strok Mountains

Valeria

Naria

Lynia

Astaria

The River Thappe

40 miles

Uteria

Deamon Caves

Rostia

HUMAN WORLD

Prologue

The goddess could remember the moment of Creation with great clarity. One minute, there was nothing, and the next, consciousness. Breath made of unseen particles filled her insides, and she was alive and whole. Waking to her experience, she saw the parallel universes as they multiplied and expanded beyond infinity. Out of the multitudes of universes, she was thrust into her own single galaxy, her own planetary system and, finally, her own solitary world where she would reign supreme in perpetuity.

The goddess Etherya was roused and resolute.

Knowing that she had been given great power, she began to build her planet with care. Tall, sweeping mountaintops crested with snow, which melted to form powerful rivers that flowed to the valleys. Luscious green trees filled the atmosphere with oxygen. Powderpuff clouds absorbed the moisture in the blue atmosphere and returned it to the soil with loving care.

Etherya's Earth was thriving.

But being a goddess was quite lonely, and she found herself longing for companionship. She would breathe out long sighs in solitude that whipped the tree branches for hours and caused the waves of the oceans to slap upon the shores.

When she could take no more, she created intelligent life.

With immense concentration, she spawned the Slayera, and they were beautiful. Gentle, loving creatures with no room in their hearts for hate or conflict. Etherya blessed them with immortality, and since they had nothing to fear, they were assured to live long lives in the infinity of the Universe.

Or, so Etherya thought.

Shortly after the creation of her beloved species, the Universe made its displeasure known. Etherya had created a flawless species but she, being imperfect herself, was not allowed to create perfection from imperfection. This would cause a great imbalance. Etherya begged and pleaded with the Universe to save the Slayera, and it took pity on her. She was permitted to create another species of immortal, one that would counterbalance the Slayera.

With her heart full of gratitude, she created the Vampyres: huge, hulking creatures skilled at fighting, combat and strategy. They were all things that were absent in the Slayera. At the Universe's command, she made both species interdependent upon each other. The Slayera would rely on the Vampyres for protection, and the Vampyres would need to drink Slayera blood to survive. Although her world was currently peaceful, she now recognized that the Universe could be fickle and volatile. Since the Slayera were innocent and vulnerable, having the Vampyres' protection gave her extra peace of mind.

They were two imperfect species living as one.

A yin to the yang.

The Universe also commanded that Etherya let humans exist and evolve on her world. They had done quite well on another planet, in a far-distant galaxy, and their ingenuity and intelligence would need to be tested in a new environment. The goddess had no need for humans, which she saw as bumbling and useless, especially in their mortality. But it was a small price to pay if she could keep her two beautiful species, both created from her womb, and envelop them in the harmony of her exquisite world.

Deamons also evolved, another species of immortal, but they were weak and chose to live in the darkness of their underground caves. The goddess regarded them as insignificant anomalies, beings that would never bother her precious species.

For thousands of years, the Slayera and the Vampyres coexisted in peace. Etherya would reward them with blazing sunsets, good harvests and sun-kissed days that turned into long, balmy nights. She was grateful for the abundance of happiness she felt when she smiled down on her small, precious sphere.

And then, in what was perhaps the blink of an eye in the span of things, all was shattered.

The night of the Awakening had come.

Excerpt from The Ancient Manuscript of the Slayera Soothsayers
Book 3 – The Awakening

Death's foul stench spread over the green grass of the Vampyre compound of Astaria.
Dense rain fell from the sky to mingle with the tears of few and the blood of many.
Hearts ceased to beat; souls that had lived so carefree were released to the Passage.
Lives of love and laughter perished, leaving behind only carnage and demise.
This was the night of the Awakening.
Our great and powerful King Valktor struck down our enemies, King Markdor and Queen Calla, with the Blade of Pestilence.
Once great allies turned upon us, choosing to call us "Slayers" instead of our formal name of Slayera.
Our people responded bravely, and the War of the Species began.
The balance of Etherya's Earth was destroyed.
Etherya was very angry and withdrew her protection from our people, showing her as the false goddess we always knew her to be...

Chapter 1

The Slayer compound of Uteria, 1000 years after the Awakening...

Miranda rode her stallion to the clearing by the river from where Kenden had radioed her. She probably should've stopped back at the main house and gotten one of the four-wheelers but she had already been riding Majesty and his large, black corpus felt reassuring beneath her. As she neared the clearing, she softly whispered to him.

"Whoa, boy. We're here."

With a caress of his silky mane, she jumped down and neared the few soldiers who were crowded around her cousin. Early morning light fingered softly through the clouds, and she could barely see his thick brown locks over the heads of the others.

"Kenden," she called softly, "what do we have?"

The soldiers parted, and her cousin motioned to her with his arm. As she neared, she huddled down to kneel beside the girl. Hair, black as a raven's wing, was down to her waist, wet and curled. Extremely pale skin covered her face except for the veins in her head, blue and angry.

"She's a Vampyre," Miranda breathed, struggling to keep her composure. "How did she come to be here?"

"She must've fallen in the river and hit her head," Kenden said as he lifted the hair near her nape to show a deep purple bruise along her thin neck.

"How is she not dead? She's been exposed to the sun."

Kenden shook his head. "I don't know, but she's alive. We have to figure out what to do with her."

Miranda nodded and stood, wiping her hands on her camouflage pants. "Get her to the castle and put her in the room by the gym. The one with no windows. No one is to see her, and you are to bind her hands and feet. Understood?"

Kenden nodded, reaching down to pick up the Vampyre. She was large, as all Vampyres were, but he lifted her as if lifting a feather from the ground. Such was the strength of the cunning Slayer commander. "Do you want to give her blood?"

"Yes." Miranda's eyes narrowed. "Have Sadie bring some up from the infirmary. No one else is to enter her room but you and Sadie. I want you there with me when she wakes." Walking up to her cousin, she added in a low voice, "And whatever you do, don't tell Father. He'll have a conniption if he knows there's a Vampyre on the compound. She may prove to be useful, and I want to question her before he has the chance to kill her."

Kenden nodded and loaded the Vampyre woman into his four-wheeler as the soldiers piled in after him. Inhaling a deep breath, Miranda walked back to inspect the site where the woman had been found. The river flowed onto their lands from the main Vampyre compound of Astaria, which was located some forty miles north. It seemed impossible that she could've floated the entire way, but in the land of Etherya, these were strange times and peculiar things happened more and more often lately.

"Who are you, Vampyre, and why did you wash up on our shores?" Turning to Majesty, she nuzzled his mane and sighed. "Ready to go, boy?" she asked, jumping onto her saddle, which rested firmly on the horse's back. "It's time for me to nurse a fucking Vampyre."

* * * *

Once back at the main house, Miranda did her best to avoid her father until after she had spoken to the Vampyre. Although she had become more adept at concealing her thoughts over the past centuries, she didn't want to lie to him unless absolutely necessary.

As she entered her chambers, she pulled the black fleece over her head, throwing it carelessly on the large four-poster bed. Catching a glimpse of herself in the armoire mirror, she grimaced slightly. Large, almond-shaped eyes the color of ripe green olives stared back at her, tired and wary. Straight black hair fell to her shoulders, and her slightly crooked nose bunched up in the reflection as she studied herself. With her black tank top, camouflaged pants and army boots, she looked more like a soldier than a princess. *As it should be*, she thought, giving herself a terse nod in the mirror.

Her mother had been a great beauty. According to the soothsayers who lived on the outskirts of the compound and told sweeping stories of days long past by the light of the campfires, Rina had been the most majestic creature that had ever lived amongst the Slayers. Void of vice, pure of spirit and true of heart, she had been a vision of all that was good and perfect for her people.

Rina's father Valktor, Miranda's grandfather, had been the first Slayer King, created from the womb of Etherya herself. He had been a resplendent figure and a magnificent king until his fateful decision to murder his Vampyre counterparts in cold blood.

No one had ever been able to account for Valktor's actions on the fateful evening of the Awakening.

Some said that he'd grown tired of having his people bank their blood for the Vampyres in exchange for protection and felt that he had the means to raise a strong and competent army himself.

Others proposed that he was looking for an alliance with the humans, and when that failed, he blamed it on the Vampyre King and Queen.

Still, others postulated that he simply went mad. For, shortly before his murderous rampage, his daughter Rina had been kidnapped by Crimeous, the evil Lord of the Deamons. Until Rina's kidnapping, the Deamons had been the most inconspicuous group of immortals, choosing to live in the darkness and recluse of their underground caves. After her abduction, the Deamons became a serious threat.

The Dark Lord was no longer content to live in the shadows and wanted dominion over all of Etherya's Earth.

It sure wasn't a great time for the Slayers, Miranda thought as she headed into the bathroom to give her face a quick wash and brush her teeth. Her people had transitioned from a peaceful, loving species to a kingdom besieged by war with two powerful foes. One thing she knew for certain? If this Vampyre woman had any importance to anyone of note at her compound, she would sure as hell exploit it to her people's full advantage.

The Slayers had lived in the shadows too long. Hunted by the Vampyres for their blood, and by the Deamons because of their own sick, twisted pleasure. Circumstances had to change.

She couldn't remember much of her grandfather, as she had only been eight years old when he'd perished after his murderous actions. But when she did reflect back on him, she thought of the valor and strength in his deep green eyes, the same color as her mother's; as her own. He had carried himself with the regal carriage of a great leader of a magnificent species, and it was time that she helped her people regain their footing in this world.

No one was going to hand them back their dignity. She was going to have to grab it from the clenching fists of her worst enemies. And damned if she wasn't up to the task. The time for cowering was over. Fate had sent them an opportunity in the form of a Vampyre washed up on the riverbank, and Miranda wasn't going to squander the chance to take the offensive.

With one more look of firm resolve at her reflection, she dried her face, threw the towel down on the bathroom counter and exited her chamber with a renewed sense of purpose.

* * * *

Arderin slowly came into consciousness with the knowledge that someone was nailing a hundred tiny screws into her brain. Any other option was unimaginable due to the splitting pain she encountered as she tried to suck in a breath. Finding that nearly impossible, she attempted to lift her hand to her throbbing head but realized, after a brief struggle, that she was restrained. Slowly, she lifted her lids.

As the room came into focus, she could see that she was on a large bed with four wooden posts at each corner. The room was dark, save for the dim light on the bedside table, and her feet and hands were bound with thick ropes, one to each bedpost. She was still wearing her dark blue dress from the party they'd been having in honor of Lila's birthday. She tried to piece together how she'd ended up in this strange place.

She remembered drinking a bit too much. Sathan had approached her and told her that she shouldn't have any more wine. Her oldest brother was quite protective of her. Although she loved him dearly, it sometimes infuriated her, causing her to overreact. She had spouted some diatribe to him about how she was her own woman and he couldn't tell her what to do. Then, she had left the party to go outside and get some air under the light of the full moon.

The last thing she could remember was standing by her favorite spot at the riverbed, in the shadow of the thick oak tree, wishing the gurgling water could take her anywhere but Astaria, which sometimes felt like a prison. Looking up at the stars, she had begged Etherya to take her away...somewhere...anywhere but there.

And then, she'd heard a rustling in the nearby bushes...hadn't she? Perhaps a beaver or a mole. And then—

Darkness.

Struggling to remember, she tried to sit up straighter, which was quite unfeasible due to her bound limbs.

Her head snapped toward the door as it opened, and two people, a man and a woman, entered. *Slayers*, she thought ruefully. The situation had just gone from bad to worse. She was being held captive by her people's sworn enemies.

"Who are you?" she demanded, wishing that her voice wasn't so shaky. "Release me at once! You have no idea how powerful the people are who are looking for me!"

The female Slayer walked toward the side of her bed and studied her. "We were hoping that was the case," she said, her eyes roaming over Arderin's form, most likely to make sure her bonds were still tight. "What is your name?"

Arderin kept silent, trying to determine what course of action was best. If she told them that she was the Vampyre princess, sister to the Vampyre King Sathan, she could become a powerful bargaining chip for blackmail. If she lied and told them she was no one, a commoner, then they might judge her as dispensable and kill her.

"I see you contemplating your options in your mind, Vampyre, and while I admire your spirit, it will do no good to lie to us. We will find out eventually who you are and will employ every means necessary to obtain the information."

Fear snaked around her heart, writhing and coiling, and she found herself wishing this were all a bad dream. How many times had Sathan warned her that her rebellious streak was going to eventually create a situation that he couldn't save her from? Looking to the sky, she made a silent promise to Etherya. She would never argue with Sathan again. Hell, she would tell him a hundred times over that he had been right and she had been wrong...if the goddess would be kind and spare her life.

"Praying to your goddess will do you no good here. Etherya abandoned our people after the night of the Awakening, and we consider her a false prophet. Appealing to her will only anger us more."

"You know nothing of Etherya," Arderin spat, enraged at the denigration of the goddess whom her people held dear. "She abandoned you because your people are sniveling weaklings who were only put on this Earth to be our food!"

The Slayer fisted a large mass of Arderin's hair in her hand, exacerbating the pounding that already existed there, and lowered her face so that their noses almost touched. "Antagonizing me isn't going to help you. Now, tell me your name and your station at Astaria."

Arderin studied the woman through her pain. How did she know that she hailed from the compound at Astaria? Was she bluffing? The Slayer woman's eyes were the deepest green she'd ever seen, and her hair was as black as her own, although it sat in a straight cut that fell to her shoulders, unlike Arderin's waist-long, curly tresses. Upon further reflection, she realized that the woman looked much like the Slayer Princess Rina, whom she had studied in her childhood when she was learning the history of the realm.

"You're Miranda, the Slayer princess," Arderin said, her voice tinged with a bit of wonder and a slice of fear. "If you think I'm going to tell you *anything*, you are sorely mistaken. I would rather die than help you. Go ahead and torture me or kill me, or whatever other plan you have, because I swear to the goddess, I'll never talk!"

The Slayer sighed and rolled her eyes, releasing her death-grip on Arderin's hair. "Good grief, are all Vampyres so dramatic?" Looking to the male Slayer in the room, she said sarcastically, "Remind me to brush up on *Days of Our Lives* this week so I can deal with Susan Lucci over here." The chestnut-haired male Slayer stood immobile, arms crossed over his chest, except for the slight lift of the corners of his lips.

"Look," she said, turning back to Arderin, "regardless of what you think, I have no desire to kill an innocent woman, even if she is of an inferior race." Arderin felt her nostrils flare with fury. "However, I will torture or even kill you if you don't give me what I want, so you have three hours to decide. After that, no more Ms. Nice Slayer, okay?"

When Arderin didn't answer her or even nod, the Slayer continued. "I'm guessing you understand me even though you're not answering. Our house doctor, Sadie, will be in later with some blood for you to drink from our infirmary. She's a hell of a lot nicer than me, so I expect you to be kind to her. Understood?"

Shaking her head at Arderin's lack of response, the Slayer turned to leave. "You have three hours, Vampyre. Think hard about how important living beyond tomorrow is to you. See you soon."

Arderin watched the Slayer exit the room, her male counterpart following behind. The door closed with a firm thud. Closing her eyes, she let the emotions swarm her, the pain overtake her, and allowed herself to cry.

The Vampyre Compound of Astaria

Something was very wrong. Sathan knew this in his gut even though he had no proof. After ruling his kingdom for a thousand years, he had learned to listen to the voice in his head. Instinct was something to be treasured, especially in these dark times, and it now had him coiled in its dark web.

Arderin was missing.

After she blew up at him, she had stormed out of the castle. Frustration led to him letting her go, realizing she needed to calm herself. She would've headed to the riverbank, her favorite patch of vibrant green grass under the oak tree beckoning to her. He had watched her stew in that spot many times after arguments, albeit from afar and without her knowledge. When they argued, he always felt terrible, promising himself he would be more patient with her next time.

His sister was a frustrating creature. The epitome of his beautiful mother, who had been slain before his eyes when he was only ten years old. He had never forgiven himself for what happened that day. Had he only stepped in, only pulled out the knife from his belt, all would be different. But he had stayed silent, frozen with fear. His inability to save her was his greatest failure.

He had vowed from that day forward to avenge his mother, his father and his people. Even at the tender age of ten, he knew that he would be the sworn protector of the realm. His need to protect his sister consumed him. As she grew into a woman and went through her immortal change in her twenties, she began to look more and more like Calla. Ensuring that she lived a full and happy life was his vow. He would protect her as he hadn't been able to protect his mother. He realized that this angered her and sometimes stopped her from seeing how desperately he loved her. Family was sacred, and he knew that his two brothers, Latimus and Heden, agreed.

Looking out the window of the king's royal office chamber, he could no longer ignore the feeling of anxiety in his lower stomach.

"No sign of her," Latimus said, his voice brisk as he rounded the corner of the entrance to the large room. "We have to send out a search party."

"Yes," Sathan said with a nod. Turning to Latimus, he sighed deeply. "I should've never engaged with her last night. She was having fun, and I was embarrassed that she had been drinking so much—"

"Regret is a waste of time," Latimus interrupted. His brother, less than two years younger than he, was known for his terseness and lack of giving a damn about politeness or courtesy. He was a man of few words and even fewer emotions. As the commander of the vast Vampyre army, Latimus was a warrior first and always. Pleasantries had no place in his world of war and strategy.

"I know," Sathan said, rounding the large mahogany desk to stand in front of his brother. Of all the siblings, Latimus favored Arderin the most. They shared the same raven-black hair, angular features, ice-blue eyes and long, thick eyelashes. Sathan had made fun of Latimus' eyelashes once when they were teens, comparing them to a girl's. His brother had proceeded to bash his face in, and although Sathan put up a good fight, it had been a losing one. He'd never picked on his brother's appearance again, that was for damn sure.

Such was the way of brothers. Although he and Latimus both had alpha personalities, dominant and domineering, they had an unbreakable respect for each other as men, soldiers and brothers. In a dire situation, he could think of no better ally than Latimus.

"Let's mobilize a search party within a fifty-mile radius. I'm sure she went to the river to stew after we argued. The dogs should be able to find her scent there."

Latimus nodded. "We'll find her." His boot steps sounded under his six-foot-nine-inch frame as he exited.

Sathan ran his hands over his face, his heart clenched with fear. "Damn it, Arderin, where the hell are you?"

Silence was the only answer from the empty room.

*Excerpt from **The Ancient Manuscript of the Slayera Soothsayers***
*Book 4 – **The Blade of Pestilence***

Our powerful lord and protector, King Valktor, used the Blade of Pestilence to strike down the evil King Markdor and Queen Calla at the Awakening.
Afterward, he traveled to the Cave of the Sacred Prophecy.
The Blade had been fashioned from poisoned steel so that the Vampyres' self-healing abilities could not save them from its wrath.
Inside the Cave, our King drilled into a large rock and placed the Blade inside.
Using his omniscient power, he placed a spell on the Blade.
It could only be excised if lubricated simultaneously by the combined blood of the first-born of a generation of his lineage and the first-born of a generation of Markdor's lineage.
The combined blood must fall straight from both first-borns' vein.
And so, with the War of the Species, the Blade is destined to sit still and unused for eternity...

Chapter 2

Arderin woke with a start and rubbed her tongue to the roof of her dry mouth. It tasted like sandpaper and salt. Thirst consumed her, and she wondered how long she'd been captive. Twenty-four hours? Forty-eight? Too much longer and she would be at risk of falling unconscious due to lack of Slayer blood.

She struggled against her binds, and a soft voice came from beyond the foot of the bed. "Oh, no, no, please, don't struggle," the tiny Slayer said quietly as she approached Arderin on her right side. "It will drain your strength, and the binds are so tight it's a waste of your energy. Here, drink this."

The Slayer lifted a metal cup to Arderin's lips, full of life-sustaining blood. Swallowing heartily, she licked her lips when finished. "Thank you. You must be Sadie. The Slayer bitch said you'd be nice to me."

"So, yeah, I'm going to pretend I didn't hear that. Blasphemy against our princess is a capital offense leading to severe punishment." She went back to the table at the foot of the bed and continued rummaging around. Arderin couldn't see much in the darkened room, so she listened to the Slayer's movements for any sort of clue on how to escape.

"I can't see your face," Arderin said.

The Slayer's motions ceased as the room grew quiet. Slowly, she approached the bedside again. "Do you want more?" she asked, her face obstructed by the hoodie she wore. Arderin could only make out the tip of her tiny nose and the shadow of thin lips.

She shook her head, unable to fathom drinking any more blood right now, as her stomach was queasy. "Do you hide your face on purpose?"

The Slayer returned to the foot of the bed, and the clink of the cup could be heard as she set it down. "I took a blood sample from you," she said softly. "As part of my Hippocratic oath, I feel compelled to tell you that. A patient shouldn't be tested without their knowledge."

Walking back over to the bed, the Slayer rested her palm against Arderin's forehead. "Due to your self-healing abilities, the cut on your neck is completely healed and you don't have a fever. Miranda will be able to tell by the purity of your blood how old your lineage is. If you are an aristocrat, I would tell her before the results come in. She is determined to use you, but I think you misunderstand her intentions."

Resting her hip on the side of the bed, she bit her lip with white teeth barely visible under the hood. Arderin got the sense she was choosing her words very carefully.

"I don't want to overstep, but our princess has become very progressive lately, diverging from her father, our king, on many matters to do with Vampyres. She is a kind-hearted leader looking to find a way to regain her people's freedom from persecution. Sometimes, one's greatest foe can become a great conspirator if they find a shared interest."

The Slayer rose from the bed. "Think about it."

"Wait," Arderin said, reaching for the Slayer but coming up short due to her bindings. "You are a trained doctor?"

"Yes."

"Where did you train?"

"I have trained with the humans in several specialties over many centuries. My small stature allows me to blend in with them quite nicely."

Arderin nodded. "I would like to train to become a physician one day as well. My family has a hard time understanding this because Vampyres have self-healing abilities, but I've always believed that knowledge can be used in many circumstances if one only chooses to look."

The Slayer might have smiled under the hood but Arderin couldn't be sure. "It is a noble profession and one that has brought me great joy. I don't have much in my life and being able to heal has given me a purpose."

"Is this why you conceal your face?"

The Slayer sighed and lifted her hands to the hood. Slowly, she eased the fabric from her head, and Arderin gasped. The woman's entire right side was burned to a mangled pulp. Grafts upon grafts of skin were layered together in a puzzle whose pieces would never fit. Saying that her appearance was grotesque would be putting it mildly.

"I was burned in the Purges of Methesda when I was young," she said, her tone sad. "There was nothing anyone could do."

In the dim light of the room, Arderin could see that the left half of her body appeared completely normal. She had pretty, light hazel eyes and short, chestnut brown hair, although it only covered one half of her head.

"I know someone who could help you."

The Slayer's expression lit with a brief flash of hope that was extinguished just as quickly. "I've visited the best human burn centers on the earth and no one can help me. But thank you all the same. I have learned to live with my scars and understand that my life was meant to be spent helping other people."

Even in her distressed state, kidnapped and bound, Arderin felt sorry for this woman. She reminded her of the wounded birds she sometimes found by the river. She would do her best to nurse them back to health, but even when their wings were repaired, their spirits never regained the will to fly.

"I know someone who has more knowledge than any human doctor—"

"You're very kind," Sadie interrupted. "Please, show some of that kindness to our princess. She is very interested in saving our people, and if she feels that you can help her do this, she will be amenable to getting you home safely. Good luck."

With that statement of finality, the Slayer lifted her hood back over her head and turned to leave the room.

Arderin's thoughts began to churn, and for the first time since her abduction, she felt a surge of hope. She was going to find a way to ingratiate herself to the Slayer princess bitch and get the hell out of this mess.

* * * *

Miranda exhaled in short, quick breaths as she neared the end of her workout. James Hetfield beckoned her to take his hand off to never-neverland and sleep with one eye open. Good advice. Humans were pretty useless in the broad scheme of things but they sure knew how to make some damn good music.

Finishing her run, the black belt of the treadmill came to a stop, and she grabbed for her towel. Rubbing it on her face, the water bottle beside her was drained in short order. Kenden entered the workout room as she stepped off the machine.

"Still listening to that human garbage?" he asked, one eyebrow arched.

"Blasphemy!" she joked, throwing the empty bottle into the blue recycle bin. "You'll hurt my boyfriend Lars Ulrich's feelings."

"If only he was so lucky," he said. "Speaking of, do you even care that Kalil is scheduled to visit next month?"

Miranda rolled her eyes. "Of course, I don't care. Father's been trying to get me to marry him since before the eight-shooter was invented. You'd think he'd get the hint by now."

"Your father, or Kalil?"

"Both," she muttered. "What's going on? Are the Vampyre's blood results in?"

Kenden nodded. "Her blood is purer than I've ever seen in all the samples we've collected from fallen soldiers over the years."

"Meaning?" Miranda asked.

"I think she's the king's sister. I looked through the soothsayer manuscripts for Queen Calla's picture, and she's a dead ringer."

"Holy shit," Miranda breathed. "We hit the jackpot."

"Yes," Kenden said, but his tone was hesitant. "I'm just not sure I trust the circumstances. I mean, the sister of the Vampyre king washed up on shore just like that? It seems so..."—he gestured with his hand, searching for the right word—"*convenient*. What if it's a trap?"

"Set by whom?" she asked. "Her brother, to entice us to contact him and then ambush us when we try to return her?"

"Maybe. Or perhaps by Crimeous. Perhaps he kidnapped her from Astaria and is trying to instigate further conflict between us and the Vampyres. The more we fight each other, the less time we spend tracking down the Deamons and destroying their caves."

Miranda inhaled deeply, contemplating. "Well, we know Crimeous isn't above such actions."

Kenden's expression transformed into the same one of love, pity and anger that it always did when they spoke of her mother's kidnapping and eventual murder by the Dark Lord of the Deamons. "Yes, we do," he said softly.

"I don't know. It does all seem a bit convenient but it's also a huge opportunity that I don't want to waste. I've been looking for a way to get the upper hand on the Vampyres for centuries. Those bastards have terrorized us with their raids long enough. If she truly is the king's sister, I have to take advantage of it."

Kenden nodded. "And what about Marsias?"

Miranda rubbed her forehead in frustration. "Father will never understand any attempt to negotiate with a species we are at war with. All he understands is conflict and battle. It's so fucking annoying. Instead of fighting with guns and fists, we could will them into submission. If she is the king's sister, he would most likely agree to anything to save her life. Even releasing his captive Slayers or stopping the raids."

"That's a large bet to place on a brother's love. Especially when it would be traded for the nourishment of all of the people of his kingdom. Most leaders would choose to sacrifice one for the sake of many, even if it were their sister."

"What if it were me?" she asked, looking up into his chestnut brown irises. "What would you do?"

He looked to the ceiling for a moment and considered. "I would find another way. One where I could still feed my people but also get the person I loved home safely."

"Okay." She sat on the black, padded workout bench and thoughtlessly tapped her fingers on her bottom lip. "What is the ultimate goal here, beyond the Vampyre woman and all the raids and battles? It's to end the fighting. To resume our lives without war with any species."

"Yes, that would be ideal. How would you accomplish that with one Vampyre hostage?"

"What if we could use her to help defeat the Deamons as well?" she continued, lost in her musings.

"I'm not sure we have a play with the Deamons here."

Standing up, she brushed off his mild objection as the gears in her mind shifted and swirled. "What if I could leverage this to get our hands on the one thing we know will defeat the Deamons? What if I could finally get the Blade of Pestilence?"

"The Blade of Pestilence?" Kenden said, taken aback. "Randi—"

"The king's blood for his sister's life," she interrupted. "Don't you see, Ken? It would allow me to have the upper hand over both species!"

"And you think the Vampyre king will just hand over the Blade to you once you pull it from the bloodstone?" he asked, his tone incredulous.

"I'll let him think I want a truce," she said, excitement for her plan overtaking her as she plodded on. "I'll tell him that we'll return his sister to him in exchange for helping me release the weapon. That we'll become allies and defeat Crimeous together and that our people will bank our blood for his again."

"But this will be a lie?"

"Yes," she said, running her fingers over the tiny black tail she'd pulled her hair into before her workout. "Once our shared bloodstream releases the Blade, I'll plunge it into his black, eight-chambered heart."

"Miranda," he said softly, always so calm in the face of her emotion, "you'd never be able to do it. To lie like that? To live with yourself afterward? To murder another in cold blood under less than honest circumstances? It would kill you."

"Bullshit," she said, frustrated that he couldn't see the brilliance of her plan. "Those monsters have raided our compound for centuries and killed our people without giving so much as a damn. I don't care what circumstances I kill them under. Any of them!"

"It's not you," he said. He stood firm in his belief in her goodness. "Whatever you think now, you would never be able to falsely negotiate a truce and then betray it. You're too noble."

"My grandfather was noble too and look where it got him. Where it got us!" she said, her anger palpable. "He finally took a stand and murdered those bastards."

"And look where we are now. Ravaged by war." Placing his hands gently on her shoulders, he continued, "You're better inside than any person—any leader—I've ever seen. You have more integrity in your little finger than anyone I've ever met, including your father or your grandfather. I won't let you talk yourself into doing something that isn't worthy of you."

"I'm tired of being worthy while my people suffer," she said and pushed his arms away. "Either you're with me or against me on this."

"I'm not going to waste time arguing with you when you're agitated," he said. His cool composure furthered her ire. "There are other options, and we need to look at all scenarios before we make a decision."

Before either of them could speak, a voice bellowed from the hallway, "Miranda!"

"Shit, it's Father," she said. "He must've found out about the Vampyre."

"Don't engage with him now, Randi," Kenden warned. "You're not in the right state of—"

"I'm in exactly the right state, and don't start fucking speaking to me like a child, Ken. I'm the princess of this realm and I'll be damned if I let you or my father or anyone else keep us on this path of destruction. Someone has to take the offensive, and I plan to be the one to do it."

"Miranda!" her father's voice beckoned once more.

"Go," Kenden said, shoving her toward the door. "I can buy you ten minutes to cool down."

"Screw your ten minutes," she said as she walked out the door. "It's about time he saw me angry."

Excerpt from The Ancient Manuscript of the Slayera Soothsayers
Book 5 – The Prophecy of the Death of the Deamon Lord Crimeous

Before the great King Valktor took his life in the Purges of Methesda, he had a great vision: The Dark Lord Crimeous, King of the Deamons, would be killed by one of Valktor's own lineage. This Slayera descendant of Valktor would kill the Dark Lord with the Blade of Pestilence. The Blade would strike him down with one sure thrust.
Knowing this prophecy was abiding and true, King Valktor sacrificed his life to the Purges of Methesda.

Chapter 3

Her father stood in his royal office chambers stooped over the window, his palms resting flat on the sill. Fury emanated from his stiff, hunched shoulders. Miranda stilled and took a moment to silently observe him. Sadly, this had become the norm for them. Their relationship had deteriorated so badly that she sometimes feared it was beyond repair.

Her first memory of her father was of him smiling at her as they had their weekly tea parties. Sitting on the floor across from her, the tea cup where she deposited her pretend liquid always looked so small in her father's large hand. He would lift his little finger and smile at her with love shining in his eyes as he sipped the nonexistent drink.

Even after thousands of years, she still remembered how he would shower her with affection. "You're so beautiful, my darling girl, just like your mother," he would say, and she would beam with his praise. "You are all that is good and just in this world. Daddy loves you with all his heart." He would slide his fingers in an X across his chest and then lift his hand to blow her a kiss. She would mime catching it with her tiny fist and giggle up at him.

Those first years had been so precious and so few. When she was eight years old, her mother had been kidnapped by Crimeous, and her grandfather had murdered the Vampyre royals. All had changed in the blink of an eye. Her father, who had loved her mother with intense passion, had quite literally become another person. Consumed with despair that he couldn't locate his wife and new threats from the Vampyres, he channeled all his energy into defending his people. Miranda devolved into an afterthought of his; a daughter he still cared for but whom he had no time to nurture.

Miranda had never blamed her father. She still didn't. He had dedicated his life to saving their people. How could she fault him for that? Knowing that he hadn't the capacity nor the time to focus on her, she became independent very quickly. At just thirteen years old, she approached Kenden, asking her cousin to train her to fight. At first, he resisted, but she had been so steadfast and resolved that he began training her at night so her father wouldn't find out. The Slayers were a traditional people with long-standing defined roles for women. Being a skilled warrior was absolutely not on the public agenda for Miranda.

On her eighteenth birthday, she had been surprised to find a small, wrapped box on her bed with a pretty black bow on top. Thinking that it was from her father, she was thrilled, as this was the first time he'd remembered her birthday since the Awakening. Instead, she was horrified to find that the box contained a severed finger. Inside, there was a small piece of folded paper that read:

I have decided to kill your mother slowly, as she no longer pleases me.

To say that her innocence was shattered that day would be a vast understatement. She ran to find her father, but he was held up in a meeting with the military leaders. When she finally cornered him later in the day, he'd snapped at her.

"What's so important, Miranda? I have too much work to do to have dinner with you this evening. Just have the cook prepare something for you."

"But Father—"

"Not right now. We think the Vampyres might attempt another raid tonight. We'll talk in the morning."

He had placed a quick kiss on her forehead and stalked off to the war room.

In that moment, she realized several things. One was that her father would never see her as an equal. She couldn't be sure if this was due to the fact she was female, or that she was still so young, but it was true, nonetheless. Second, she realized that she was an inconvenience to her father. A distraction from his true job of protecting his people. Lastly, she realized that with her mother's kidnapping and the threat to her people, he might not have any capacity left to love her.

Vowing to be strong as a princess should be, she kept the devastating "present" to herself. A few days later, during one of her evening training sessions with Kenden, he had noticed her mood.

"Your heart's not in it today, Randi. What's going on?"

"Nothing," was her quick reply. "Let's go another round."

"Not until you tell me what's up," her cousin had prodded, his worry for her evident in his deep brown eyes.

Deciding that she needed to tell someone, she'd led him to her bedroom and pulled out the tiny box. Allowing her weakness to show to him, whom she trusted fully, she had cried on his shoulder as he held her. Afterward, they'd trekked to Miranda's favorite spot by the river. The moonlight cast a pale shade under the gnarled branches of the nearby tree as they buried the small digit in the soil of the grassy riverbank. Saying a soulful prayer of remembrance, he'd held her shoulders with his firm arm, giving her strength. Water flowed in tiny ebbs over the smooth rocks as they stood in stony silence. An unbreakable bond had formed between them.

Every year, on her birthday, she would find a small wrapped box with a pretty black bow on top of her bed. Every year, it would contain a finger or toe from her mother's hand or foot. Twenty years, twenty digits. And then, the boxes stopped coming. Miranda knew that her mother was dead.

She and Kenden would still take time each year to visit the riverbank. They would stand mostly in silence, lost in their thoughts, taking solace in each other's strength. After saying a prayer for her mother, they would then return to the compound to rejoin her father, who never knew of the boxes or the ritual.

Miranda figured she should be alarmed that someone was able to penetrate their compound each year and leave the boxes on her bed. Who were they from? Were they delivered by Crimeous himself, or one of his minions? Instead, she'd always felt a bit grateful. Someone was delivering a piece of her mother to her that she could bury and remember. Fear no longer had a place in her world and losing her ability to feel that emotion would bring heartache down the road.

As the centuries wore on, they fell into a pattern. Kenden continued to train her, and her father continued to rule the kingdom and ignore her. Eventually, Marsias found out about her secret training sessions and scolded her in his ever-condescending manner. But he didn't make her stop. Perhaps he realized that if she was occupied with becoming a soldier, she wouldn't have time to bother him.

Looking at him now, both angry and dejected, caused a small bit of guilt to pinch her gut, but she dismissed it. Now was not the time to be timid. Inhaling deeply, she came to stand in front of his large mahogany desk.

"Father," she said.

"Goddamnit, Miranda," he said, not turning from the window. "What the hell are you doing?"

"If you give me a minute, I think you'll see that we have a great opportunity here—"

"We?" he yelled, rotating to face her. "We?" He began to approach her slowly. "*We* had no part in sheltering a Vampyre on this compound. How dare you keep this from me? If you were anyone but my daughter, I would have you executed for treason!"

Her chin jutted up and she looked her father in his coffee-colored eyes. They were so much like Kenden's except they lacked the warmth she always saw in her cousin's. "She is the sister of the Vampyre King. We have a huge opportunity to negotiate her release."

"You misunderstand your place here, Miranda. I am the king of this species, and I make all negotiating decisions. You had best remember this and explain to me why you didn't notify me right away of her presence on this compound!"

"These are my people too, Father!" she said, exasperated. "I only want to help! I'm so tired of the endless war and abduction. Don't you see that we're slowly killing ourselves? We have to find another way out of this mess, especially with the Deamons attacking us too. I thought we could figure out a way to negotiate her release to help us defeat both species."

His responding laugh was full of anger and indignation. "And what do you know of negotiating? You were just a child during the Awakening. You know nothing of the cost of war."

"Of course, you relegate me to the position of child even though I've been a woman for centuries. A fully grown, strong, smart woman who could help you rule this kingdom if you gave me half a chance!"

"Not again, Miranda. I'm not getting pulled into this age-old argument we always have. You have the blood of Valktor running through your veins. It is time you got married and produced an heir so that he can fulfill the prophecy. That is how you can help your people."

She shook her head and gave a humorless laugh. "Because the one who frees the Blade must be male."

"Of course, he must be male," he said.

"The prophecy states that a descendant of Valktor's will kill Crimeous with the Blade of Pestilence. It never mentions that the descendant must be male. What if I am the one who will slay the Dark Lord?"

"Ridiculous," he said, bringing his index finger and his thumb to pinch his nose in frustration. "You are no soldier. I let you fight with Ken because it seems to make you happy. However, you will always be a woman, smaller and weaker than any man. Women have no place fighting in combat. Do you really think that you could slay Crimeous, who killed your mother and has evaded us for centuries?"

"Yes." She nodded firmly, crossing her arms. "If I had the Blade of Pestilence, I believe I could."

"This is nonsense," he said, dismissing her with a wave of his hand. With a long exhale, he sat on the edge of his desk. "Your decision to harbor the Vampyre woman and to hide her from me is inexcusable. I'm sending out a royal decree that you are to be sanctioned. I'll be sending you to Restia, where you will stay with Kalil's mother. She's already expecting you, and I've promised her you'll be biddable and willing to spend time with Kalil. It is time you married and produced an heir, Miranda. That is your duty to your people, and I have let you shirk it for too long."

"How dare you," she said. Her arms slid to her sides, her fists clenched so hard her fingernails must be drawing blood. "You have no right."

"I have every right. I am the king of the species, and you are their princess. If you won't choose to do the right thing, then I'll force you to. If it takes a royal decree, then so be it."

She studied her father's expression, so impassive, so firm. How had it come to this? She had placed herself on the front lines countless times during the raids over the past centuries. She had fought valiantly, showing her love for her people in a way that she considered much more powerful than jailing herself in a loveless marriage.

"How can you doubt my love for our people?" Emotion crushed her throat, and she fought to keep it out of her voice. "How can you think that I don't strive every day to protect them?"

"When you harbor the enemy under our roof and keep it from your king, you are harming your people. Not to mention committing treason."

"Treason," she said, her tone mocking. "You really want to go there?"

"What choice have you left me? Your constant defiance cannot go unchecked. I won't allow our people to suffer because you are an impetuous child who refuses to grow up."

"And I won't allow our people to suffer because they are ruled by a king who refuses to do anything but constantly go to war. If you won't even consider negotiating, I will have to consider the detriment you're causing our people."

"Meaning?" he asked.

"Meaning that I will no longer support you as king."

As she said the words, her heart constricted, and sadness swamped her. She loved her father intensely and thought him a magnificent and strong leader. Her support was important to his rule, and tiny pangs of hurt fluttered in her belly as she contemplated how her words must have wounded him.

His face contorted into an intense expression of fury.

"You forget your place, Miranda."

"No," she said, shaking her head firmly. She straightened and lifted herself to her full height. "I think it's time I finally remembered my place, Father. If you choose to banish me by royal decree, I will have no choice but to publicly separate from you."

He scoffed with rage. "So, this is the path you choose to take? Although you are my daughter I have no qualms about banishing you from Uteria." He stood and loomed over her. "I will give you the night to think it over. Tomorrow, I will send out the royal decree. It will either detail your sanction to Restia or your banishment from our realm altogether. Don't force me to choose."

A dull, ringing sound pounded inside her ears. Heart beating furiously in her chest, she understood that she was at the crossroads of the most important moment in her life. One path led to giving her standard apology to her father and having him send her to Restia. Once there, she was sure that she could eventually figure out how to get out of marrying Kalil and find her way home.

The second path was obscure, unclear. Filled with self-doubt and unknowns. It was the path that would force her to do the one thing she had never been able to do: defy her father. It also opened the door for her to accomplish what she coveted above all else: peace for her people.

"We always seem to get here, don't we?" she asked. Lifting her hand, she placed her palm over his heart. "For centuries, we've danced the same dance. I defy you, you scream at me, I apologize, and you forgive me. That's some sick, twisted form of love in itself, isn't it?"

Placing his hand over hers on his chest, he sighed. "I've tried to love you as best I could. It was just so hard when your mother was taken and after the Awakening. I see now that I've failed you in so many ways. This is not a punishment, Miranda. It is my attempt to do the right thing. You must know that."

In that moment, she knew he spoke the truth. He was attempting to do what he thought was right. Unfortunately, she thought, as her heart splintered, she and her father no longer shared the same definition of right and wrong. Knowing what she must do, she leaned in and hugged him with all her strength.

"I'll be ready to go to Restia in one week's time," she said, her cheek against his chest. "What do you plan to do with the Vampyre girl?"

"Kill her, of course." His words vibrated from his throat against the top of her head. "I'll tell Kenden to drug her and shoot her with the eight-shooter after she's unconscious, so that she won't suffer or feel any pain. It's the least I can do for an innocent woman who had the misfortune to wash up on our riverbank."

"That's very kind," she said, her voice hoarse. "I'm sorry I didn't tell you."

"I know, darling," he said, kissing her on top of her head.

"I love you, Father."

"I love you too. You will make Kalil a fine wife and have so many beautiful children. Your mother will look down from the Passage and be so proud of all of the children you spawn."

"Yes," Miranda said, knowing this was what he perceived her value to be. A brooding mare for Slayer heirs.

Disengaging from him, she walked to the door, then turned back to look at her father for what might be the last time. "See you tomorrow."

It was the first outright lie—not just a lie of omission—that she had ever told him.

* * * *

As soon as she left her father's office, Miranda knew what she must do. She had little time and even fewer people she could trust with her plan.

She found Kenden in his shed, which sat near the compound wall, quite far from the main castle. This was his private place where he came to be alone with his thoughts. Over the centuries, he had lined the wooden walls with rare weapons he had collected. Some human, some Vampyre, some Deamon...they all were precious pieces to the Slayer commander. He was a thoughtful student of history and strived to understand the outcome of every war that had been fought so that he could strategize more effectively for his people.

When she entered, he was sitting at the cedar table he had fashioned for himself, studying maps of the Deamon caves. The pale light filtered over his brown hair and broad shoulders. His looks favored her father's so much, and she knew that leaving him would be a thousand times harder than leaving anyone she'd ever known.

"Well, he's banishing me to Restia," she said, trying her best to keep her tone light. "It's been nice knowing ya."

Kenden's head snapped up and he scowled. "What?"

"He's sending me to Restia to marry Kalil. He's going to ask you to kill the Vampyre woman later this evening. I'm wondering if I should ask you to just off me too since getting married might be worse than death."

"Wow," he said, his cheeks puffing as he blew out a breath. "That's harsh."

"No less than what I deserve, I guess, for harboring a Vampyre and hiding it from him."

"Right," Kenden said, his tone flat.

"Well," she said, kicking the ground with her shoe, "I wanted to say thanks for helping me with the Vampyre and all. I really thought that this was a chance for us to have the upper hand, but my fossil of a father just wants to keep us in a state of constant war. Oh well, he'll have to live with that, I guess. I'm off to bed. Just wanted you to know that, um, I really appreciated your help with...everything," she finished lamely. "Night."

"Whoa," her cousin said. He stood and walked toward her. Grabbing her lower arm, he turned her toward him. "What are you doing, Randi?"

"Going to bed. I just told you."

"Uh huh. Just like that. No fight? No argument? Just, '*Oh, my dad's sending me to another compound to get married,*' and you're going to bed?"

"Yep," she said, gazing up at him, trying to control her broken smile. "I love you, you know."

"Fuck, Miranda," he said softly, grabbing her other arm as well. "You can't do this. It's insane. You'll die the moment you step onto their compound. I won't let you do it."

Her heart squeezed with love for this man who would always be the most important person in her life. They had shared so much. So much pain and loss. So much war and hate. He was more of a father to her than her own had ever been. More of a brother than a cousin. "I don't know what you're talking about, Ken. It's late. I'll see you in the morning."

"Enough," he said softly and pulled her toward the table so that they could both sit. "You don't know me at all if you think I would let you engage with the Vampyres without protection." Pulling out a notebook, he grabbed a pen. "Let's make a plan. Quickly, since we don't have a lot of time."

Heart swelling with love, they began discussing the plan that would change her future and, if all went well, the course of history for her people.

They decided that she would take a Hummer with dark tinted windows so the Vampyre's skin wouldn't burn. Kenden would send two soldiers along with her to guard and protect them. He also persuaded her that Sadie should accompany them. Although she didn't like the idea, the Slayer physician could help keep the Vampyre in an unconscious state and bring her to consciousness when needed. Miranda felt wary about putting her friend in danger but ultimately agreed that it was the right choice.

Understanding that they needed to ensure their compound wouldn't be raided for blood while Miranda was traveling with the Vampyre princess, Kenden agreed to bank the soldiers' blood from the infirmary and deliver it to an agreed-upon spot outside Astaria's wall daily at dusk.

Finally, after almost an hour, the plans had been solidified.

Giving her cousin one last hug, Miranda pulled away from him to return to the castle.

"Take this," he said, handing her a small cell phone. "You won't have service when you get past the Portal of Mithos, but until then, you can call me anytime. It will be untraceable by your father."

"Thank you, Ken." Taking the small device, she gave him a tiny smile and exited the shed.

Once in her chambers, she showered, put on her camouflage pants, black tank top and boots, and loaded up a backpack with supplies. Then, she headed to find the Vampyre whose fate, whether she liked it or not, was now inexorably tied to her own.

Excerpt from The Ancient Manuscript of the Slayera Soothsayers
Book 6 – The Vampyre Raids

Needing Slayera blood to sustain them, the Vampyres raided Uteria.
Their reserves had run dry, and they were no longer receiving the shipments of banked blood from the Slayera, their now-sworn enemy.
In the darkness, they came, their savage screams waking the sleeping Slayera.
Our powerful King Marsias grabbed his sword and fought with strength and valor.
That night, thirty Slayera men were lost.
Showing a twisted sense of honor, the Vampyres did not abduct any women or children.
King Marsias knew there would be more raids and began to build a powerful army to protect his people.
He enlisted his nephew, who was cunning and resilient, to form the military.
Our noble Commander Kenden proceeded to build a great militia and awaited the next raid.
The raids would continue for eternity, as peace had become a distant memory.
All hope for a reconciliation of the tribes was lost...

Chapter 4

Kenden contemplated why he didn't try to stop her. As her closest advisor, he could've talked her out of the seemingly impossible plan she was embarking on.

And yet, he'd let her go.

After their meeting, he showered and sat down in his bedchamber to prepare for the next morning's training with his army, feeling restless. He hadn't stopped her because, deep down, he knew she was right. Their people could not go on like this. They had lived with unending war and persecution for centuries. Unless the cycle was broken, there was no end to the pattern. They were no better than rats on a wheel, doomed to live in a cage of their own making.

Knowing he would get no sleep this night, he waited for Marsias to summon him to execute the Vampyre, unaware that Miranda would have already absconded with her.

His cousin was the descendant of Valktor. Being a woman in their tiny world of tradition, she had always been dismissed by his uncle. But he knew her to be strong—so much stronger than she, or anyone else, gave her credit for. He hoped Miranda would call upon all of her strength for the road that lay ahead. Their people were in dire need of a new vision, a new leader.

He had absolute faith that she was up to the task.

Around four o'clock in the morning, he heard the banging. Opening his bedroom door, the king stood on the other side. "Where is the Vampyre?" he asked.

"I don't know," Kenden replied. At least this was truthful.

"Where is Miranda?" Marsias asked.

Kenden contemplated lying to his king, an action that held considerable consequences. "She's gone."

"And you let her go?"

Kenden felt his lips draw into a thin line. "I think the time of you or I letting Miranda do anything is over."

Anger flashed in his eyes. "You would dare betray me too, the commander of my army and my own nephew?"

"You've grown paranoid, Marsias," Kenden said, keeping his tone calm and clear. "I'm still here and will fight and defend our people until our last days. But Miranda is Valktor's heir. His blood runs strong through her. We must give her the latitude to protect our people in whatever way she sees fit."

"I knew it was a mistake to let you train her," he spat. "You've filled her head with notions of grandeur that will be her undoing!"

"And you've denied her the right to rule her people for too long. I won't fight you on this, Uncle. I will set out to train the troops at daybreak as I always do. But don't ask me to choose between you. I think you know who I'll pick."

"Treason," the king whispered, anger seething in his brown eyes.

"No, just reality. Have faith in your daughter. She's stronger than you've ever been able to see."

"I see her just fine, insolent child."

"No, you don't," Kenden said, struggling to contain the small bubble of anger that was welling in his chest. "You don't know half of what she's struggled with in this life." He thought of all of the times he'd held her by the riverbank. "She's lost so much. You should be grateful that she hasn't yet lost the ability to fight for her people."

Marsias scowled. "I'll figure out what to do with this situation—and with your insolence—tomorrow. Don't let anyone know that she has defected. I want them to think that she is at Restia."

"You have my word," Kenden said with a nod.

After another scowl, Marsias stalked off.

Closing the door, Kenden said a silent prayer for his cousin. The one remaining descendant of Valktor was very important. He was determined to make sure his soldiers kept an eye on her and that she stayed alive.

The future of their people depended on it.

* * * *

Sathan lifted the binoculars and scanned the horizon for any sight of his sister. She had now been gone almost three full nights, and he realized that with every passing moment, the chances of finding her alive were diminishing.

"Nothing is disturbed for twenty miles," his brother said from behind. "We should keep moving down the river."

"It's almost daybreak," Sathan said. He threw the binoculars on the ground and screamed a loud curse. "How can we find her when we're relegated to searching in the dark like animals? I'm so tired of this fucking curse. When will Etherya realize that we are still her faithful servants and end this?"

Latimus latched his beefy hand onto Sathan's shoulder. "One day, brother, the sun will shine upon us again. There must be an end to the darkness if we only keep our faith."

Sathan ran his fingers through his thick, wavy hair. "I hope so. Gather the party. Let's get back to the compound. No good will be done if we incinerate ourselves while searching for her."

Latimus placed his index finger and thumb in his mouth and let out a loud whistle. The members of the search party all scattered to the various four-wheelers to head home.

Once back at the compound, Sathan went to his royal office chamber and poured a hefty amount of Slayer blood into the metal goblet that sat upon his desk. Ingesting the liquid, he reveled in the taste of it, rusty and dense. If only Etherya hadn't created a world where Vampyres needed Slayer blood to survive. How different would his life be now? What world could he have built for his people? He swallowed the rest of the blood, along with a good bit of bitterness, and headed down to the dungeon.

Once there, he walked along the darkened hallway past the cells, many of them containing a male Slayer who had been captured in their last raid. Coming to the end of the hallway, he entered the infirmary and addressed the man in the white lab coat.

"How many are left, Nolan?"

The doctor turned away from the counter scattered with medical equipment and looked at his king. "Only eight, I'm afraid. They keep killing themselves even though we've promised them no harm if they bank quietly and peacefully."

Sathan studied the human. Dr. Nolan Price had come to live on his compound under the most peculiar circumstances. Due to his actions to protect Sathan on the fateful day they met, and his discovery of the Vampyres, Etherya had granted the man immortality. For three hundred years, he had lived on the compound and used his medical knowledge to try to extend the lives of the Slayers they abducted.

His job was quite difficult though, as the bastard Marsias had commanded all abductees to commit suicide upon capture. This left Sathan with a rather strange task. He must abduct Slayers so that he could bank their blood, but also wanted to extend the prisoners' lives so that he could perform fewer raids on their compound. If only their idiot king could see how futile this was.

He had tried over the centuries to show some sort of goodwill and gestures of kindness to the inferior species. He had never abducted any women or children and made it illegal for any soldier to do so. No matter how bloody the war, he wished to retain as clean a conscience as possible.

The orders were clear: abduct only twenty to thirty men at a time. The people of his kingdom, with their four compounds, could survive on the banked blood of thirty Slayers. A Vampyre needed to drink Slayer blood every two to three days to stay alive. Based on that knowledge, he thought the Slayer king would give up the first thirty soldiers after the first raid and be done with them.

But no. The Slayer king was stubborn. This frustrated Sathan to no end. Couldn't he see that he didn't want to murder his people? That the raids were a blight on his soul that he could barely tolerate?

"Of course not," he muttered to himself, rubbing his forehead in frustration.

"What was that?" Nolan asked.

"Nothing. Do everything you can to keep this batch of soldiers alive. I don't want to plan another raid while we're still searching for Arderin."

"Will do," the human said. "I miss my little student with her big smile and curious mind. I hope you find her soon."

Sathan nodded. "Me too. I'm happy to hear that she smiles at you. At least I know that someone makes her happy."

"You're a good brother, Sathan," he said. "She loves you with all her heart. She's just stubborn and willful. Like some others I know," he finished wryly.

"Truer words, my friend," Sathan said, patting the doctor on the shoulder. "Keep them alive," he commanded once more before turning to walk back down the dark corridor. When he was in the middle of the murky hallway, surrounded by the Slayers in their cells, he spoke to them in the darkness.

"I do not wish to harm you, Slayers. I only wish to harvest your blood to keep my people alive. Each one of you who dies represents another soldier that we have to rip away from their post, from their loved ones. I know your king has given you orders to end your life but think of your fellow Slayers. They benefit from you staying alive."

His statement was met with mutterings from the dim cells. *Fuck you, Vampyre...blood sucking murderer...I'll die before I feed one more Vampyre scum...*

He'd heard it all before but it still never ceased to amaze him how deep the hatred was. They would rather sacrifice their life, and the countless lives of their fellow soldiers, than feed his people.

And didn't that just fucking suck.

With a resigned sigh, the Vampyre king exited the dungeon.

Excerpt from The Ancient Manuscript of the Slayera Soothsayers
Book 7 – The Invention of the Mighty Eight-Shooter

Due to their self-healing abilities, our mighty Commander Kenden found the Vampyres extremely difficult to injure.

Their capacity to die in battle was even rarer.

Knowing that he had to create a weapon that would stop our slaughter by our evil enemy, the great Commander Kenden invented the eight-shooter.

The weapon, fashioned from wood and later from steel, would deploy eight small bullets at once.

The bullets would pierce each chamber of a Vampyre's eight-chambered heart simultaneously.

This meant certain death for the Vampyres, and our great people began to emerge as equals in the War of the Species.

Chapter 5

Marsias could remember the first time he saw Rina. Clear as day, the image was burned into his brain like a brand on a grazing animal's skin. He had been so young, a man of only twenty, full of hope and life. His father, the great Slayer aristocrat Attikus, had sent him to the castle to meet with King Valktor. Attikus was ready to retire from the council and wanted Marsias, his first-born heir, to take his place. The king had agreed to meet with him to assure he was worthy, and he was determined not to let his father down.

As he approached the castle, with its cold gray stones and imposing mahogany doors, he heard the most amazing sound. Like a melody that was played by the sweetest symphony, a woman was laughing nearby. Turning his head, he looked through the window of the castle.

She sat on a high-backed chair, holding a glass of champagne. Surrounded by other women, she was the only one who existed in his eyes. Opening her perfect, pink lips, she threw her head back, laughing so thoroughly that he wished he'd heard the joke. The slim line of her neck beckoned for his caress, and her straight, raven-black hair fell to her waist since her head was tilted back.

Unable to move, he stared at her, the most beautiful creature he'd ever seen. As if Etherya herself slowed the progression of time, the woman slowly raised her head and turned her face to him. White teeth formed a glowing smile as she locked onto his eyes.

Any breath that was left in his now shaking lungs was expelled when he saw the deep green of her irises. His shattered mind could only form one word: *mine*.

Regaining his composure, he met with Valktor, and the king, whom he'd always found to be kind and jovial, approved his request to take his father's place on the council. Pride surged through him that he would be able to represent his people with honor.

After their meeting, Valktor walked him to the sitting room.

"Ladies," the king said, addressing the five women who were sitting in the plushy chairs, "this is Marsias. He will be taking his father's place on the council."

The women all rushed to shake his hand. After all, a handsome young aristocrat was a valuable asset to an unwed Slayer female. Only one hung back, refusing to leave her seat. After greeting the other women, he approached her.

"Hello," he said, bowing. "It is a pleasure to meet you, Princess Rina."

She gave a nod and saluted him with her champagne glass. "The pleasure is mine. I am very fond of your father. I hope you have what it takes to replace him."

Marsias smiled. "I look forward to impressing you, princess."

She'd arched one of her dark, perfect eyebrows. "That's not easily accomplished."

"Challenge accepted," he said, lifting his own brow.

Her response was another brilliant laugh, causing his heart to pound in his chest. Vowing to claim her, to win her, he got to work.

Their courtship was encompassing. Filled with laughter and joy, frustration and tribulation. For Rina was her own woman. She knew what she wanted and pushed Marsias to be better, to give her more than he'd ever known he could give.

She'd made him a better person, and he'd loved her mindlessly.

They married in a beautiful ceremony, flowers swirling around them as they dropped from the altar under which they stood. The sun shone bright in the sky, and the Slayers rejoiced. Valktor had shaken his hand, sadness in his eyes, and made Marsias promise to protect his daughter with his life. It was a promise that he took very seriously.

Their marriage was amazing and intense. Rina was a force to be reckoned with, exhibiting a stubborn streak and an annoying habit of always thinking she was right. Her nature was also quite reckless, and Marsias would scold her when he found her swimming too close to the rapids in the river or riding her horse outside the compound's walls.

But she was also the most amazing person he'd ever met. Her beauty was ethereal, and her heart was full of compassion and love. She spent her days doing her best to improve her peoples' lives. At night, when he would hold her, he would pray to Etherya, thanking her for his breathtaking wife.

After a while, a kernel of fear began to grow in his gut. Happiness, like he'd never even dreamed, had pervaded his world. What if something happened to her? How would he go on? In the dimness of their bedchamber, she would hold him and tell him not to worry. Promises of forever fell from her lips as he loved her, always needing more, telling himself not to ruin their joy.

When she got pregnant, he thought his heart might burst. Seeing her round with his child was a fantasy come true. She would laugh in her melodic way when he placed his ear on her stomach to listen to the baby's heartbeat.

Their daughter, Miranda, was born on a sunny day, like most were on Etherya's Earth. As Marsias held the tiny creature in his arms, he'd looked into her stunning green eyes and promised to love her as best he could. And yet, he was quite afraid, for his love for Rina was so consuming it absorbed most of his energy. He hoped he could find room in his heart to love his little girl too.

He did grow to love Miranda, always enjoying their tea parties and times when she would sit on his lap and look up at him with adoration shining in her eyes. But he would've been lying if he didn't admit that time spent with his daughter was bided time, spent so that he could be in Rina's presence once more.

When Miranda turned eight years old, they threw her a grand birthday party. Marsias had smiled broadly at his two girls as they sat at the head of the table, both mirror images of each other. A few days later, Rina had saddled her horse for a ride.

"I don't want you to go out today. I think it's going to rain," Marsias said.

"I'll be fine, darling," Rina said, patting his cheek. "I like the rain. Please, don't worry about me. Miranda will be home from school soon. Make sure you hug her when she comes in the door. Sometimes, I worry that you don't even see her when she comes home. She's always so excited to see her daddy."

"I see her," he said, pulling her in for a hug. "How could I not? She looks just like my beautiful wife." He gave her a peck on her pink lips.

"I love you, Marsias. Let's take a trip soon. Maybe to Astaria. We haven't seen Markdor and Calla for a while. It's time that Miranda formally meet Sathan and Latimus."

"I agree. Maybe next month."

She'd given him that gorgeous smile and ridden away as the clouds gathered above. Marsias had returned to the castle, frowning as he stepped inside and realized he hadn't told her he loved her back. She knew, of course, but he wished he'd said the words. Promising himself he would tell her ten extra times that evening, he went to his study to do some paperwork for the council.

Sadly, Rina never returned. Valktor went mad, unable to live with his daughter's disappearance, and after killing Markdor and Calla, he burned himself to death in the Purges of Methesda. Miranda, the next in line to the throne, was deemed too young to ascend. Marsias, as Rina's husband, assumed the throne in her stead.

For a thousand years, he struggled to avenge his wife. Hatred for the Deamons and the Vampyres consumed him. Vowing to never rest until the last Vampyre took his breath and until Crimeous perished by Miranda's heir, he felt himself going quite mad.

Miranda was a nuisance to him. He hated to admit it, but it was the truth. Without Rina around to temper him, he grew angry with her when she tried to connect with him. She brought out an intense frustration in him that he couldn't seem to squelch. Couldn't she understand that his sole focus should be killing their greatest enemies? Anything else was futile and useless.

Eventually, she left him alone. Kenden seemed to love her in a way he couldn't, and he took solace in that. Her one purpose was to have an heir and ensure that he fulfilled the prophecy and killed Crimeous. It was imperative that he push her toward that goal.

And now, look where it had gotten him. He and his daughter were so distant they might as well live on separate islands upon Etherya's Earth. Sighing, Marsias ran his hands over his face as he sat at the mahogany desk in his office. It had all gone so wrong.

Pulling the top drawer of his desk open, he picked up the picture of Rina that sat there. An artist had drawn it when she was pregnant with Miranda. Hope glowed in her almond-shaped green eyes, and her smile was bright.

"I'm sorry, my love," he whispered, rubbing the picture with the pad of his thumb. "I've let you down terribly. I hope you can forgive me."

Tears welled in his eyes, and he felt the familiar emptiness inside. It seemed to pervade every aspect of his life. Once he killed the last Vampyre and ensured

Crimeous' death, he was sure it would abate. Those were his goals, and he wouldn't let anyone obstruct them. Even his own daughter.

Placing the picture back inside the drawer, he closed it and latched onto his hate. It was always there and that was comforting. His rage never left him, as Rina had. As long as he had it, he felt he could survive. Resolved, he decided to have a glass of scotch before heading to bed for another night where he would get no sleep.

* * * *

It turned out that transporting a six-foot-tall Vampyre princess was no easy task, as Miranda found out the hard way. After making her way down to Sadie's infirmary, she had asked the doctor to prepare a syringe with enough force to knock the woman out for several hours. Then, Miranda sat her down to explain her plan in detail. She informed Sadie that she needed her to come along to ensure the Vampyre stayed healthy and strong. Appealing to the doctor's Hippocratic oath was a bit of an underhanded tactic but Miranda knew it would work. Sadie had reluctantly agreed. And just like that, Miranda thought, another person had been dragged into this mess she had created.

They had gone to the windowless room where the woman was being kept, and Sadie had injected the entire syringe into her arm. After unbinding her, Miranda worked furiously to load the Vampyre onto the stretcher she had wheeled up from the infirmary. Her five-foot, six-inch frame was barely up to the task.

They had wheeled the unconscious woman to the black SUV Hummer and deposited her in the large trunk. Sadie had climbed in the back with her to monitor her vitals.

Two Slayer soldiers appeared, informing Miranda that they had been tasked with protecting her and her captive on their journey. One of them handed her a note from Kenden:

Randi: Blane and Zander will accompany you. They are at your command and will guard the woman while you journey with the Vampyre king. They will hold her at the abandoned cabin near the juncture of the River Thayne and Astaria. Your father is furious, but I will take care of him. He is choosing to let the kingdom believe you are vacationing at Restia. Please, be safe and smart. I love you and have always believed in you. Ken

Reveling in her love for her cousin, she held the note to her chest and said a silent thank you to him. And then, it was time to get moving.

Miranda drove along the unpaved gravel road that ran parallel to the river. As she passed the spot where she and Kenden had buried the pieces of her mother, she said a quiet prayer.

Mother, please, send me the strength to help our people. I need you more than ever.

She could have sworn she felt a gentle caress on her arm. Or was she simply going crazy? Doubt crept in as she drove along. Did she really think she was going to negotiate her people's future with the unconscious Vampyre in the back seat? Without the help of her father? Good god, she really was insane.

Realizing that self-doubt did her no good here, she drove to the part of the river where the tall stone wall stood. The Wall of Astaria was said to be blessed by Etherya herself. No one could get in or out of the compound due to its protection.

"Well, here we go," she said to herself, a sort of impromptu pep talk. "You can do this, Miranda."

Exiting the car, she walked to the back and opened the trunk door. "Make sure her wrists and ankles are bound and then bring her to consciousness," she said to Sadie.

Nodding from under her hoodie, the doctor complied.

Ten minutes later, the groggy Vampyre lifted her head.

"You'll want to stay in the car since it's still light out," Miranda warned. "Sundown won't come for another thirty minutes at least."

Miranda reached into the pocket of her camouflage pants and pulled out a cell phone. "I took this from you while you were out. I'm going to call your brother with it. He'll want proof that you're alive. I also have two armed soldiers standing five feet from us. Don't do anything stupid, understand?"

The Vampyre woman nodded. She seemed resigned to the fact that she had no hand to play in this situation.

"Password?" Miranda asked.

"Three nine eight seven," the woman replied.

Miranda entered the code and brought up the contacts list. It was listed there plain as day: *Sathan*. With her heart pounding in her chest and her mind struggling to keep her shaking hands at bay, she hit the call button.

After three rings, she heard her greatest enemy's deep voice.

"Arderin? Where are you? We've been looking for you for three nights!"

Miranda stood frozen, her insides locked in battle: confidence in her cause versus self-doubt.

"Arderin?" the deep voice said through the phone.

The Vampyre began screaming from the SUV. "Sathan! Sathan! She has me!"

Miranda gave a quick nod to Sadie, and the doctor immediately placed a large piece of duct tape over the woman's mouth.

Inhaling deeply, Miranda calmed herself and proceeded.

Lifting the phone to her ear, she said, "As you can hear, I have your sister."

The man began cursing, threatening her through the phone.

"I would stay calm if I were you," she said, her tone firm. "I have no wish to kill her, but if you anger me, I won't have a choice."

Silence. And then, "What do you want?"

"Meet me at the intersection of the Wall of Astaria and the River Thayne. Come alone. If I see anyone else with you, I will kill her. I have an eight-shooter trained on her heart at this very moment."

The Vampyre king's wrath was almost palpable through the phone.

"Don't harm her. I'll do as you wish. Give me an hour."

"Thirty minutes," Miranda said, unwilling to let him dictate any part of this negotiation. "Or she's dead."

"Understood." The line went dead.

Miranda let out a long exhale. Looking at the women in the back of the SUV, she allowed herself a shaky breath. *Well, Randi, you've stepped in it now. Better be able to finish it.*

Walking to the passenger side, she began preparing the eight-shooters for her meeting with the Vampyre king.

* * * *

"You have to let me come with you, Sathan," Latimus said. "I won't let you go alone to be slaughtered."

"She said to come alone, and so I will," Sathan replied, his tone firm. "Arderin is still alive, which means that the woman who's holding her hostage must want something from me. I'm not taking any chances with her life."

"Let us come to the edge of the wall with you at least," his youngest brother Heden said. "We can't let our king go alone into a hostage negotiation."

Sathan nodded. "Okay, you and Latimus can come with me to the edge of the wall, but no further." He lifted his finger, pointing back and forth between them. "Understood?"

"She's our sister too, Sathan. It's ridiculous to suggest that you're the only one who can help rescue her."

"I'm the one the abductor called. I see no reason to put you both in danger."

"Bullshit. I could take her out with one shot from atop the wall," Latimus said.

"Enough," Sathan said, feeling drained. "I haven't slept in three fucking days and I don't want to argue with either of you. You'll come with me to the wall and that's it."

Heden approached him and held out his hand. A small, black device sat in his palm. "This is a transmitter. It will allow us to hear you. Latimus and I will breach the wall if we feel that you're in danger. You can ask us not to, but you know that we will."

Sathan smiled at his little brother, his heart swelling a bit in his chest. Heden was youngest of his siblings and had only been a toddler during the Awakening. He had never lived in a world that was at peace and yet had grown up to be the most lighthearted member of the royal family. Possessing a kind disposition, he was always ready to crack a joke if the mood was too heavy.

Latimus, who was deathly serious, often mocked Heden for his carefree attitude. Heden would just smile and pat his brother on the back and tell him to go chug a beer. Or get laid. Sathan admired his happy-go-lucky attitude in their imperfect world.

"Thanks," he said, lifting up the tiny device. "Where do I put it?"

"That's what she said," Heden laughed.

"For the sake of the goddess, Heden, now is not the time to joke," Latimus said. "Arderin is being held hostage, and our idiot brother thinks he can save the world all by himself."

"Relax, Latimus. I won't do anything stupid. I fully trust in all of the training I've received as part of your army."

"Oh, and don't call your king stupid," Heden chimed in. "The penalty for that is five years in the dungeon."

"You're both ridiculous," Latimus said angrily. "I don't have time for this shit. You can find me in the barracks when you're ready to deploy." He stalked out of the room.

"Well, he's a riot as always," Heden said with a roll of his eyes. "Give me five minutes and then I'll meet you in the barracks. You want to take the Hummer?"

Sathan nodded.

"Put the transmitter in your pocket. I've accounted for sound muffling, so we should still be able to hear you loud and clear."

"Okay," Sathan said, placing the tiny device in the pocket of his black army pants. Besides being the much-needed comic relief on the compound, Heden was also a whiz at technology. Sathan was thankful that someone in the royal family had that ability, as he and Latimus were soldiers and at a loss when it came to anything to do with technology.

"Thanks," he said. "I'll see you in ten."

With a nod, Heden exited the room. Sathan ran his fingers through his thick, wavy hair. It was time to get his sister back.

* * * *

Latimus muttered to himself as he stalked down the corridor to the barracks. His anger, and that alone, accounted for him almost plowing down Lila in the hallway.

Hearing her breathy, "*Oomph*," he grabbed her arms to stabilize her and then pulled his hands away as if they'd been burned.

"Whoa, I didn't see you," she said, her voice soft and gentle as always. His stupid heart skipped a beat as she looked up at him and smiled. "Are you okay?"

Motherfucker. He was supposed to say something here, right? Yes, he was sure he should. But he couldn't get his damn lips to move. How could anyone be expected to function with this woman staring up at them? White teeth framed by soft, pink lips...perfect upturned nose...lavender irises that seemed to glow in the dimness. Mentally shaking himself, he struggled to get away from her as soon as possible.

"Yes, I'm fine. Sorry." Brushing past her, he stalked away.

"Great," he heard her say behind him. "Any word on Arderin?"

Refusing to answer, he continued to march to the barracks. He had no time to waste on this woman. This woman who belonged to another. This woman whom he had loved since he could remember what the word meant. This woman who was betrothed to his brother.

* * * *

Well, that was rude, Lila thought to herself as Latimus stalked off. But what did she expect, really? He had always been discourteous and impolite to her, so why should tonight be any different?

She had always struggled to understand what she had done to him to make him dislike her so. Early on, when they were children, she and Latimus had been great friends. She remembered laughing with him as they played alongside the riverbank. They had fought mock duels and captured toads in their makeshift containers. And then, one day, when they were still so young, he had just...stopped. Stopped talking to her. Stopped acknowledging her. Stopped seeing her.

When she was a baby, the goddess Etherya had declared her the betrothed of the future king, Sathan. As the daughter of the realm's most distinguished diplomat and his wife, descended from a distant cousin of Markdor, her blood was the closest thing to royalty without being in the royal family. As a warrior, Latimus didn't have much respect for blue-blooded aristocrats, whose lineage was seen as too valuable to be wasted on enlisting in the army. But she had always hoped that they could rekindle their friendship, as she would one day be married to his brother and bear his nieces and nephews.

Being a good servant to the royal family, and to Etherya, she had never resented her betrothal. Sathan was a good man and a magnificent ruler. But in the darkness of night, when she lay in her bed, she would be lying if she didn't admit that it was Latimus' face she imagined looming over her...his lips kissing her own...his muscular arms holding her as they slept...

Shaking her head, she forced the images from her mind. She was extremely lucky to be betrothed to Sathan. He had given her freedom for all these years. Centuries ago, he'd sat her down and explained that he didn't want to bond until they could have the ceremony under the light of the sun, for all their people to see. She had agreed, and they had begun living mostly separate lives.

Sathan visited the pretty women who lived at the edge of the compound from time to time. Perhaps it would have made another woman angry or driven her insane with jealousy, but Lila had never been jealous where Sathan was concerned. He had become like a brother to her, and although she loved him as her king, she doubted she would ever love him passionately, as a woman loves a man.

Resigned to this fate, she appreciated that he let her have her freedom on the compound. It allowed her to live her life, study her history and collaborate with Heden on important projects.

She hoped that one day, the War of the Species would come to an end, and she could follow in her father's footsteps to become a great diplomat. Both of her parents were now long deceased, and she wished to continue their legacy.

Finding her way to Sathan's study, she observed him talking into the speaker phone on his large desk. "I'm heading down now." He punched a button to disconnect.

"Did you find Arderin?" she asked hopefully.

"Yes. It's a long story, but yes. Latimus, Heden and I are going to get her now."

"Thank the goddess," she said, placing her hand over her heart. "I was so worried."

"Me too," he said, coming around to stand in front of her. "I realize that I haven't seen much of you lately. We have to make time to have lunch soon. I want to hear about the tunnels you've been working on with Heden."

"Of course," she said with a nod. "I'm at your disposal as always, my king."

He chuckled and placed a kiss on her forehead. "Always so regal. Maybe you can teach my brother some manners. He seems to be grouchier than ever these days."

"Yes, I just ran into him in the hallway. Literally. He is, of course, anxious to recover your sister."

Sathan nodded. "I have to go. We'll get together next week."

"Go get our girl," she said, her voice full of hope.

Excerpt from The Book of the Goddess, King Markdor Edition
Article 4 – Cross-species Procreation

Upon creation of her two species, the Goddess Etherya regarded her children.
The Slayera, so lovely and fair.
The Vampyres, so strong and magnificent.
Knowing that the Vampyres would find the Slayera as beautiful as she did, Etherya made it impossible for cross-procreation between the two species.
Although the two species could mate, their mating would never result in a child.
Therefore, the species remained separate, choosing to mate and procreate with their own kind.
And all was peaceful on Etherya's Earth.
Thanks be to the Goddess.

Chapter 6

Latimus pulled up to the barrier that surrounded the compound. As the three brothers exited the black Hummer, he addressed Sathan. "Be careful. We're here if you need us."

Sathan nodded and walked to the wall. The stones were cool against his palm under the dark sky and silver moonlight. The force-field that Etherya had implemented around the wall vibrated against his hand. Pushing against the rocks, they swung open, and he walked through.

About twenty feet away, he saw a black SUV, the headlights bright. He walked slowly toward the car.

"That's far enough," a female voice said.

"Where's my sister?"

"She's being held in a safe place not far from here."

The woman walked forward, and he studied her in what little light he had. Silky, raven-black hair fell straight to her shoulders. Camouflage pants were tucked over black army boots, and she wore a black tank top. Approaching him, he noticed how small she was. Probably about a foot shorter than his six-foot, eight-inch frame.

She stopped about two feet in front of him and lifted her chin, training her gaze on his. He felt a sharp clenching sensation in his solar plexus when he saw her irises. Like wet leaves that glistened on the tree after a rainy day, they were the deepest green he had ever seen.

"You have dragged me here," he said, regaining his composure. "What do I have to do to get her back?"

"Do you know who I am?" she asked. Her voice was clear and firm, without a trace of fear.

"The Slayer Princess Miranda," he said.

She nodded and looked down at the grass for a moment. He wondered if she was more nervous than she appeared. Looking back up at him, she said, "I have no wish to hurt your sister. I wish to use her to ask you to help me."

"*Force* me to help you," he said, bitterness lacing his tone.

"If you like," she said with an absent shrug of her shoulders. "Our people have been at war for a thousand years. We are locked in a stalemate that neither side seems to be able to win. I have come to the conclusion that we need to change our tactics."

"I'm listening."

She inhaled a deep breath before continuing. "I've grown weary of fighting your people. I wish to form a temporary truce with you so that I can accomplish something of great importance."

"Right," he said, his tone suggesting that he trusted her about as far as he could throw her. "And what is it you need from me?"

"As the first-born descendants of Valktor and Markdor, our shared blood stream could release the Blade of Pestilence. Once I have it, I will use it to kill Crimeous and I will return your sister to you."

Sathan blinked a few times, unsure he'd heard her correctly, and then he laughed incredulously. "Wait, are you serious?"

She stood still and mute, her chin thrust up in the air, waiting for his response.

"You want me to travel to the Cave of the Sacred Prophecy with you, release the Blade of Pestilence and then just let you go on your merry way after you've kidnapped my sister?"

"Yes," she said, as if his statement hadn't been dripping with sarcasm. "Except that I didn't kidnap your sister. She washed up on the shore of our riverbank. I actually employed our doctor in nursing her back to health. You're welcome, by the way."

What a patronizing, cocky little bitch, Sathan thought. Although, he had to admire how she stood her ground against him. His physical dominance over her alone should've had her cowering. He tested her will by taking a step forward, closing the distance between them. She stood firm, tilting her chin up even more to hold his gaze, and reluctant admiration for her courage coursed through him.

"You want me to thank you for keeping alive a hostage that you're now using to negotiate with me?"

"It would be nice," she said flippantly, "but I won't hold my breath. So, what's it going to be?

She stared up at him expectantly, as if she hadn't just asked him to trek over four hundred miles with her to rescue a weapon from an ancient prophecy.

"No. Now, give me my sister. I don't know what game you're trying to play, but you're obviously physically outmatched here. I'll give you five seconds to hand her over, or—"

A sharp pain stabbed in his chest, and he gasped. Lowering his gaze to the left side of his chest, he realized that the woman had stabbed him with some sort of contraption.

"It's a mini-blade-loaded eight-shooter, you fucking bastard," she said, spittle flying from between her clenched teeth as she pushed the contraption further into his chest. "The blade on the top of the barrel will only hurt, since you fuckers seem to heal like some goddamn miracle. But if I pull the trigger, it will deploy eight tiny bullets right into your black fucking heart. Don't make me do it."

Pain coursed through him as well as a healthy dose of anger. And yet, as he looked down on this tiny she-devil of a woman, he felt a jolt of respect. She had gotten the upper hand on him. Bracing himself, he pushed his chest further into the blade. An intense pleasure ran through him when her eyes widened in surprise.

"Go ahead," he said, daring her. "Shoot me, princess. Let's see if you have the courage."

Tiny nostrils flared as she struggled to compose herself. Moments stretched by in silence as they stood locked in a dance of wills. "Well?" he jibed. "Haven't you the bravery to kill me?"

Stepping back, she pulled the blade from his chest but kept the weapon aimed at his heart, her finger on the trigger. "Just like a stupid man," she said, disgust lacing her voice. "Killing someone does not indicate courage or bravery. It's the will to find a peaceful solution that shows one's true strength."

Huh. He didn't expect that one. Not from the princess of the people who were his sworn enemy. He lifted his hand to put pressure on his bleeding wound. "Releasing the Blade of Pestilence will not find you peace. It will lead to more war if you wish to use it to kill Crimeous."

"Perhaps," she said. "But like I said, our tactics have to change. If you help me release the Blade, I promise I will return your sister to Astaria unharmed."

He realized he believed her. Although she was a Slayer and had just stabbed him in the chest, she betrayed a firm genuineness. "And what about your father? The raids we hold against your people? Surely, you cannot ask me to journey with you to the Cave knowing my army will attack your people in another fortnight."

Her face contorted into a withering scowl. "Yes, of course. How terrible of me to deny you the sport of hunting and killing my people."

Remembering his earlier visit to the dungeon, he shook his head. "And now look who's stupid."

"What does that mean?" she asked.

Choosing not to answer her, he continued. "We're almost out of rations from our last raid. If we don't obtain more Slayer blood over the next fortnight, my people will begin to starve. Ruler to ruler, what would you have me do?"

"My cousin, our army commander, has agreed to supply your compound with blood from the injured soldiers we currently have in our infirmary. He will bank it for you daily and deliver it to this spot while we travel to the Cave."

"Well, you've just got it all figured out, haven't you?" he asked sarcastically.

"It's better than continuing this madness that's been going on for centuries, isn't it?" she asked, her tone just as biting. "Surely, you can agree that it can't hurt to employ new tactics in this age-old war. I mean, ruler to ruler, right?" She placed her free hand on her hip and her eyebrows jutted up as she waited for him to answer. Snarky little minx, this one was.

"Even if I agreed to your plan, how could I guarantee that my sister would be safe? For all I know, you could have your guards murder her as soon as we leave on our journey."

"You'll just have to trust me, I guess."

"Says the woman holding the eight-shooter to my chest."

Ever so slowly, she lowered the weapon to her side. "I don't want to hurt her. I'm sure you understand that if you hurt me, she will be immediately killed. I am trusting you not to harm me until I have the Blade in my possession. After that, once you return to your compound and I return to mine, we can assess how...*cooperative* we've been toward each other and chart a course forward."

And just like that, Sathan thought, the world had gone insane. The Slayer princess was standing in front of him asking for a truce so that they could work together to rescue the centuries-old blade that her grandfather used to kill his parents. Fucking insane.

But what was even more insane was that he was considering it. After all, he had become frustrated with the current state of events as well. This cycle of endless war and destruction had them on a constant loop with no end in sight. What if he could actually work with the princess to change the course of history?

"Your father is on board with this plan?" he asked.

"Yes."

Studying her, he narrowed his eyes. "I am intrigued by your proposal but I need to discuss it with my brothers. If we are going to move forward with this, I would ask that you turn my sister over to me and trust that I will keep my word. How am I supposed to trust you if you do not trust me in return?"

"Good try, but no fucking way," she said, shaking her head. "This trust thing is going to go one way and one way only. You'll trust me to keep her alive and you'll *earn* my trust by helping me."

"She is an inexperienced female not used to the world outside our walls. I worry for her health—"

"She's doing just fine. All you men think that we women just sit around waiting for you to let us live our lives. Your sister is strong and has already threatened to kill me about a hundred times. She's got more spirit than I've seen in half our soldiers. I don't wish to hurt her, and I won't as long as you help me."

His heart warmed at the thought of Arderin putting up such a brave fight against her captor. "I need twenty-four hours to discuss with my brothers. I will meet you back here then."

"I want an answer now—"

"No," he said, lowering his hand from his now-mended chest. Self-healing abilities really were amazing. "The fact that I'm even considering your plan is making me doubt my sanity. I need to discuss with my brothers, who are my closest advisors. If you can't grant me that, then we are at an impasse."

"Fine. I'll give you until sunset tomorrow. I'll be here. Don't be late."

With one last look at the impertinent little princess, he turned and exited through the wall. His brothers were going to think he'd gone mad for even considering this. Of that, he was sure.

* * * *

Miranda let out a huge sigh and lifted her hand to rest against her beating heart. Good god, that had been the most intense moment of her life. She hadn't been prepared for the hulking man who had appeared from the stone wall under the moonlight.

She had expected someone old and ugly, as she imagined most Vampyres to be. Instead, the Vampyre king had looked young and full of strength. He must have gone through the change in his late-twenties, she guessed. That would have frozen his features at that age for all time. He had dwarfed her by over a foot, and his arms had bulged out of the sleeves of his black t-shirt. Black pants had encased burly legs the size of small tree-trunks. Angular features, similar to his sister's, had lined his face, and his irises were pitch-black. She wondered if that made it easier for him to hunt in the dark. Blood-sucking bastard.

The deep timbre of his voice had vibrated through her as they spoke. White fangs had distended below his full, red upper lip. Had he ever plunged them into a Slayer? Shivering, she tried to erase the mental image, wondering why she was imagining him scraping them over her neck. Dark, thick hair had rounded out his features. Overall, he was quite attractive. Not that she gave a fig. The game she was playing here was far from a spin on Match.com, she thought wryly. His appearance was no concern of hers.

Well, that was nerve-wracking, she thought to herself as she headed toward the Hummer. She had tried her hardest to keep any waver out of her voice and to not show any fear. Hopefully, she had accomplished her task.

"You did well, princess," came a low-toned voice from behind.

She whirled around, lifting the eight-shooter, searching for the man who had addressed her.

"Relax, Miranda," the unseen man said calmly. "If I wanted you dead, you would be already. Trust me."

"Where are you?" she asked, rotating back and forth as she held the weapon. "I'm armed with an eight-shooter and I'm prepared to shoot you on sight."

"Yes, yes, we all know how agile you are with an eight-shooter, my dear. In fact, bravo for stabbing the king in his heart. Well done."

Slow claps came from behind her, and she whirled around again to see an image form in front of her. Slowly, a man came into sight. "Who are you?" she asked, puzzled as to how a person could materialize out of thin air.

"C'mon, Miranda. You can do better than that. Don't make me do all the work. Use the brain in that tiny little head. I know you can do it." He tapped on her forehead as he spoke in a condescending tone.

Smacking his hand away, she lifted the eight-shooter. "You've got about five seconds before I blow your head off, buddy."

Rolling his eyes, the man faked a yawn and lifted his hand to pat his open mouth. "*Borrrring*," he said, the word stretched out as he mocked her. "Let's try again. I have all night. I'm guessing you have, oh..."—he looked down at the non-existent watch on his wrist—"until sunset tomorrow."

Furious, Miranda studied the man. In the dimness of the moon she could see his short, buzz-cut hair, small features and greenish-looking eyes. It was his ears, however, that gave it away. Their tips came to small points at the top, reminding her of the elves she had read about in her fantasy books as a child.

"You're a Deamon."

"Very good," he said with a nod. "Although, I would say that I am *the* Deamon. I guess it's all about perspective. But most would say that I am the most powerful Deamon of all. Even more powerful than my father."

She sucked in a breath. "You are Darkrip, son of the Dark Lord."

"Finally," he said, rolling his eyes as he smirked. "Let's hope you can keep up, princess, because I don't have all night."

"What do you want?" she asked, still pointing the weapon at him.

"A piece of the action, of course," he said, looking down at her. She figured him to be a bit taller than six feet. "I see you sizing me up and let me save you the trouble. I am the son of the Dark Lord Crimeous. His blood runs through me and makes me more powerful than anyone on this godforsaken planet. I can transport myself with a thought, kill someone with my mind and fight with the strength of a hundred soldiers. I like your spunk, but you'd be dead in a second if you tried to fight me."

Placing his index finger on top of the barrel of her weapon, he lowered it. "Knowing all that, let's put this away. I wouldn't want you to hurt yourself before I say what I've come to say."

"And what is that?" she asked angrily.

"You've gotten a good start here, Miranda. When I knocked the Vampyre princess unconscious and sent her down the river to you, I wasn't quite sure what you'd do."

"That was you?' she asked, shock evident in her tone.

"Of course," he said with a shrug. "I was tired of waiting on you or the Vampyres to get things started."

"What things?" she asked, her suspicion growing like an evil flower blooming in her chest.

"The next phase of my plan," he said, his tone menacing. "You see, I've grown tired of serving my father. He's become a bit...deranged in his old age. He's obsessed with destroying the Slayers and the Vampyres, and it's getting in the way of what I desire most."

"And that is?" she asked.

"Becoming the leader of the Deamons myself, obviously. With him standing in the way, I can't become who I was meant to be—which is a leader, like you."

"I'll never be anything like you," she said through gritted teeth.

After a condescending *tsk, tsk, tsk,* he continued, "Don't judge one whom you do not yet know, my dear."

"Stop calling me that," she said, throwing the eight-shooter to the ground and shoving his chest.

"Shoving me isn't a good idea, *my dear*," he said, his eyes flaring with laughter as he saw her anger escalate.

Realizing that she needed to remain calm, she inhaled a breath. "How does my alliance with the Vampyres help you achieve your goal?"

"If the prophecy is true, I need you, as the lone descendant of Valktor, to release the Blade and kill my father. Only then can I ascend to his throne and rule my people as it was meant to be."

"And are you as evil as Crimeous?" she asked. "Or will you rule them in peace in the underground caves and let us be?"

"Evil is such a dirty word, Miranda. I prefer resolute. And I am certainly resolute in my desire to kill him. I have been watching you for centuries now. Your longing to end the War of the Species is noble, and I feel that we can also form an alliance. My first goodwill gesture was sending the Vampyre princess to you."

"You almost severed her head," she said. "We're lucky she survived."

He shrugged. "A beauty such as her? She's lucky I didn't rape her before I sent her to you. I certainly thought about it but decided that there's always another time and place to have my fun."

Miranda shivered at the ice in his words. "I have no desire to align with a Deamon."

"And yet, you've already aligned with me just the same. By accepting my *gift*." He nodded toward the woods where the Vampyre was being held.

She studied him, this evil Deamon who stood before her. Muscles bulged from a thick chest under his black turtleneck. He wore a fashionable belt, fitted and unwrinkled pants that ended at what looked to be very expensive black loafers. At first glance, he looked more suited to be heading out for a night on the town rather than the son of the Dark Lord. How deceiving looks could be.

"There, there," he chided, lifting his hand to pat her shoulder and chuckling when she swatted it away. "It's not so bad to work with a powerful Deamon such as myself. My abilities could come in handy in times of strife for you."

"I'd rather die than use powers that are evil."

"We'll see," he said, his gaze firm on hers. "Regardless, you're on the right path here. Keep it up. The Vampyre king needs to agree to your plan for all of us to survive on this pissant excuse for a planet." His eyes narrowed. "He was attracted to you. Use that to your advantage. Women have always been able to lead a man around by the nose as long as attraction is involved."

Miranda snorted. "As if I would ever encourage attraction from a Vampyre. The species that has murdered my people for centuries? You must be mad."

"I think you were a bit attracted to him too," he continued, as if she hadn't spoken. Rubbing his chin, he contemplated her. "This could get interesting."

Exasperated, she lifted her hands and waved him away. "I don't have time for this—"

"Take heed," he interrupted, lowering his head to whisper in her ear. "There are many on the Slayer compound who support you over Marsias. The blood of Valktor does not run through his veins as it does yours, and many think you are the true ruler of the Slayers. I have listened unobserved to many conversations about this by your kinsmen. Know that when you return with the Blade of Pestilence to Uteria, you might have to take your father down. How magnificent it would be to see you in your righteous glory, claiming your throne as the one true leader of the species."

"You're insane," she said, his words causing alarm bells to ring in her head. Could this really be true? Were there Slayers who supported her usurping the throne? Surely, this was treason. Wasn't it?

"Perhaps," he said, straightening to his full height. "Or perhaps we are more alike than you want to admit. Both of us struggling to push out our fathers and claim a throne that should be ours."

"I'll never betray my father," she spat, angry at herself that she had even considered his treacherous words.

"We'll see," he said with a slight shrug. "That is a matter for another time. Stay the course, Miranda. I'll be watching to make sure your journey with the Vampyre king is a safe one. Have no doubt that regardless of what you think of me, I want you to succeed in freeing the Blade."

And with those parting words, he proceeded to vanish. Literally. She blinked her eyes and shook her head, wondering if it had all been a dream.

"Shit," she muttered to herself. "Things just got *really* complicated."

Excerpt from The Book of the Goddess, King Markdor Edition
Article 5 – Betrothal of Prince Sathan

Prince Sathan, the firstborn heir of King Markdor and Queen Calla, was betrothed on the first day of the fifth month in the year eight P.A. (Pre-Awakening).
To keep the bloodline pure, Etherya decreed that Prince Sathan's betrothed be of great lineage. The Aristocrat Lila, daughter of the Great Diplomat Theinos and Gwen the Aristocrat, was chosen by Etherya to be the Crown Prince's betrothed and future Queen of the Realm.
And all was peaceful on Etherya's Earth.
Thanks be to the Goddess.

Chapter 7

"No fucking way!" Latimus' voice boomed so fiercely that Sathan was sure he could be heard all the way to the Slayer compound. "If you think I'm going to let our king travel to the Cave of the Sacred Prophecy with a Slayer intent on killing him, you've lost your mind."

"Sit down, Latimus," Sathan said, gesturing toward his brother's unoccupied seat. They were all gathered around the large conference room table, which was mostly used to plan the raids. Heden and Lila sat to his right. He had asked his betrothed to sit in because she was level-headed and usually could see different angles to a situation than he and his brothers. Latimus scowled and sat down to Sathan's left.

"I didn't get the feeling that she actually wants to kill me—"

"You've got to be kidding me."

"Stop interrupting me. I'm trying to see this as a possible opportunity. You all know that I've become tired of hunting the Slayers. It's a drain on our soldiers as well as our finances. Now that the Deamons attack us frequently, keeping up the army has been taxing to say the least. This could present a viable alternative."

"She has Arderin," Latimus growled. "How can you be so flippant about this?"

Anger bubbled in Sathan's chest as he addressed his brother. "I'll caution you not to describe me as flippant about our sister again. I want her returned safely, as you all do, but I see what the Slayer princess is attempting to accomplish. She seems as tired of this war as we are."

"You can't go alone," Heden said. "It would be suicide."

Sathan nodded. "I think that you should come with us. Latimus can stay behind. As commander of the army and the second in line of succession, if something happens to me, he can ascend the throne."

"I don't want to ascend the throne, as I've told you a thousand times. All the diplomacy and bullshit of being a ruler is everything I detest. Let me go with you instead of Heden."

"We need you to stay behind as a symbol of strength. Our people look to you as a leader, Latimus."

"Ridiculous," he muttered, sitting back in his seat. "I'm a soldier. That's all I've ever wanted to be."

"If I may say something," Lila interjected, continuing when Sathan gave her a nod, "I actually see more of a benefit to Latimus accompanying you. The trail to the Cave of the Sacred Prophecy is said to be quite treacherous. His strength might be better used helping you and the Slayer. Heden and I can stay behind and take care of the realm." She placed her hand on Heden's forearm, reaffirming how close the two of them were. "If that's okay with you?"

"Sure thing, buttercup," Heden said, his smile genuine as he teased her with his favorite nickname. He was always quoting the movie *The Princess Bride*, and Lila reminded him of the main character. "I'm down for whatever helps us get Arderin back as quickly as possible. It will also give us time to finish the tunnel plans. We're really close to being able to implement underground travel between all our compounds, and I'm anxious to get everything finished."

Sathan mulled over his options. "Okay, let's say Latimus and I went to the Cave with the Slayer. I'm thinking it would be about a ten-night journey. We'd sleep during the day and navigate by night, of course. Am I being too ambitious with the timeline?"

Latimus placed his large hands on the map of Etherya's Earth that sat on the table in front of them. "No," he said, tracing it with his index finger. "It will be tough, but it's doable. The Slayer will have to keep up."

"She seems to want this badly. I'm not sure I've ever met someone with that level of determination in their eyes. She is intent on freeing the Blade and killing Crimeous."

"And what if she resects the Blade and plunges it right into your heart? It's how her grandfather killed Mother and Father, after all. This has 'trap' written all over it. I still think it's ridiculous to even consider it."

"And what would you have me do? Let her kill Arderin? Continue the Slayer raids for eternity? Fight two species of immortals until we all kill each other? I understand how unorthodox this is, but it's an opportunity for us to change course. What kind of leader would I be if I didn't at least attempt another alternative?"

"I agree," Lila said in her soft voice. "We used to live in harmony with the Slayers, and if there is any opportunity to restore peace, we should take it."

"Why is she here?" Latimus said, directing his question to Sathan. "She's not a member of this family and doesn't understand what's at stake. This is a matter for the royal family."

"Stop being a dick, Latimus," Heden said. "Lila is as much a member of this family as we are—"

"Not until she bonds with Sathan, she isn't. I'm tired of having a thousand fucking opinions about everything. Let's decide this between brothers."

Lila sat up straighter in her chair. "I am only trying to help."

"Well, you're not," Latimus said, his tone nasty. "You're a born diplomat amongst soldiers, and there isn't any time to waste. If you want me to go with you, I will," he said, turning to Sathan. "But let's decide and be on our way. My sister is out there, and I'm not going to have a fucking summit in order to get her back."

"Fine," Sathan said, giving a reassuring look to Lila. His brother had become so unpleasant toward her, and he struggled to understand why. "Why don't you two let me plan the journey with Latimus? I'll come find you once we chart our course. Thank you, all of you, for your input. It is imperative that we remain unified."

Lila stood up, her flawless skin paler than usual. "Thank you, Sathan. I'm only trying to help. I'm sorry to have upset you, Lattie." Looking at Heden, she said, "I'll be down in the tech room."

"Okay, sweetie," he said gently. "I'll be there in a few."

Upon her exit, Latimus cursed. "I've told her a thousand times, I hate that fucking nickname. I think she uses it just to piss me off."

"Well, she should," Heden said. He stood and pointed across the table. "You've become a real asshole, Latimus. I'm surprised she doesn't deck you across the nose. That woman has more grace and humility in her little finger than you can fathom. The fact she even tolerates you, with the way that you treat her, should tell you something about her character. I'm sick of it." Turning to Sathan, he gave him a nod. "I'll be downstairs if you need me." With that, he stalked out of the room.

Sathan sighed and ran his hand over his face. "I don't know what's gotten into you, but it's got to stop. I need us all to work together. She will be my bonded someday. You can't speak to her that way."

"Sorry," his brother replied, in a tone that suggested he was anything but. "I'll apologize to her before we leave. I just don't think she has a place at this table. She's not family."

"Lila brings a perspective that the three of us could never have. You underestimate her. I expect you to honor your word to apologize to her." Reaching down, he grabbed the map and pulled it toward him. "Now, let's start planning this journey. It's not going to be easy, and we have to consider that the Slayer princess can only travel about half as much ground per night as we can. I say that we use the Hummer and start to follow the river here..."

Minutes bled into hours as the brothers plotted their journey.

* * * *

Miranda watched the wall open and the Vampyre king walk through exactly two minutes after sunset. The bastard was testing her by cutting it close.

"One more minute and I would've killed your sister. You're lucky you made it in time."

Another hulking Vampyre spoke from behind the king, this one even taller and more formidable, if possible. "It's an empty threat. If you kill our sister, you have no hand left to play."

Ah, so this must be one of the Vampyre king's brothers. Judging by his size, he was most likely the warrior Latimus.

Kenden, with a true soldier's cunning, had reticently told her that he admired Latimus. He had built the most powerful army on Etherya's Earth. Kenden felt that he would be a fool not to study his every move and try to emulate him. She had to admire Ken for his ability to look past his hatred and see his Vampyre counterpart as a worthy opponent.

"True. Although, remember that if any harm comes to me, the captors I've installed to guard your sister will kill her immediately. So, I guess that makes us even." She smiled sweetly, although the gesture was filled with sarcasm.

"Enough," the king said. As he came closer, she was forced to tilt her head back to look into his eyes. "If we are to be successful, we cannot keep exchanging barbs and insults at each other. Our task is to get to the Cave of the Sacred Prophecy. My brother and I have mapped it out, and it will take ten nights. I don't care to argue with you the entire way. My only goal is to save our sister." He extended his hand to her. "Will you agree to a truce? We have to be cordial if we are going to complete this journey and get on with our lives."

Miranda studied him. Reluctantly, she joined her hand with his, and they shook. She tried not to notice how small her hand felt encased in this creature's massive grip. And she definitely didn't allow herself to acknowledge the tiny butterflies that flitted in her stomach as his palm heated hers.

"I'm assuming he's your brother? The Vampyre army commander?" She jerked her head toward Latimus.

"Yes. But I can't vouch for him being pleasant. It's hard enough to get him to be nice to us."

Detaching their hands, she studied their large black vehicle through the opening in the wall.

"We will take our Hummer since it will allow us to navigate the unpaved roads from here. We'll have to travel through the Strok Mountain pass to the Portal of Mithos. From the Portal, we'll navigate to the Cave, but we'll have to leave the Hummer about fifty miles from the Cave and travel that last bit on foot. Are you up to the task?"

Miranda nodded. Clenching her hands on the straps that fell over both shoulders, she jerked her head to the backpack she was wearing. "I have rations for ten days, a tent and all the gear I'll need. Hopefully, you boys can keep up."

Turning on her heel, she began to walk from them. "Bring the Hummer through the wall. I don't want to waste any more time."

"She's bossy," the larger Vampyre said.

"Tell me about it," the king muttered.

A minute later, Miranda heard the vehicle behind her and climbed into the back seat when it came to a stop.

"How long do you anticipate before we get to the foothills of the Strok Mountains?"

"It's a twelve-hour drive since the roads aren't paved. Sathan and I will take shifts," Latimus said from behind the wheel. "Get comfortable, Slayer. We've got lots of time."

Miranda looked around the backseat, all black leather and complete with tinted windows to block out the sun from the Vampyres' frail skin. "Twelve hours. Great," she muttered, sitting back and crossing her arms over her chest. "I guess it's too much to hope that you heathens like Metallica?"

They both turned to scowl at her.

With a *harrumph*, she rolled her eyes and popped in her ear buds. This was going to be a long journey indeed.

* * * *

They made it to the foothills of the Strok Mountains in just under twelve hours. Miranda grudgingly admired the Vampyres for keeping them on task and driving diligently. They had only stopped for short breaks when one of the passengers needed to pee—most of those times, Miranda being the offender. *Don't these guys hydrate?* she thought as she'd squatted over a bush about thirty feet from the car. She guessed they weren't as up on the whole 'eight glasses a day' thing as she was.

Once they made it to the foothills, dawn was barely stroking the horizon with a dull glow of blue and yellow.

"Let's set up camp," Sathan said from the front seat. "Latimus, can you scope us out a good spot where we'll be shielded from the sun and can build a fire?"

With a nod, the Vampyre exited the car.

"Grab your gear and everything you'll need at camp. We'll leave the Hummer here while we sleep during the day."

Miranda grabbed her pack and shoved it on her back after she exited the car. Upon hearing that Latimus had found them a place to camp, she followed the king into the nearby woods. The Vampyre commander had secured a spot about a hundred feet into the forest and was already working on lighting a fire. "You can set up over there," he said to his brother. Sathan nodded and started unpacking.

Miranda found a smooth spot about ten feet away and started to set up her tent. She made quick work of it and turned to the king, who was still kneeling down attempting to put his tent together.

"Need help?" she asked, her tone baiting. "Since you're busy murdering my people, you probably don't get out to camp much."

Eyes narrowed, he scowled up at her. "I'm just fine, thanks. But you're right. It's been a while since I've been camping. We don't all have our father to run our kingdoms for us. Some of our fathers were murdered, so we have extra responsibilities."

Anger flashed through Miranda as she stared down at him. "I help my father run our kingdom just fine, you blood-sucking bastard."

"Right," he said in a disbelieving tone.

"Screw you," she bit back, crossing her arms. "I'm going to watch the sunrise back by the Hummer. Something you'll never be able to do. Enjoy putting up your tent for the next two hours."

With that, Miranda stomped her way back to the vehicle. Finding a soft patch of grass, she sat and watched the sun grow higher and higher in the sky. What must it be like to never see such beauty? She wondered if the Vampyres missed the sun. Closing her eyes, she inhaled the rich air of the woods and meadow around her. With all the chaos in her life, this moment of stillness was quiet perfection.

* * * *

"She put up her tent faster than you," Latimus said.

"Uh huh," Sathan said, putting the finishing touches on the tent he would share with his brother. "Annoying."

"I'll say," Latimus replied and went to sit by the fire. Opening their thermoses, they sat in silence and drank the Slayer blood inside.

"Pretty sure she'd have a conniption if she saw us drinking blood. How long do you think she'll stay in the sunlight?"

Sathan tilted back his head to look at the thick canopy of trees that gave them the much-needed shade. "I don't know. But if I was lucky enough to watch the sunrise, I wouldn't waste even one day inside."

Latimus' lips drew into a thin line. "My greatest goal is to find a way to let us walk in the sun again. I won't rest until I do."

Sathan looked at his brother, his ice-blue eyes reminding him so much of Arderin. By the goddess, how he missed his sister. He hoped that she was safe and knew that they were doing everything they could to bring her home. "I know you won't," he said, placing a hand on his brother's shoulder and squeezing. "Since Etherya took away our ability to be in the sun so that we could only hunt the Slayers at night, perhaps, by helping this Slayer, we're one step closer to seeing the sunrise again."

Latimus remained impassive. "You have a lot of optimism to think there's hope in aligning with someone who kidnapped our sister."

"It's her only hand. And she's using it magnificently. I can't imagine how much courage it took for her to come to us and demand I help her release the Blade. She says her father is on board, but I have my doubts."

"Many think that he's a false leader. That Miranda should've been made queen after the Awakening, since the blood of Valktor does not run through him as it does her."

Sathan contemplated his brother. "Where did you hear this?"

Latimus shrugged. "Sometimes, we torture Deamons before we kill them to get information they've gained by observing the Slayers." Sathan grimaced. "Well, brother, someone has to do it. We have a functioning army with the best intelligence of the immortals. Sometimes, that information has to be coerced. It's not for the faint of heart but it does yield valuable info."

"I wish that you didn't have to do such things," Sathan said softly. "I feel it's hardened you to a point where you've forgotten how to feel."

Latimus scoffed. "Feelings are overrated. Believe me. I'm fine, thanks."

"You're not. You're completely closed off and you've turned into a pretty big asshole."

"Well, don't blow up my ego all at once, bro," Latimus said. "Like I've told you in the past, the army is what I am. It's what I was put here for. Being commander is my greatest accomplishment, and the other shit is just crap that I'm not cut out for."

Sathan was saddened that his brother only focused on his army. He was fiercely loyal and trustworthy—good qualities in a potential husband and father. "You could have so much more."

"I don't want to talk about this shit." Standing, Latimus took his empty thermos to his backpack and pulled out a bottle. "Macallan 18," he said, waggling his eyebrows.

"Now, there's the good stuff," Sathan said, lifting his empty thermos so that his brother could pour some in. "I knew you wouldn't leave the good scotch behind."

Latimus took a swig straight from the bottle. "If you're going to ask me to leave my army for over a week to camp with a Slayer, I need this." Sitting back down beside his brother, they chatted in the darkness and waited for the princess to return.

Excerpt from The Book of the Goddess, King Markdor Edition
Article 6 – Drinking Directly From Slayera

Let it be known that drinking directly from a Slayera's vein will allow access to that Slayera's thoughts, memories and emotions as long as the blood flows through the Vampyre's body.

Being that Etherya wished to protect the privacy of the Slayera, our valiant King Markdor declared direct drinking illegal.

All blood is to be banked and stored in barrels during the annual Blood-Banking Festival.

Anyone found violating the decree will be sentenced to death.

And all was peaceful on Etherya's Earth.

Thanks be to the Goddess.

Chapter 8

Dusk arrived, and the three packed up their camp and climbed into the Hummer. The road that connected the foothills of the Strok Mountains to the Portal of Mithos was unpaved and winding. Miranda clutched the door handle so hard that her knuckles turned white. Swaying back and forth even with the seat belt on, she worked furiously to eradicate her mind of images of the vehicle overturning...with them inside.

"How much longer?" she asked.

"Thirty minutes," came Latimus' terse reply. His driving was aggressive to say the least.

When they arrived at the Portal, daylight was just beginning to peek out from behind the mountaintops. As they had done the day before, Latimus scouted a campsite for them in the nearby woods, and they went to set up their tents.

"I'll race you," Miranda taunted Sathan, pulling out her tent. "First one to set up gets the first swig of the good scotch your brother's been hiding."

Sathan smiled, the first real smile of his Miranda had ever seen, and her heart jumped like a hot popcorn kernel in her chest. His teeth were white against his full lips, and she could see the slight points of both of his fangs. It should've disgusted her. Instead, she felt hot.

"Good try, but I'm not in the habit of making bets I can't win." Lowering down, he began setting up his tent. "Didn't peg you for a scotch drinker."

"Why, because I have a vagina?" she replied, angry that she noticed how nice his smile was.

He chuckled and shook his head. "No, but I can't say that I know many women who like scotch. I just figured that you'd gravitate toward fine wine or whatever else you all drink when you have your royal parties."

Miranda ran her fingers over the soft fabric of her tent as she contemplated. "We don't have parties anymore," she said softly. "We did when I was very young, but my father stopped once he realized my mother wasn't coming back. He said that it was disrespectful to her memory to enjoy fine things when she had suffered death at the hand of Crimeous."

Sathan was quiet for a moment. "I didn't realize..."

"It's fine," she said with a shrug, picking up one of the tent poles. "There hasn't been a lot to celebrate over the past, oh, thousand or so years. What with my mother being kidnapped and murdered, the Vampyres raiding our compound for blood and the Deamons doing their best to end our species. Parties aren't really our jam in the grand scheme of things."

"I didn't mean to—"

"I'd rather not talk about it," she said and they continued their tasks in silence. "There," she said triumphantly a few minutes later. "All set. Now, how about that scotch?"

Giving her another one of those annoyingly gorgeous smiles, he poured her a generous amount.

* * * *

Sathan studied Miranda as she sat by the fire, her back propped up on a log that Latimus had found nearby and dragged to the campsite. He was exhausted from driving, so he had already headed into their tent to sleep.

Watching the Slayer, he had to admit that she was stunning. As king of his, realm he had first pick of any of the beautiful women he chose to fraternize with. Wanting to respect Lila, he usually would go to the cottages at the edge of the compound where the army widows lived. They were all quite pretty and still very attached to their husbands' memory, which led to very uncomplicated, no-strings-attached liaisons.

But none of them were as striking as the woman sitting across from him. Everything about her was so tiny, but a resolute strength also pulsed from her. Cute, pert ears, perfect cheekbone structure and those olive eyes... He had never met anyone with eyes as deep green as hers. They reminded him of the wet grass that had glistened with rainwater on sunny days when he was a child. Her nose was slightly crooked but that only added to her appeal somehow.

"How did you break your nose?" he asked.

She looked up from her thermos, her eyes glassy in the light of the fire, and he realized that his little Slayer was well on her way to being plowed. "Huh?"

He stood up and walked over to sit next to her by the log. "Your nose is crooked. How did you break it?"

"Which time?" she asked and promptly proceeded to hiccup.

"Okay," he said, gently pulling the container from her hand, "enough scotch for the day. We have a long trek ahead of us."

"I'm fine," she said, waving a hand, but let him set the thermos down beside him. "The first time was when Kenden began training me."

"Your cousin teaches you to fight?"

"Obviously," she said, rolling her eyes dramatically, and he fought not to snicker at how tipsy she was. "What kind of Slayer princess would I be if I couldn't defend my kingdom?"

"Indeed," he said with a nod. "So, you were fighting your cousin...?"

She sat up straighter. "He was getting so pissed at me because I wasn't protecting my face and kept telling me he was going to teach me a lesson if I kept it up. Of course, I did, and of course, he whacked me—bam!—right in the knocker. I bled like a motherfucker," she said, gently rubbing her nose with her finger, "but I never forgot to protect my face again."

Sathan chuckled, thoroughly charmed by her story. And maybe by her, but he'd be loath to admit it. "Not a very nice way to learn a lesson."

"Screw that," she said. "I never want any special treatment because I'm the princess. I told Ken that from day one. You can't learn if you're being shielded. Your enemies certainly won't hold back. I got what I deserved and it made me stronger for it."

Even though he tried to tamp it down, admiration for this tiny creature crept through him. As the princess, she had every right to live a luxurious life and let her army fight her battles. Instead, she chose to train alongside them. As much as he hated to admit it, there was a nobility to that.

"And the second time?" he asked.

"Um, yeah, that story is not so grand. One of the diplomats was visiting from Restia, and my father had promised him I would show him around. My father is always trying to put me in the position of showing around *eligible men*," she said, making quotation marks out of two fingers on each hand, "so that I'll do my duty and procreate. I was showing him the back lawn after dinner one night. He got the wrong idea and leaned down just as I was lifting my head to say something, and his chin hit me right on my nose."

"Yikes," Sathan said.

"Let's just say that he was of the many bachelors who ran away once they realized what a disaster I really am."

"Is it that bad?"

"Yes. Absolutely. One-hundred percent. I am completely unmarriable. Is that a word?" She looked up at the trees above, contemplating. "Well, I say it is. And maybe they can put my name next to it in the dictionary!" She lifted her index finger in the air, accentuating her point.

Sathan couldn't stop his grin. "But you'll have to marry eventually. All good rulers must, in order to fulfill their duty."

She exhaled loudly, her lips vibrating together. "Duty, schmooty. I'm over it. My father is a great ruler. He'll do just fine if I never procreate. And who are you marrying anyway?" she asked with a skeptical expression.

"Etherya declared my betrothed to be the aristocrat Lila, daughter of Theinos and Gwen," Sathan replied.

"Sounds like a real love match," she said, one dark eyebrow raised sarcastically.

"Not all of us get to bond for love. Or marry, as Slayers call it. I think very highly of Lila and will be honored to be her bonded once we decide to move forward."

"You've had a thousand years. What are you waiting for?"

Sathan considered her question. Why had he waited so long to bond with Lila? When they were young, he'd sat her down and given her some excuse about wanting to bond with her under the sun, but that had been centuries ago. Truth was, he could've done it many times over the years. The time had just never seemed right to him. But why?

"It just isn't time yet," he said, unwilling to search his feelings further. "But she is a wonderful woman, and any man would be lucky to have her."

"Says every man who breaks up with a woman. Man, your love life is as whack as mine. Good lord. Give me back the Scotch." Her hand outstretched, she wiggled her fingers.

"Not today, Miranda," he said, lifting to his feet and offering her a hand. "We have a long journey when the sun sets."

"Buzzkill," she murmured but grabbed his hand and let him lift her up. "Tomorrow, we drink the vodka."

"How do you know my brother has vodka?"

"He doesn't. You do. Don't play dumb. I saw it fall out of your pack when you were failing miserably at putting your tent together." And with that, she entered her tent and zipped up the fabric behind her.

Observant little minx, he thought as he checked to confirm the vodka was still in his pack. At least she hadn't stolen it. Yet. He wondered what other talents, besides snooping, he would discover in the Slayer. With surprise, he realized that he was looking forward to finding out.

Excerpt from The Post-Awakening Vampyre Archives
Archive #7 – The Son of the Dark Lord Crimeous

Let it be known that the Dark Lord Crimeous has borne a male heir named Darkrip.
The son of the Dark Lord possesses many of the abilities of his father, including object manipulation, dematerialization and the ability to read images in others' minds.
Take heed, as he is quite powerful.
Now that we are at war with the Slayers, and our young king is only seventeen years old, we must be extra cautious.
Thanks be to the Goddess.

Chapter 9

The lone man walked quickly and solemnly through the caves of the Land of the Deamons. When he reached the twenty-foot wooden doors, he commanded them to open with his mind. They flew open as if made of toothpicks.

He walked into the murky, dreary lair, hate flowing through his veins as it always did. Hate for himself. Hate for what he was. Hate for an infinite future that would never end. Hate for his father. He hated the Dark Lord most of all.

"My lord," he said firmly, coming to stand before the large wooden desk. "I have information on the Slayer princess and the Vampyre king."

Slowly, the high, leather-backed chair turned, revealing the Deamon King sitting on the other side. Pale, pasty skin the color of cement covered a shriveled body shrouded in a flowing purple robe. A bald head sat atop beady black eyes with razor-thin eyebrows and no soul. A long, narrow nose led to lips paler than the moon, slim and chapped, forming a humorless smile.

"What is this news you bring me, son?" he asked in his raspy baritone.

Darkrip gritted his teeth. He hated when he called him "son," not wanting to be reminded that he was spawned from this hateful creature. "They have fared well on their journey so far and have set up camp at the entrance of the Portal of Mithos."

Crimeous brought his long fingers together, tapping the ends of his V-shaped nails simultaneously. The noise grated on Darkrip's nerves.

"Excellent," the Dark Lord replied. "I have no doubt that Miranda will kill the Vampyre once she unsheathes the Blade. She pretends to be noble, but hatred always brings out one's worst impulses when they have an insurmountable advantage. This will empower us to attack the Vampyres and finally conquer them."

"And the Slayers?" Darkrip asked.

Crimeous waved a dismissive hand. "They will most likely break into civil war once Marsias realizes his daughter has killed the king, repeating the sins of her grandfather. Marsias' supporters will attack the Slayers loyal to Miranda, and they'll all kill themselves before we have a chance to. I'm more worried about the Vampyres. Their army is mighty."

"The Vampyre commander travels with the princess and king. This leaves their compound open to attack now."

"Yes,"—the Dark Lord nodded—"but I would rather attack them when they've lost their king. It will be so...*demoralizing*. And I love nothing more than when a species has lost all hope."

"Will that be all, my lord?" Darkrip asked pointedly.

"Yes, my son, you have served me well. I will call on you early in the morrow. For now, rest."

"Thank you, my lord." He turned to exit the room.

"Darkrip!" Crimeous called loudly.

"Yes?" he replied, not turning around.

"Will you ever find it within you to call me Father?" he asked, his tone almost amused.

Turning, Darkrip looked at the creature whom he loathed with his entire being. "No, my lord," he replied willfully.

Crimeous laughed hatefully, the sound filling the room. "Do you despise me, my son?"

Darkrip swallowed, choosing not to answer.

"Good," the Dark Lord said firmly. "Your hate makes you strong. Do not ever forget this."

Darkrip remained silent, a muscle clenching in his jaw.

"Be gone then. Your refusal to throw your hate in my face makes me sick!"

"Yes, my lord," Darkrip said, hoping the continued formality would anger his father one last time. Exiting the room, he closed the doors behind him with his mind.

Angry footsteps echoed down the cavern until he came to his bedchamber. He showered in his bathing room, wishing to wash away every piece of the Evil Lord from him. And yet, how could you wash away half of yourself? Sighing with revulsion, Darkrip stepped back into his bedroom and rubbed his chest. If he had a heart, he would guess that he was feeling something akin to loneliness. Since that was impossible for a creature such as him, he dismissed it altogether.

Unashamed of his nakedness, he stalked down the cavern until he came to his father's harem. Hundreds of Deamon women splashed in the large pool that sat in the center of the room. "My lord Darkrip," one of them sighed, "are you here to let us pleasure you? Please, my lord, it would be our honor."

Darkrip looked down at his cock, always engorged, always aroused. It was a curse that he'd endured for eternity and it made him question why humans created pills to sustain erections. He only coveted one moment of peace when his body was truly relaxed.

"I wish to have only one of you tonight," he called to the harem. "Whom shall I choose?"

Shrieks of pleasure echoed off the walls as the naked girls raised their hands, all vying for his attention. "You," he commanded to one of the faceless women. "Come with me."

He grabbed her wrist and led her down the cave to his bedroom. Pushing her face-down on the bed, he seized her wrists and secured them to the headboard with the ropes that always hung there. Circling her ankles, he did the same to them at the bottom of the bed. Wetting his fingers with his saliva, he rubbed the moisture over the woman's opening to ensure she was ready. Positioning the head of his cock at the entrance of her sensitive tunnel, he plunged in with one hard thrust.

The woman "ooohhhed" and "ahhhed" from the bed, unabashedly enjoying his domination of her. Darkrip pumped into her as waves of revulsion at who he was threatened to strangle him. After what seemed like an eternity, he pulled out and spurted his seed on her back but still remained hard and turgid. Untying the woman from the bed, he sent her back to the harem.

Placing his arm over his eyes, he willed himself to sleep, cursing his father as he sank into nightmares.

* * * *

On the other side of the realm, Arderin was about to die. Literally shrivel up and die. Of boredom. Lifting her fingers, she counted today's activities. Frick and Frack, the Slayer soldiers, had tied her up in a musty cabin somewhere near to where her brothers had come through the wall to start their journey with the Slayer bitch.

Then, the same brown-haired, good-looking guy who had been there when she'd woken up at the Slayer compound had come to check on Frick and Frack. He'd told them he had three barrels of Slayer blood that he'd be depositing at the wall. That was nice.

After that, the friendly Slayer doctor had checked on her, sympathy swimming in her eyes, but had still made sure her bonds were tight. With a sigh, Arderin looked up at the cabin ceiling. Was it day? Night? She had no idea. All she knew was that if she didn't have a conversation with someone soon, she'd gnaw one of her limbs off just to have some excitement.

"Hello?" she called out, hoping to get Sadie's attention. "I need to use the bathroom."

Silence. Frick and Frack must be off in the woods grabbing firewood or having a contest to see who was dumber. Idiots.

"Hello?" she called again, her voice desperate.

The nice Slayer appeared, hoodie in place. Arderin could hear the smile in her voice. "You just went twenty minutes ago. If you have to go again so soon, I think I might need to examine you for a bladder issue."

"But this is so *boring*," Arderin wined, rolling her head on her shoulders as she sat on the floor, her back propped up on the wooden wall. "I swear, Sadie, I'm going nuts here. If you won't let me get up and walk around, at least hang out with me and chat."

"I don't think that's a good idea," the Slayer said hesitantly.

"Oh, who's it gonna hurt?" Arderin asked, excited that she was considering it. "Just us two girls, hangin' and chattin' and, you know, girl stuff. Please?" Her voice dripped with sweetness. "Just for a few minutes?"

"Okay," Sadie said and dropped down beside her. *Thank the goddess.* "What do you want to talk about?"

"Hmmm," Arderin said, wracking her brain. "Who do you think is hottest on Insta right now? Like, I really like Nick Jonas and Shawn Mendes but Zac Efron will always be the hottest in my mind."

Sadie slowly shoved her hoodie down to her neck, revealing her face, which was a mask of puzzlement. "What is an Insta?"

"Instagram," Arderin said, as if she was daft. "You know, one of the greatest inventions of the humans in the last hundred years?"

Sadie shook her head and smiled, her unburned cheek reddening a bit. "I don't really have any use for human achievements unless they involve medicine."

"Wait, what?" Arderin said, sitting up straighter. "You've never used Instagram?"

"Sadly, no," the Slayer said with a chuckle. "I'm sorry to disappoint you."

"Oh sister, we have a *lot* to cover. Wait until I teach you about Snapchat. Their filters will make you look like a supermodel."

Looking at the ground, she smiled softly. "Probably not me."

"Nope," Arderin said firmly. "Even you. I swear, Sadie, you'll be amazed. Go get your phone, girl."

The Slayer laughed softly and rose from the ground. "Okay, what can it hurt? Let me grab it from my bag."

As Arderin watched her, she felt almost sad that she was going to use this caring creature to escape her bondage. Although she hated the Slayer princess bitch with a passion, Sadie had been nothing but kind to her. In fact, she actually *liked* her. However, she could tell that the doctor lived in self-imposed exile, which made it very easy to befriend her. Chewing on her bottom lip, Arderin's heart squeezed at the pain Sadie would feel when she realized she had used her to escape.

But then again, a girl had to survive, and she'd had enough of this captivity. As Sadie approached and sat back down beside her, Arderin contemplated how long it would take to convince her to untie the bonds at her wrists and ankles. She gave the Slayer twenty-four hours, tops. Using this as her goal, she got down to business.

"Okay, let's start with Insta..."

Excerpt from The Post-Awakening Vampyre Archives
Archive #14 – Humans

The Universe declared that humans would exist on Etherya's Earth. They would evolve as they did on the Earth in the Milky Way Galaxy, their world here a mirror image of that far-off world. The parallel species would share the same history, successes, tribulations and technological advances.

Humans on the other Earth eventually destroyed themselves with their mistakes and inability to control their less-than-noble impulses. But they were also creatures of great love and compassion.

Therefore, the Universe wished to give them an opportunity to try again.

Their world is separated from us by the Ether created by Etherya. It surrounds the world of immortals and is invisible to the human eye. Moving through its density is difficult, and due to its thickness, one can only bring through what they carry on their body.

Immortals are able to enter different periods in the human world, as the space-time continuum flows unorthodoxly there. This has allowed us to learn much from them over the centuries.

We travel to their world to learn of their advancements and implement them in our world, but they never travel to ours as they do not know of its existence.

Thanks be to the Goddess.

Chapter 10

As soon as the sun set, the three travelers set about to traverse the Portal of Mithos. The Portal, which connected the Strok Mountains to the woods of the Cave of the Sacred Prophecy, was quite treacherous. Miranda tried her best to focus on the music coming out of her earbuds as Sathan drove through the various dirt roads and small streams.

Large oak trees with gnarled branches seemed to pop up in the middle of their path every hundred feet. Sathan would swerve, causing Miranda's stomach to lurch, and she cursed herself for eating the waxy granola bar earlier. Pretty soon, she was going to hurl it right into Latimus' slick hair.

Green bushes dotted with red flowers lined the edge of the dirt road. Large yellow bees buzzed back and forth under the moonlight as they fought for position to suck the life-giving nectar from the pretty buds. Since it was dark, she searched the tall, thin-stalked grass for nocturnal vermin. A pair of beady eyes shined at her in the moonlight as the car sunk down into a large hole. Sathan cursed, revved the gas, and the Hummer groaned as it was extricated from the indention.

The Portal of Mithos was an undeveloped part of Etherya's Earth. Past it, there was only the Cave of the Sacred Prophecy and the Purges of Methesda. After that, the land of Vampyres and Slayers ended, and the human world began.

Traveling into the land of humans was something that immortals rarely did. Miranda had never been and doubted she ever would. Traversing to the Cave would most likely be her most adventurous journey.

Several hours later, they made it to the edge of the woods. This was where their journey in the Hummer ended. They all packed the gear they needed, locked up the vehicle and started into the woods on foot.

About ten miles in, Miranda started to get tired. The trail was narrow and filled with stones she kept needing to navigate around or over. No less than four blisters had formed on her feet, and she cursed the new hiking boots that she'd changed into.

Not that she'd tell either of the Vampyre bastards who were hiking in front of her any of this information. She would rather cut off her own foot than let them know she was in serious pain. She remained mute until Latimus came to a stop around the eighteen-mile mark.

"Let's camp here for the day. I think the Slayer might pass out if we continue any further, and the sun is about to rise."

"I'm absolutely fine," Miranda said, her chin lifting in defiance. "In fact, I could hike the entire fifty miles if you all aren't too tired to keep going."

"No, thanks," Sathan said, removing his pack and lifting one arm to massage his shoulder. Miranda absolutely did *not* notice his bulging bicep as he worked his hand into his flesh. "I'm good to camp here. There's a clearing over there." He motioned his head to the nearby patch of soft grass. "Looks as good as any to me."

Nodding, Latimus went to scope out the clearing and beckoned them over with his hand.

After the tents were set up, Miranda sat down inside hers and removed her boots. The four blisters, two on each foot, were bleeding and swollen. Pulling out her first-aid kit, she began to methodically clean them, hissing each time the alcohol-laced swab touched the battered skin.

"How's it looking?" Sathan asked from the door of her tent, which she had stupidly left unzipped.

"Fine," she snapped, shooting him a scathing glare. "And I would ask you not to invade the privacy of my tent."

As if she hadn't uttered a damn word, the Vampyre stalked in and sat down across from her. "Your blisters look bad, Miranda. I don't want them to slow us down. I can help you heal them if you want."

"I'd rather ask for help from a snake," she hissed, sounding much like the creature she referenced. "Get out of my tent."

Squinting his face, he looked toward the top of the tent and rubbed his chin with his fingers. "And here I thought we called a truce and said we would be cordial with each other on this journey."

"Oh, for god's sake! I'm trying to be cordial, but it's hard when you're invading every inch of my privacy, creepy stalker. Get out of my tent and let me clean my blisters. I promise I won't slow us down. I'm tough and will keep up with the pace tomorrow."

"That, I absolutely believe," he said in his calm baritone, and she felt her defenses lessen a bit. "But why should you suffer in pain if I can help you?"

Sighing in annoyance, she asked, "Okay, and how exactly can you help?"

"A Vampyre's saliva carries healing properties."

"So, you want to lick my feet?" she asked, her voice ending in a squeak. "That's super weird—"

"I'm glad you find my attempt to help you so funny," he said, exasperated. "I was suggesting that I wet one of your cloths with my saliva and you can rub it on your blisters." He shifted to stand. "But if you would rather suffer..."

"Wait," she said, grabbing his forearm so that he remained seated. "Okay, I get it. It's really nice of you to offer. Here." She thrust a clean cloth in his face. "Maybe you could spit on there?" She began to chuckle and then broke out into a full-on laugh. Sathan watched her as she sat rocking back and forth, hugging her waist, gasping as she walloped with laughter.

"What the hell is so funny?" he asked. He looked so ridiculous holding the white cloth, his expression baffled, that she broke into another round of laughter.

"Okay, forget it." Standing, he threw the cloth at her. "That's the last time I try to help you."

"I'm sorry," she gasped, attempting to stand up but still gasping air between lingering laughs. "I swear, I—ouch!" Losing her footing, she fell back to the floor. "Those little suckers hurt!" Looking up at him, she held up the cloth. "I want to try. Please, put your spit on the cloth. I promise I didn't mean to laugh at you. It's just been such a long day, and I break into fits like that sometimes. It drives Ken crazy."

Sathan raised an eyebrow and reluctantly sat down in front of her again. Lifting the cloth to his mouth, he spat into it several times and rubbed the moisture in.

"This is so gross," Miranda said.

"Here," he said, thrusting the cloth toward her. Grasping it, she began to rub it on her feet, and what do you know? It actually made her blisters feel better. "Geez, we need to bottle this shit. It's good stuff."

"Once it dries, the healing properties expire. That's why it's always most effective to lick a wound directly to close and heal it quickly."

With those words, an image flashed in Miranda's mind of this Vampyre thrusting his fangs into the vein at her neck, sucking her blood as his hands wandered her body. Then, upon finishing, this massive creature with black eyes and full lips would begin to lick her wound with his wet tongue. He, her greatest enemy, giving her pleasure unlike anything she'd ever known or even tried to imagine.

Miranda shook her head to clear her thoughts. What the fuck? She must be in desperate need for sleep, that was for damn sure. Did blisters affect one's mental health? She'd have to look into that.

"Thank you," she said softly, not trusting herself to look him in the eyes lest he catch a glimpse of the madness that had overtaken her brain. "This was really helpful. I think it's time I turned in."

Acknowledging her, he stood and left the tent. "Good day, Miranda."

"Good day," she said softly, watching him zip the tent behind him.

Later, as she was attempting to fall asleep, she berated herself in the darkness. He was the leader of the species who abducted and murdered her people for blood. She'd do well to remember that. She continued to scold herself until she fell into a restless slumber.

* * * *

Sathan noticed that Miranda was packed and ready to go before he and his brother had bundled their tent the next evening. If she was trying to send a message that she wasn't holding them up, she had succeeded. Reluctant admiration coursed through him as he finished packing up camp.

Several hours later, she was leading the group, trudging along the winding path at a pace that even he found hard to navigate. She certainly wasn't weak, that was for sure. He and his brother had underestimated how quickly she could move. He found himself wishing that half his soldiers could be armed with her steely determination.

The view wasn't half-bad either. Hiking behind her, with Latimus bringing up the rear, he had a first-class ticket to the fine show her backside was putting on. She'd opted for some sort of black yoga-legging-looking things today, and they surely didn't disappoint. Regardless of the species—Vampyre, Slayer, human or Deamon—he was sure every male could appreciate a great ass in yoga pants.

He imagined placing his large hands on the juicy globes, one on each cheek, and spreading her apart from behind. That, unfortunately, made him grow rock hard, and he rushed to adjust himself so he could keep up the pace. His brother gave an asinine *"ahem"* behind him, and Sathan turned his head to give him a hateful glare. Latimus just jutted an eyebrow at him as if to say, *Keep it in your pants, asshole, we've got work to do here.* Bastard.

They hiked about twenty miles and decided they would camp for the day and trek the remaining twelve miles to the Cave the next evening. As usual, Miranda made quick work of putting up her tent and then disappeared.

"Where did the Slayer go?" Sathan asked, trying to conceal any care or concern for her from his voice.

"Wouldn't you like to know?" came his brother's sardonic reply. "Careful, Sathan. She's not one of your war widows. She's the princess of our sworn enemy."

Sathan felt a muscle clench in his jaw. "I'll choose not to honor that with a response." Rummaging in his pack, he found the bottle of vodka and stalked from the camp.

He found her sitting on a clearing of green grass, arms around her tucked-in knees, head tilted to the sky, eyes closed. A perfect picture of tranquility. It made him long for his grassy spot on the hill at Astaria, under the large elm tree—the only place he ever felt peace.

Judging by the dim light on the horizon, the sun wouldn't rise for an hour or so.

"Mind if I join you?"

Annoyance clattered inside him as she scowled and turned her head toward him, drilling that lush-green gaze right into his. "As if I have a choice? You seem intent on invading any moment of privacy I have, so why not this one?"

Arching a dark brow and lifting his lips into a grin, he held out the bottle. "I brought vodka."

Narrowing her eyes, she contemplated. "Good negotiating. C'mon over."

With a chuckle, he sat beside her. Her tiny hand palmed the bottle, unscrewed the cap, and she took a long swig. Her neck was long and smooth in the waning moonlight, and he imagined tracing a finger lightly down the vein he saw pulsing there.

When she lifted the bottle to take another shot, he cautioned her. "Whoa, slow down, killer. We've still got a decent hike tomorrow."

Holding the bottle in her left hand as that elbow perched on her upturned knee, she looked over toward him. "You'd love my father."

"I don't think so," he said derisively.

"Seriously. I've never met two men who like to scold me more. It's absolutely fucking annoying." Lifting the bottle to her lips, she sputtered when he grabbed it away and took a large swig himself. "Hey!"

"Maybe someone should've taught you to share. Having many siblings, this is something I learned early on. It's called manners, princess. And you could also say, 'Thanks for the vodka, Sathan.'"

She pursed her lips and regarded him. "You're so full of yourself, you know that?"

"And you're a brat." He took another sip from the bottle.

Her laugh washed over him like a warm wave in a calm ocean. Looking over at her, he found himself mesmerized by her smile. All of those white teeth surrounded by her bronzed skin. It had been so long since his people had seen the sun that he barely remembered what tanned skin looked like. He ached to run his hands over her, to feel her golden-brown complexion. Instead, he took another swig.

"Hey! Who's not sharing now?"

Smiling, he handed the bottle back to her.

"Aren't you going to burn up and die or something, being out here at dawn?"

Sathan shrugged. "As long as I get back to camp before the sun rises, I'll be fine. I always liked the dawn. When I was a kid, after we lost the ability to walk in the sun, I'd stay outside before the sunrise as long as I could to see how far I could push it. I think I hoped that one day I would discover Etherya had lifted her curse. Eventually, I gave up hope."

Miranda was silent for a moment, a rarity for her. "If you stop hunting my people, won't she lift the curse?" Her gaze was focused on the faint horizon but her posture indicated that she knew the gravity of what she was asking.

"Probably," he said softly.

"Then, why haven't you?"

He inhaled deeply, followed by a long exhale. Sad and contemplative. "I wish nothing more than to stop abducting your people. A few centuries after the Awakening, we tried to negotiate with your father. Unfortunately, our attempts at negotiating peace were unrequited."

Miranda took a long swallow from the bottle and handed it back to him. "Drink," she commanded. "And then tell me what the hell you're talking about."

After complying, he continued. "I was only ten years old at the Awakening. When I assumed the throne, everyone in the kingdom was upset about my parents' murder. Of course, I was furious too, but what does a ten-year-old child know? I let my advisors council me that war was the only option. That it was my duty to attack the people of the man who had murdered my parents and drain their blood."

Miranda shivered next to him. "Are you cold?" he asked.

"No." She shook her head, pushing her boot-clad toe into the ground. "It's just so surreal. I was only eight at the Awakening. I was deemed too young to ascend to the throne, even though I was the rightful heir as Valktor's surviving blood descendant, so my father stepped in. I can't imagine how you took over a kingdom at ten years old." She lifted those amazing eyes to his. "You never got to be a child."

Swallowing, he drilled his gaze into hers, silently thanking her for understanding. Perhaps she was the only other person on the planet who could. "No. But I didn't have time to focus on that. So, I just went about my duties, full-force. One of them being hunting the Slayers."

She grabbed the bottle from him. "Go on."

"It was thrilling for a while, growing into my immortality, going through my change, watching my brother build a powerful army." He began absently pulling at the grass, looking down at the ground as he continued. "But eventually, it became burdensome. I found it hard to sleep before each raid, knowing I was separating Slayers from their families for what would certainly be forever."

"My father's suicide decree," she said softly.

Sathan nodded. "I don't understand why he would issue such a decree knowing that it would mean we will have to continually replenish our supply of blood."

"Because capitulating to you and allowing our soldiers to stay alive is a form of surrender. I assure you, my father would never allow that."

"And what about you?" he asked, regarding her in the shadowy light. "Do you agree with the suicide decree?"

Miranda propped her head on her hand, her elbow resting on her pulled-up knee. "I do," she said. "We have to show you that we're not weak. That we will never surrender and will be a worthy opponent till the death."

He felt a severe sadness at her words. "Well, that seems shortsighted to me. In a world where we have a more powerful army than yours, it's only a matter of time until your people are exterminated."

"And what will you do then?" she asked angrily. "If our species dies, yours will as well."

"True. This is why I tried to form a truce with your father centuries ago. I wrote him many official letters explaining that I understood both of us were on a trajectory of eradicating our people if we let the war continue. I told him that I was open to any possible solutions and would be honored to sit with him in a royal summit and discuss. My letters went unanswered. After a few years of trying, I gave up. Then, the Deamons started attacking us too, and I refocused on protecting our people at all costs."

"Son of a bitch," Miranda said, the last word drawing out with a long "shhhhh", and he realized she was buzzed. "My father never told me that."

"I wish he had. Perhaps you could've talked some sense into him. Whether you want to admit it or not, I believe we have similar aspirations. We both want our people to live in peace, without war and destruction."

"And how do I know you're not lying?" she asked. "Perhaps you're feeding me false information in order to drive a wedge between me and my father."

"I think you're smarter than that, Miranda."

"Don't mansplain to me how smart I am, you arrogant ass!" Standing up, she thrust the bottle into his chest. "My father would never omit to tell me something like that! I don't believe you as far as I can throw you. I know you hate me for holding your sister hostage, but if you think I'm dumb enough to believe your lies, then you've severely underestimated me."

She stalked away from him but not before turning and yelling, "Oh, and thanks for the vodka, you arrogant fucking asshole. I hope you burn to death while I sleep!"

Letting her go, Sathan sighed and took another long swig from the bottle. Tiny wisps of red and yellow were on the brink of becoming brighter. He needed to return to camp.

Whether the Slayer realized it or not, they had made some progress tonight. He now understood that she was the one he should've attempted to negotiate with all those centuries ago. When he had spoken about their people living in peace, an expression of longing had come over her face. She wished to end the war as much as he did. That made them comrades of sorts. A plan began to form in his mind, one he knew would take much convincing on the part of his brothers, his advisors and his people. But one he also knew would work.

He was going to have to align with the Slayer princess and convince her to overthrow her father. It wasn't going to be easy but it was going to end the war. In the grand scheme of things, that was all that mattered.

It was imperative that he plant the seed of their alliance before they finished their journey. Once she returned home, it would be extremely difficult to influence her from Astaria. He screwed the top back onto the bottle and walked back to the camp, confident in his strategy.

Excerpt from The Post-Awakening Vampyre Archives
Archive #354 – The Last Entry

Let it be known that this will be the last entry in the Vampyre archives.
Until the war is over, our great King Sathan does not wish to record the instances of death and hate.
King Sathan believes that there can be peace again and the sun will shine upon us once more.
We, the Vampyre archivists, leave you with wishes of prosperity and hope.
If, in the future, you find fault with some of our entries, please know that we did our best to put our people and our kingdom first.
It is sometimes better to record what is right in your heart than what is right in the moment.
We look forward to resuming our important work once harmony reigns and the sun shines again.
Until then, peace be with you, with our great King Sathan and with Etherya above all.

Chapter 11

Heden held his palm to the stone wall at the edge of the compound and the invisible door opened. Stepping through, he approached the Slayer on the other side. Tall and fit, he must be one of their soldiers.

"I have your banked blood for the evening," he said, motioning his head to the three wooden barrels beside him. "You're not the soldier who has been coming to meet me to collect the shipment."

"No, I decided to come in his place tonight." Stepping closer, he extended his hand. "I'm Heden, brother to King Sathan."

The Slayer seemed surprised at the kind gesture of the greeting. "Kenden," he said, joining his hand and giving a firm shake.

"The Slayer commander," Heden said, a bit of surprise in his voice.

Kenden nodded.

"I didn't think you would actually deliver the barrels yourself."

"This mission is too important to allow subordinates. We have your sister, and your brothers are sequestered with my cousin in dense woods with no cell service. I felt it important that I keep an eye on as much as I can without interfering with her mission."

"Do you have an update on Arderin? Is she okay?" Heden asked.

"She's fine, I assure you. Two of my best soldiers and our compound's physician are with her, making sure she stays strong and healthy. We have no desire to hurt her. My cousin only wants to free the Blade so that she can challenge and ultimately kill Crimeous. She has grown tired of endless war and has finally decided to take action."

Heden studied the brown-haired Slayer, noting that he looked nothing like the black-haired Slayer he had seen depart with his brothers through the opening in the wall several nights ago.

"She and I are related on her father's side. Her father and mine were brothers. The blood of Marsias' line runs through me. The blood of Valktor runs through her."

"I didn't—"

"I could see the question churning in your mind," the Slayer said.

"My brother Latimus has spoken to me of you."

Kenden lifted an eyebrow, his expression skeptical.

"He says that you're the greatest strategist he's ever seen. That it would've been almost impossible to create a competent army from a weaker species, unaccustomed to fighting before the Awakening, but that you were able to do it magnificently. He has studied your practices and although he wouldn't admit it, I think he admires you a great deal."

"Weaker species comment aside, thank you," Kenden said.

"It's hard for us, knowing that we were created to protect you," Heden said, looking down at Kenden from his six-foot-six height. Although he estimated the Slayer was probably six-foot-two, he still towered over him and outweighed him by a good seventy-five pounds.

"We never asked for this war. It is a product of the mistakes that the generation before us made. Hopefully, my cousin, and perhaps your brother, can succeed in finding a solution."

Heden found his words encouraging. "I hope so. My brother has grown long-tired of the fighting, and we spend much time battling the Deamons now. Our people deserve more."

"We find ourselves fighting the Deamons with increasing regularity as well," Kenden said, his expression grim. "I have developed a weapon, comparable to the eight-shooter for Vampyres, that has been quite effective at killing them in one shot."

"No shit," Heden said, his technological mind spinning into overdrive. "Is it based on the irregularity of their third eye?" Deamons had a vestigial third eye that had never evolved into an organ. Located on their forehead, between their two normal eyes, it was a thick patch of round skin said to be extremely vulnerable and sensitive.

"Yes," the Slayer responded.

"How does it work? Is it shot directly into the head? Or leveed by a contraption that is attached? I have schematics for something that I tinkered with centuries ago. I could show you tomorrow evening when you deliver the barrels." He could barely contain the excitement in his voice. His love of invention ran deep.

"I think it's best that we wait to see how my cousin and your brother's mission turns out before we start sharing secrets," Kenden said, his voice deadpan.

Wow, this guy's a real barrel of laughs. But he did have a point. "Sure, sure," Heden said, reminding himself that they were sworn enemies. "Well, good luck with it. Those Deamons are a bunch of bastards."

"Truer words." Extending his hand, Heden shook it firmly. "Nice to meet you, Heden."

"Nice to meet you, Kenden."

The Slayer got into a black four-wheeler, revved the engine and drove off, following the road along the river.

Heden loaded the barrels onto the crate and then pulled it back through the opening, the stones materializing behind him.

Neither of them noticed the pair of deep green eyes watching them from the darkness behind the trees of the nearby forest.

* * * *

Miranda awoke with a mixed sense of excitement and trepidation. This was the night she would unearth the Blade. She would be lying to herself if she didn't admit that there was a small amount of fear she wouldn't be able to extricate it. What if the soothsayers were wrong and the prophecy was false? What if her and Sathan's shared blood couldn't free the weapon?

Pushing her doubt aside, she arose and walked outside, disappointed to realize that it was still daytime. She walked further from the thick canopy that hung over the campsite and saw that the sun was still close to two hours from setting. Deciding to use the time to her advantage, she grabbed her toiletries bag and set out to find a pond or river to bathe in.

She found one about a hundred and fifty feet away, a large lake whose water seemed to be clean. Lucky for her, the waning sun was still shining on the shore, and knowing that her companions would never come anywhere close to the sun, she stripped off her clothes and set to bathing.

As she ran the soap-sudded cloth over her skin, she reveled in how good it felt. Other than the hand rinses she'd done with her cloth and water rations over the past few days, she hadn't had a decent bath since she'd left the Slayer compound.

She also thought about what a lying bastard the Vampyre king was. As if she was stupid enough to believe for one second that her father wouldn't inform her if their greatest enemy had contacted him offering to negotiate a truce.

Something nagged at her though, as she ran the wet cloth over her arm. He would tell her...wouldn't he? She had always known that her father had his issues with her, but she assumed that for the most part, he trusted and wanted her council. If for nothing more than the fact that she was Valktor's granddaughter, and by tradition, that meant she must be recognized as at least a partial ruler of the realm. Her father was nothing if not a traditionalist. That was for damn sure. Resolute in her belief that the Vampyre must be lying, she dismissed the doubt.

Finishing up, she stepped out of the water and took one last stretch in the sun, allowing her skin to dry naturally.

"Well, what a nice view," came a voice from the woods.

Shrieking, she grabbed her towel and wrapped it around her body, clutching the top to her chest with her fists. "Who's there?"

"It's just me, Miranda, calm down," Darkrip said, his voice chiding. "I'd rather you save the view to seduce the Vampyre king."

Miranda took a deep breath and exhaled slowly, trying to calm her furiously beating heart. "Hard to believe from a man who was discussing raping an innocent woman last time I saw him."

The Deamon's eyes narrowed as he glared at her. Miranda felt something shift in her chest as she looked at him. She couldn't quite place her finger on it but she felt a strange sense of familiarity in his green-eyed gaze. Only for a second, and then it was gone. "I have no interest in raping you, Miranda. You understand nothing. It's hard for me to deal with species such as yours and the Vampyres. Both of you, so slow and stupid." Sighing, he lifted his hand in a dismissive wave. "No matter, I don't have a lot of time since the Vampyres surely heard you shriek, and I've come to update you."

"Update me on what?" she asked angrily.

"Your cousin made contact with the youngest Vampyre royal, Heden, earlier this evening. It was a good exchange. They were quite amicable. I see them being loyal to our cause."

"*We* don't have a cause," Miranda said through her clenched teeth. "I told you that I have no wish to align with a Deamon, and if you're not careful, I'll kill you with the Blade after I dispose of your father!"

"Oooohhhhh," he said in a jibing tone, "so snarky. Your Vampyre must love that." His upturned lips formed a sarcastic smile. "I'll bet he just can't wait to whisper words of love in your pretty little ear—"

"Fuck you, asshole." She started to lift her hands to shove him but realized that would cause her to drop her towel.

His laugh made her want to vomit. "Now, now, Miranda. Calm yourself. You get too worked up, and we both know your spur-of-the-moment decisions are...shall we say...less than ideal. The Vampyre is good for you in that way. He has a calmness that will help you navigate your impulses, and you have a courage that will help him take action. It's a good match."

"My god, you're infuriating. Please, leave me alone."

"In due time. Take heed to what I said about your cousin and the king's brother. I'll be watching you. Make sure to pull strongly on the Blade."

Miranda was about to tell him she was going to pull strongly on his neck as she strangled him but instead, she turned her head toward Sathan's voice, coming from the woods. "Miranda! Are you okay? We heard you scream. I'm coming to help you."

Turning back, she discovered that Darkrip had vanished.

"I'm fine," she shouted, annoyed that yet again her privacy had been compromised. "I was just taking a bath. I'll be back to camp in five minutes."

So much for a soothing dip in the lake. Scowling, she donned the clean clothes she'd brought with her and then headed back to camp, wondering the entire way what the son of the Deamon king really wanted with her.

Chapter 12

They hiked the remaining twelve miles in record time. Latimus found a clearing with a dense tree overhang about a ten-minute walk from the opening of the Cave of the Sacred Prophecy. As they prepared, Miranda heard him speaking to Sathan.

"Be careful as you navigate the Cave. It's been centuries since anyone has been in there, and the foundation might not be secure. The archives say that it's only a short distance to the Blade but that was written after the Awakening. Who knows if it's true?"

"I'll be careful," Sathan said, shaking his brother's hand in a way that Miranda found quite formal. If Kenden were here, she'd hug him until he couldn't breathe. Feeling lonely, she blew out an impatient breath. "It would be great if we could head up there before the next century passes. I'm getting pretty tired of hanging out with Vampyres all day and would like to get this over with."

Sathan shot her a look. "Enough, Miranda. It's a short walk, so leave your pack here. The less we carry, the faster we'll go."

"Thanks for your instructions, *Dad,*" she said, rolling her eyes, "but I think I'll hang onto my knife, thank you very much. Can't be too careful." Giving him her sweetest smile, she batted her eyelashes, stuck her knife in the belt that held up her camouflage pants and turned to walk toward the path that led to the Cave.

"Maybe just kill her once you've loosened the Blade," Latimus said. "Prophecy or not, she's a pain in the ass."

Miranda heard the remark and turned to give a retort but noticed Sathan giving the same look of warning to his brother that he had just given her. Well, fine then.

She continued on and heard Sathan's footsteps behind her.

A short time later, they came to the mouth of the cave. As she began to enter, he grabbed her wrist.

"Let me go first," he said.

"I'm perfectly capable—"

"I know you are," he said, squeezing her wrist. "But I don't want you to get hurt. It might not be sturdy. Let me lead."

"Fine," she said, pulling her arm from his grasp.

Sathan entered, and she ignored the slice of terror that shot through her spine as she followed him. Turning on the flashlight she carried on her belt, she walked through the darkness.

Drops of water fell from the slick, rocky roof, the sound echoing like tiny pings in her ears. Although she was loath to admit it, she was thankful to have Sathan's hulking body in front of her. She didn't know why, but she believed he would save her if the cave started to collapse.

Time seemed to stand still as they trekked through the dimness. Eventually, something gleamed in the beam of her flashlight. Approaching slowly, they came to stand in front of the rock that sheathed the Blade.

The roof of the cave was only eight or nine feet tall where they stood, and claustrophobia threatened to choke her. As they stared at the rock, the Blade it held seemed to wink at her in the shadows. Was it a sign? Ominous or hopeful? She didn't know.

The large brown stone that held the Blade, and crested at her breastbone, beckoned to her. The last person who had stood here was her grandfather. Emotion clenched her throat as she contemplated the task before her.

"So much pain and death resulted from this Blade," Sathan said, his voice sober. "Are you sure you want to unsheathe it?"

Miranda lifted her gaze to his black one, not understanding how she could still see his irises in the murkiness of the cave. And yet, they seemed to tunnel into her very soul. "We have a chance to change the course of history. To end the death and destruction. I have to try."

A moment passed, and he gave her a firm nod. Words were futile. It was time to act.

Lifting a small knife from his waistband, he raised his left wrist, hand fisted over the Blade. Miranda placed the still-lit flashlight on the ground and stood to mirror him, with her left hand fisted over the Blade. With his right hand, he sliced his knife over the pale skin of his wrist, and blood began to ooze from the wound. Handing her the knife, she cut an incision into her own wrist and handed the knife back to him. Lifting their fists, they watched their blood drip and pool onto the juncture where the Blade met the stone.

Silence stretched around them like an invisible casing. Miranda felt tightness in her chest and her breathing became labored. After several moments, a trickle of frustration set in.

"Patience," Sathan murmured.

Miranda's reply was a scathing glare, but he just stared calmly back at her. Intensely annoying, especially when she was trying not to notice how badly the cut on her wrist throbbed.

And then, after several moments that seemed to last for eternities, the ground began to shake under her boots. Exhaling a quick breath, she latched her free hand onto the handle of the Blade, attempting to pull it from the rock, but the stone was unforgiving.

"Keep pulling," Sathan said as he joined his wrist with hers so that their twin wounds were touching, mingling. Miranda felt a jolt at the contact that she neither wanted nor cared to acknowledge.

"It's not budging," she said through her clenched teeth.

"It will."

And then, as if it had only been encased in a cloud of air, the Blade slipped from the stone, and Miranda held it in her hand. Breaking contact with the Vampyre, she held up the Blade, wonder in her expression.

"We did it," she said, her eyes wide.

Sathan nodded. "Come," he said, grabbing her bleeding wrist. "We don't know how stable the cave foundation is. We need to get outside before we close our wounds."

His words echoed into her mind as if they'd been spoken from a chamber a thousand miles away. An energy entered her body, and she looked up at her companion. Her foe. Her greatest enemy. Pulling her wrist from his, she placed that hand on the handle as well, wielding it like the soldier her cousin had trained her to be.

"Miranda," he said, his expression puzzled. "We have to go. The ground is not solid."

One stroke. That was all it would take to strike him down. Like her grandfather before her, she could plunge the Blade into his heart and end him right here. It was made from a special poisoned steel that his self-healing body would never recover from.

She knew the moment he realized what she was contemplating. Resignation overtook his expression as he lowered his hands to his sides and turned to face her.

"Think long and hard about what course you want to take, Miranda," he said, the soothing tranquility of his voice causing her further annoyance. "In your quest to rewrite history, I would hope that you don't instead repeat it."

Anger bubbled up from her throat to her voice. "You've killed so many of my people," she said, glaring at him in accusation.

He nodded, but the move was filled with resignation. "I've made many mistakes and live with the regret of every life lost in this endless war. But you have the power to change that. Killing me will be rewarding, for a moment perhaps, but my brother awaits outside the cave."

"I'll kill him too!"

"And how many others?" he asked, lifting his hands in frustration. "Will you kill until you become the monster you accuse me of being? Where will that leave you?"

Miranda felt her chin quiver but was too enraged to be embarrassed. Suddenly, the ground shook beneath them, and small rocks started falling from the roof.

"The cave is collapsing, Miranda."

"Stop. Being. So. Calm." The muscle in her jaw clenched. "I hate you so much. I could kill you right here, and your brother after you, and then Kenden could attack your compound. And my father would be proud. So proud of me."

"Yes, he probably would be. But you're better than that. I don't know you well but I've seen enough to know what a magnificent leader you can become. You said yourself, on the night we met, that it takes strength to find a peaceful solution instead of just killing your enemy. Show me how. We can do this together." Slowly, palm up, he extended his hand toward her. "Take my hand. We have to get out of this cave."

In reaction, she clenched the weapon tighter, lifted it higher. Ready to strike. Loud grumblings echoed around them as the cave continued to shake and moan.

Letting fury overtake her, Miranda gritted her teeth and swung the Blade.

Sathan grunted and shifted out of the way, causing her to lose her balance. Quickly, she recovered and lifted the weapon to strike again.

Quick as a lightning, his hand grabbed her belt, and he spun her so that her back was to him.

Giving a loud "*oomph*" when she crashed into his body, she tried to lift the Blade again. His massive arm snaked around her waist, holding her to his front. As she struggled, he pulled the Blade from her hands, throwing it to the ground.

"You son of a bitch!" she sputtered, trying to escape the death grip he had on her.

"Goddamnit, Miranda," he said in her ear, the deep timbre of his voice sending shivers through her furious body. "I thought there was a possibility you'd try to kill me when you had the Blade but I hoped you wouldn't. Guess it was too much to ask."

Lifting the knife that he had sheathed in his belt, he deftly swung it so that the hilt faced out. With the speed of a cougar, he knocked the base of the knife into her skull.

Miranda's last thought was that her Vampyre had some serious skills with a knife. And then, all she saw was darkness.

* * * *

As soon as Miranda crumpled to the ground, Sathan picked her up in his arms and grabbed the Blade. Small rocks falling from the ceiling of the cave had turned to larger ones, and he knew he didn't have much time to get them to safety.

Running through the dusky tunnel, he didn't contemplate her actions. There would be time for that. Until then, he needed to make sure they both survived.

Once he reached the cave's entrance, Latimus rushed to him. "What the hell?" his brother asked.

"Take her," Sathan said, handing Miranda over. "We need to move further from the cave. It's collapsing."

With a nod, his brother began to carry her down the trail, and Sathan followed, licking his wrist to close the wound. Miranda's cut would need attention but not until they reached their camp.

After the ten-minute hike to their campsite, Latimus lowered Miranda to rest on a large log that sat by the fire pit. Scowling at Sathan, he began to build a fire. "What the fuck happened?"

Sathan sat beside Miranda and lifted her wrist to examine her wound. "Hand me the towel and the water."

Latimus grumbled something unintelligible but gave his brother the items he requested. Sathan went about cleaning Miranda's wound.

"She tried to strike me," Sathan finally said, "once she had the Blade."

His brother turned, his expression filled with incredulity. "What? And you let her live?"

Turning her arm over as he worked, Sathan continued in his calm manner. "Besides the fact our sister will die if she is harmed, yes, I let her live. She is special. The past few days have taught us both that. The blood of Valktor runs strong through her. We're on the verge of something different here, Latimus. We have to put the past behind us."

"Bullshit," Latimus said, standing now that the fire was lit and rubbing his hands on his black pants. "She's the princess of our greatest enemy and she just tried to kill you."

"There was a fair bit of hesitation along with her hatred. Her indecision gives me hope. I've grown so weary of this war, of this life. It's time to start a new chapter." Lifting her wrist, Sathan began to lick it, ever so gently, to close the wound with his healing saliva.

"Uh huh," his brother said behind him, his tone mocking. "From the looks of it, maybe you just want to keep her alive so that you can fuck her. For the sake of the goddess, Sathan, have you really been blinded by Slayer pussy? She's hot, but this is ridiculous."

Sathan's shoulders tensed. He focused every ounce of will on closing the Slayer's wounds instead of turning around to punch the hell out of his brother. "I'll caution you not to speak to me like that again." Finishing up on his patient, he dropped Miranda's wrist to her side, noticing that her head dipped a bit as she sat unconscious. Her bottom lip was slightly removed from her top, and he could see the tiny pink tip of her tongue. That, along with licking her smooth, tan skin, made him hard with arousal.

But he'd die before admitting that to his brother.

Inhaling a breath, he stood and faced him.

"You're my brother, Latimus, and my closest confidant, so I've let you slide on matters of respect. That ends today. I am the king of our people, and with that comes a huge burden that you will never understand." Anger began to seep into his tone, although he tried to keep it in check. "Every time we abduct a Slayer from his family and he dies in our dungeon, I feel a black mark across my soul. Sometimes, I feel my heart is so blackened that I will never be welcomed into the Passage. Etherya has forsaken me, and our people live with constant darkness and death."

Inching closer, he lifted his finger and jabbed it toward his brother's face. "If you trivialize this for one second and make it about anything else than my undying desire to free our people from this prison of war, then you are no longer welcome in my council. You can go live with your Slayer whores at the edge of the compound for all I care."

Latimus lifted an eyebrow. "Are you done?" he asked, his tone unreadable.

"Actually, no, I'm not. Stop being such an asshole to Lila. I don't know what your problem is with her, but she has been nothing but gracious to you, and you treat her like shit. Her council is valuable to me, and if you can't be a decent person to her, I'll ban you from our sessions."

Latimus scowled and crossed his arms over his chest. "Stop jabbing your finger in my face, Sathan. I get it. You want to fuck the Slayer and keep fucking Lila. Good for you. Some of us are serious about fighting for our people. Honestly, man, what has happened to you lately? You used to be stronger than this."

Sathan fought the urge to deck his brother right in his long, structured nose. By the goddess, it would feel so good. But that would get him nowhere. Clenching his teeth, he struggled to keep his voice calm.

"I'm taking the Slayer into her tent and I'll stay there with her today. It's almost dawn, and I'm exhausted. Take some time to think about which side of history you want to be on, Latimus. I'm tired of this war and I'm intent on ending it. I'm also intent on uniting with the Slayers and taking Crimeous down. You can either join me, or wallow in self-imposed misery at the edges of the compound for eternity. Your choice." Lowering down, he picked up Miranda and the Blade and began walking to her tent.

"Oh," he said, turning just before he entered the tent, "and I don't fuck Lila, for your information. She has remained a virgin, as the goddess decreed the king's betrothed would do, and will until I bond with her. So, I guess you don't know everything, do you, asshole?"

Something that looked like pain, or perhaps surprise, flashed across his brother's face as it glowed in the light of the fire. And then, just as quickly, it was gone.

Sathan entered the tent and bundled Miranda up in her sleeping bag. He then sheathed the Blade and locked it in the weaponry case they had transported with them. Lowering himself beside her, he closed his eyes for some much-needed sleep.

Chapter 13

Kenden tasked Larkin with continuing to deliver the banked blood to Astaria. The Slayer soldier was one of his best, and he trusted him immensely. After transporting the barrels for the past several nights, and meeting the king's brother, he felt that Larkin could take over for him so that he could begin a new mission.

He had wanted to follow up on the old soothsayer gossip for some time, but life had gotten in the way, and his responsibilities at Uteria were vast. Now that Miranda had taken action, it was imperative that he follow the lead.

In his room at the castle, he packed a bag, knowing he would be gone for several days. Hopping in one of the Hummers parked in the barracks behind the main house, he revved the engine and began to drive.

He followed the River Thayne past the satellite Slayer compound of Restia, which sat some twenty miles south of Uteria. Once past, he drove another thirty miles southeast until he came to the blurry wall of ether.

Parking the Hummer, he exited, locking it so that it would be there upon his return. Clutching his bag to his chest, he checked to make sure his gun and knife were secured to his belt. Closing his eyes, he began to wade through.

As he navigated the thick and stifling ether, he imagined in his mind where he wanted to exit on the other side. Immortals could enter any destination and time period of the human world if they focused intensely enough.

Fresh air hit his face, and he opened his eyes, pleased that he was in the spot he had imagined. Lush green knolls of the beautiful Italian countryside welcomed him. The blazing sun was setting in the distance, creating a magnificent display of red and yellow dotted clouds. Inhaling deeply, he began the trek to the old man's house.

The thatched-roof cabin sat high atop a hill, a lone light shining in the window of the now dusky sky. Kenden approached and knocked on the door. A man, his face wrinkled and withered, with kind blue eyes opened the wooden door.

"Ciao," the man said. "Posso aiutarla?"

"Do you speak English?" Kenden asked, more familiar with that language than any other human tongue.

"Yes," the man said with a nod.

"I've come to ask you about Evangeline."

The man's eyes widened. "Come in, please."

They sat upon cushy chairs as Kenden asked his questions. The man spoke with mischief twinkling in his eyes.

"There was always something about her. She never seemed to age. She was my favorite lover, and I've had many," he said, waggling his powder-white eyebrows.

"There was a sadness to her, and a mean streak a kilometer wide, but I loved her for the few years we shared together."

"You were together over sixty years ago," Kenden said. "Have you heard from her recently? Do you know where she might be?"

The man gave an absent smile. "She loved France. The magnificence of Paris always beckoned her, and her love of Bordeaux was broader than her love of Chianti. If I thought to look for her, I would look there."

"Thank you, Francesco," Kenden said, standing to shake the man's hand. The old man walked him to the door, opening it for him. Before he could exit, the man placed a hand on Kenden's forearm.

"Tread lightly. I always knew she was not of our world. As I prepare to enter heaven, I wonder if God knows that others exist here. It would sometimes give me chills as I lay beside her. Her nightmares were evil and murderous. Although I was fond of her, I was sometimes so scared of her that my blood curdled."

"I understand," Kenden said with a nod. Stepping into the night, he began to walk down the hill. He needed to find a train station and get to Paris.

* * * *

Miranda awoke with a gasp and lifted her head to assess her surroundings. With a groan, she closed her eyes and brought her hand to the back of her head, pounding with the force of a thousand jackhammers. Holy hell. Where was she? She tried to remember...the cave...unsheathing the Blade...and then...she'd tried to murder the Vampyre king. Uh oh. Heart pounding, she sat up and looked around the tent.

She was shocked to find Sathan sleeping beside her. His large back was facing her, broad shoulders filling out every angle of his black T-shirt. Where was the Blade? Sathan must have carried her out—did he grab the Blade as well?

"The Blade is locked in the case, Miranda," his baritone said below her. "Now, lie down and go back to sleep. It's the middle of the day."

Gritting her teeth, she wondered why he felt he could boss her around all the damn time. "Slayers sleep at night, for your information. I want to see the Blade." Attempting to stand up, she lifted herself and then fell back down. She rubbed the lump on the back of her head. "You hit me with your knife."

Sighing, Sathan rolled over and placed his head on his palm, his elbow resting on his pillow. His eyes were drowsy with sleep, and the thick black hair on his head was tousled. If she didn't hate him so much, he would look almost...charming. Barf.

"Yes, I hit you with my knife. I think it was because you were contemplating killing me with the Blade of Pestilence. Let me try to remember..." He squinted up at the top of the tent as he rubbed his chin with his free hand. "Yeah, you tried to plunge it right into my chest."

"Oh, fine," she spat, looking down at him from her crossed-legged sitting position. "I wasn't even really trying, anyway." Scowling, she continued to rub her head. "If I was serious about killing you, you'd be dead. Believe me."

One side of his mouth turned up in a grin. "Mmmm hmmm..."

His lips were quite thick. Would they overtake hers if he leaned up and tried to kiss her? Shaking her head, she attributed that thought to the fact that she had a traumatic brain injury.

"How did my wound heal so quickly?" Moving her hand down, she rubbed her left wrist, eyeing him warily.

"I licked it closed."

Delete mental image. She was so not going there. No fucking way.

"Now that we have the Blade, I'm anxious to get home. I want to brief Kenden, report to my father that I've accomplished my goal and plan our attack against Crimeous. And I'm sure you're anxious to have your sister returned safely."

"That, I am. We'll leave at sunset, I promise. Until then, I have the key to the container for the Blade in a safe place where you won't want to look for it."

"And where is that?" she asked, lifting an eyebrow and giving him a disbelieving look.

"In my pants pocket. Of course, if you can't stop yourself from sticking your hands into my pants, I would be happy to let you—"

"Excuse me while I vomit," she interrupted, rolling her eyes. "I'd rather touch a shriveled old Deamon than touch you anywhere near your pants." His answering smile only infuriated her more.

"Whatever you say. Wake me twenty minutes before sunset." With that, he rolled back over to sleep.

"Son of a bitch," she muttered. Rolling her head on her neck, she gritted her teeth in pain.

"I laid out some aspirin for you by the door of the tent." She looked over, and sure enough, two aspirin and a thermos of water were sitting there waiting for her. How dare he go and do something nice for her after he almost bludgeoned her to death? Jerk. Crawling over, she devoured the pills and chugged the water. Not knowing what else to do, she lay back down and tried not to focus on the constant throbbing of her head. In minutes, she was asleep.

* * * *

A few hours later, Sathan stirred and turned over to check on his patient. Miranda slept soundly on her back, soft snores echoing through the tent on every exhale. He was enthralled by how peaceful she looked, never getting to see her with her defenses down when she was awake. She must've gone through her immortal change sometime in her mid-twenties. The skin on her face was wrinkle-free and flawless. There was no rhyme or reason to when immortals went through their change. Usually, one could predict when their change would happen based on their bloodline. If one's ancestors went through their change later in life, their children were more apt to do so, but not always. The year of your change was the time that your body was locked into immortality. Sathan was pleased that Miranda's had been when she was young, if only so her beauty could be captured timelessly.

Her mother had been known as the greatest beauty that Etherya had ever created, so he wasn't surprised that he was attracted to her daughter. After all, he was only a man, and men, being visual creatures, were usually attracted to pretty ladies they came into contact with. But his attraction to her personality worried him. She was a force of nature. Strong-willed, infuriatingly sure of herself and fearless. It was a cocktail of appeal that he needed to be wary of, lest he become addicted.

He needed her as an ally, and to accomplish that, he knew he must remain completely free of any romantic entanglement. Being that she hated his guts, he figured it should remain a pretty simple task.

She murmured something in her sleep and then smacked her lips together loudly several times. Stilling, her mouth remained open as she breathed. For just a moment, he imagined making love to her, seeing that tiny mouth open to receive him as he slid in and out between her pink lips. By the goddess, it would feel so good to have her mouth around him like that, the wetness of her tongue bathing him...

And now, he was hard. Scolding himself not to be the creepy stalker she'd once accused him of, he rose and exited the tent to stretch. Enough with these ridiculous fantasies. He had a kingdom to save and was determined to have a serious talk with Miranda about his intentions. Looking at his watch and noting that the sun had set, he went to awaken his brother.

* * * *

"Sadie, I just can't tell you what a great time I'm having with you, girlfriend. Let's take a selfie together." Arderin gave the Slayer her biggest smile.

"No selfies for me, thanks," the Slayer replied, and Arderin forced herself not to clench her teeth in frustration.

"No worries. Let's see...what else can I teach you about the ways of social media?"

Sadie gave a quiet laugh and shook her head. "I think you've been more than kind. Especially for someone I'm holding hostage." Her expression relayed her sympathy for Arderin. "Do you want some more Slayer blood? You haven't drunk in a while."

"Yes, please," Arderin said, knowing that now was the time. Pushing down the guilt that rose in her gut at hurting the Slayer, she extended her bound hands. Sadie leaned toward her, handing her the cup, and Arderin grabbed the woman's shirt collar with a hard tug, pulling her to the floor. Lifting her bound legs, she placed them over Sadie's neck, holding her hostage. The woman sputtered and struggled as Arderin's heart pounded with remorse.

"Sadie, I need you to untie the binds on my hands. I don't want to hurt you, but I am much larger than you, and Frick and Frack are gone on their nightly shift change. I don't know why they always take so long or why they do it outside of the cabin, but they always go at the same time every night, and if you don't untie me, I will kill you before they come back."

The Slayer stopped struggling and froze. Arderin realized that she was terrified and made a silent promise to find this kind woman one day and make this up to her. "I don't want to hurt you, Sadie, but I will. Untie the binds at my wrists. Now!"

With jerking movements, the Slayer rotated slightly and untied the binds at Arderin's wrists. Quickly, she pulled Sadie's hands behind her back and retied the ropes around her much smaller wrists. She repeated the same moves at Sadie's ankles.

Arderin stood, massaging one sore wrist, and contemplated the Slayer, who now sat bound and defeated on the floor of the cabin. "I'm sorry, Sadie. I mean it. I didn't want to hurt you."

Sadie's throat bobbed up and down as she swallowed, most likely tamping down tears. "It's okay. I should've known you were only pretending to befriend me to escape. Miranda's going to kill me—"

"First of all," Arderin said, lowering to her eye level, "if that Slayer bitch so much as even touches one hair on your head, I'll kill her myself. And secondly, and I want you to hear this, Sadie."—she cupped the Slayer's chin and turned her so she was staring right into the doctor's watery hazel irises—"I was lucky to befriend you. You are a kind and beautiful person. Someone along the way made you believe differently, but one day, I'm going to come looking for you, and we're going to change that narrative. Now, I have to go before the wonder twins come back, but know that I mean it when I say that you have been a true friend to me. Thank you."

With that, Arderin stood and fled the cabin. Once outside, she thanked the goddess that it was nighttime and began to try to navigate toward Astaria using the moon and the Star of Muthoni, the brightest star in the night sky. The moon was waxing tonight, so if she walked northeast, she might just be able to work a miracle and get the hell home.

Chapter 14

Sathan was contemplative as they began their trek away from the Cave of the Sacred Prophecy back to the Hummer. They completed twenty-two miles before daylight declared it time to set up camp for the day. Of course, Miranda assembled her tent in record time and came sniffing around for the vodka.

Sathan rose from his squat where he was assembling the tent and looked down at her. "I have something important I want to discuss with you today. I think we should go lightly on the vodka."

"Uh oh, that sounds scary. In that case, I'm *only* talking to you if we have vodka first."

"Important, Miranda," he repeated firmly.

With a *harrumph*, she sat on the ground by the fire, resting her chin in her hand as her elbow sat on top of her chest-drawn knee. The gesture reminded him so much of Arderin. What exasperatingly annoying imps they both were.

He finally came over and sat beside her. "Where's your Neanderthal brother?" she asked.

"If you're trying to anger me, it won't work. I'm pretty pissed at Latimus myself."

"Ohhhh, do tell," she said, her tone picking up in excitement.

Sathan couldn't help but chuckle. "A story for another time. He's mulling over war plans in the tent. Fun stuff." Placing the bottle of vodka between them, he cautioned her, "We'll drink in a minute. But first, I want to ask you a question."

"Shoot," she said, eyeing the bottle.

"Why are you so convinced that your father would've shared my letters with you? *If* I wrote them, that is."

She chewed on her bottom lip, and he reminded himself not to notice how it glistened in the fire since he had sworn off any romantic entanglement with her. "Because he's my father," she said finally, "and he respects traditionalism. Any letters that he would've received from you would've had to have been automatically shared with the descendant of Valktor. He just wouldn't see any other way."

Sathan nodded, knowing he needed to tread lightly. Although he felt that she had diverged from her father on many things, she still loved him. Love could create blind spots, even to those who were determined to take a different path. "What is his plan to see you ascend to the throne? Surely, he can't rule forever. As the heir of Valktor, you will take over for him one day, right?"

Anger entered her expression, and he willed himself to remain calm no matter how agitated she became. "Listen, I have no wish to discuss this with you. You're my greatest enemy, for god's sake, and I'm sure as hell not going to sit here and tell you my future plans for my realm."

Staring into the fire, Sathan trudged on. "I believe that your father is intent on never letting you ascend to the throne. That he has become accustomed to ruling and justifies in his mind that he is doing a service to you and your people by continuing to rule in perpetuity."

"Absolutely not," she replied firmly. "One day, when we both are ready, I will take the throne and rule our people. This has always been our plan."

"When, Miranda?" he asked quietly. "What is he waiting for? What big event will make this happen?"

"When I kill Crimeous," she said, her voice soft as she looked at the fire. "Surely then, he won't be able to justify keeping the throne any longer." There was a quiet questioning in her tone, as if she barely believed this herself.

"Are you sure this will be the tipping point? When he didn't even support your mission in the first place?"

She gave a humorless laugh and shook her head, looking at the ground in front of her. "Nice fishing attempt. You must think I'm really stupid. Try again."

Becoming frustrated, he willed himself to stay the course. "In fact, I think you're extremely intelligent. I've realized over the past few days that I've been attempting to negotiate with the wrong royal. I should've reached out to you directly centuries ago."

"I would've just directed you to my father. We work as a team."

"Perhaps in the past. But I feel that you've moved in a different direction. Choosing to defy him and unsheathe the Blade was very courageous. Whether you realize it or not, you are coming into your own, Miranda."

She gave a *pfft* and waved her hand. "I don't need flattery from you, Vampyre. But thanks anyway."

Reaching for the vodka, he unscrewed the top and poured some into two thermoses. Handing her one, he continued, "The days to come are going to be difficult. I believe that your father will reject your unsheathing of the Blade as nothing more than a folly on your part. I think he will demand you lock it up and forbid you from attacking Crimeous. He will pull the support of the army from you and see you as a threat to his throne."

"Wow," she said, sipping from her thermos. "Sorry your parents were killed. You have a real fucked-up view of parent-child relationships."

"This is not a joke. I know it's easier for you to joke about these things. It's a pattern you fall into when you're not willing to see the truth in something."

"Oh, because you know me so well. Thanks, Sigmund Freud. Maybe you can help diagnose the complex I have about my mother being murdered too. Do you charge by the hour?"

Reluctantly, he smiled. Although her joking was a pain in the ass, she was pretty damn funny. He supposed he could use a bit more humor in his life. "See, you always go there. Don't get me wrong, the comic relief is nice, but it holds you back from seeing the truth."

She sighed and lifted her head to look at the trees above. "What do you want me to say? That I believe my father's going to fuck me over? Even if I did believe it, I would never admit it to you, my greatest enemy on the damn planet."

Sathan regarded her in the firelight. Her eyelashes were so long and seemed to turn white right at the end. Rosy cheeks, warmed by the fire, bookended her soft, pink lips. "Are we still such great enemies? Even after I helped you retrieve the Blade? Surely, that has to count for something."

"What will you do when I return to my compound, and you return to yours? Will you continue to hunt my people?"

"That depends," he said softly. "Will you continue to bank blood for us? Will your father allow that?"

Miranda's eyes dropped, and he could see her brain struggling to find a scenario where the answer was 'yes'. Unfortunately, they both knew that would never be the case. "I don't know."

"Yes, you do. You and I both know that he is intent on dragging out this war until one or both of our species is extinct."

"Well, what would you have me do? Align with you?" she asked angrily. "Do you think my people would just accept it if I stood up and announced, '*Oh, hey everybody, it's me, your princess. We're gonna become besties with the species who have hunted and murdered us for a thousand years. Yay?*'" She shook her hands in the air as if she was cheering at a football game.

Sathan shook his head. "If you said it like that, then no, I'm pretty sure people wouldn't take kindly to it."

"What you're asking of me is impossible. I want to end the fighting as badly as you do, but the damage is too deep. I don't see how our people can ever be allies again. I think the best we can hope for is to live separately and peacefully for eternity."

"And who will fight the Deamons? Surely, someone will rise to take Crimeous' place if you succeed in killing him." An unreadable flash washed over her face, as if he had stumbled upon something he shouldn't know, but it was just as quickly gone. "Are you aware of plans that someone has to overtake the Deamon kingdom?"

"Of course not," she said, waving off his suggestion. "But I think you're living in la-la land if you think that Slayers and Vampyres will align their armies to fight the Deamons."

"Look at us. We're getting along." He laughed at the sardonic look she gave him. "Seriously. We've succeeded on this mission beautifully."

"Because I'm holding your sister hostage."

"I don't really like her anyway," he joked, shrugging his shoulders.

"Stop it," she said, punching his upper arm.

"Easy there, killer," he said, happy that her anger had evaporated slightly. This woman really did ride a roller coaster of emotions. He wondered how she had the stamina. "It's been an honor getting to know you on this journey. Regardless of our people's past transgressions against each other, I feel that you and I have similar goals. We both want our people to be happy and free. If we had the courage, we could align together to accomplish that goal. Two armies working together will always be better than one."

She sighed, long and sad, and shook her head. "I just don't see how it could work now. My father will need time to come around. Perhaps, once I kill Crimeous and change the way he sees me...but until then, I can't offer to align with you. To do so under false pretenses wouldn't be truthful, and I at least owe you honesty for helping me free the Blade. Oh, and for the great vodka." With a broad grin, she took another sip.

Honesty. Loyalty. Freedom. These were lofty goals to aspire to, and this woman embodied them all. Admiration swam through him, and he knew he had chosen the right ally. He also knew that her father would do as he'd said and forbid her to attack Crimeous. Hopefully, this conversation would open the door to her asking for help when that happened. The future happiness of his people depended on it.

Deciding he'd pushed her hard enough for one night, he changed the subject to something lighter. "So, Metallica, huh?"

"Hell yeah. They're fucking awesome."

"How in the heck did you get into human music? They're heathens."

"Of course they are, but they make some damn fine music. As I'm always telling Ken, one day, you'll all come around and realize the awesomeness of 'Enter Sandman.'"

Sathan laughed and shook his head. "I don't think so. I just can't get over the human thing. Do you know, Etherya told me that in one of the parallel universes, there was a planet similar to our Earth where humans were the dominant species?"

"Yes," Miranda said, excited. "Our soothsayers told me the same! How is that even possible? Humans are absolute morons. They think that Vampyres live in the shadows and can be killed with garlic and crosses. And that they drink the blood of humans just for fun and sport. Can you imagine such a thing? Drinking human blood? Ew."

"Humans also believe that Vampyres have no reflection. How would I comb my beautiful hair in the morning?" he joked, running his hand over his thick black hair.

"Okay, Romeo," she said, snickering with him. "It's all so absurd. And what about the Slayers? Humans think they're teenage girls with names like Buffy and Willow. What the hell? They relegated an entire species to sixteen-year-old girls?"

"It is farcical, to say the least," he said, enjoying the ease of their conversation. "I wonder what they think about Deamons?"

"Who knows? At this rate, they could be the rulers of the planet!" They both erupted in laughter and spent the rest of the hour coming up with even crazier scenarios. As Sathan drifted off later, beside his brother, he realized that it was the first time he had ever laughed so hard with a woman.

Chapter 15

In the Deamon caves, the mood was quite a bit darker. Darkrip stood in his father's study and watched him flip his desk over, as if it were weightless, in a fit of rage. "Why didn't she kill him?" the Deamon Lord screamed. Spittle flew from his mouth, and muscles corded tight as strings under the pasty skin of his long neck.

"She pulled the Blade and attempted to, but he was too quick. He knocked her unconscious and fled the cave with her."

"She's so fucking weak," his father said, his beady eyes narrowing.

"Yes," Darkrip said, trying to disguise his hatred. It would do no good to undo centuries of gaining his father's trust just to lose it now. He had worked too hard and sacrificed too many years for that.

Crimeous sighed and rubbed his hand on his forehead. Long fingers stretched into pointed claws; he truly was repulsive. "Fine. At this point, we must mount an attack on one of the compounds. I'm wondering which one is more vulnerable. Astaria because the king is absent, or Uteria because the Slayers have let their defenses down."

"It is my opinion that we should attack Restia," Darkrip said.

His father's head snapped up, angry. "A satellite compound? That would never send a strong enough message. Why are you suggesting this?"

Darkrip shrugged. "It would send a message that we're coming for every angle of the Slayers' existence. The Vampyres only ever attack Uteria. If we attack a less fortified compound, our chances of success are greater."

Crimeous mulled over his son's idea. "It is true that they don't fortify Restia as well, although the gate is heavily guarded."

"If I lead the attack, I can assure that their guards are disabled quickly."

The Dark Lord arched a thin eyebrow, surprised. "Your initiative is encouraging, my son. I did wonder when you were young if you had the strength to be a great leader. I see that you are embracing your evil more and more each day. It makes me proud."

Darkrip struggled to tamp down the bile that bubbled in his throat at his father's compliment. "Thank you. I would like to get to work on an attack plan. It would be best to attack at night, possibly tomorrow evening, if we can rally the troops."

"So be it," his father said with a nod. "I'll give you a hundred soldiers. Kenden's troops will surely kill them all, but our men should be able to cause many mass casualties before that happens."

So little regard this ruler had for his people. A hundred men that he was sending to their sure death. How did one become so evil?

"I will report back before we depart." Bowing to his king, Darkrip turned and left the chamber. He had some planning to do if he was going to manipulate this attack to his will.

* * * *

Lila and Heden sat in the basement of the castle at Astaria in what they lovingly called the "tech room." Heden, being a super geek of giant proportions, and Lila, who was fascinated with helping him succeed in his endeavors, usually found themselves here plotting their new ideas.

"I'm so excited for these tunnels," Lila said, pointing to the schematics on the large flat-screen in front of them.

"Totally," Heden said, typing something on the keyboard. "Look at this." He lifted his hand to point at the screen. "The high-speed underground rail will be able to get from Astaria to any of the three satellite compounds in under thirty minutes. We'll be connected like never before."

"You're a genius!" she said, smiling broadly at him.

"Damn, Lila, when you smile at me like that, it makes me want to murder my brother so that I can whisk you away and bond with you myself. Is that treason?" he asked, rubbing his goateed chin as he contemplated.

"Stop it," she said, slapping him playfully on his chest. He truly was one of her favorite people on the entire planet. He popped a Starburst into his mouth and chewed as he proceeded to furiously type and stare at the screen. Lila observed the thick, corded muscles of his neck, which sloped into a wide chest and thick build. The goatee had appeared a few centuries ago, and although his brothers mocked him for it, Lila thought it was quite cute.

The royal siblings all shared similar features: black hair, ice-blue eyes (except for Sathan's irises, which were pitch-black for some unexplained reason), strong bone structures, angular noses. Heden, Arderin and Sathan all shared their thick, wavy hair. Only Latimus' raven hair was straight and long, stopping just before his shoulders. He always secured it with a leather strap so that it formed a tiny tail at the back of his head. Lila had witnessed many a jibing session between Heden and Latimus where they debated which was worse: Latimus' ponytail, or Heden's goatee. Not surprisingly, Latimus usually won. Mostly likely because his hand always seemed to end up squeezing Heden's throat before the youngest sibling could laughingly call mercy. It was all in good fun though, as Lila had never seen a stronger bond between siblings than the royal Vampyres.

She had longed for a sibling as a child. Some sort of companion she could share her innermost thoughts with. Latimus had been her best childhood friend, and he had secured that spot in her heart for a few precious years. But responsibilities and duties could ruin even the strongest of friendships if they took precedent in one's life. Perhaps she was partly to blame for Latimus' dislike of her, as she had wanted so badly to be the perfect betrothed to the king that she lost focus on anything else.

"Hey, buttercup," Heden said, chucking her on the chin, "you look sad."

Smiling, she shook her head. "It's nothing. What else can I do to help you here?"

"The schematics are done, thank the goddess. Next will be the tunnel construction, which will take about a year if we assign a good deal of men to it. When we'll really need you is for the roll out of the trains. Our people aren't exactly early adopters and getting them to trust our underground railway won't be an easy task. Luckily, your diplomatic skills will save the day. As you ride the rail with the governors of each compound, do press conferences and engage our people, you'll become the face of the railway. So exciting. You're like our very own Kate Middleton. Or Princess Diana, if we're sticking with the same hair color."

Lila flipped her waist-long, platinum blond hair over her shoulder. "My hair is my best feature."

"Um, I'm not sure if you've looked in a mirror lately, but every feature is your best feature, sweetie. I feel bad for other women of our realm. Sathan's a damn lucky man."

Lila grinned shyly, thanking him in her own silent way. She had no idea why people found her so beautiful. Her coloring was very rare for a Vampyre. As a child, she'd been told that her hair would change from its almost platinum-blond color as she matured, but unfortunately, when she went through her change in her early thirties, it was still there. Most Vampyres had light eyes and dark hair, and she had always felt awkward. Deciding that she might as well go with it, she had grown out her hair until it fell long and wavy to her waist. The length, if not the color, was something that she could control.

Lila's eyes were strange too, as they were a shade of deep lavender that she had never seen on a Vampyre—or any other species for that matter. When she was young, the other children would make fun of her and call her "Ugly Eyes." Latimus had always stood up for her, defending her honor. But that was a lifetime ago. She had no idea why, after so many centuries, the memories were still there, just as vivid.

Normal, average features made up the rest of her face. With her Vampyre-pale skin, she sometimes thought she looked like one of the human ghosts that were depicted in their movies. But for whatever reason, Heden always told her she was attractive. And she loved him all the more for that. Over the years, he had become her best friend, besides Arderin, and her confidant as well. Not wanting to bother Sathan with trivial matters, she usually went to one of them if she needed anything, which was rare.

As a child of the aristocracy, founded long before the Awakening, she was raised by the belief that duty was the number one aspiration of her life. Duty to the realm, to the king, were priorities above all others. At all times, she must speak in a pleasant manner, strive to perfection and do her best to bring peace to the realm. Due to this, she was extremely excited to be the ambassador for the new rail system. Harmoniously joining the compounds together would be the culmination of a thousand years of rearing and training. She was ready.

Standing, she squeezed Heden's shoulder. "I'm going to head to my chamber. It's almost daylight—"

A loud noise from the hallway outside the tech room caused her to pause. She thought she heard a woman calling her name.

"Did you hear?" she asked.

"Yeah," Heden said, standing.

Then, they were both running from the room, up the stairs, to the main foyer of the Vampyre castle. The black and white tiled floor of the foyer glistened under the light of the massive chandelier, and they ran past the large, carpeted spiral staircase. They both stopped short in surprise.

"I'm home," Arderin said, her arms outstretched as tears ran down her face.

"Arderin!" they both called, running to her and embracing each other in a massive group hug.

"How did you...? When did you...? What happened?" Heden asked, running his hands over her wet cheeks, happiness glowing in his blue eyes. "We were so worried."

"I know," she said, nodding and wiping mucus from her nose onto the sleeve of the blue dress she had been wearing all those nights ago when she disappeared. To Lila, it seemed an eternity ago. "I escaped."

"I'll be damned," Heden said with wonder, giving her another big hug. "Don't fuck with my sister! Those Slayers should've known!"

Arderin laughed. "They should've. I missed you guys so much."

Lila hugged her once more and took her hand. "Come, let's get you out of this dress and into a warm shower." Leaning closer, she whispered into her ear, "They didn't hurt you, did they?"

"No," Arderin said, smiling at Lila through her tears. "I'm fine. But yes, I need to get out of this fucking dress. For the love of the goddess, I just need a shower and some sweatpants right now."

Lila laughed and pulled her friend toward the large staircase. "Let's get you cleaned up. Heden, go prepare some Slayer blood for her. We'll be back down within the hour. I can't wait to hear the whole story."

Lila's heart was full as she led her friend up the stairs. Taking care of people was her highest honor. Taking care of Arderin, whom she loved dearly, was the highlight of her year.

Chapter 16

The next two nights' hike back to the Hummer were uneventful. Once they reached the vehicle, they drove back to the mouth of the Portal of Mithos, choosing to camp there for the day.

Miranda noticed a thick tension between the Vampyre brothers and did her best to steer clear.

The next evening's journey back through the foothills of the Strok Mountains was easier than the first pass had been, and they all found themselves camping under a thick canopy at daylight, knowing that the next night's journey would be their last together.

Sitting by the fire that he had built, Latimus took three thermos cups and divided the last of the scotch between them. "To a successful mission," he said, lifting his cup.

"To a successful mission," Sathan and Miranda repeated, and they all clinked their cups together.

"So, now that you have the Blade, what is your plan of attack? Will you storm Crimeous at the Deamon Caves?" Latimus asked.

Miranda studied him, not wanting to divulge her secrets but understanding that as an extraordinary soldier, he could possibly give her some useful suggestions. "I was thinking so, yes. Kenden has plotted and mapped their caves with great accuracy. I believe I know where to strike to do the most damage and find Crimeous the most vulnerable."

"His spies are many. They'll know you're coming almost before you do."

"Yes. I've anticipated that. Ken will help me break our troops into many different battalions. The constant onslaught of fresh troops will be devastating for them. As you must know, the Deamon army is vast but their fighters are weak. They have no strong general, such as you or Ken, and their training is basic at best. We have been able to defeat them so far."

Shifting, she sat up straighter, uncrossing her legs and stretching them in front of her. "But we have seen an evolution in their army as well. They're getting stronger and more cunning as the centuries wear on. Eventually, they will be formidable."

"We've seen the same. Up until now, they have been a nuisance, draining our energy and our money. But that won't last forever. It would be best to defeat them now, before they grow stronger."

"Well, that's my goal." She took a sip of the scotch. "Defeating Crimeous will send the Deamons deeper underground. They're not smart or capable enough to function above-ground without him. Whereas Slayers and Vampyres have our functioning societies, and the humans have their own, unaware of us, the Deamons are not that advanced. Killing Crimeous is the key."

Latimus' gaze was focused on her, and it gave her time to truly study him. Unfazed by his scrutiny, she looked at his jet-black hair, pulled back by a leather strap, his long, angular nose and full lips. "I would take any advice from you if you wish to give it. It isn't often that I have the greatest general on the planet's ear."

The side of his mouth turned up. "Flattery, is it?" he said in his firm baritone. "That seems beneath you."

"Nothing is beneath a ruler when their people's lives are at stake."

A look passed between Latimus and Sathan, who had stayed remarkably—and a bit infuriatingly—silent during this exchange.

"What?" she asked, her voice relaying her annoyance.

"I'm just imagining your cousin's face when he hears that you called me the greatest general on the Earth instead of him."

"He would admit the same to you. Kenden is humble and devoid of vice. If someone is better than him, he says it. He wasn't meant to be a commander; he was forced to be. You, on the other hand, were born for it. It emanates from every fiber of your being. Kenden respects that being an expert general comes naturally to you."

"Well, he's done a fine damn job. That fucking eight-shooter has been a thorn in my side since he invented it. It changed the game for us, and we had to step up our training to a whole other level."

"He would be proud to hear it," Miranda said, offering the Vampyre a smile.

"Okay, fine," he said, looking at his brother. "She's not as bad as I thought. But I still don't like her."

Sathan chuckled, and Miranda waved her hand. "Hi. Um, yeah, sitting right here. I can hear you, jerk."

"I take it back," he muttered, sipping his scotch.

"You can't take it back!"

"Okay, kids," Sathan said in a playful tone. "Calm down. This has been a long journey, and we will all be happy to get home tomorrow evening. Latimus and I are excited to be reunited with Arderin."

Miranda felt a pang in her chest at the mention of going home and stared absently into the campfire. How angry was her father going to be at her? Pretty damn angry, if she had to guess. She would just have to work hard to convince him that her cause was just and noble. And she couldn't make any mistakes when attacking Crimeous. She had to kill him swiftly and effectively for her father to respect her. Finishing the last of her Scotch, she placed the cup on the ground and chewed on her lip as she watched the blazing fire.

"Miranda." Sathan's voice came from above her. Looking up, he was standing over her. "Were you daydreaming? Latimus turned in for the day. You ready?" He extended his hand down to her.

Grabbing it, she let him pull her up. He must have overestimated her weight because she flew up and banged into his chest. "Ooph," she said, rubbing her nose.

"Oh no," he said, tilting his head to inspect it. "Did you break your nose again?"

"Ha ha," she said, giving him a sarcastic look. They were now standing chest-to-chest, the top of her head barely coming to the bottom of his thick neck. The proximity caused her heart to start beating faster, and she knew she should take a step back.

She didn't. His Adam's apple, in her direct line of view, bobbed up and down as he swallowed thickly.

"Are you okay?" he asked, bringing his right hand under her chin and tilting her face up to his.

"Yes," she whispered, hating that she didn't have control of her voice.

With his left hand, he extended his index finger and, ever so softly, traced the bridge of her nose. Involuntarily, her eyes drifted closed at the gentle touch. "It doesn't look broken." His voice was gravelly and so deep that she felt her insides vibrate from the sound of it.

"It's fine," she said, lifting her lids to look up at him. Into him.

Slowly, as if not to startle her, he ran his right hand from her chin, over the soft curve of her lower jaw, to cup her cheek. The scratchy pad of his thumb began a whisper-soft caress over her bottom lip. Desire, unchecked and wanton, curled in her stomach.

"Don't," she whispered.

His dark irises whisked over every angle of her face. "You're so beautiful."

He slid the pad of his thumb that had been resting on her lower lip, dipping it just slightly onto the wetness of her inner lower lip. She sensed a change in his body, a tightening of muscles, and knew he had grown hard. Imagining how large someone like he must be in that state, she felt the desire that had been swirling in her stomach pool between her thighs in a rush of wetness.

Exhaling, he closed his eyes and stilled. He inhaled sharply and then looked down at her, a blazing desire haunting his gaze. "What is it?" she asked, her voice so soft in the darkness.

"I can smell your arousal."

Her skin flushed with the knowledge that she couldn't disguise her yearning from him. Feminine power jolted down her spine. It was exhilarating.

Testing, she lifted her tongue and touched the tiny red tip to his thumb. At his resulting growl, she closed her lips fully.

Cursing, he pulled his thumb from her mouth and slid the hand to the back of her head, gently gripping her hair and tilting her face up toward his. Miranda gasped at the act, so primitive, so primal. And then, he devoured her.

Large, strong lips surrounded her own pink ones, and he melted into her as they kissed. Needing more, his tongue plundered her lips until she let him in, all the way. His tongue swept her mouth, and she lifted hers to battle with his.

"By the goddess, Miranda," he breathed and continued to ransack her mouth with his. He slid his free hand up her arm and cupped her neck, massaging the tense muscles there. Slowing, he pulled back to lick her lower lip and then to nibble at the juicy flesh there.

Suddenly, her sanity returned. What the hell was she doing? Was she really kissing her greatest enemy? Self-revulsion shot through her.

"Stop." She placed a hand on his chest.

Confusion swept over his features under the pale shade of the trees. "Miranda—"

"I said fucking stop, okay?" she said, shoving him with both hands. Fury ran through her that he wasn't even budged by her push. "I don't know what your angle is, but if you think I'm going to sleep with the person responsible for murdering countless Slayers over the centuries, then you're batshit crazy."

Sathan sighed, lowering his hands to his sides. "You're angry at yourself, not me."

"I'll be angry at whomever I want to be. And don't touch me again. Ever. Got it?"

"There's no angle here, Miranda, and I don't play games. I'll tell you straight up, so that there's no doubt left in your stubborn little head." He took a step closer, and she stood her ground, lifting her chin up defiantly. Heat radiated between them. "I'm attracted to you, and you are to me. Don't bother denying it," he said, pointing a finger in her face when she started to sputter in dissent. "I can smell your arousal. Vampyres have heightened senses for these things."

Miranda clenched her thighs together, mortified that she was so wet in her most private place. Just from kissing him. Good fucking grief.

"I have no angle except to help my people and hopefully get you to see that I want to end this war as much as you do. I'll apologize for crossing any boundaries you set because I'm a gentleman, but I won't apologize for kissing you." His voice softened as his face moved closer to hers. "And if I fuck you one day, I won't apologize for that either. The way you responded to me, I think you could use a good tumble with someone who isn't scared that you're a princess and who can make you forget who you are when you come."

Her palm crashed against his cheek with all of the force she could muster. He barely flinched. "Fuck you," she said through gritted teeth.

"One day, if you're lucky," was his angry reply. And then, he turned and stalked into his tent.

Miranda picked up her thermos top and threw it into the woods, yelling in frustration. What a conceited, pompous ass! Thank all the gods this trip was almost over. Otherwise, she'd strangle the bastard herself.

She put out the fire, wishing it was as simple to tamp down the shaking in her limbs from the heated exchange and mind-blowing kiss. Why did the jerk have to give her the best kiss of her life anyway? Annoyance gnawed at her insides.

As she lay in the tent attempting to sleep, she took a moment to contemplate why she had reacted to him that way. How could she be so attracted to a Vampyre? The monster who had slaughtered her people? Hating herself, her traitorous body fell into a fitful slumber.

* * * *

Evie ran her hands over the lush red grapes. Longing to taste one, she pulled it from its stem and placed it in between her rouged lips. Flavor burst on her tongue as she chewed, closing her eyes in pleasure.

"Mademoiselle," the wine maker called behind her. "We hope you have enjoyed the winery tour. Now, it is time to head back for your complimentary glass."

"Thank you," she said, walking over and patting the man's cheek. His brown eyes glowed with desire. Tilting her head, she contemplated him. He was quite handsome, with his curly brown hair, goatee and brown eyes. She figured him to be in his mid-thirties, which hopefully meant he knew how to navigate a clitoris. Younger men were always terrible at that, too consumed with finding their own pleasure. Deciding she might let him try later, she gave him her sultriest smile and headed inside.

She'd done this wine tasting solo, as she preferred to do most things in life. Of course, she'd made friends, so as to blend in and not call attention to herself, but she cherished her solace and loved spending time at the beautiful wineries in France.

Once inside, the sommelier poured her a glass of Bordeaux, and she headed to the porch to watch the sunset. Sitting in one of the rocking chairs, she sipped the rich liquid and watched the horizon as it tried to grab the sun. Crimson streaks battled with golden rays, and small white clouds flitted by. Birds sang their songs to her as she allowed herself to feel contentment.

Suddenly, the tiny hairs on the back of her neck stood to attention. Not wanting to appear alarmed, she slowly stood and placed her glass on the wooden railing of the balcony. Scanning the numerous vines that ran parallel on the meadow before her, she waited.

His presence was detectable, like a feather-light wrap placed over her pale skin. Unwilling to let him see her discomfort, she fought the urge to rub the chill bumps that popped up on her arms. Realizing that he wasn't going to show himself—at least not today—she lifted the glass and gave a salute. If not to him, then to the smoldering sun as it burned the far-off mountains.

He was playing with fire, whoever he was. She hoped he understood that. Finishing her wine, she gave one last scan of the vines and decided to head home.

* * * *

Miranda woke that evening, ready to see Kenden and to embark on the next phase of her journey. She also needed some space to clear her head, especially after the kiss of the century that she'd had last night with the leader of the species who had slaughtered so many of her people. She would need to analyze it when she had the privacy to gather her thoughts. For now, she was determined to act as normal as possible around Sathan.

"Good evening," she said, zipping the remnants of her tent in her pack as the two Vampyres exited theirs. "I've already packed up, so I'll meet you at the Hummer."

Throwing her pack over her shoulders, she departed for the car. Well, that was one way to act cool. Complete avoidance. *Nice job, Miranda*, she chided herself.

Twenty minutes later, they appeared from the brush. After throwing their packs in the trunk, Latimus got behind the wheel. Sathan approached her beside the car. "How did you sleep?" he asked, his expression unreadable.

"Fine. It was obviously a mistake. I'd rather not make a big deal out of it."

He shrugged and climbed into the front seat.

She sat in the back, annoyed that he didn't even seem phased by the kiss.

They drove in silence most of the way, Miranda jamming to Soundgarden through her earbuds. A few hours in, she lifted her gaze to see Sathan waving at her. "How in the hell do you function with those things so loud?" he asked when she pulled out one earbud.

Miranda rolled her eyes. "What do you want?"

"We're back in cell service range."

"Oh, thanks," she said, pulling her phone from her pack. Powering it on, she saw that she had ten voicemails and twenty-seven text messages. Whoa. Something must be wrong.

Scrolling through, the first texts were from Ken telling her that he had calmed her father...for now. He'd told the kingdom that she was vacationing at Restia, and he wanted her to comply with that narrative when she got home.

Then, the texts got more dire.

Ken: Randi, the Vampyre princess escaped. Her brothers will find out the instant you all regain service. I would address it outright and have them drop you at the wall where you first met instead of the clearing where we were holding her captive. Sending escort vehicles so they don't hurt you.

No sooner had she finished reading the text than two Hummers appeared on each side of their vehicle, keeping pace with them.

"It seems that your cousin has sent soldiers to escort you back to our original meeting point, since our sister escaped," Sathan said dryly, looking at her from the front seat.

"It seems so," Miranda said, not wanting to push her luck. The Vampyre princess was the only insurance policy she had, and she was now in dangerous territory with her two greatest foes.

"We could dump her in the river," Latimus said, "the same way Arderin was dumped there."

Sathan gave him a stern look. Turning his head, he said to Miranda, "We'll escort you to the meeting point safely. There's no need for the extra escort, but I will allow it, so you feel safe."

"Thank you," she said, suddenly feeling like an impertinent child. This large, hulking Vampyre, whom she should hate with all her heart, was now promising to get her home safely. Conflicting emotions warred inside her.

Was he truly a cold-hearted murderer? Or was he just a boy whose parents had been slaughtered—by her grandfather no less—who'd been forced to take over a kingdom? Perhaps he really had done his best under less than ideal circumstances. Abducting women and children in the raids had been banned; only the bare number of soldiers were captured when needed. He was doing his best to survive. They all were.

The Slayers were not perfect. The suicide decree was ludicrous, regardless of what Miranda had said to him as they'd sat on the plushy grass. She knew it, and so did Kenden. And what if Sathan *had* reached out to her father? Anger surfaced at the prospect that this was true and her father had lied to her. If this was at all factual, their relationship would truly be put to the test.

Rage had filled her heart for so long. Would it be possible to fill it with something different?

Her thumb scrolled through her remaining texts, and she gasped as she finished the last ones.

Ken: The Deamons have attacked Restia. Attack was strange. 100 Deamons but no weapons. They came armed but somehow the weapons seemed to vanish in their hands as they breached the gate. Think I'm going crazy. All 100 are dead but here cleaning up. Won't be at the meetup but 6 soldiers will be and I sent Kalil in my place. You're welcome.

Fucking Ken. The last person she wanted to see right now was Kalil, especially after she had sucked face with the Vampyre king last night. Kalil was extremely traditional and aligned with her father on all things Vampyre. Great. She made a mental note to strangle her cousin when she got home.

"What's wrong, Miranda?" Sathan asked, his voice laced with worry.

"The fucking Deamons attacked Restia earlier this evening."

"Restia?" Latimus asked. "Why in the hell would they do that?"

"I don't know." But she had a pretty good idea who would.

"Do you need help?" Sathan asked.

She laughed and ran a hand through her dark hair. "Um, no. My father would think I'd had a lobotomy if I told him I was bringing the Vampyres to help. We're not there yet. Let me work on him. I told you, it's not going to be easy."

Shooting her an exasperated look, he turned back around in the front seat. Thirty minutes later, they arrived at the juncture of the Wall of Astaria and the River Thayne.

Miranda jumped out of the Hummer, grabbing her pack and throwing it on her back. She addressed the soldiers that exited from the escort vehicles and thanked them for helping her. "I'm safe, guys. The Vampyres treated me very well. Let me grab the Blade from the trunk, and we'll be on our way."

* * * *

Sathan grabbed the weaponry case that held the Blade and handed it to Miranda. She looked so small as she held the large case. Those deep green eyes were going to be the undoing of him, he thought, as she looked up at him.

"Thank you," she said. Her throat moved up and down as she swallowed. "I appreciate you helping me unsheathe the Blade. I do want to end this war and promise you I will speak with my father."

"I know you will," he said. All his hopes were pinned on this small wisp of a Slayer. He hoped she was up to the task. A raven-black strand of hair from her shoulder-length bob had flown into her mouth, and he had to tamp down the urge to free it with his fingers. *No touching the Slayer princess in front of her soldiers. Not a good idea.*

A man approached Miranda and put his arm around her shoulder. "We were so worried for you," he said and placed a kiss on her silky hair. Sathan's fists clenched, and his protective instinct went into overdrive. *Mine.* The word flitted through his brain, and he struggled to remain calm. It wasn't like him to feel jealousy where any woman was concerned.

"Thank you, Kalil," she said, turning and giving the man a half-hearted smile. "This is the Vampyre king, Sathan. He took great care of me."

The man eyed him with undisguised contempt. "We're grateful that you helped our princess and found it within yourself to tame your base instincts and not drain her as you have most of our people."

Sathan felt his brother approach from behind, anger emanating from him. He held an arm to block him from moving forward. "And you are?" Sathan asked the man.

"Kalil, son of Ranju and Tema. And Miranda's betrothed."

Miranda's shocked expression would've made him chuckle if the situation hadn't been so tense. Flinging his arm off her shoulder, she turned to him. "You absolutely are not—"

"Your father made it official this morning, darling," he said, looking down at her in puzzlement. "He signed the betrothal decree and announced it to the realm. It's fantastic news. Or, it was until the Deamons attacked Restia. This has taken up the last several hours. Your cousin sends his regards."

Sathan studied the man looking down at his furious Slayer. He had smooth brown skin, reminding him of the human Indians he had learned about in school. Dark hair, white teeth, straight nose. Perfectly normal-looking, but he hated him on sight for having the gall to touch her. Taking solace in Miranda's obvious distaste at their betrothal, Sathan spoke.

"Hand me your phone."

"Why?" she asked.

Extending his hand, he shook it at her. "The sun will rise soon, Miranda. Don't be difficult. Hand me your phone."

"I would advise you not to speak to our princess that way," Kalil said, anger in his tone.

Turing to him, Miranda said something he couldn't quite hear. The man gave her a scowl but turned to walk to the car.

"He seems like a real charmer."

With a sarcastic look, she handed him her phone. He typed a number in her contacts.

"I programmed my number. I'll try my best to hold off on another raid in the hopes that I will hear from you."

Something sparked between them as her fingers brushed his, taking the phone. "Thank you," she said. Suddenly, he wished to be alone with her for one more moment, if only to memorize her stunning features in the waning moonlight.

"You're welcome."

And then, she turned, walking toward the soldiers' Hummers. Her tiny shoulders were slumped, and he almost felt a pang of sorrow for her. Almost. For he knew that only after she discovered her father's betrayal and lack of loyalty to her would his plan be able to come to fruition.

"Sorry, bro," Latimus said, patting his back as they watched the cars drive off. "I know you liked her. If evidenced by the face sucking I heard last night, you *really* liked her."

Sathan scowled at him. "Were you eavesdropping on us?"

"Pretty hard not to hear that slap, man."

"Yeah, she got me pretty good," Sathan said, turning his head to look off into the distance once again.

Latimus stared down the river to the horizon as well. Once the vehicles were out of sight, they drove the Hummer back to Astaria.

Chapter 17

"Latimus!" Arderin's voice was warm as she threw herself at her favorite brother. "I'm so glad you're home. I escaped! I showed those bastards they couldn't mess with the Vampyres!"

Latimus chuckled and smoothed his hand down her long black curls. "I've always known you were the smartest of us all." Lowering his head, he whispered in her ear, "If only our idiot brothers would listen."

She laughed and hugged him again as they stood in the large foyer of the castle. Sathan entered and approached them. "I'm so glad you're home safely, Arderin."

Disentangling herself from the hug, she slowly approached Sathan. "I'm so sorry," she said, her eyes filling with tears.

"Shhhhh," he soothed, pulling her close. "I'm sorry too. I was so worried about you."

"I know." Pulling back, she smiled up at her oldest brother. Latimus thought her the most precious thing on the planet. In his lonely world, she was the only light that had ever shined. Heart swelling, he watched his siblings embrace.

"She was so excited to see you," a melodic voice said from his side. Stiffening, he looked down at Lila. "She loves you the most, you know? You've always had such a quiet belief in her that Sathan and Heden struggle with. In your eyes, she can do anything."

Latimus swallowed, studying the gorgeous creature. "She's stronger than either of them gives her credit for. I don't know how she puts up with their shit."

The corner of her mouth turned up. "I guess we all put up with people's, er, stuff when we love them." Deep genuineness emanated from her upturned face. The woman couldn't even bring herself to say a curse word. Were there two different people on the planet than he and this fragile, proper female?

"Love is a made-up word for fairy tales and soothsayers."

"Says the brother who loves his sister with all his heart."

"She's the only one," he said, growing tired of discussing feelings with the one woman he'd tried his whole life not to have them for. "Where is Heden?"

"I think he's turned in. I didn't want to miss the reunion. It's so nice to see them getting along." She motioned with her head toward Sathan and Arderin, who was recounting her story of escape.

"Did they hurt her?" he asked softly.

"No. She was not harmed, thank the goddess. Like a good princess, her virginity remains intact."

Latimus shook his head in frustration. "That rule is antiquated. If she wants to get laid, she should. I don't see the need to follow rules that were decreed centuries ago."

"Well, look who's a feminist," Lila said, laugher in her voice.

"You should get laid too," he said, anger bubbling up at her, although he had no idea why. "Sathan fucks other women. He was close to fucking the Slayer princess. You look like a fool, waiting around for him."

All signs of laughter vanished, and she looked as if he had struck her. Guilt immediately gnawed at his gut, but he continued, wanting to hurt her for some unfathomable reason. "There has to be some poor sap on this compound who would fuck you, Lila, even as frigid as you are."

Twin dots of red appeared on her otherwise pale cheeks. He wished that she would slap him. Or scream at him. Or rip his eyes out with her fingernails. Anything but the look of severe disappointment and self-doubt she was giving him. What a piece of shit he was. He could delude himself that he didn't know why he spoke to her this way, but that would be a lie. In his heart, he hoped that if he hurt her enough, she would just leave him the fuck alone. The less he saw her, the less he was reminded that he would never be good enough for someone like her.

Instead, she pursed her lips. Her nostrils flared, and she seemed to calm herself. "Thank you for that information. It is always good to know where I stand in this betrothal. Sathan is my king, so he is free to do as he wishes."

Moisture appeared in her eyes, and she looked to the ground. He wanted to rip his heart out and stomp on it with his boots. It wasn't the first time he'd made her cry. What an asshole he was.

"I think I'll turn in for the day." Turning, she floated off, light as air, as she always seemed to be.

"Where did Lila go?" Sathan asked. "Was she upset?"

"How the fuck do I know?" Latimus said, rubbing the back of his neck with his hand. Hating himself.

"You better not have been an asshole to her." Giving Arderin a peck on the forehead, he stalked after Lila.

"Latimus," his sister said. She framed his face with her hands. "You're such a good man. I'm sorry that you can't have everything you want."

"I have everything I need," he said. His sister was the only one who had ever suspected his true feelings for Lila.

"You deserve to have it all. I'm sorry that you can't. But I love you with all my heart." Her thumbs ran over his cheeks. "And she's my best friend, besides you. Please, try harder. She has a special place for you in her heart. She wants so badly for you to like her."

"I like her fine," he said, grasping her wrists and disengaging her touch. "I'm pretty tired of getting this speech from all of you. She deserves to know that Sathan was attracted to the Slayer princess. I would want someone to tell me."

"Okay," she said, lifting to give him a kiss on his cheek. "Even when you try to do the right thing, you're an asshole. It's quite a feat."

"Quiet, you little bugger." He began tickling her sides, and she shrieked.

"I missed you," she said, after he had ceased.

"I missed you too."

Joining hands, they walked slowly down the hall as she excitedly recounted the story of her abduction and escape.

Later, he headed to the cabin he kept on the outskirts of the compound. The main castle was just too stifling tonight. Especially knowing he had hurt Lila. Again.

Sathan had dropped a bomb on him when he'd revealed he'd never slept with her. What a waste. If he had the right to touch her whenever and however he wanted, he wouldn't hesitate. Sure, she would start off so prim, so tense. But he imagined sliding his hands down her back, gliding under her gorgeous hair. Pulling her to him, he would mold his body to hers and kiss away the tension from every inch of her body until she was a quivering mess. By the goddess, watching her come would be amazing. Would she scream? Or maybe just moan with that velvet voice?

Frustrated that he'd made himself aroused, he threw on some jeans and headed to the cabin next door. Moira answered on the third knock. "Yes?" she asked, one eyebrow arched. Although her eyes were blue and her features were smaller than Lila's angular ones, she had blond hair. Not as long as Lila's, it fell to her mid-back.

"I need you."

Smiling, she opened the door wider. "Well, come on in, soldier."

He wasn't gentle. She didn't need him to be. He had been coming to her for centuries now. She was a Slayer who had been accidentally captured in the raids almost eight hundred years ago. When he had tried to return her to the compound, she'd begged him to stay. They had never discussed why, but her dreams were filled with violence. He could tell these things as he lay beside her in the darkness.

There were a few women like this. Slayers he had collected over the centuries, who chose to stay, that he fucked when he needed to rid his head of *her*. They had come to be known as Slayer whores. Slayers who lay with the king's powerful brother, exchanging blood and sex for a simple, safe life.

Sathan had outlawed the practice of keeping Slayer whores centuries ago, but Latimus didn't give a damn. It was just something they never discussed. He knew by his brother's disapproving glances that he wished he would cease the practice, but Sathan chose not to fight this battle with him.

Afterward, as he lay with the woman splayed across his chest, he absently played with her blond hair.

"You did it again."

"What?" he asked.

"Called me by her name when you came."

Latimus looked at the ceiling, cursing himself. "I'm sorry, Moira. Shit."

"It's okay," she said, rubbing her hand over the tiny hairs of his chest. "I know the rules. It's sad that you can't be with her like this."

"My sister said the same thing to me tonight."

"The world is harsh," she said, rubbing her fingernail over his nipple. He shivered under her. "You can call me any name you want. I'm thankful to you for giving me shelter here."

"You can tell me about your past, you know?"

"I know," she said, lifting up to rest on her elbows on his chest. "But I won't. Let's not make this something it's not. Oh, and I promise, I won't tell anyone what a nice guy you are. It would ruin your reputation."

Smiling at her, he lifted one eyebrow. "We can't have that."

Disentangling himself from her, he threw on his jeans and headed back to his cabin. In the darkness, he thought of Lila's lavender eyes, filled with tears. Nice guy, he was not. One day, she was going to stop speaking to him altogether. Maybe that would finally give him peace.

* * * *

Miranda asked the soldiers to drop her off at her spot by the river. Assuring them she would be fine, she needed a few moments to clear her head. Once she was alone, she placed the Blade case on the ground and looked at her mother's makeshift grave. Would she have been proud of her? She liked to think so. Freeing the Blade had also freed something in her, and she could feel it growing, like a young seedling reaching for the sun. She was ready to save her people.

"I tried my best to thwart the attack," Darkrip's voice said behind her.

Somehow, she'd known he would come to her and was unsurprised by his presence. "I'm not sure 'thank you' is appropriate in this situation."

"Ah, Miranda. Always so combative. I disintegrated their weapons as soon as they breached the wall. Your cousin's soldiers defeated them handily."

"A hundred of your men are dead. Don't you care at all?"

He shrugged beside her. "All part of the end game." His expression was impassive as he stared at the river, but the hunch of his shoulders seemed sad. She wondered if he was truly as unaffected by the soldiers' deaths as he claimed.

Miranda shook her head as she looked at the gurgling river. "So much death. Will the outcome even be worth it?"

"When you kill my father, yes. It will be. What will you do now, knowing your father won't support your venture to kill the Dark Lord?"

Miranda saw red. "Why does everyone think my father won't support me? I'm the direct descendant of Valktor, and this is my kingdom."

"Indeed." His expression was one of surprise. "I'm happy to hear you finally say it. Your father is a false ruler. It is time you took the throne from him."

"I have no wish to dethrone him. It will take time, but I will gain his support, and we will rule together."

Darkrip was silent for a moment, watching the river. "You must know in your heart that isn't true. You're too smart to think otherwise. Know that I will support you in your quest to rise to power. One needs all the allies they can get in these situations."

Gritting her teeth, she chose to stay silent. What was the point in arguing with him anyway?

"This is where you buried the appendages of your mother," he finally said.

"How do you know about that?"

"I told you that I am powerful and see many things, Miranda. You are quite hardheaded and don't listen very well."

Looking down at the ground, she ran the toe of her boot over the green grass. "That was centuries ago. She is long gone from this place."

The Deamon surprised her by closing his eyes and lifting his face to the blue sky. "I feel her here, still, after all the years that have passed. She is happy that you and your cousin still come to remember her from time to time."

Miranda felt her throat tighten, and tears flooded her eyes. "I would ask you not to speak about my mother. She hated Deamons, and you sully her memory by speaking of her."

He sighed loudly and turned to look at her. "I've told you that things are not always as they seem. You would do well to remember this. Don't let your past hurt and pain cause you blindness toward the future."

She studied him, light filtering onto his face through the branches of the tree overhead. Another flash of recognition ran though her, as it had in their previous meeting, and then it was gone. "Did you meet my mother in the caves? After Crimeous abducted her?"

He stayed still, contemplative. "Call upon me when your father denies your request. I will help you gain access to the Deamon caves. It will not be easy, but it can be done. Stay the course, Miranda." And then, he was gone.

Frustrated, Miranda kicked the ground with her boot. What an infuriating creature he was. But she was smart enough to know that war made for strange allies. She placed a hand on her mother's tree, saying a prayer. Then, she picked up the case and headed home.

Chapter 18

Miranda found Ken in his shed, standing over a map of Restia and making notes with a pencil. Looking up, he smiled broadly at her. "You're home." Rushing over to her, he picked her up and swung her around in a huge hug. "And you stink," he said, waving his hand back and forth under his nose.

"Jerk," she said, slapping his arm. "Where's Father? I want to shower and prepare before I approach him."

"He's called a meeting of the council this afternoon. Kalil informed him that you were less than thrilled about the betrothal."

"I'd rather be a withered old grandma than marry someone for duty."

"He's prepared to fight you on this, Miranda. One of the items on the council meeting agenda is to set a date for the wedding."

Grinding her teeth back and forth, she struggled for calm. "Then, I'll just have to inform the council of my wishes. The time of Father dictating my life is over."

Kenden smiled at her, admiration in his gaze. "You've come into your own, Randi. It's about time."

"We'll see about that," she said. "I need a shower if I'm going to have any chance of swaying even one of our dinosaur council members."

"I've recently returned too," he said, eying her a bit warily.

"From where?"

"The human world. I was following up on some antiquated soothsayer gossip."

"Do I need to be worried?" she asked, wondering what he was searching for.

"I'm not sure yet. It might be nothing. I came back here to check on things before I could really do any digging. Thank goodness, since I was here when Restia was attacked."

"Is everyone there okay?"

He nodded. "It's fine. Such a strange battle. I feel like so many bizarre things are happening in our world right now."

Miranda thought of her meetings with Darkrip and sucking face with the Vampyre king. Yep, definitely abnormal, that was for sure. Deciding that now wasn't the time to discuss those things with her cousin, she narrowed her eyes.

"Do you need my help? With the human thing?"

"No," he said, shaking his head. "Let's deal with your father first. That's the most important thing. We have to prioritize."

"Okay," she said, clutching his hand and giving it a squeeze. "See you at the meeting."

Miranda walked to the compound through the barracks and took the back stairs of the main house to her bedroom. Before she got there, she ran into Sadie and threw her arms around the tiny doctor.

"Are you okay? I know the Vampyre woman escaped. Did she hurt you?"

"No," Sadie said, only half her face visible under her hoodie. "But I'm so sorry I let her escape. It was all my fault—"

"Stop it," Miranda said, rubbing Sadie's unburned upper-arm. "You're not a soldier, and it wasn't your job to guard her. The soldiers who let her escape are to blame, but I've got bigger fish to fry. Everything worked out. Don't sweat it."

"I'll make it up to you—"

"Good lord, I'll be mad if you think about it for one more moment. And that's an order, straight from your princess. Got it?"

A thin smile formed on her lips under the hoodie. "Got it."

"Good. Now, I have to go meet with the council. Wish me luck!"

Miranda reached her bedroom and pulled off her camouflage pants and tank top, throwing them on the bed. When her bra and underwear came off, she groaned with pleasure. The warm shower was the best she'd ever had.

With a sense of renewal, she dressed in black slacks, a white turtle-neck sweater and heels. She hoped the more traditional dress would be one more thing that could placate her father. He hated it when she wore camouflage pants or leggings.

Marsias preferred the more traditional dress of the aristocracy. Those Slayer females usually wore long, flowing gowns and donned faces full of makeup. Miranda had always thought applying makeup an incredible waste of time. And the dresses were just absurd. How in the hell did women maneuver in those things?

The middle-class subjects usually wore more casual outfits such as jeans and sweaters. Only soldiers wore camouflage pants, but she considered herself a soldier, so why not wear what she was comfortable in? She usually chose to wear those or soft yoga pants, as they were easy to move in.

Today would be different though. She needed to ingratiate her father to her in any way possible. Too stubborn to don a dress, the slacks and heels were at least more acceptable to him than her usual attire.

After running her hand over the case that held the Blade, she locked it in the large safe that sat in her bottom drawer. She'd had it installed centuries ago when a staff member had absconded with some of her mother's jewelry. Resolved, she set off to the conference room to confront the council.

The various council members, all men, were milling around the room as she entered. They ranged in age from two centuries all the way back to before the Awakening. One of the younger members, Aron, approached her.

"Miranda, we hear that you have freed the Blade of Pestilence," he said, his head lowered so that their conversation could be as private as possible.

"Yes," she said. She liked Aron immensely and had always felt that he wished to end the fighting as much as she did. "A page has turned. It's time for me to fulfill my destiny and kill Crimeous."

"And the Vampyres?"

"Their king was very kind to me on our journey. He wishes to find a way to end the raids. We finally have a chance to change things."

Aron squeezed her forearm, offering her his alliance. "I support you, Miranda. Many of us do. Know that your allies are strong in our belief that it is time you rule our kingdom."

"Thank you," she said. "Your support means more to me than you know."

"Order! Order!" one of the men called, and Miranda took her seat at the table, at her father's right hand.

King Marsias spoke to the group of twelve once they all had been seated. "As you can see, my daughter is home safely." He gazed down at her, eyes cold and angry, causing her to shiver. She had rarely seen him so furious. "She has freed the Blade of Pestilence and wants to fulfill the prophecy to kill our great enemy Crimeous."

"Hear, hear!" came the response of a few of the men.

"However," Marsias said, standing to his full height, "I have decided to take a different course. Miranda will marry Kalil and produce an heir. Since that child will have the blood of Valktor, he will be the one to kill Crimeous once he has been trained."

Silence blanketed the room. Clenching her fists together, Miranda had to mentally restrain herself from standing up and punching her father. How dare he?

"King Marsias," Aron said, standing at the other end of the table, "your plan is wise, but I would like to offer another. As the current descendant of Valktor, I believe that Miranda should be the one to attack Crimeous."

Murmurs of agreement and descent echoed throughout the chamber.

"Your suggestion is noted, Aron," her father said, "but we cannot send our remaining descendant of Valktor—a female, no less—to fight the Dark Lord. It would be the end of his line, and once deceased, there would be no hope of fulfilling the prophecy."

No longer able to stomach everyone discussing her as if she wasn't there, Miranda stood. "Enough," she said, training her angry gaze on her father. "This *female* is sitting right here and can speak for herself." Looking to the council, she addressed them. "I understand the concern about sending me to kill Crimeous. However, the time has come to take a new path forward for our people. I will not wait another century to attack him. By then, his army will be more powerful, and we will have lost countless soldiers. I have the chance to prevent that and I won't squander it. As the descendant of Valktor, you either support me, or you don't."

"Miranda just returned and is quite tired," her father said, rubbing her upper arm. Placating her. She hated it when people placated her.

"Enough, Father," she said, pushing his arm from her, drawing a gasp from several of the council members. "I won't have this division between us anymore. I have let you rule for ten centuries unchallenged. I am the rightful heir to this kingdom, and I'll be damned if I let you, or any man, dictate what I can and can't do."

Turning, she fully addressed the table. "I am the granddaughter of Valktor, first and beloved father and king of our great people. Your loyalty should lie with me. If it does not, then you are no longer welcome on this council."

"Miranda," her father said, his expression shocked. "We should discuss this in private—"

"It has been discussed between us for centuries, Father. I'm tired of talking. Now is the time for action." Turning, she addressed the men. "I propose a council vote. Either I am allowed to attack Crimeous, or I marry Kalil and produce an heir. I am confident that all of you will make the right choice."

Hushed voices swirled through the room as the men bent their heads toward each other and discussed. Finally, Aron lifted his head. "I second the vote."

Miranda nodded to him, thanking him with her gaze.

"This is absurd," Marsias said, his disgust evident.

"This is ruling, Father. We are a kingdom full of competent people and should not be run like a dictatorship. I have let this go on long enough." She looked at the member sitting to her father's left. "Runit, please cast your vote. We will go around the table."

Miranda's heart pounded as each member cast their vote, hoping that she hadn't misjudged the amount of supporters in the room.

"It's a tie," Marsias said, giving a humorless laugh. "Even our council members are divided on this plan. We must take more time to strategize, Miranda. I won't have our people break into civil war because you've finally decided you want to play queen for a day."

What a pompous asshole her father was. Fury surged up her spine, and she thought seriously for several seconds about slapping the condescending expression right off his face.

Thankfully, Kenden spoke from the doorway. "In the event of a tie on council committee votes, the army commander is allowed to cast a vote. And I vote for Miranda's plan."

Miranda's heart swelled in her chest. "Then, we have all the votes," she said firmly, looking up at her father and daring him to challenge her again in front of the men. "Seven to six, I move forward with my plan. There is no time to waste. I would like a battalion assigned to me."

"Miranda," her father said, "let's discuss this further in my study."

"The discussion is over and the votes have been cast." Addressing the men, she asked, "Do you all recognize the validity of this vote?"

They all responded with an "aye," some more supportive than others.

"Then, it shall be. Kenden, please prepare a battalion of your best men so that we can begin to train. Thank you all for your support. I hope that I can begin a new path for our people."

The council members rose and several of them approached her to shake her hand and offer support. Many of them also advanced toward Marsias, whispering words of dissent in his ear. Miranda wasn't naive enough to believe that the traditionalists' minds could be changed so quickly. But she was sure that killing Crimeous was the first step in the right direction.

Finally, she was left in the large room, alone with her father. She called to him softly, not wanting to argue.

"What you did today was reckless, Miranda," he said, disappointment swimming in his eyes. "You have a responsibility as the last descendant of Valktor. If you get killed, we all will be lost."

"Would you care because your daughter would be dead, or only because I am Valktor's blood?"

"That is a ridiculous question," he said, anger in his voice.

"Is it?" She shook her head. "I'm sorry that it has to be this way between us. I want your approval, but I want to save our people more. Perhaps one day, you will come to understand this."

"I won't live in a world where my daughter is a soldier, sympathetic to Vampyres." Miranda opened her mouth to argue, but he rushed on. "Kenden told me about the banked blood he delivered while you were on your journey. It is unacceptable. They are our greatest enemy, Miranda, whether their king helped you unearth the Blade or not. I won't give that murderer another drop."

Miranda studied him, the lines of his face seeming more pronounced with his hatred. "You would fight forever if you could," she said, sadness lacing her voice. "Your revulsion runs so deep that you would lock our people in a prison of war before choosing to let go of your anger. That is truly sad, Father."

"That is strength, Miranda. You would do well to remember this."

Shaking her head, she regarded him. "Did he write to you? The Vampyre king? Asking you to negotiate a way to end the war centuries ago?"

With a humorless laugh, he narrowed his eyes at her. "Did he tell you this? And you believed him? My god, what a perfect way to sow dissent between us. It's a sad day when you believe the Vampyre king over your own father."

"I didn't believe him," she said, realizing that she was lying. After her father's behavior today, she was firmly convinced that Sathan had sent the letters. Not wanting to escalate their argument even further, she continued. "I told him that there was no way he could've sent you those letters without you informing me. As the descendant of Valktor and the princess, it was your duty."

"Then, we are wasting time discussing it," he said, his mouth drawn into a thin line. "Tread lightly, Miranda. There are many who do not like the path you took today. The council members will spread the word, and many of them support my plan and my rule. I have been a noble ruler to our people and tried my best to do what is right. If you're not careful, you will cause a civil war."

"My goal is to end wars, not start them. Although we disagree, we can find a way to work together, Father. We always have. Please, have faith in me."

He swallowed thickly, and she thought that his eyes grew a bit glassy. "I had faith in your mother. You look so much like her. She was also strong and brave. And reckless. That recklessness got her abducted and eventually killed."

"Father—"

"I have work to do," he said, clearing his throat of the emotion sitting there. "I will see you for dinner."

Brushing past her, he exited the room.

Miranda exhaled a large breath, contemplating their tense exchange. Civil war? Good lord, she hoped not. Surely, her father would come around and support her, especially now that she had the vote of the council.

Doubt gnawed at her, but she dismissed it. He would come around. Of that, she was sure.

Miranda headed back to her room, anxious to start training with her battalion. She changed into her training clothes—camouflage pants and a tank—and remembered the weaponry case sitting in her safe. Walking over, she retrieved it, unlocked it and lifted the top.

Then, she let out a huge curse.

Pulling out her phone, she dialed the Vampyre.

* * * *

Sathan's phone rang. Checking it, he saw it was an unidentified number. "Hello?" he said into the phone.

"You son of a bitch."

By the goddess, he was actually happy to hear her voice. "Miranda—"

"You and your asshole brother must be laughing your heads off that you pulled one over on me. Well, great job. Now, how do I get it back? I've got a Deamon to kill."

"I wanted to have some negotiating power so that you would continue to bank blood, if only for a short time, until we can attempt to figure out a truce."

"Truces don't usually start with one side being a bold-faced liar."

Smiling, he decided he had missed her. "Fair enough. I'm sorry. Now, let's move on and discuss next steps. Did you confront your father about my letters?"

"Yes. He denied he ever received them."

"He's lying."

"Well, that sounds really reassuring coming from the bastard who stole my Blade!"

"I'm sorry about the Blade, Miranda. Truly. I have a peace offering of sorts. Let me offer twenty of my soldiers to help you when you attack Crimeous."

"Twenty of your spies, you mean?"

"Your cause is noble. I want to help, if you'll let me. You know our soldiers have ten times the strength of yours. It can be our first attempt at working together."

"Absolutely not. My father would have a conniption if he knew I was even communicating with you. I plan to attack Crimeous in two and a half weeks' time, under the light of the full moon. Save this number. You'd better have the Blade back to me by then."

"I'll return it the night before the full moon. At our meeting place outside the wall. I expect you to keep supplying banked blood nightly until then. Otherwise, we have no choice but to raid your compound."

"Fine. But you listen to me, you blood-sucking bastard, you'd better honor your word. Otherwise, I'll kill you myself."

He chuckled and swore he could hear her teeth grinding through the phone. "I wouldn't have it any other way." The line went dead. His little Slayer was mad as a hornet. Would she be that passionate in bed? Damn, he'd sure love to find out.

* * * *

Miranda went to the meadow behind the barracks to meet her battalion. Kenden was already there, as she knew he would be. Sometimes, she wondered if her tireless cousin ever slept.

"I figure we can get two good hours in before it gets dark."

Kenden nodded, turning toward the men. "Soldiers, as you know, we have a special mission for you. Our princess has decided to fulfill her destiny and attack the Deamon Lord Crimeous." The warriors broke into cheers. "I have trained her well in combat, but she needs to bond with you all as your leader and commander. Listen to her as you would me. We'll start with combat drills. She will come around and spar with each of you one-on-one to assess your advantages. You have been selected because you are the best, and we thank you for your service." That elicited another raucous cheer from the men and they began to pair off to spar under the waning light of the blue-gray sky.

"Thank you, Ken," she said, fighting off tears at his unending support. That wouldn't be warrior-like at all. "I don't know where I'd be without you."

From behind, they heard a commotion. Miranda's head snapped, and a sense of foreboding snaked up her spine. It took her only a moment to realize that she was being ambushed. By a battalion of her own troops.

Soldiers dressed in brown and gold, the colors of her father's house, surged from the barracks, weapons in hand. The battalion of soldiers that Kenden had assigned her, dressed in their camouflage training gear, roared in retaliation.

Pulling her sword from her back, Miranda began to fight. Countless men, faceless and enraged, fought each other on the open field that butted against the barracks. One swung his sword at her, and she blocked him, turning to hold her sword at his throat.

"I don't want to hurt you," she said, knowing she had the upper hand.

"Marsias is my true ruler," the man said, his eyes filled with hatred. For her. By all the gods, she had never expected it to come to this. Not wanting to kill one of her own men, she walked behind him as she held the blade to his neck and then knocked him unconscious with the hilt.

More men followed, one after one. It became increasingly harder not to kill them as they were all furiously trying to harm her. Where the hell was Ken? She looked behind her to see him fighting valiantly, protecting her. Doubt swelled in her as she fought, and she wondered if she had made the right decision defying her father's wishes. Even though they were stuck in perpetual war, wasn't it better than fighting each other?

"Enough!" her father bellowed, standing on a platform at the edge of the barracks. His expression was cruel in the light of the waning sun, and his gaze leveled on hers as she stood twenty feet away on the field, her sword still raised in protection.

"As you can see, Miranda, our troops support my rule. Your defiance of me can only mean that the Vampyre king poisoned your mind toward me, and to our people, on your journey. You have been manipulated by our enemy. Therefore, you are not of sound mind to rule. I hereby command that you are committed to the care of the infirmary, where a professional can treat your condition properly."

Miranda stared at him. She felt apart from her body, drifting in a world where reality had vanished. After all, how did one respond when someone they loved betrayed them so deeply? Every heartbeat seemed to fracture off a piece of the treacherous organ, shattering it into tiny pieces in her chest.

At that moment, she had no choice but to admit that her father was her greatest foe. Not Crimeous, not the Vampyres. Her own father. Wetness pooled in her eyes but she didn't care. Unashamed, she spoke. "I am Miranda, descendant of Valktor, and the rightful heir to the Slayer throne. For all who can hear, I declare myself Queen of the Slayers. You accept me as your queen, or you will be designated a traitor. This goes for you too, Father." Lifting her sword, she pointed it directly at him, standing in the semi-darkness of the barracks across the field. "What is your decision?"

"I am King!" he bellowed, pounding his chest with his fist. "Attack her and all who support her! I don't want one soldier on her side left alive."

Voices mixed in various yells as the men resumed fighting. Miranda fought off her attackers. In between bouts, she looked at the field and observed that the fifty men Kenden had assigned her were still fighting against her father's men. Of course, her cousin had been smart enough to assemble a group of soldiers most loyal to her. It was imperative that she pulled them from this battle. Not only were they fighting their own men, they wouldn't have enough troops left to fight Crimeous when the time came. Making a firm and fast decision, she yelled, "Retreat!" Lifting her sword, she ran across the field toward the woods.

Boot steps and labored breath sounded behind her, and she knew that her men were following. In the distance, she heard her father yell, "Cease fighting. The enemy has retreated. We will fight them another day." His men cheered in support.

Miranda led them to a clearing, knowing they didn't have much time to regroup. Catching her breath, she did her best to stand tall. "How many casualties?" she asked.

"Only two, my queen," the soldier named Larkin answered.

"Two," she said, shaking her head in anger. "That's two too many. Let this be a warning for us that we must always be on alert. The Earth is changing faster than we know, and we must take care to protect what we love."

The men mumbled in agreement. Miranda realized they were in need of a serious pep talk. The Slayers had just broken into civil war. Worst-case scenario was upon them.

"Soldiers, I know your families are at home, on Uteria or Restia, and I believe with all my heart that no harm will come to them. My father's anger rests with me, and his betrayal is meant for me only. Although he has lost his way, know that we both only wish for our people to be free of war." Lifting her hands, she stood taller, spoke louder. "My grandfather's blood runs true in me. I ask that you trust me as your commander. I have a plan to defeat Crimeous and to return home with his head and claim my throne. You all will be rewarded tenfold for your bravery and support. Let's restore our great kingdom to the bloodline of Valktor, the first Slayer. Our true king!"

A roar sounded from her men and they began whistling and clapping. She took a moment to revel in the feeling, the surge of pride, and then she sobered.

"My father will send his spies after us. I plan to lead us down the River Thayne. We must trek smartly since we are on foot. I am going to make some unorthodox decisions over the next few days. I ask you to trust me as your leader and your queen. I promise you that I will fight for our people's future and peace until my dying breath."

Turning, she began the long journey northward on the river, the men falling in line behind her. She wondered where Kenden was and asked Larkin as he fell into step beside her. He was a competent soldier, and although she didn't know him well, Ken had always spoken of his bravery and loyalty.

"He is not with our battalion," Larkin said. "But I didn't see him fall on the battlefield either. It is quite possible he has retreated on his own to strategize, now that civil war is upon us."

Miranda nodded. "Thank you, Larkin. Please, keep me updated on the morale of the men. I need you to be my eyes and ears."

"Yes, ma'am," he said, giving her a salute. "Everyone in our battalion is a loyalist to Valktor and his bloodline. Your support is vast within this group, and I will make sure that it stays that way."

"I appreciate your support," she said. Nodding, he fell back to march with the troops.

Miranda pulled out her phone and began to text as she walked.

Miranda: Need your help. Father attacked my battalion as we trained. Civil war imminent. Meet me at the wall. Bringing 50 soldiers. Will accept your offer of 20 more. We will train at your facility. Hope your offer to align still stands.

She waited with bated breath for the light to blink on her phone, indicating that he'd written back. Finally, several minutes later, the screen glowed.

Sathan: Yes. ETA?

Well, a soothsayer he was not. No long, drawn-out prose for this Vampyre. Way to under-emphasize the moment. Geez.

Miranda: Sunset tomorrow. We're on foot.

Sathan: We'll be at the wall.

Well, shit. She'd just aligned with the species that sucked her people dry. One day, she was gonna write a fucking book. For now, she marched, followed by her men, into the darkness.

Chapter 19

Kenden caught up with them halfway through their journey to Astaria. He was driving a Hummer and pulled up beside her. She commanded the soldiers to take ten minutes to rest and relieve themselves if needed and stepped to the driver's side of the Hummer to speak to her cousin as he exited the vehicle.

"Crap, I thought you were wounded. Thank god you're okay."

"I grabbed the Hummer so that we'd at least have that."

"Good thinking," she said with a nod.

His brown eyes glowed in the light of the morning sun.

"I don't want to separate from you, Randi, but I need to follow up on the lead I was researching in the human world."

"What is it?" she asked, her heart starting to pound. "It must be bad if you feel it necessary to follow up with this much urgency."

"I believe that Crimeous had another child and that she lives in the human world. If this is true, she could be a powerful ally in our quest to best him. It's said that Darkrip shares his father's unique powers. If she does too, I want to try to sway her to fight with us. We'll need every ounce of support we can get."

Miranda inhaled sharply. "Wow. You just dropped a bomb on me. Okay, let me think." She rubbed her forehead with her fingers. "I don't really need you to be at Astaria with me while we train to attack Crimeous. How long do you think it will take to find her?"

"I don't know," he said, shaking his head. "She's extremely elusive. I'm determined to find her and speak to her. Traveling to the human world is taxing, and I don't want to have to keep making trips there. If I go, I won't come back until I make contact with her."

"Okay," Miranda said, breathing out of her puffed cheeks. "You have to go. Aligning with someone who shares Crimeous' powers would help our cause immensely."

Concern filled his handsome face. "I'm worried to leave you with the Vampyres without my protection. Do you feel safe going to their compound without me?"

Inhaling deeply, she nodded. "Sathan and Latimus were extremely kind to me throughout our journey. They wish to end this war as much as we do. I feel that our agreement on that ensures my safety."

His chestnut irises darted back and forth between hers. "Are you sure?"

"Yes," she said, her tone firm.

Exhaling, he looked to the sky, contemplating.

"Okay," he said, lowering his gaze to her. "I'll head into the human world and try to locate this woman and prove she's Crimeous' daughter. If she is, I'll try to sway her to our cause. I won't have cell service there, so I'll work as quickly as possible. I hate to leave you, but our troops are strong. I assembled the best fighters for you. Larkin is extremely capable and can take command in my absence."

"Okay," she said, terrified to be without him but understanding that another ally with Darkrip's powers would give them a significant advantage.

He wrapped his powerful arms around her, and she fell into the hug, pulling him as close as possible. "I'm scared," she whispered. It was something she would only admit to him.

"I know," he said, his low-toned voice reverberating over her head. "But you're the most amazing person in this world, Randi. Your grandfather's blood runs so strong in you. You can do anything you set your mind to." Pulling back, he gazed into her as he held her upper arms. "I love you more than anything. Please, remember that."

"I love you too," she said, hugging him once more. "Please, be safe."

"You too," he said, placing a kiss on her hair.

They called Larkin over and explained their plan in detail. He nodded in assent and headed to command the troops to march again.

With one last squeeze of her hand, Kenden hopped into the Hummer and drove away. Anxious heartbeats pounded in her chest.

"Ready, princess?" Larkin asked beside her.

"Ready."

With firm resolve, she led her men to Astaria.

* * * *

Sathan met her at the spot where the river intersected the wall, the dim light of dusk above her head. Fifty soldiers marched behind her tiny frame. And yet, there was a strength about her that was undeniable. Some people were just born leaders. His Slayer had come into her own, and she was magnificent.

Stopping only two feet from him, she tilted her head back. "It was as you predicted. You can gloat, or we can work together. It seems that you are now my greatest ally in our quest for peace."

"My only wish is to find a solution where both our people can live without war."

Silently searching him with her gaze, she seemed to struggle to believe him.

"Come," he said, gesturing toward the opening in the wall. "Darkness has fallen, and I want to get you and your soldiers behind the safety of the wall."

Inhaling a deep breath, she nodded and waved toward her men to follow her. There was no turning back now. Once inside the wall, Sathan motioned toward the eight-wheeled camouflaged tanks. "Each can fit fourteen men. The rest can ride in the Hummer with Latimus. You'll ride in my Hummer so that we can discuss details on the way to the compound."

Turning, she instructed her men to load into the vehicles and gave Latimus a nod of thanks. He scowled at her in return, and Sathan shot him a glare. Jumping into the driver's seat, he extended his hand to her to help her. Her expression told him to pound sand. Grabbing the handle above, she hopped in and buckled her seatbelt.

"I've made accommodations for your soldiers to bunk in the vacant cabins at the edge of the compound. The lodgings are bare but not lacking. Each house will sleep ten men."

"And I will bunk with them?"

"No, I want you at the main castle. You're too valuable to be left unsecured."

A muscle twitched in her jaw, and her hand clenched, still fisting the handle above her window. "I'm trying not to tell you to fuck off right now but I'm finding it increasingly hard," she said. "I'm thankful for your help, but you've got another thing coming if you think you're making decisions for me."

"It's only practical, Miranda. The main house is most secure. You'll have access to Wi-Fi and cell service, which is spotty at best by the cabins. Don't make this difficult. You have enough challenges right now."

"Fine," she said, staring blankly through the windshield. His heart squeezed at her dejected expression. How must she be feeling, now that her father had betrayed her? Attacked her? He wanted to ask but felt she needed space.

The rest of the ten-minute drive was filled with mundane information. His staff would prepare meals for the troops three times per day. Although Vampyres ate food to savor the flavor, blood was their main source of sustenance. Assigning members of his staff to feed the Slayers was warranted. Twenty of his warriors would train with her men every night, dusk till dawn, so that they could coalesce as a team and form a strategy to attack Crimeous.

Sathan pulled up in front of five thatch-roofed cottages. As her men piled out of the vehicles, they lined up so she could address them.

"Take tonight and the day tomorrow to rest and prepare, troops. We begin to train at dusk tomorrow alongside twenty Vampyre soldiers. This is a first for our people, and I hope that you all understand the importance of working with the Vampyres. I will not tolerate petty infighting or animosity between species. We are all one team. Our people are on the verge of peace, and we must keep our eyes on the prize."

The men responded with several chants of, "Hear, hear," and loud whistles through their fingers. They all piled into the cabins, and she turned to him.

"Ready or not, we're aligned. I hope they're ready."

I hope you're ready, he thought, assessing her impassive expression. "Let's get to the castle."

* * * *

Miranda was silent most of the short drive to the main house. As they approached the large castle, the dark stones seemed to glow in the moonlight. It was a bit larger than the castle at Uteria, and she figured it probably had a few more bedrooms than her home. Balconies jutted from some of the rooms on the second floor, and four towers formed points at the corners. Statues of goblins and gargoyles hung from the stones, warning away foes.

After driving through a large meadow, they pulled up to what looked to be a large, enclosed warehouse. This must be the barracks, as they looked similar to what they had at Uteria.

Sathan parked the Hummer in the dim barracks warehouse and led her through the cavernous space to a back-door entrance to the main house. After navigating a dim hallway, they walked through a sizeable room that she assumed they used for parties or balls, and then, into a large foyer. A grand, spiraling staircase stretched up to a second floor. The chandelier above sparkled and looked to be made of diamonds.

"Miranda, this is Lila," he said. A woman, the most beautiful and perfect she'd ever seen, seemed to float toward her. Waist-length blond hair fell in bouncy curls from her scalp. Flawless pale skin was mostly hidden underneath her cream-colored gown. Lavender eyes gazed down on her as her pink lips formed a kind smile.

"Hello, Miranda. It is nice to meet you. I've heard quite a bit about your journey with our king. I'm here to help in any way I can."

"You must be the betrothed. Nice job," Miranda said, shooting a glance at Sathan. "I think you're the most beautiful woman I've ever met. Slayer, Vampyre, or any other species."

The Vampyre blushed, only adding to her beauty. "That is very kind. Although, your mother was said to be the fairest of all of Etherya's creatures. If she favored you at all, then I would believe it."

"Yeah, I packed up my modeling career years ago to fight for my people. Much more noble in my eyes."

"She likes to joke," Sathan muttered to Lila.

The woman nodded in consent. Although she was gorgeous, there was a stiffness about her. She reminded Miranda of Kalil, formal and unyielding.

"Lila will show you to your chambers. She can lend you some clothing. It won't be the right size but hopefully, you can find something that will work. My soldiers will supply yours with training clothes and gear." He smiled at the blond woman, and Miranda felt a tiny twinge of...jealousy? No, it couldn't be.

"Thank you, Lila." Placing a soft kiss on her forehead, he left the room. And there was the twinge again. For whatever reason, she didn't like the Vampyre kissing the woman he was supposed to marry. She figured there would be time to unpack that later.

"Come," the woman said, turning to float up the stairway, and Miranda followed. Did they teach that floating thing in Vampyre etiquette school or something? She'd have to check into that.

Reaching the top of the stairs, the woman turned down a dimly lit hallway. They passed several closed doors and then, she led her into a bright bedroom. "This is my chamber. We'll take a look at my clothing and see if we can find some things that will work. You seem to be about five-foot-six and a size four, right?"

"Yes," Miranda said, shocked at how ornate the room was. Everything, from the four-post canopied bed to the curtains to the drawers, was so *feminine*. She had more pillows on the bed than Miranda even knew existed on the planet.

"Here," she said, opening the door to her walk-in closet. "We'll start with the closet, and I'll look through my drawers."

About an hour later, Miranda was set with the three pairs of yoga pants, two sweaters, three t-shirts, two tank tops and some satiny shorts and tank top combination that the woman had insisted were pajamas. They weren't perfect fits, but since she was mainly going to be training on a field with soldiers, she guessed that didn't really matter.

"Thank you," Miranda said, holding the clothes in her arms.

"Of course," Lila said, kindness emanating from her every pore. Was this woman real? She seemed devoid of vice or anger. How did one exist in this world and not feel rage at the constant state of war and death?

"Follow me, I'll show you to your room."

The woman led her past several more closed doors and finally opened one on the right side of the hallway. "This room has light and a balcony that faces east. We can't use it, but Sathan thought you might like to watch the sunrise in the morning after you train. I can't imagine being a soldier. My parents were diplomats and aristocrats, so following tradition was all I was ever trained for. Perhaps you could teach me some of your skills one day."

Miranda looked up at her, realizing that she really liked this Vampyre. A stab of guilt ran through her as she remembered that she'd sucked face with her betrothed only days ago. "I would be happy to."

"Wonderful. Then, I will leave you to rest. My chamber is just down the hall if you need anything."

Miranda looked around her room, inspecting the bed, the chest of drawers and the small bathroom with a stand-up shower. Opening the glass door, she walked onto the balcony and inhaled the fresh air. Under the cover of darkness, she allowed herself to finally process where she was. On the retreating side of a civil war. Against her father. Aligned with the Vampyres. Sheltered in their compound. If she took too much time to digest it, she was sure she would drown in an ocean of self-doubt.

Instead, she changed into Lila's silken pajamas and allowed herself to sleep.

* * * *

The first night of training was grueling. Her soldiers appeared on the large field in front of their cabins at dusk. Twenty Vampyre soldiers, led by Latimus, arrived shortly thereafter.

"I will be helping to train the soldiers," he said. "I expect you to allow me to lead. It will be much more effective—"

Miranda held up a hand, cutting him off. "If you think I'm stupid enough to deny the greatest general who ever walked the Earth from training my troops, then you've gravely underestimated me. I will do anything to improve their skills so that my people can have peace."

His mouth opened as if to speak and then closed. "Good," he said finally. "Let's begin."

They trained valiantly throughout the night, under the reflection of the moonlit clouds. Miranda made sure she rotated through the men to spar with each one, confirming her skill to them and ensuring that they understood she was worthy of their support.

Latimus stood up on the hill, assessing the men as they trained. Watching Miranda, he was impressed. The tiny Slayer switched from warrior to warrior, each one of them seeming to dwarf her more. Her skill was superb, but her cunning was her best weapon. She always seemed to sense her opponent's move and block the attack, allowing her to thrust her weapon at a vulnerable spot on his body.

Sathan came to stand beside him. "She is magnificent," Latimus said, continuing to observe the troops as they sparred. "And tireless. She was born to be a soldier."

"She was born to be a queen," Sathan said, his profile juxtaposed against the darkness. "She has been denied too long. It's her time."

"And what of our time?" Latimus asked. "You're in such a rush to align with her. Etherya once loved the Slayers more than us. We were an afterthought of her creation. Be careful that you don't push our people more into the darkness by helping to lift theirs."

"It is possible for us both to live in peace."

"I hope you're right." Latimus spat out the gum he'd been chewing onto the grass. "I'm going down. See you at dawn."

Chapter 20

Miranda's body was battered and bruised by the time the horizon began to turn a reddish yellow. Invigorated, she wished the troops a good morning, happy to see that the main household's staff had arrived to prepare breakfast for them.

Bounding back to the house, she went in search of Sathan. Once in the large foyer, she headed down a long hallway. Portraits, ancient and sacred, hung along the walls. Coming to a stop, she regarded one of a beautiful dark-haired woman who favored the Vampyre that had washed up on their riverbank weeks ago. To Miranda, that fateful day seemed like a century ago. How could she have known that so much would change so quickly? The coward in her longed to go back to the days when her head had been buried in the sand, and her father ruled the kingdom. But what good would that do her people?

"That was my mother, Calla," Sathan said beside her, his baritone shattering her silent thoughts.

"She was very beautiful. Much like your sister."

"Yes, she is the spitting image of her. Something that my sister despises, as it makes me quite overprotective of her."

"How so?" Miranda asked.

"She wants to go to the land of humans to train as a doctor. I've forbidden it. She's an exceptionally talented and smart woman, and I wish for her to take her royal duties more seriously. I don't mind if she travels anywhere in the Vampyre kingdom but I just can't justify letting her go to the human world. I would never forgive myself if I let her die as I did my mother."

What a burden he must have carried as a ten-year-old boy, not being able to prevent his mother's murder. "It wasn't your fault," Miranda said, pushing away the insane urge to place her hand in his and squeeze.

"I know. But it still burns."

"Judging by her escape, your sister seems to be pretty tough on her own. Maybe you should just let her protect herself. So far, she's proven more than capable."

Tilting his head toward her, he asked, "Have you two been comparing notes? She says the same thing to me almost daily."

Miranda smiled. "We women are used to men thinking you have to save us. It's infuriating. Maybe one day, you'll realize that we're stronger than you've ever dreamed of being."

"No doubt," he said, turning his body to face her fully. "I was watching you train earlier. You're a capable soldier."

"Thank Kenden for that. He's been training me for centuries. Thank goodness, because I'm going to need it now more than ever." Lifting her chin, she added, "I need to ask you something."

"Okay."

"Do you still have Slayer prisoners in your dungeon?"

His expression was wary. "Yes."

"How many?"

"Six."

Miranda nodded and rubbed her upper arms. "I would like to ask you a favor."

"You seem to be racking them up."

She shot him a droll look. "I want you to release them. Back to the Slayer compound. We have a physician there who will nurse them back to health. It will show my father that you are willing to change course."

His face was impassive, his dark irises boring into hers. "And how would I feed my people?"

"I will have my forty-eight soldiers bank their blood after training every other morning. Surely, that will be enough to sustain your compounds for months."

Inhaling deeply, he looked toward the ceiling as he contemplated.

"Please," she said softly.

"Sathan," he said in his low, velvet tone.

"What?"

"My name. You've never called me by my name. I find that odd. It's always Vampyre or blood-sucker or asshole." The corner of his mouth lifted at that. "But never my name. Why?"

"Yes, I have," she said.

"No, you haven't." He moved in closer, and she stood her ground, refusing to be intimidated. Her traitorous heart began to pound furiously in her chest.

"So, what's the big deal?" she asked, defiant. "I'm sure Miss America says your name all the time between the sheets. Why do you care if I do?"

Confusion crossed his features. "Lila?" he asked. At her nod, he chuckled. "Jealous?"

A sarcastic laugh jumped from her lungs. "You wish."

Moving closer, she swore she felt his body heat. The fabric of his t-shirt grazed the top of her shoulder, bare because of the tank top she wore. "Call me by my name, and I'll release your soldiers from the dungeon."

"Blackmail? That seems beneath you."

"As you said, what's the big deal?" Gently, he threaded his fingers through her hair, one large hand on each side of her head. Sliding them back, he cradled her head and tilted it further up toward him.

"Don't touch me."

"Sathan," he said. "Don't touch me, Sathan." Damn it, he was mocking her.

"You're an asshole."

"Sathan," he said, his lips curved in a sexy smile. Motherfucker, she was drowning.

The skin on her face tingled as his breath caressed it. He was moving closer to her, inch by inch.

She exhaled a gasp when his lips touched hers, feather soft. "Say it."

Tiny pants exited her mouth, and she was mortified that he could work her body into this kind of frenzy so easily. He clenched his fists in her hair, and she moaned, the pinpoints of pain on her scalp arousing. Being a strong woman, she had always dreamed of having a dominant lover. Someone who would declare dominion and relieve her, if only for a few moments, of her need to be in control. Her knees almost buckled beneath her.

"Say it," he breathed against her mouth.

"Sathan," she whispered, causing him to groan against her lips. Sliding one hand down her back, he gripped the ripe curve of her bottom, lifting her against him. Lost to desire, she lifted her arms around his neck, clutching him. Moving his other hand down, he cupped her and lifted her to straddle him. Wrapping her legs around his waist, he slammed her back into the wall beside his mother's portrait.

Thick lips consumed hers. Holding nothing back, she slid her tongue into his mouth. Growling, he sucked it deep, tangling it with his, and pushed his erection into the juncture of her thighs. Mouth open, she tilted her head back, allowing him access to her neck.

Wet lips placed small kisses along the vein of her neck. Then, in a reckless gesture, she felt his fangs scratch along her delicate skin.

"No," she said, lowering her head to look into his eyes. "You can't drink directly from me. You know that. I won't have my privacy invaded that way."

He lowered his forehead to rest on hers, breathless.

"Put me down."

Slowly, he lowered her, so that she stood before him. Something akin to hurt swam in his eyes. "I would never drink from your vein without your consent, Miranda. Although I desire you, I would never cross the line like that. No matter how carried-away I get. You must believe that."

All she knew was that her entire body was shaking and she felt like the floor was about to collapse underneath her. She needed to get her attraction to this Vampyre in check *now*. Although she was sometimes reckless in other parts of her life, she had never been so with a man. Albeit, she had never desired a man as she did this one. And that made him dangerous.

Needing space, she conceded. "I believe you," she said. "Now, I've given you what you wanted. I want to see my men before they are released."

Stepping back from her, he regarded her, his expression sullen. "Go shower and meet me in the dungeon in forty-five minutes. Lila can show you the way." He turned and stalked off.

Sighing, Miranda ran her hand through her hair. She didn't have time for this crap. Muttering to herself, she navigated her way to her chamber.

* * * *

Lila stood in the shadows of the hallway, her heart beating rapidly at what she had just seen. Her betrothed had all but devoured the Slayer. Their desire had been undeniable.

Was that what true passion felt like? She touched her fingers to her lips. Would she ever be kissed by any man in that way? She didn't know much about the logistics of infatuation, but she knew enough to understand that her betrothed was extremely attracted to Miranda.

Lila lifted her hand to her chest, a small kernel of fear beginning to grow. She wasn't jealous. Not being attracted to Sathan herself, that wasn't something she had ever felt.

But she was worried. If he continued to desire the Slayer, perhaps he would decide to call off their betrothal. She had trained her whole life to be queen. It was all she knew. What if it was suddenly denied to her after all these years?

Lost in thought, she returned to her chamber. Perhaps she was blowing this out of proportion. Sathan had always seemed firm in his commitment to bond with her. Yes, she was just being paranoid. Her king would never cast her aside; he was too noble.

A few minutes later, a soft knock sounded on her door. Opening it, she looked down at the gorgeous Slayer. The nagging fear returned.

Putting on a brave face, she smiled warmly at Miranda and led the way.

* * * *

Sathan watched as Lila led Miranda down the steps to the dungeon. When they got to the bottom, Sathan thanked Lila and gave her a broad smile. After she'd returned up the stairs and they were alone, Miranda spoke.

"Look, I don't know what kind of Stepford Wives thing you and the Nicole Kidman-ScarJo mash-up lady have, but I don't want any part of it. It's inappropriate that you kiss me while your betrothed is completely oblivious."

Sathan figured she had a point, but he and Lila had come to an agreement ages ago. Still, he didn't want to hurt her in any way. He had to be careful about allowing his desire for Miranda to surface. It was quite a feat, as he hadn't been so attracted to a woman in centuries. Maybe longer. Maybe ever.

"She and I have an arrangement." She shot him a look, unamused. "It's not as nefarious as your expression would allow. But you're right. I owe that to her." He extended his hand to her, and she eyed him suspiciously. "The walkway is narrow, and the dungeon is dark. Come on." Shaking his hand at her, he declared a small victory when she placed her small one in his and let him lead her.

The thin walkway led to the infirmary, and he felt a jolt of happiness at her wide smile. Six Slayer soldiers were lying on the hospital beds, and he felt as if he was giving her a great gift.

"Princess," one of the men called, his voice raspy.

"I'm here," she said, approaching the man and grabbing his hand. "It's going to be okay. We're sending you home."

Sathan observed as she walked to each bed, grasping the hand of each prisoner. Murmuring words of comfort, she soothed them, running her hand over their hair and clutching their hands to her chest. In that moment, he truly understood how deep her love ran for her people. Pride surged in him. A strange emotion to feel, but he felt it nonetheless. He was proud to be her ally.

"And who do we have here?" Nolan asked, coming to stand beside Sathan.

"Nolan, this is Miranda, the Slayer princess. Miranda, this is Nolan."

Having finished soothing her men, she walked toward them, her expression thoughtful. "You're human," she said with wonder.

"Quite right," Nolan said, smiling. "I'm also a physician. I have tried my best to keep your soldiers alive so that the Vampyres don't have to, er, visit you as often."

Miranda lifted those curious green eyes to his. "You tried to save our people when they were abducted?"

"Yes," Sathan said. His voice sounded gravelly and far-away, most likely a result of her heartbroken expression. "I tried my best. It allowed us to space out the raids longer."

Lowering her gaze to the floor, a tear slid down her cheek, and she batted it away. "My father's stupid suicide decree."

"He made it quite difficult to keep your men alive, but we did our best—didn't we, Sathan?" Nolan said in his always affable tone.

Sathan nodded, the moment rife with emotion.

"Thank you," she said, looking up at Nolan. He found himself wishing she would look at him that way and then scolded himself for being ridiculous. "I would like to repay you but I don't know how."

"Not necessary, princess. I hear you have a great battle before you. Please, let me know if I can help."

As she smiled at Nolan, Sathan found himself frustrated at her unwillingness to thank him as she did the doctor. After all, he was the one who had employed the damn human. He was the one who was assigning his troops to her. Would it be so terrible for her to gaze up at him with those gorgeous eyes and give him one of her brilliant smiles?

"Nolan will be helping to bank your soldiers' blood at sunrise each day. Being human, he can tolerate the sunlight. I'll leave you to your men. I have work to attend to."

Turning, he tracked out of the dungeon, his boot steps angry on the ground.

Chapter 21

Sadie stood frozen as her king paced back and forth in front of her. He had been questioning her for almost an hour, and she wanted to melt into a puddle and disappear. Unfortunately, the laws of physics prevented that.

"And you're sure that there's nothing else you can tell me?"

"I'm sorry," Sadie said, swallowing thickly. "I never actually saw Miranda and the Vampyre king together."

Marsias scowled, making him look ugly. "I am worried they have aligned together. Can you imagine? My own daughter, the blood of Valktor, aligning with Vampyres? It makes me sick!" He sliced his hand through the air.

Sadie had been aware of Miranda's views on Vampyres softening for decades, so she kept her mouth shut. Although the princess always spoke of her hatred for Vampyres, she also seemed to understand she would need to negotiate some sort of peace with them to end the wars of her people.

Marsias came to a stop in front of her and exhaled a deep breath. "Thank you, Sadie. That will be all."

"You're welcome, Your Majesty," she said, practically running from the room.

Once in her infirmary, she pulled out her cell to text Kenden.

Sadie: Marsias wants to find Miranda. Would he be crazy enough to attack Astaria? Hope u r ok.

Kenden hadn't answered her texts in days. He'd called her on his way to the human world, informed her of his plan and sworn her to secrecy. Was it possible that Crimeous had another child? What if she was as evil as the Dark Lord himself?

Sighing, she checked on a few of her patients and began writing in their charts. As she worked, her mind wandered back to Marsias. She was becoming increasingly concerned that he was unhinged and would attack the Vampyre compound of Astaria. That would be a disaster, as his soldiers were no match for the Vampyre warriors.

After finishing her charts, she headed to her room and packed up her backpack. If she needed to flee the compound, she'd better be ready. Heading into the world with her scarred body was extremely frightening to her. However, it ranked higher than dying in a civil war. Telling herself to be tough, she pulled out her tablet to read the day's medical headlines before falling asleep.

* * * *

Darkrip gasped for air, his hands flailing as his eyeballs threatened to pop from his head like two pieces of burnt bread escaping a toaster. The choke-hold his father was executing with his mind was straight-up Darth Vader, and his throat was paying the price.

Suddenly, he fell to the floor. He gasped large heaps of oxygen into his lungs.

"It was your idea to attack Restia," his father yelled. A loud bang sounded, and then something shattered as he threw one of the metal objects on his desk across the room.

"How dare you fail? Or was that your plan all along? Are you trying to sabotage me, son? Has your hatred of me finally capitulated to treason?"

"You're paranoid," Darkrip said, standing and rubbing his throat. "We did not fail. The Slayers have broken into civil war as we speak."

"No thanks to you," he said, spittle flying from his thin lips. "You are an abomination!"

At least on that, they could agree. "The Slayer princess will come to attack you under the light of the full moon in two weeks' time. As I told you, I have been visiting her. She is beginning to trust me and she is overly curious. I will be able to lead her to you, to a place in the caves where she will underestimate your strength."

Crimeous scowled. "I am becoming tired of your scheming. Make sure you don't fail again. I'm not opposed to torturing you as you die, as I did your mother. It is no less than you deserve."

Darkrip bowed and skulked from his father's chamber, bile rising in his throat. He had witnessed his father's long, skillful torture of his mother. It was something he wouldn't wish on his worst enemy.

Entering his chamber, he kneeled at his bedside and clasped his hands in front of his face. He had never prayed in his life, much less to Etherya, whom he hated with all his heart due to the cruel curse she had placed upon him. But the end of days had come, and that could change any man.

Closing his eyes, he prayed to the goddess he detested to give him strength to finish what he had set out to accomplish.

* * * *

Miranda found herself loving the nights of training. The Vampyre warriors were extremely skilled, and she felt her body growing stronger as she sparred with them. It was hard to read her men when she had announced that she wanted them to bank their blood, but they all had complied. That was something. Ready to attack Crimeous, she would show her people that she was a valiant leader. In her mind, defeating him was the only way to convert her father's supporters to her cause.

She was also doing her best to avoid Sathan. For some reason, he had been unusually grumpy toward her over the past few days during their brief encounters. Having not the time nor the inclination to analyze a Vampyre's moods, she felt it best to leave him the hell alone.

One thing that surprised her? Her growing relationship with Latimus. He exhibited a tireless dedication to training all of their troops, and she was grateful to him. They fell into a seamless pattern as they worked together, and she was quite thankful.

There were only a few nights left until the full moon. Miranda spent hours going over Kenden's Deamon cave renderings with Latimus. Thankfully, he had emailed her a copy before he entered the human world. She worried for him but also knew that there was no other person more capable of surviving than Ken.

Sliding into bed, she closed her eyes, knowing she needed sleep so that her body would be strong. She was still getting used to sleeping during the day, but the blackout shades in her room helped.

As she awoke, she inhaled a deep breath. It was time to train. After brushing her teeth, she donned her bra, underwear and a pair of yoga pants that Lila had given her. As she pulled the tank top over her head, she heard a grave voice behind her.

"I am afraid you will not be attacking my father during the full moon."

She whirled, observing Darkrip as he stood by the bed, and lowered the hem of her shirt to her waist. "Why in the hell do you always appear to me while I'm in some state of undress? It's creepy."

She expected a quip back from him, but he remained silent. Worry crept into her chest. "Why won't I be attacking your father?"

His green eyes bore into hers. "Yes," he said.

"What?" she asked, confused.

"You asked me if I knew your mother, after my father abducted her. The answer is yes."

Emotion swamped her. "When did you see her? How often? Did she—?"

"There's no time for that now." He came to stand in front of her. "She looked so much like you." Lifting his hand, he brushed the ends of her hair with the backs of his fingers.

Miranda shivered, expecting to be repulsed by his touch but instead feeling drawn to him. "Why are you telling me this now?"

His expression was one she had never seen on him, pensive and serious. "I need you to trust me. The world is crumbling beneath our feet. I find myself worried that you will die. It is the first time I have ever been scared to lose someone, and it is...strange. One such as me, with the blood of the Dark Lord, generally doesn't feel these things."

Sadness rushed through her. What a lonely life he must lead. Although he was a Deamon, she felt something akin to sympathy for him. "I'm not scared of your father. If I die trying to fulfill the prophecy, then at least I die knowing I tried. It's more than I can say for most."

"Your courage is noble, but it is not my father you should be afraid of. It is your own. Hurry. He marches upon the compound as we speak. His mind is crazed and he is determined to kill you rather than accept a truce with the Vampyres." Sober emerald eyes stared down into her soul. "Stay the course."

Like all the other times before, he vanished.

Miranda threw on her army boots and ran to warn the others—for she somehow knew that the Deamon told the truth.

Chapter 22

Sathan sat at his large mahogany desk, buried in the paperwork of the realm. As the sole ruler, he was responsible for signing off all licenses, applications and requests. It was the least favorite part of his duty. He much preferred strategizing with Latimus and Heden about how to better the lives of his people.

Miranda burst into the room, breathless.

"He's coming," she said.

Sathan stood, his heart's pace quickening. "Who?"

"My father. He's marching here with his troops. Tonight."

"Let's go," Sathan said. Walking with purpose, he led her to the barracks.

Latimus' head popped up from his task of cleaning his AR-15 rifle. "What is it?" he asked.

"Marsias is leading an attack on our compound. Round up the troops and head to the wall. We'll meet them outside."

Resolute, his brother stood and followed his orders.

Ten minutes later, he was racing toward the wall in the Hummer, Miranda sitting beside him. She looked tense and pensive.

"It will be all right," he said, trying to comfort her. "We won't let him defeat your cause."

"I know," she said. He saw her throat bob as she swallowed. "That's what I'm worried about. His hatred makes him weak." Turning her head, her eyes pleaded with him. "Promise me you'll take him alive. I don't want him to die."

Sathan grabbed her hand and squeezed. "I promise."

Reaching the wall, they exited the vehicle. Several large tanks pulled up, each carrying ten Vampyre soldiers. The Slayer troops had come as well. Tonight, the battle lines would be blurred as Slayer fought with Vampyre to defeat Slayer. The world had gone mad.

Sathan addressed the soldiers. "Men, Latimus is your general this evening, but I am your commander-in-chief. I order you to take King Marsias alive. He is not to be harmed." The men yelled their acceptance of his order.

Turning, he regarded Miranda, standing to his right. Such a large burden had been placed on her small shoulders. He could see the emotions warring inside her.

"Come, Miranda," he said, jerking her from her thoughts. "It's time."

Sathan led the soldiers to the wall and placed his palm against the stones. A doorway materialized, and the troops began to march through.

He saw Marsias standing a hundred yards away, men lined in up formation behind him.

"I would guess he has two hundred men," Latimus said, coming to stand on his left. Miranda stood silently to his right.

"He will be slaughtered. We have four hundred."

Latimus nodded. "What do you want to do?"

Sathan rubbed his forehead with his fingers, frustrated. He hadn't spent the last few centuries trying to decrease the frequency of the Slayer raids so that he could kill two hundred of them this night. "Let me try to negotiate with him."

Miranda grabbed his arm, concern in her expression. "He will never negotiate with you. It is not in his nature."

Sathan placed his hand over hers on his forearm. "Let me try. If not, we will attack, and I promise we will take him alive."

She gave him a small nod, and he started forward.

When he was within earshot of Marsias, he spoke. "King Marsias, we have no wish to fight this night. Your daughter has aligned with us and sees the advantage in finding a nonviolent solution. Our wish is the same: a peaceful existence for our people. Lay down your weapons and let us negotiate peace."

Marsias gave a cruel laugh and stepped forward a few paces. "Slayers will never align with Vampyres. Your people have slaughtered and murdered ours for centuries. My daughter has no official capacity to negotiate with you, and if continue harboring her, we will consider it an act of war."

"We recognize Miranda as the true queen. Valktor's blood runs strong through her."

"I am the true ruler of the Slayers!" Marsias said. Spittle shot from his mouth, and his eyes were crazed. Sathan knew that a truce was unlikely.

"I will give you one more chance before we attack. Otherwise, draw your weapons."

In response, Marsias lifted the sword he held in his hand. Locking his gaze onto Sathan's, he screamed, "Charge!"

Chaos broke loose. Sathan turned to run as the Slayer men approached. They were armed with everything from eight-shooters to semi-automatic rifles to swords. He heard Latimus yell, "Attack!" and the cries of war broke out.

Reaching his men, he turned to fight. From the time he was young, he had always had skill with a knife. Pulling the knife he kept at his belt, he charged.

Out of the corner of his eye, he could see Miranda wielding the sword competently. Unbeknownst to her, he had been secretly observing her train each night with the troops. Watching her was mesmerizing, though his need to do so was puzzling. He had yet to understand why he was becoming obsessed with being connected to her in some way. Even if she didn't know he was there.

One of the Slayers aimed an eight-shooter at his chest, and he knocked it away. Another charged him, and he plunged his knife into his stomach and lifted up, gutting the soldier. Hating that he was killing, he screamed in frustration as another soldier charged.

They fought for a small eternity. Soldier against soldier. Slayer against Vampyre. Slayer against Slayer. Eventually, the troops began to tire.

"Assessment!" Sathan yelled to Latimus.

"We've lost about twenty, but they've lost almost ninety. It is just a matter of time before they are defeated."

Sathan acknowledged his brother's statement and then turned to fight the oncoming Slayer behind him.

It was Marsias.

The king gave a crazed roar as he lifted the eight-shooter to Sathan's chest. Thinking fast, Sathan shoved the barrel of the weapon down, and the Slayer shot the bullets into the ground. He gave a frustrated cry that created an opening. Sathan seized it. Grabbing Marsias, he held the knife to his neck.

"I have your king!" he bellowed, trying to make his voice as loud as possible. Marsias struggled against him, his back to Sathan's front as he held the blade to his neck. "Cease!" Sathan said.

Slowly, like a wave spreading, the fighting stopped as the men realized that the Vampyre king held the Slayer king hostage. Once he had the attention of all the soldiers, Sathan said, "I have your king. The battle is over. Slayers, return to your compound. Otherwise, I will kill him on sight."

Miranda rushed toward him. "No!" she said.

Those gorgeous green eyes pooled with fear. "Trust me," he said quietly.

Slowly, she stepped back a few feet.

Marsias continued to sputter against him. "I will not hold him much longer. Retreat, or watch your king's throat slit open. It is your choice."

One of the larger Slayers turned to the troops. "Retreat!" he said. The Slayers gave a valiant cry and turned to follow the river home.

Once they disappeared from sight, Miranda rushed toward him. "Let him go!"

"No," Sathan said, understanding that she was overcome with emotion. "Latimus, I need the restraints."

Latimus came over, restraints in hand, and lifted his sword. With the butt of the handle, he delivered a blow to Marsias' head, knocking him unconscious.

Miranda screamed and rushed to her father's side, falling on her knees beside him. Fury filled Sathan that she could have such concern for the man who had betrayed her time and again.

He grabbed her upper arm and pulled her to her feet. "Not here, Miranda," he whispered angrily, not wanting her soldiers to hear. "You can see to him once we're off the battlefield."

Anger filled her features, and she pulled her arm from him. "Don't manhandle me. Latimus knocked him out!"

"Latimus did what he had to do. It is easier to restrain him this way. We'll take him to the barracks and question him there."

Hatred swam in her gaze, further inflaming his anger.

"I will question him."

"We both will," Sathan said.

"No fucking way."

"It's not a debate, Miranda. Now, gather your men and give them a good speech. They fought valiantly tonight, and they need acknowledgement from their leader."

A muscle twitched in her jaw as she gritted her teeth. She stalked toward her men and began to address them. Watching her, emotions warred within him. Her stubborn, passionate streak was both an asset and a hindrance. While it motivated her to take action, it sometimes caused her to react too impulsively. In the centuries since he'd assumed the throne, he had worked hard to rule with restrained passion. He wanted to help her in any way he could to do the same. It would make her an even better leader.

When she finished speaking to the troops, Sathan gave Latimus a nod. His brother picked up the Slayer king and headed toward the opening in the wall. Once everyone was through, Sathan closed the opening.

He ordered Latimus to transport Marsias back to the barracks and was surprised when Miranda jumped in his brother's Hummer. "I'm riding with my father. I'll see you at the barracks."

Deciding not to engage—on this battle at least—he got into his Hummer and followed them back.

* * * *

Once at the barracks, Latimus tied Marsias to a chair, making sure the bonds were tight. The three of them regarded him as he began to moan.

"Father," Miranda said, rushing to kneel beside him.

Latimus gave Sathan a look, but Sathan shook his head, silently warning him off. He saw no harm in letting her soothe her father, as long as it wasn't in front of the soldiers.

"Miranda," her father said, looking around the dim room. "Where are we?"

"You're safe," she said, rubbing his arm. "We've got you."

Sathan saw the exact moment when recognition lit in the king's eyes. Followed shortly thereafter by rage. "You're holding me hostage with two Vampyres? How could you?"

"You gave me no choice," she said. "You led an attack on the compound. Why? Do you hate me that much?" Sathan could hear her trying to hold back tears.

"I hate the fucking Vampyres," he said, his neck muscles straining. "I thought you did too. They are murderers!"

"Not anymore." She stood and removed her hand from him. "We have to evolve past that, Father. They wish to end this war as much as we do."

"Lies!" he said, his eyes bulging with hate. "They wish to dethrone me so that they can install you as queen. A woman. Weak and filled with emotion. Then, they can attack us and abduct us all!"

Miranda jerked as if she'd been struck. How awful it must be to hear these things from a parent. Wanting to help her, Sathan spoke up.

"We wish for peace, Marsias. An end to this war. That is all we want."

The king gave a hate-filled laugh. "You are so weak, Miranda, to believe his lies. He wants nothing more than total annihilation of our kingdom."

Miranda shook her head, bringing her hand up to cover her mouth. "I won't watch you devolve into this," she said. She turned, and he felt something shift inside him. The pain swimming in her eyes rocked him to his core. "Keep him here until he's ready to be reasonable. I need a few moments in my chamber."

Nodding, he watched her leave the barracks and enter the main house.

Latimus pulled him toward the outside opening of the barracks, not wanting Marsias to hear their exchange. "We are most likely going to have to kill him. I see no other way if he won't consider a truce."

"I know," Sathan said, rubbing the tense muscles at the back of his neck. "But let's not rush things. Keep him secured, with four soldiers guarding him at all times. I will work on Miranda."

"She is too emotional," his brother said, scowling.

"I don't think you're giving her enough credit," Sathan said. "Her love for her people is vast. She'll do what she needs to when the time comes."

"You place too much faith in her," his brother said, unwavering.

"We need to let her come to the conclusion on her own that her father must die. It's a tough fate for anyone to accept."

"Fine," Latimus said. "I'll assign the guards. But work on her quickly. She listens to you, even when you think she doesn't."

"What do you mean?"

"She and I have been working together every night. She has told me on more than one occasion how she admires your ability to lead such a mighty kingdom, especially since you assumed the throne as a child."

Sathan felt a surge of pleasure at his brother's words, knowing this was something Miranda would never tell him herself.

"I'll do my best to push her along."

"I'm counting on it." Pivoting, he went to gather the guards.

Sathan entered the house to speak to Miranda. She would be angry that he wasn't giving her space, but the stakes were too high, and time was of the essence.

Chapter 23

Miranda covered her ears at the pounding on her door. "Go away!"

"We must speak, Miranda. Open the door."

Yelling in frustration, she threw one of the decorative trinkets on top of the dresser at the wooden door. "Leave me alone!"

The pounding continued until she thought she might go mad. Having no choice, she pulled open the door.

"I hate you."

"Yes, you've told me that many times during our acquaintance," he said, walking past her as if she wasn't there. Standing beside the bed, he motioned to it. "Sit down. We have to talk."

Realizing that it was the only way to make him leave and get the privacy she was craving, she complied. She sat at the foot of the bed and crossed her legs under her. He perched on the edge, by the pillows, facing her. Once again, he was calm as he stared at her. It was infuriating.

"I am not your enemy," he said, breaking the silence.

She scoffed and shook her head. "At this point, I feel like everyone's my enemy." She clutched her knees to her chest, resting her chin on them. "Who will I have if he's gone? Ken is unreachable in the land of humans, and half my people support my father as ruler over me."

"No one said ruling was easy. It took me many centuries to feel assured in what I was doing. You will find a way. Over time, your allies will show themselves, and you will gain confidence in your abilities."

Her cheeks puffed as she exhaled deeply. "I don't want to rule without him."

Sathan's expression was filled with understanding. "I didn't want to rule after my parents were slain. It was terrifying. I did the best I could and learned along the way."

"You want to murder him," she said, struggling to keep her eyes from filling with tears.

"I can't think of a scenario where he lives and we both get what we want. Peace for our people. We are aligned in this, Miranda. He is not. I am open to suggestions if you have any."

She swallowed, hating that it had come to this. Of course, she had always wanted the best for her people. But she had never imagined a scenario in which that meant killing her father. The thought made her sick.

"I need time to think."

He studied her, his dark irises so deep and brooding. "Unfortunately, the longer we take to act, the weaker you will look. Especially in the eyes of his supporters."

Miranda picked at a nonexistent piece of lint on her pants, knowing he was right. "Give me the rest of the night. I owe him that. Let me try to think of a way."

He stood, his body so large, muscles straining from his black pants and tight black t-shirt. Tilting her head back, she gazed up at him as he towered over her. Gently, he lifted his hand and ran it over her hair. Soothing her. It had been so long since she'd been comforted by anyone, and she ached to crawl into his big body and let him hold her. Instead, she pulled away.

His eyes narrowed, and she sensed his frustration. "I'll come looking for you at dawn."

The door closed with a firm thud, and she dropped her forehead to her knees. What the hell was she going to do?

* * * *

Miranda spent several hours trying to find a solution to the rift with her father. Surely, there had to be something she could do. She thought of sequester or banishment, but he would still be alive. With his many supporters, that would always leave them open to a surprise attack.

She contemplated trying to reason with him and change his mind. If only he could let go of his hatred and choose peace. Unfortunately, she knew that would never happen.

She even considered maiming him. Making it so that he couldn't walk or perhaps unable to lift his arms to hold a sword. But for someone like her father, that fate would be worse than death.

Knowing that she couldn't give up, she walked quietly down to the barracks where he was being held. Upon entering the dimly lit, large warehouse, she saw him sitting in the chair. Hands and feet bound, he wasn't struggling. Four Vampyre soldiers guarded him.

Approaching the soldiers, she said, "Leave me with him."

They all looked at each other, and the one she knew as Bryan spoke. "We cannot, princess. We are under orders from Latimus."

"I don't give a crap if you're under orders from Etherya herself. Leave me with him," she said through gritted teeth.

"It's fine," Latimus said, approaching from the darkness. "Take ten." The soldiers saluted him and headed out toward the field that adjoined the open part of the barracks.

"Thank you," she said, looking up at the hulking Vampyre.

"Ten minutes," he said, his expression impassive. "Don't do anything stupid." He skulked off into the darkness.

She turned to her father.

"So, have you come to save me?" he asked.

"I don't know if I can," she said, her tone consumed by sadness.

Some of the madness had disappeared from his expression, and he seemed resolute. "Untie me, Miranda."

"You know I can't," she said softly.

He seemed to be attempting to communicate something with his gaze. "Untie me."

Lowering down, she loosened the bonds at his feet and then his wrists behind his back. He rose to his full height and looked down upon her as she came to stand in front of him.

"My life has never been the same since your mother was taken." He lifted his hand to cup her cheek. "I tried to do the best I could but I was so bitter. So filled with rage. I'm sorry I didn't do better by you."

Tears ran down her cheeks, and he wiped one of them away with his thumb. "I can't live in a world where Vampyres and Slayers are at peace. The only thing I understand is war. It's all I've known for a thousand years."

"You can change, Father. Please. I know you can."

Wetness entered his eyes as he smiled gently down at her. "You lie to yourself too well, Miranda. You always have. It is a defense mechanism that you must let go of if you are to become the ruler I know you can be."

"I want to rule with you," she said, swiping her cheek.

"You are the true ruler. I know that deep inside. Even though I believe it, I will never accept it. And you will never accept it while I'm alive. Therefore, I must make a choice for both of us."

His gaze never leaving hers, he spoke into the dimness. "Hand me the Glock you're holding."

Latimus stepped forward from the shadows. She gasped, unaware that he had been watching. Stretching out one arm, Marsias grabbed the weapon from him and pushed Miranda into the Vampyre's chest with the other. Latimus placed an arm over her, holding her to him as she began to struggle.

"No!" she screamed.

Marsias held the barrel of the gun to his head, his hand shaking.

"May the goddess be with you," Latimus said above the buzzing in her ears.

The loud bang of the gun echoed off the darkened walls, and Miranda ran to pull her father's crumpled body toward her. "No, no, no, no, no..." she cried, rocking his lifeless body in her arms.

She felt Latimus behind her, knowing that he would prevent anyone from entering while she wept. Air heaved in and out of her lungs as she tried to accept that her father was gone. Broken-hearted, she clutched him to her, cursing the Vampyres and the Deamons and Etherya herself. What had any of them done to deserve such pain?

Eventually, the tears began to dry. Lifting her head, she ran her fingers down his arm and clutched his hand. She wondered if her heart would ever truly recover.

"We need to bury him," she said softly. "A ceremony by the River Thayne. I want to make sure he receives a proper entry into the Passage."

Latimus gave her a nod, and she was thankful for his silence. After several minutes, she rolled her father onto his back and crossed his arms over his chest. "May the Passage welcome you with peace, Father."

Standing, she looked up at Latimus. "You'll prepare his body?"

"Yes. I will take care of it."

Nodding, she swiped the moisture under her nose with the back of her arm. "I need a shower." What she really needed was to go back in time and erase all the terrible decisions she had made since the Vampyre woman had washed up on her riverbank. Sadly, that wasn't an option. Dejectedly, she walked to her room, showered and lay down on the bed, only to break into another bout of tears.

Chapter 24

The next evening's almost-full moon cast a soulful, dim light over the small group as they marched solemnly to the river. Reaching the riverbank, Miranda lifted the hood from her head. She had borrowed a black dress from Lila. Knee-length on the Vampyre, it fell almost to her ankles. The cloak she wore over it was as black as her mood. And possibly her soul.

Sathan, his two brothers and Larkin had carried her father's body on the bamboo stretcher. Lila and Arderin, whom Miranda had yet to run into in the large castle, had decorated the stretcher with white flowers. Her father wore a crown of multicolored flowers that Lila had banded together.

The six of them, including Lila, stood in silence as the river gurgled by.

"Do you want to say anything?" Sathan asked softly.

She shook her head, unable to think of any words that could come close to honoring the moment. She had nothing left to give. Sathan nodded at the men, and they lifted the stretcher. Walking over to the riverbank, they placed it in the water. Miranda's throat closed up as she watched her father begin to drift away. All of her tears had been shed, so she stood resolute as he faded into the distance.

She could've sworn she saw a pair of green eyes watching them in the darkness, behind a tree in the forest on the other side of the riverbank. Or perhaps her mind imagined it, in its grief.

"Fare thee well, Marsias, King of the Slayers. You were a great ruler and a worthy opponent," Sathan said.

Slowly, they walked back to the main house. Miranda noticed that Lila held hands with Sathan's brother Heden in front of her. They must be close. She'd store that away for another time when she was able to experience curiosity again. She felt Sathan's hand brush hers as he walked beside her. Drawing her arm in close, she ensured that he wouldn't touch her again. Dealing with her desire for him alongside all the other fucked-up things in her world wasn't an option.

They made it back to the house, and Larkin headed off toward the cabins. Entering through the barracks, the five of them headed to the foyer. Once there, they took off their cloaks.

A female Vampyre bounded into the room, nose buried in a book. Noticing everyone, she froze, her long black curls bouncing behind her. She removed the pair of spectacles she was wearing, tucking them in the 'V' of her shirt. "Hi," she said softly to the group.

It was the first time Miranda had seen Arderin since all the weeks ago when she had left her to free the Blade. God, that seemed like a lifetime ago. She knew the woman hated her but was unable to muster up the energy to spar.

"How did the ceremony go?" she asked, looking at Lila.

"It was very respectful for a great king." Placing her arm across Arderin's shoulders, she began to usher her from the room. "Let's go dig up something to eat. I'll tell you about it."

"I'm sorry," Miranda blurted out.

The two women stopped and turned toward her.

"When you washed up on our riverbank, it gave me an opportunity. One that I seized. I see now that I made many rash choices and so many have been hurt. Holding you captive was not personal. I just wanted to help my people. I'm sorry."

Feeling her throat begin to close, Miranda rushed toward the spiraling staircase and all but ran to her room, leaving the Vampyres behind.

Closing the door behind her, she rested her back against it and looked up at the ceiling. How could she possibly go on feeling this empty? It was as if every nerve ending in her body had shut down, and she wanted to crawl into a hole and disappear. She wasn't sure she could go on like this. Grief was choking her to death.

* * * *

Sathan watched Miranda flee from the room, hating to see her in such pain. Sighing, his gaze rested on Arderin.

"I didn't say anything!" she said. His impertinent little sister, always trying to dodge the blame. Fortunately, this time, she had no reason to.

"I know," he said. "She's understandably upset. I think she truly feels bad for holding you hostage."

"Well, she should," his sister said. Her lips formed a pout. "I mean, I had to slum it with Slayers in a dusty old cabin for days—"

"Okay, I think that's enough," Heden chimed in, rushing over to her and Lila and placing one arm over each of their shoulders. "I think I heard something about food? I'm starving."

"Well, I'm not going to feel bad because the Slayer bitch finally decided to apologize."

"Enough, Arderin," Latimus said. Sathan couldn't believe he was standing up for Miranda. How things had changed. "She said she was sorry. Leave it alone."

Arderin shot her brother a mean look but was quickly whisked away by Heden, as he led her and Lila down the hallway toward the kitchen.

"You should go check on her," Latimus said.

Sathan studied him. "You have grown fond of her."

"Don't make a big deal out of it. I like her, okay? She needs to be tended to. I'm sorry that her father is dead, but her kingdom is without a leader. She needs to set that right. She also still needs to kill Crimeous. Her father's loyalists won't accept her without that validation."

"I'll go talk to her."

Latimus gave a nod and exited the room.

Sathan walked up the stairs, wondering what he could say that would possibly reach his little Slayer in her moment of grief. Suddenly, an idea began to form in his mind. Coming to face her door, he knocked softly.

She opened the door slightly, looking up at him. So many emotions rested on her flawless face. "I want to show you something. Will you come with me?"

Sighing, she looked down. "I just want to be alone."

"Please?" He smiled at her and extended his hand. She eyed it warily. "I promise you'll like it."

She lifted those magnificent jade eyes to him, hesitating. Moments later, she pulled the door open and took his hand. Clutching her, he fitted his palm to hers and twined their fingers together, giving her support even if she didn't want it.

He led her to a large room near his office. Walls lined with books surrounded them, and he reveled in the glow of her curiosity.

"A library?" she asked.

"Of sorts," he said, leading her to a bookshelf filled with old manuscripts. Pulling her hand from his, she fingered them gently. "How old are these?"

"Some are from before the Awakening. Others from just afterward. They are the archives of our people, stored here lest we forget our history."

She pulled out one of the books and laid it on the nearby table. Careful not to harm it, she opened it to one of the pages in the middle and read aloud.

"On this, the twentieth day of the fourth month of the fourth century, our sacred King Sathan has honorably declared that women no longer have to bond with a man to own property."

"That was a good day," Sathan said, grinning down at her.

"It took you four centuries to grant equality to women?" His smile grew larger, happy that she was reclaiming a bit of her snarkiness.

"To formally grant it, at least. I had believed that from the time I was small. My mother was a great female who ruled side-by-side with my father. She instilled equality in me from a very young age."

Miranda looked back down at the weathered book.

"I wanted you to see this," he said, pulling a large leather-bound book from the shelf. Placing it on the table, he opened it to one of the first pages.

"My parents hired an artist to capture images from all the blood-bankings before the Awakening. I don't remember them, but they were said to be great festivals of peace and laughter."

Gasping, she looked at the page he had opened. Staring back at her was Rina, smiling and beautiful. "Mother," she whispered, tracing her finger softly over her features. Turning the pages, her smile grew with each rendering.

"There's my father," she said, love filling her expression as she pointed at the page. "The man beside him, is that Markdor?"

"Yes," Sathan said. "That's my father. They were once great friends."

"So sad that he forgot these times. I wish I could've shown this to him."

"Look at this one," he said, flipping to the next page.

"Grandfather!" she said, awe filling her features. "Oh, he looks so happy. The artist even colored his eyes the right shade of green."

"Deep olive," Sathan said, "like yours. The color is striking. I have never seen it on another."

Lifting those gorgeous eyes to his, she shook her head. "This is...amazing. Thank you. It's been so long since I've seen his face. I remember him as a child, but it was so long ago. It's as if he only exists under mists and clouds."

Reaching down, he closed the book and placed it in her hands. "I want you to have it."

"Oh, no, I couldn't," she said, thrusting it back toward him. "It's part of your archives, your history. I can't take that from you."

"*Our* history," he said, gently pushing the book back into her hands. "We shared peace once, long ago, and I want to share it again with you. Please, keep it. The road ahead will be long and winding now that your father is gone. If you get lost, this will remind you what you're fighting for."

For the first time since he'd known her, she gave him a brilliant, heartbreaking smile. It almost knocked the breath from his lungs. The force of her beauty was overwhelming.

"Thank you," she said softly. All trace of hate was gone. He felt a sense of renewal and purpose.

"You're welcome."

Her gaze dropped to the ground and then lifted to bore into him.

"You were right last night," she said, clutching the book to her chest.

"Now, those are words I never thought I'd hear."

She shot him a look.

Smiling, he asked, "What was I right about?"

"Comforting my father in front of my men. I shouldn't have."

He remained silent, feeling it important to let her keep going.

She placed the book on the table and blew a breath out of her puffed cheeks. "How in the hell do you stay so composed all the time? I'm stubborn and hardheaded, and it gets me into trouble."

"You?" he asked, arching an eyebrow and smiling. "I hadn't noticed."

"Very funny." She rolled her eyes. "I'm serious though. Is it something you've worked on over the centuries?"

"I've done my best to learn to control my impulses so that I can make decisions free of passion. A passionate decision is usually just but not practical."

"Don't I know it. How did you learn to do it?"

"Through many years of trial and error. It took me five centuries to write your father, asking to negotiate. I should've tried earlier but I was young and arrogant. These things take time."

"And now, you're just old and arrogant," she said, her lips curling into a smile.

"Something like that." He grinned.

"There's something inside that drives me to push," Miranda said. "I want better lives for my people, and I get so frustrated when I can't accomplish that. I'm sure that sometimes I just make it worse."

"Your passion is one of the things I admire most about you. Your desire to help your people is inspiring. It's not something you should lose, just something you should control. I know it's hard for you to take advice from me, but I would be honored to try and help you. I had to learn on my own. There's no self-help book for becoming a competent ruler."

"You had the weight of the whole world on your shoulders," she said, her gaze filled with compassion.

"As you do now. Perhaps I'm the only other person who can truly understand how you feel."

She absently chewed on her bottom lip as she contemplated him. "You know, it's much easier to hate you than to do...*this*,"—she gestured back and forth between them with her hand—"whatever *this* is...with you. I don't know how to feel when you're nice to me."

"I'm nice to you," he said, feeling his lips form into a small pout.

"You've been grumpy to me for two weeks."

"You've been training. I thought it best to leave you alone. And it pissed me off that you fawned over Nolan."

Her mouth gaped open. "I did not fawn!"

"You did. It was annoying."

"You're jealous!" she said. "Of a human? Wow. That's low. Even for you, Vampyre."

He laughed and shook his head. "I think I'll just let that one go."

"Coward," she said, smiling up at him.

They were flirting. It was something he'd rarely done in his life. He quite liked it.

"Thank you for making me laugh." She grabbed his hand and squeezed. "It's obviously been a hard few days. My father was the only family I had left. Except for Ken, and he's unreachable."

Sathan squeezed her hand back and mourned the feel of her soft skin when she dropped it back by her side. "Do you think that Crimeous really has another child?"

She shrugged. "I don't know. But if he does, Ken will find her. He's the smartest person I've ever known and my closest confidant. I miss him so much."

"I don't want you to feel alone. I'm always here for you, Miranda. I've grown quite fond of you. And if you tell my brother I told you that, I'll deny it until my dying breath."

She laughed, and twin splotches of red appeared on her cheeks. His little Slayer was embarrassed.

"I guess I'm fond of you too. Considering that I stabbed you in the chest on the night I met you and tried to murder you in the Cave, we've definitely come a long way."

"We have." Those memories seemed like a lifetime ago and yet they had happened so recently.

"It's just all happened so fast. I can't believe my father killed himself," she said, sorrow creeping back into her tone.

"He knew he was defeated. He had no choice."

"I'm going to choose to believe that in his final moments he chose peace, in his own way. Is that delusional?"

"No," Sathan said, unable to resist the urge to draw her close. Pulling her to him, she wrapped her arms around his torso and nuzzled into his chest. "There is something I'm wondering though."

"Hmmm?" she asked, as he held her.

"How did you know he was going to attack?"

She stiffened slightly in his arms and detached from his embrace. "I just knew," she said, shrugging. "Like a feeling in my gut or something."

"A feeling in your gut," he said tonelessly.

"What can I say? We women have this intuition that you guys just don't have."

He had the distinct impression that she was lying to him but decided to fight that battle another time.

"I know you're mourning, Miranda. The loss of a parent is devastating. Your father's betrayal of you only compounds that. But you must find the strength to forge ahead. Your men are counting on you, and your people are without a leader. If you don't hurry, you will lose this opportunity, and one of Marsias' supporters will assume the throne. I speak from experience on this. But I did what I had to do, and so must you."

She nodded and absently rubbed her upper arms. "You're right. Kings and queens don't get the luxury of mourning, do they?"

"Unfortunately not. I'm so sorry. I wish you had more time."

"Me too. But I'm a big girl, and I need to get my shit together. I've got a kingdom to rule and a Deamon Lord to kill."

"That, you do."

Those tiny teeth appeared as she chewed on her bottom lip, sending his heartbeat into overdrive. He found the habit so fucking sexy.

"What?" he asked.

"You're one of the only people in my life who isn't scared of me. Most people do what I tell them, when I tell them. You put me in my place. I like it."

There were several places that he'd like to put her at the moment. All of them involving him and her in bed. *Keep it in your pants*, he scolded himself.

"You put me in my place too. It's infuriating. But it makes both of us better."

"Agreed," she said, gazing down at the book he gave her. "I'd like to look at some of the other archives you have here. Do you mind?"

"Take all the time you need. When night falls tomorrow, we will need to address the troops together. Think about what you want to say and what course you want to chart. Let's meet in the conference room three hours before dusk to plan. I'll invite Latimus as well."

"Okay," she said. Triumph surged when she didn't argue or accuse him of ordering her around. Perhaps she was coming to see him as a true ally. He hoped so.

"Good night, Miranda."

"Good night," she said softly.

* * * *

Kenden was embroiled in his mission and growing tired of being in the land of humans. Narrowing his eyes, he observed his target. The scarlet-haired woman sat in the French café, laughing amongst friends as she drank a glass of red wine. He sat across the street, the lone man at a table set for four on the sidewalk. Humans buzzed by, lost in their phones and their conversations, never conscious that he wasn't one of them. They were an amazingly oblivious species.

Kenden snapped a picture of the woman with his phone. Touching it with two fingers, he spread them apart so that the image of her grew larger. Her pale skin was flawless, but he hadn't gotten a direct shot of her face. Damn it.

Deciding to try again, he lifted the phone. And then, he froze.

The woman stiffened and turned her head, locking her gaze onto his. It was filled with a warning. *I know you're watching me, Slayer.* The voice seemed to travel through his brain. Startled, he stared back at her, refusing to be intimidated.

He couldn't deny what he saw.

Her eyes were the same vibrant olive green as Miranda's.

Giving her a nod, he acknowledged her awareness of him.

She lifted her glass, saluting him through the window of the restaurant.

Heartbeats pounded in his chest.

Rising, he dropped a few euros on the table and stalked off.

Chapter 25

Miranda arrived promptly, three hours before dusk, and sat at the conference room table beside Sathan. Latimus sat on his other side.

Looking refreshed and renewed, she thrust up her chin and spoke with confidence. "I need to return home and inform my people that Father is dead. I have come up with a plan. I welcome your thoughts."

She informed them that the first phase was to march home with her soldiers. She would assume the role of ruler until she could be formally coronated. In the meantime, she would work on helping her people assimilate to a life without Marsias as king.

Phase two was attacking Crimeous. She planned to attack him during the full moon in three months' time. This would give her enough time to ensure her people were safe and work out logistics of banking blood for the Vampyres. Once she defeated Crimeous, she would return home and officially claim her throne. Any remaining supporters of Marsias would have to choose between accepting her rule, or banishment.

Phase three would be her coronation as queen.

"So, what do you think?" she asked, looking back and forth between them.

"It's a solid plan," Latimus said. "I would like to send our twenty men to stay at your compound and support you through the transition."

"Thank you. I accept. We welcome their help, and they have become part of our team."

"Who are you going to enlist to bank blood?" Sathan asked.

"I haven't decided yet. I think I'll ask for volunteers and see if anyone offers. There were many who spoke to me of wanting to negotiate with the Vampyres for centuries. Now is the time for them to put up or shut up."

Sathan was pleased at her turnaround. She seemed to have come to some sort of acceptance with her grief and she appeared strong and ready. They strategized about minor details for the next several hours and then went to address the troops.

Under the light of the waning moon, Miranda stood on a wooden box she had carried from the barracks and addressed the men. They stood still, in front of the cabins, their attention focused on her words, her confidence. A small seedling of some unidentifiable emotion began to grow in his gut. Her bronzed skin glowed in the moonlight, under the twinkling stars, and he truly felt that they had a chance at peace. With this magnificent creature by his side, how could they go wrong?

Finally, she stepped down, and the troops returned to their cabins. Jumping in the nearby four-wheeler, Latimus drove them back to the house. She was set to leave at nightfall the next evening, hoping to navigate down the river under the light of the waning moon.

He wanted to be by her side as she marched into Uteria, her soldiers at her back, but knew that she must claim that moment alone. The future of her rule depended on it. Of course, they would see each other again, as their alliance continued to forge, but he suddenly felt sad at the prospect that she wouldn't be sleeping under his roof anymore.

In his chambers, he felt restless. Pulling off his clothes, he threw on a pair of sweatpants. Pouring blood into his silver goblet, he walked onto his balcony to soak up the last hour of darkness before sunrise.

He smelled her scent before he saw her. Smoky, spicy and filled with a hint of jasmine. Gazing to find her, she was seated on the plushy grass, arms around her upturned knees, looking at the moon.

He knew he shouldn't bother her; the woman loved her privacy. But he found himself calling her name.

Straight, silky hair snapped around in a shiny curtain as she gazed up at him. "Didn't know you had a balcony," she said. He could hear the annoyance in her voice. And something else too. A breathy anxiousness.

"Come up and see it. The view is much better up here."

"I'm fine," she said, shaking her head. "Us Slayers like hanging in the grass."

He shrugged. Let her sit on the damn ground if she wanted. Stubborn woman.

She sat in silence for many moments, and then, he heard her exhale loudly. "Well, if you're gonna stand up there and gawk at me, I guess I'll come up. Stalker. Open the door when I knock. Maybe leave a sock on the door. Your house is a fucking maze."

He chuckled as she stomped inside. It seemed she had regained her sense of humor.

A soft knock sounded, and her eyes traveled over his chest when he opened the door. "You don't own a t-shirt?" she asked.

Smiling, he ushered her in. She scowled when he set the goblet on his bedside table. "I can't change who I am, Miranda."

"I know," she said, waving a hand at him. "Show me this amazing balcony."

Grabbing her hand, he pulled her outside. The night was warm and breezy. Her hair whipped in her face, and he longed to brush it away. Instead, he leaned his forearms on the railing. "So, what do you think?"

Inhaling deeply, she closed her eyes and tilted her head back. The line of her throat was splendid against the backdrop of the darkness, and he felt himself harden as he watched her. Opening her eyes, she regarded the sky.

"So many stars. So many universes. Do you think they even know we exist? Our problems seem so big, but to them, we're just dots in the night sky."

Who knew his little Slayer was a philosopher? "I would imagine that although we're separated by distance and our problems are not the same, all species feel the basics of emotion. Fear, hope, anger, love." He paused on that last one, checking himself.

While he found the Slayer immensely attractive, love was a word that he had never used with a woman and felt he never would. As a ruler, he was practical. When he bonded with Lila, it would be for duty, heirs and the betterment of his kingdom. He could think of nothing more noble.

Ridding his head of his momentary insanity, he chalked up his mention of love to being lost in the moment with a beautiful woman under the moonlight.

"You're probably right," she said, dragging him from his thoughts. "I hope whoever's suffering out there tonight will find some peace."

He would miss her terribly when she returned home tomorrow night. He wouldn't even try to lie to himself on that one. "I am always here if you need me, Miranda. I'm only a phone call away."

"I know," she said, reaching over to place her hand over his. It was rare that she voluntarily touched him, and it set his body on fire. Slowly, he turned to face her. Swept up in the moment, and their imminent goodbye, he wanted so badly to drag her to him and imprint himself onto her. Into her.

She locked onto him with those eyes. Lowering them to his chest, she studied the dark hair there. He was aching for her but was determined to let her make a move. He had always been the one to initiate their heated kisses, and he wanted to know if she burned for him as he did for her.

Lifting one hand and then the other, she placed her palms on his pecs. Moving slowly, gently, she ran them over his copper nipples, causing the muscles underneath to tremble, and then, over his eight-pack. She stopped at the 'V' of black hair that ran from his navel into his pants.

"You're so massive," she said, moving her hands back up his chest. "I feel so small next to you."

He remained silent, determined to let her have control. Finally, she raised her eyes to his. "The world has gone mad," she said, as his heart beat furiously under her palm. "Why shouldn't we have a piece of the madness?"

"What are you asking me, Miranda?" He reveled in her shiver at his voice.

She lowered her gaze to his chest again, contemplating.

"I won't allow there to be any doubt as to who decides what comes next." Lifting her chin with his fingers, he looked into her soul. "What do you want?"

Fear mingled with desire in her voluminous eyes. He saw the moment when the desire won out.

Reaching up, she pulled his face down to hers and lifted to her toes, joining their lips together.

Placing his arms around her, he lifted her so that she straddled his waist, her ankles crossed at his back. Heading inside, he lowered her to the bed and devoured her mouth. Little pants of her wanton desire filled him, and he struggled to retain control. Reaching down, he tunneled his hand under her shirt, touching the soft skin beneath. Her tiny groan urged him on, and he cupped her small breast over the satin of her bra, his hand engulfing it.

Frustrated, he wanted to lose the barriers. Lifting up his head, he raised off her, placed two hands at the bottom of her shirt and ripped it in two. Gathering the fabric, he threw it to the floor.

"You couldn't just pull it off?"

"Shut up," he said, reclaiming her mouth again. She kissed him back passionately, and he moaned into her. Reaching behind her, he undid her bra with a snap. Pulling it off, he looked at the tiny mounds of her breasts.

"My god, Miranda," he breathed, supporting himself on one side while he caressed her small breast with his hand. Running the pad of his thumb over her nipple, lust constricted his throat when it hardened into a tiny point at his touch. "So fucking beautiful." Lowering his head, he took her into his mouth.

Her hips shot off the bed, and he thrust his hand into her hair, grabbing it to hold her in place. He wasn't a gentle lover, but she seemed to like it when he took control, so score one for them. She gave a little mewl from above him, and he kissed a path to her other nipple. She squirmed when he took it into his mouth.

"Sathan," she moaned.

"I love it when you say my name," he murmured against her breast.

He lathered her sensitive nipple with his tongue, reveling in how taut her body was beneath him. Disentangling his hand from her hair, he slid it down her body as he sucked her. Moving his palm over her mound, he could feel her wetness through her soft yoga pants.

Desire almost choked him as he cupped her. "You're so fucking wet," he said against her skin.

"I always am around you. It's never been that way for me before. I don't understand it."

Growling, he looked into her eyes. "Don't tell me that. Now, I'm going to imagine you drenched every time I see you."

Biting her lower lip, she pushed her mound into his palm, testing his restraint. Little minx. She knew exactly what she was doing to him.

Grabbing the band of her pants, he stood and pulled them off. She was naked underneath, and he murmured in approval. Opening her legs, he kneeled and placed them over his shoulders. Pulling her to the edge of the bed, he examined her.

"So pretty," he said, running his fingers over her hairless mound.

"I wax," she said from above him, her voice breathless.

"It's so fucking sexy."

Rubbing his finger around her wet opening, he reveled at seeing her most private place. "My god, you're dripping." Gently, he nudged his finger inside her.

She moaned and opened her legs wider on his shoulders. "More, please, Sathan. I need..."

Her voice drifted off, and he added another finger. She purred in approval. He wanted so badly to taste her but knew that if he waited much longer, he'd explode.

Settling for a quick sip, he removed his fingers and kissed her deepest place. Touching the tip of his tongue to her tiny bud, she all but exploded off the bed. Promising himself that he would finish her down there later, he stood and pulled off his pants.

She looked at him, her eyes glassy as she lay across the bed. Since they were different species, there was no chance of pregnancy or disease, so he didn't bother reaching for a condom in his nightstand drawer. Lowering himself onto her, she hooked a leg behind his thigh.

He clenched his teeth when she grabbed his full length, squeezing, testing. A question was in her eyes.

"I'll fit," he said, pulling her hand away; aligning his body to hers.

"Are you sure?"

"I'm sure. Trust me. I promise I won't hurt you."

Lifting her hand, she cupped his cheek. "I know," she said softly.

That one trusting statement meant more to him than any words of desire she could've spoken. Touching his tip to her opening, he began to push inside her.

He went slowly, grinding his teeth as his eyes closed, needing to keep his promise to her as she adjusted to him. Sweat poured from his body, wetting her skin, as he nudged into her.

Opening his eyes, he looked down into hers. He felt his heart slam into overdrive. Never had he shared such a connection to a woman when making love. It was overwhelming, and for a moment, he felt a flash of terror.

And then, it was gone, as she looked into him and whispered, "Harder."

By the goddess, this woman would be the death of him. Gripping the tops of her shoulders, he plunged into her wetness. Tiny, curved hips rose to meet his, and he took a moment to bask at how deep he was inside her. The flesh of her walls squeezed him tight, and he thought he might die from the pleasure.

He began moving in and out of her, watching her face as he impaled her, slowly losing the ability to think. Silky hair feathered on the comforter as she rocked her head from side to side. Quickening the pace, his cock pulsed inside her wetness as he watched her breasts bounce up and down while he plundered her.

"Come for me," he growled, pulling gently at her hair again. Tilting her head back, she moaned and moved underneath him.

He pumped harder into her, needing to give her as much of the intense pleasure as she was giving him. "Come," he commanded again.

Suddenly, her body shot off the bed, and she screamed out, shaking in violent spasms. The muscles of her tight channel clenched his engorged shaft, and he knew he was lost. Shouting a curse, he slammed into her until he felt his body might shatter. Emptying himself into her, he cradled her head and felt his body jerk with pleasure.

What felt like an eternity later, he felt someone tapping on his arm. Lifting his head, he looked down at his Slayer; her lips swollen, her cheeks reddened. An unnamed emotion swamped him as he felt himself drowning in the pools of her eyes.

"You're crushing me there, big fella," she said, smiling up at him.

He smiled back, stroking her hair. "You have rendered me motionless. I guess we'll just have to stay here all day."

She moved her hips around him, causing his body to jerk again involuntarily. "Hey, no fair," he said, rubbing his hips against hers in return.

"As much as I'd love to lie here all day, you outweigh me by about two hundred pounds. So, unless you're after 'death by crushing,' I think you have to let me up."

"Minx." He grinned as he kissed her. Lifting his head, he said, "Wait here."

"Not going anywhere, Vampyre. At least, not till tomorrow."

* * * *

Miranda tried to still her beating heart as she listened to Sathan rummage around in the bathroom. She was sure that she had made the absolute biggest mistake of her life. Knowing she had an eternity to beat herself up, she decided to enjoy the moment.

Sathan returned with a warm cloth. Spreading her legs, he gently wiped the evidence of their loving from her. The kind gesture brought tears to her eyes.

Telling herself not to be a romantic dope, she watched his broad back as he walked to the bathroom again. Say what you want about Vampyres, but Sathan was one hell of a good-looking man.

Lifting her exhausted body up, she pulled back the covers and crawled underneath. She hadn't slept well since...well, she couldn't remember when she'd last had a good night or day of sleep. Yawning, she felt herself growing drowsy.

She heard him switch off the lamp on the bedside table, and then, he crawled in behind her, pulling her to his chest, spooning her. She wasn't much of a cuddler, but she was too tired to argue.

"Sorry, I'm so sleepy all of a sudden." Yawning, she wiggled her butt into him.

"Don't do that, or you'll never get any sleep," he said.

She chuckled and sank into the pillow. "Round two soon...just need to sleep for one minute...then we'll..."

She never finished her sentence.

* * * *

Miranda jolted, awakening to unfamiliar circumstances. Her eyes darted around the room, and she tried to remember where she was. Last night. Balcony. Sathan. Shit. She had slept with the Vampyre. Lifting her hand, she placed it on her forehead and cursed.

"Glad to know how you really feel," came his deep voice beside her.

Turning her head, she saw him lying on his side, half his face resting on the pillow. "Sorry," she mumbled. "I'm a deep sleeper. I usually wake up not knowing where I am."

"I know," he said. She wanted to slap the arrogant grin off his face. "You snore."

Gasping, her mouth fell open. "I do not!"

"You do," he said with a chuckle. "It's cute."

"Liar. I'll never believe you." She would die before she conceded to him.

Lifting his hand, he rubbed her cheek. It was all too touchy-feely for her. She was not a morning person and was usually cranky for at least an hour after she woke up.

"I need to go shower," she said, attempting to push the covers off and leave the bed.

"Whoa," he said, gently placing his arm across her chest. "Don't go yet. It's midday. We have several hours before you need to meet the troops." He looked adorable, his thick hair mussed, as his eyes pleaded with her. Bastard.

"I need to go over my plan—"

"You need to run, is more like it." Gritting her teeth, she told herself to stay calm.

"I'm not running from anything. I just like to be prepared."

Shifting, he slid his body on top of hers, trapping her.

"No fair. You're bigger than me."

His lips curved into a sexy grin. "I know. Some parts more than others."

She rolled her eyes. "Lame."

"Come on," he said, caressing her cheek. "Let me be with you one more time. You have eternity to run away from me."

She studied him. His handsome face, angular features, thick black hair. God, he was gorgeous. "It was a mistake," she said, her voice gravelly.

"I know," he said, gently kissing her with his thick lips. "Let's make another one. Then, we can ask for forgiveness for both together."

"I feel bad for Lila—"

"I told you, we have an arrangement. It's not like that between us. I respect her immensely and would never hurt her."

Miranda chewed on her lip and contemplated him. "How are we ever going to act normal with each other again? This was so stupid."

"We're both adults, Miranda. Who happen to be extremely attracted to each other. This is what happens when that occurs."

"And then, we get emotionally involved, and one of us kills the other with the Blade of Pestilence."

"Wow. You went really dark there." He continued to rub her cheek, the sensation soothing her. "Let's just agree that we won't let our emotions get involved and we'll be adults about this. I can do it if you can."

She remained silent.

"When you chew on your lip like that, it makes me so hard," he said, rubbing his erection into her thigh.

She wanted him again. So badly. But something was holding her back.

"I'm not sure I can remain unemotional," she said finally. "I'm not saying I'm all 'in love' with you or anything," she said, making quotation marks with two of her fingers. "I just think this might get messy."

"You've already tried to murder me once, and I've proven that I can best you, so we'll be fine."

She scoffed. "I wasn't even trying, blood-sucker. Believe me, if I make a real attempt, you're a goner."

"Well, then, I'll need to accomplish all my goals before you do away with me. The most recent being that I promised myself I would make you come with my mouth, and I am a man who keeps his promises." He waggled his eyebrows at her and lowered his head under the covers.

Miranda allowed herself to relax as he kissed his way down her body. She figured she didn't want to be responsible for him not keeping his promises either...

* * * *

Hours later, Sathan stroked her hair as she lay sprawled out on his chest. They had made love twice more, and he felt a twinge of guilt that she would have to lead the troops on so little sleep.

But, by the goddess, it had been worth it. His little Slayer was everything he had imagined she would be in bed and more. He felt immensely grateful that she had come to him and chosen to spend her last night in his bed.

"I have to go shower," she said, picking at the tiny hairs on his chest. "I think I need to borrow one of your shirts since you ripped the one I came in."

Kissing the top of her head, he rolled out of bed and threw on his sweatpants. Grabbing a t-shirt from his drawer, he walked back toward the bed. When she stood, he placed the shirt over her head. She punched her arms through each armhole and then lifted them, assessing the size of the garment. She looked so damn cute, standing there dwarfed in his black shirt.

"Thanks. I guess," she said dryly.

He chuckled as she grabbed her yoga pants and slipped them on.

"Um, okay, so...yeah. See ya at the cabins."

Grabbing her wrist, he pulled her to him and placed a kiss on her lips.

"Thank you, Miranda. For being with me last night. I am honored to have lain with you."

Her face scrunched up, and then she laughed. "Wow. Super formal. I'm not sure what to do with that."

He shook his head. She was so damn impertinent. "You say, 'Thank you, Sathan, for a wonderful evening,' and then kiss me goodbye."

"Yeah, the fourth century called and wants its traditions back. No thanks." Pulling her hand from his, she walked to the door.

A huge sense of disappointment washed over him until she turned, standing in the open doorway. Smiling, she blew him a kiss.

Laughing, he rubbed his hand over his chest, right where his heart sat, beating a little too quickly as it always did in her presence.

He prepared for the evening and headed downstairs to complete some administrative work. When it was time to meet the troops, he walked down to the barracks. He could tell himself that he wasn't searching for her, anticipating the moment when she would appear, but he would be lying.

She approached from the house in combat boots, camouflage pants and a tank top. Her hair was pulled back into a ponytail. His tiny warrior was ready to claim her destiny.

She climbed in the Hummer with him, and they drove to the cabins. After collecting all the soldiers in the various army vehicles, they drove to the wall. Once there, Sathan opened the portal, and the soldiers began to drive the trucks through.

"We're giving you five armored vehicles. If you need more, just call," Latimus said to Miranda.

"Thank you," she said. "I've learned so much from you. I'll call if I need anything."

Then, she seemed to float toward him in the moonlight. "I guess this is goodbye for now," she said, her face glowing as she looked up at him. "I have the book you gave me in my backpack." She reached behind to pat it with her hand. "Thank you so much. It's a beautiful gift."

"You're welcome," he said softly.

"I also have the Blade. Made sure you didn't pull one over on me this time."

He felt his lips curve at that one.

"No regrets?"

"No regrets," he said, longing to pull her to him for one last kiss. Knowing that was impossible, he settled for smiling into the eyes he would forever see in his dreams. "I'm only a phone call away."

"I know," she said, nodding. "Talk soon."

And then, she was gone. She hopped into the front seat of one of the armored vehicles, and the engines roared as they rolled past the wall, along the river and out of sight.

"Let's go," Latimus said, patting him on the back with his beefy hand. "It's not safe out here."

Nodding, he followed his brother inside, unable to shake the feeling that his Slayer had taken a piece of him with her.

Chapter 26

Miranda approached Uteria with mixed emotions swirling in her busy mind. On the one hand, she was ready to claim her throne. She felt stronger and more confident than ever. Her people would know peace if she had to fight to her dying breath.

On the other, becoming queen without her father present would be hard. Grief for him sat like a rock in her gut, and she focused on feeling it without letting it weigh her down. She had always imagined her father at her coronation, smiling as she was crowned queen. Knowing that would never happen made her heart squeeze in pain.

She also felt apprehension about how her father's supporters would receive her. Being that they had attacked her only a few nights ago, she must approach them with caution. They must know by now that her father had passed. How would they take the news?

The armored vehicles rolled into the compound. People lined the streets to watch the commotion. As her vehicle came to as stop in front of the main castle, she exited and looked up at the gray-stone mansion. So cold. Emotionless. Had it always been this way?

Entering through the large wooden doors, she headed through the foyer and into her father's office. Stopping short, she saw Kalil sitting at his desk.

"You're home!" he said, standing and rushing to hug her. "Thank god. We were so worried."

"I bet you were," she said, looking to see if any of her father's other supporters were around. "You seem quite comfortable keeping my father's seat warm in his absence."

"The compound doesn't shut down in moments of crisis, unfortunately," he said.

Disentangling herself from him, she moved to stand by the door. She wanted to have any points of attack covered. "I will be taking over all administrative duties."

"But your father—"

"He's dead," she said, her voice firm and unwavering.

"What?" he said, falling back. "How? I thought he was captured alive—"

"It doesn't matter. Don't tell me you didn't support his raid on the Vampyre compound as they sheltered me there. I know you always supported him over me."

"He is my king," Kalil said.

"Not anymore. I am your ruler now. Follow any other, and you will be executed for treason."

Disconcertion laced his expression, and his tone turned sullen. "You are not yourself, Miranda."

She lifted her chin, defiant. "I am finally who I was meant to be. Get on board, or be left behind, Kalil."

"Please" he said, coming toward her and grabbing her arm, "let me take you to see Sadie—"

"Let go of me," she ordered, her teeth clenched.

"Princess, do you need help?" One of the hulking Vampyre soldiers eyed her from the doorway.

"No, thank you, Takel. Please, stay close just in case."

Kalil looked at her in shock. "You brought Vampyres onto our compound? Vampyres? My god, Miranda, what has come over you?"

"I have been denied my true calling for a thousand years. The time of me cowering to my father, or any other man, is over. The Vampyres are here to protect me and my supporters. If you support me, then you have nothing to fear."

"You are mad," he said, his voice hoarse with disbelief. "I won't stand here and watch you turn into this person." Shaking his head, he left the room.

"Well, screw him," Miranda muttered to herself. He had always bored her to tears anyway. She walked over to her father's desk, looking at the paperwork strewn across it. She figured that tomorrow, she would have to get to work on that too. Yuck.

Sitting in his chair, she opened his drawers, absently snooping. She noticed a small hole in one drawer on the bottom right. Sticking her finger in it, she pulled the wood to find that it was a false bottom. Underneath, hidden in the dark back corner, were a bundle of letters. Pulling them out, she slid one out and read:

His Royal Highness, King Marsias of Uteria
The ninth day of the tenth month of the year five hundred and thirty-three
Dear Marsias,
I write to you again hoping that your lack of response means you have not received my other letters. Our rations are low, and we will need more blood within a fortnight. We have no wish to raid your compound or abduct your people. The time for bloodshed is over. Please, consider banking barrels and depositing them at the wall so that we may begin to negotiate peace. Our peoples' futures depend on it.
Sincerely,
Sathan, King of Astaria

Suddenly, Miranda began to laugh. Large, bellowing gasps as her eyes filled with tears of mirth. Hiccupping, she wiped the wetness from her eyes, overcome with crazed rage. How could her father have kept this from her?

Seething with fury, she untied the bundle and began reading all the letters. Sathan had written to Marsias for over a decade, pleading with him to negotiate peace. As she read each of the letters, holding them with her shaking hands, she felt intense sadness. Had her father ever loved her? Had he even respected her at all?

Surely not, if he could keep something like this from her. His hatred had run so deep.

Closing her eyes, she inhaled a large breath. Although she hated Etherya, she said a prayer to her, thanking her for giving her the strength to finally defy her father. How many more men would've died if she hadn't found the courage?

Images of the faces of so many fallen soldiers ran through her mind. Men she had fought with, side-by-side. Wives whom she had comforted after their husbands were taken. Children who would grow up without a father. So much of it could've been avoided.

Standing, she grabbed the letters and stormed out of the study. Takel's worried gaze met hers.

"Are you okay?" he asked.

"Fine," she said. "Get me some matches and meet me behind the castle. Larkin will know where to find them."

Stomping out of the large mahogany front doors of the castle, she plodded to the back meadow. With a curse, she threw the letters on the ground. Takel appeared with matches, Larkin standing behind him.

"This ends now," she said, crouching and lighting the letters on fire in several different places. "I'm so tired of the constant war and death. My father did a great disservice to our people. *All* of our people," she said, looking at Takel, needing him to understand that Marsias had wronged the Vampyres as well.

The three of them stood in silence, watching the letters burn. Miranda clenched her teeth as they turned to ash. Once they were no more, she turned to look at her two strong soldiers.

"We have to unite the species. I need your help. You both are immensely important to this cause. I won't let our people live with hate anymore. I'll pull it out of them with everything I have. Do you understand?"

"Yes, princess," they said in unison.

"Good. Thank you for your support. It means more to me than you know." Inhaling a deep breath, she straightened her shoulders. "Now, I need to prepare for tomorrow. I'll see you both then."

Resolute, she headed inside, ready to unite her people with the Vampyres.

* * * *

The next morning, at nine o'clock sharp, she took her place at the podium in the main square of the compound. The sun was bright in the sky, illuminating a beautiful day. Two Slayer soldiers flanked her, one on each side. She figured that Slayer soldiers would help to soften her message more than Vampyre ones.

Miranda had always thought Uteria such a beautiful place. It was a compound of about twenty thousand people, comprised of aristocrats, soldiers and middle-class subjects. The smaller Slayer compound of Restia was comprised mostly of laborers and laymen. Restia only housed about eight thousand Slayers, and it had a certain small-town charm.

She'd always felt Uteria buzzed with a quaint but elegant energy. The large wall that surrounded it provided privacy and safety, as no one lived outside the wall. With their wars, that would be too dangerous. It was mostly country living here. Very few people had cars, choosing to walk the paved sidewalks and trails that Marsias and Miranda had laid over the centuries. She'd always loved the projects that consumed her days: building parks, planting trees and making their home more beautiful for her people.

The aristocrats mostly lived near the main castle, their large houses built to show off their wealth. The middle-class subjects lived closer to the wall, not needing fancy things or tons of space. They were a simple people who enjoyed the mostly sunny days that pervaded their world. Immortals lived in a primarily temperate climate, so the weather was usually mild, and the rain was seldom. When it did rain, farmers near the walls of both compounds would cultivate their crops, harvesting them so that their people could eat.

The main square of Uteria sat a few blocks from the castle. It was comprised of tents from various street vendors and small stores that thrived on local business. Miranda looked at the crowd from her elevated position, excited that so many had gathered to hear her speak.

Life seemed to flow all around. Merchants selling fruits and trinkets. Children chasing one another as their parents observed. Dogs barking at each other as their owners struggled to pull them apart by their leashes.

She tapped on the microphone, causing a loud screech to sound. The congregation quieted, ready to heed her address. Standing tall, she began.

"My people, thank you for taking time from your busy day to meet with me. I have several announcements, and when I am finished, I will be happy to speak to each one of you individually, even if it takes the rest of the day or several days. As your princess, I am always here for you."

A murmur ran through the crowd.

"You may have heard many things lately about the state of our kingdom, and I want to set the record straight with you, from my lips to your ears." Scanning the crowd, she continued.

"I know this will come as a very sad shock to most of you, but my father Marsias has passed from this world and is now on his way to spend eternity in the Passage." Gasps echoed from the people.

"I loved my father deeply and am truly saddened by his passing. My only solace is that he will soon be reunited with my mother, the daughter of Valktor and his one true love."

She paused a moment, letting the news sink in.

"It is also true that in my father's final days, he and I came to disagree on many things. He believed that we should continue to fight the Vampyres until the last Slayer takes his last breath. Now that the Deamon army grows stronger, that fate is closer than we know.

"I disagreed with his position. I felt that it was worth at least trying to negotiate with the Vampyres. After all, they had shown a bit of compassion by only abducting men, and not women or children, during their raids."

"Fucking Vampyres! Blood-suckers! I hope they burn in hell!" one man's loud voice screamed from the crowd.

"I understand your hate," Miranda said, reclaiming control of the crowd, her voice loud and firm. "Believe me, it is hard to negotiate with a species who has raided us for centuries.

"But I ask you, what other choice do we have?" Lifting her arms, she held her hands, palms up, to the crowd. "Do you all wish to die? Knowing that the Vampyres will eventually come for our women and children, once all the soldiers are gone? Is that to be the fate of our people?"

"No! We support you, Miranda," a loud female voice called.

Taking strength from the small show of support, she straightened her spine. "I argue that the fate of our people is more magnificent, more hopeful, than we ever could've imagined. Although the Vampyres are inferior, we must find a solution and live with them in peace." She glanced at her Vampyre soldiers below her, begging their forgiveness for her 'inferior' comment. They nodded in acknowledgement, and she breathed an inner sigh of relief. Her people would need time, and she had to placate them a bit to move them along.

"We can become the great people we once were. I'm tired of living in fear. I no longer want to lie in bed, anticipating if this will be the night our soldiers are taken. I want to have the strength to find a solution. Will you help me find a solution?" she said, her voice loud through the microphone.

Cheers rang out through the crowd, and she felt a swell of support.

"There are those who support my father's plan of endless war. Although I respect them for doing what they think is noble, they are wrong. I ask you to help me convince them that this new path is right. It won't be easy, but it will be worth it. All I want is a peaceful existence for our people, free from war and death."

The people roared below her, thrilling her with their energy.

"In three months' time, I will fulfill the prophecy as Valktor's one true descendant and kill Crimeous." Opening the case sitting on the table beside her, she pulled out the Blade of Pestilence, lifting it high, so everyone in the crowd could see. Whispers and gasps traveled across the town square.

"The Vampyre king was valiant as we traveled to free the Blade. He has made his position clear. He wishes only for his people to live in peace. Our goals are aligned."

Lowering the Blade, she held it at her side as she spoke. "Once Crimeous has fallen, there is nothing to stop us from achieving our true greatness. Peace and prosperity will reign!"

She reveled in the cheers of her people, wanting so much for them to be free and happy.

"Thank you for your support, my people. I will wait for the coronation until I have rid the Earth of Crimeous. It will be a magnificent day, with a long and glorious festival. It has been too long since our people celebrated, and I will make sure we put an end to that. Until then, I ask for volunteers willing to bank their blood so we can begin negotiating peace with the Vampyres. Sadie will be helping me with this, and if you wish to volunteer, please sign up with her today."

With her hand, she gestured to Sadie, standing below the podium to the right, a lab coat covering her t-shirt and jeans, a baseball cap on her head. Shyly, she waved to the crowd, and Miranda smiled at her. "Thank you, Sadie. We are grateful you're here." The doctor saluted Miranda with her unburnt hand.

"And now, I will take your questions one-on-one. First, I would like to speak to those who have lost family members in the Vampyre raids. Then, I will speak to anyone else who wishes. Please, be patient, as I want to speak to all of you."

The next several hours were filled with conversations with her people. First, she asked everyone who had lost soldiers to the Vampyres to sit with her in the grassy park, located one block from the town's main square.

Nearly five hundred Slayers gathered around her as she sat underneath one of the tall redwood trees that lined the park. With patience and understanding, she let them say their piece. Many of them were angry, unable to understand how she could align with the great enemy who had murdered their loved ones.

After each one spoke she would hug and console them. Wading through the crowd, she encouraged them all to voice their concerns. Afterward, she stood under the redwood, holding the microphone in her hand. Her voice bellowed from the speaker that Larkin had set up at the base of the tree.

She told them of Nolan and his efforts to save the abducted soldiers. Wanting them to comprehend Sathan's efforts at peace, she explained to them about the letters he sent and berated her father's ridiculous suicide decree. Eventually, some of them softened, if only a little, and a tiny spark of hope flitted in her chest.

Several hours later, she spoke to the others who had lined up for her. Many of them had apprehensions about the future but were steadfast in their support of her. She stayed at the town square until long after the moon had risen in the sky, wanting to make sure none of her people felt left behind.

Finally, the last of her people dissipated. Alone, she walked the few blocks back to the castle and headed to her bedchamber.

Entering her room, she felt restless. She changed into her nightshirt and lay on the bed. Lifting up her phone, she texted the one person she promised herself she wouldn't:

Miranda: Went well today. You should've seen it. We're on our way. Will keep u updated.

She watched the screen for a while, hoping that the text bubble would show up to indicate that he was typing, and then she threw the phone on the bed with a groan. For god's sake, she was acting like a lovesick teenager. Disgusted with herself, she went into the bathroom to brush her teeth.

A few minutes later, she climbed into bed, wincing as she felt a pain down below. Well, wasn't that just dandy. Like she needed another reminder that she had let the Vampyre bone her brains out.

She had only been with a handful of men in the past, more consumed with her desire to train and defend her people than any desire she'd felt for a man. And then, there was tradition. Young Slayer women were taught to save their virginity for marriage. She'd always thought that incredibly sexist, as Slayer men were expected to sow their oats before getting married. Not giving a fig for any rules that some old curmudgeon decreed centuries before the Awakening, she'd decided early on that if she felt comfortable with a man and cared for him, she would sleep with him.

There had been Sam, the sweet boy she'd dated in her first century. He had been so timid, quite innocent in his avowals of love for her. Then, there was Madu, and Ergon after him. They were both badasses who liked heavy metal too. She admitted to herself that she'd only dated them because it infuriated her father.

After that, there had been a long break with no dating and much training. Around the eighth century, she had dated a nice man named Goran. He had been a bit boring for her taste, but she had been lonely, and he filled the gap. Sadly, he had eventually enrolled in the army and had been abducted by the Vampyres in one of their raids. Had Nolan treated him, trying to extend his life? Had he met Sathan in the dungeon? What if she had charted this course earlier? Could she have saved him?

Questions swirled in her mind, driving her mad. Thankfully, her phone lit up, saving her from drowning in her self-doubt.

Sathan: I saw. Heden is a whiz at these things. Don't ask me how, but he transmitted your whole speech to the tech room. You were amazing. Proud of you.

Her heart fluttered, and she scowled at her phone, annoyed.

Miranda: Thanks blood-sucker. Will keep you updated.

She wanted to type, "Miss you," and then promptly decided she should be checked into Sadie's infirmary to be diagnosed with mental illness. Forcing herself to put the phone down, she turned off the light and tried to sleep.

Chapter 27

Evie sat on the balcony of her tenth-floor condo, absently twirling a strand of her scarlet tresses around her thin finger. Narrowing her eyes, she thought of the chestnut-haired Slayer. It had been centuries since she'd seen a Slayer, and she wondered what the annoyingly curious man wanted with her.

Sighing loudly, she clenched her teeth, attempting to tamp down the rage that loomed inside her. It was ever-present, and she found herself drowning in it more times that she wanted to admit.

The war within her was constant. She wanted so badly to be good but honestly felt that it just wasn't in her. It should've been. She'd tried so hard. Smirking, she shook her head. Well, not in the beginning, she admitted. When she was young, she had been a monster.

Death and destruction had been her mantra during the first centuries of her life, and she'd reveled in them. Nothing made one feel more powerful than crushing another's life in your hands. But eventually, that began to feel old and staid, and she'd tried to move on.

As the practice of human psychology grew, she'd seen the best therapists and paid gobs of money, exhausting her resources. Unfortunately, they couldn't help her, for they truly didn't know what she was. Humans would never be able to understand the evil that was her father. She barely understood it herself.

Standing, she looked down at the humans as they blazed through the streets. Tiny ants, idiots who thought their lives meant something. They should know better. Life was a futile folly in which one had to do everything they could to survive. It was a terrible dilemma. She'd thought about killing herself so many times but had never had the guts to do it. Instead, she let herself suffer, knowing it was what she deserved.

And now, the Slayer with the confident gaze and firm chin had shown up looking for her. It pissed her off immensely. Why couldn't he leave her the hell alone? If he didn't, she was going to lose her temper. And, wow, that wouldn't be pretty. He'd most likely pay for it with his life. Deciding he was too handsome to kill, she hoped he gave up his quest and remained in the land of immortals. His future depended on it. Otherwise, he would be sorry. Very sorry indeed.

Standing, she entered her condo through the glass doors, closing them behind her with her mind. Choosing one of her sexiest dresses and styling her hair and makeup, she headed out into the night. Nervous energy coursed through her. She hadn't had a truly great lay since Francesco, all those decades ago. Oh, how she had cared for him, a rarity for her. Dematerializing, she reappeared inside his living room, within the small house that stood on the Italian hill.

He was old now, and gasped from his cushioned chair.

"Evie," he said, slowly standing on his crooked bones. "Bella."

"Hello, Francesco. How nice to see you."

He sighed and shook his head. "I should not have told him where to find you. I'm sorry, my dear."

"No, you shouldn't have. His presence has dredged up things in me that I longed to push away. You've made me very angry."

Fear entered his blue eyes. "So, you have come to kill me."

She nodded. "I have."

"I always knew you would. Somewhere deep inside."

Approaching him, she caressed his wrinkled cheek. "I will show you mercy, so that you don't suffer."

His thick fingers touched her hair. "You have goodness in you, bella. Don't let the darkness win."

Tears prickled her eyes, causing the rage inside her to enflame more. She hated feeling emotion of any kind.

"I wish that were true." Inching toward him, she placed a soft kiss on his red lips. Grasping his head with both hands, she snapped his neck, quick as lightning.

As he crumpled to the ground, she felt a small bit of something in her gut. Perhaps pain, perhaps regret, perhaps the thrill she always felt when killing. It had been a while since she'd done that as well.

Lifting her thin fingers to her lips, she blew him a soft kiss. Dematerializing back to Paris, she entered a fancy restaurant and sat at the bar. The male bartender smiled at her with undisclosed lust. Smiling back, she decided she would let him have her tonight. She would lay with him and imagine he was Francesco, all those years ago when he'd been in his prime.

Touching her lips to the smooth wine glass, she drank and allowed the man to flirt with her for the next few hours, until he took her home and fucked her emotionless body.

* * * *

The next week was a whirlwind as Miranda instituted her new policies. More Slayers than she could've imagined volunteered to bank blood, and she felt extremely grateful. She began completing the paperwork her father always had, finding she had a knack for approvals and budgets and licenses, but she still didn't like them all the same.

She preferred being with her people. Hearing their fears and assuring them that peace was coming.

Unfortunately, her respite was short-lived.

On the first day of her second week home, her father's supporters marched upon the castle. They came wielding weapons and threatened to rip her from the building. Her soldiers gathered them up and placed them in the cells that were used to hold the occasional Deamon or Vampyre prisoners of war.

Once they had been sequestered for a day, she went down to address them. Standing in front of their cells, she had urged them to fight for peace. To see that aligning with the Vampyres was the only way to prosperity.

The men, forty-two of them in all, spat at her from their cells and groaned of their hatred for her and the Vampyres. Saddened, she had to acknowledge to herself that they were truly lost. Even Kalil had joined them, and she thanked the heavens that she had plotted a different course that didn't include marrying him. She wished she knew how to handle the dissenters. To make them see her vision.

At night, she would have dinner with Sadie or Aron. Sometimes, she invited other Slayers to eat at the castle's large dining room table so that she could listen to their worries and fears. As she sat with them, trying to put on a brave face, she couldn't help but feel that something was missing.

Only in the dead of night, when she was alone under her covers, would she think of him. His corded muscles, thick neck, heated gaze. In her dreams, he came to her, soothing away her fears and loneliness.

And in the morning, she would rise, realizing that she was stuck in a fantasy that had no future. She berated herself constantly, angry that she had latched onto something that wasn't real.

On the second night of her third week home, the Deamons attacked.

She would never forgive herself for being unprepared.

Their screams rang out as the sun sat low in the sky, about to be pulled into the horizon by the clouds.

Hundreds of them scaled the compound wall, unprotected by Etherya as the wall at Astaria was. They wielded weapons of all sorts but none deadlier than the semi-automatic weapons that killed multiple Slayers with one swipe.

Her soldiers fought valiantly, and she alongside them. The twenty Vampyre soldiers were extremely helpful, and finally, under the darkness of the night sky, Larkin shot the last Deamon dead.

The battle lasted for hours. The Deamons had been murderous. They had entered some of the homes near the wall and raped the women inside before killing them and their families.

Miranda toured the compound, tallying the dead. One hundred and forty-one. Seventy-one soldiers, thirty-four men, twenty-one women, fifteen children. The bastards had slaughtered children.

As she and Larkin toured the cottages by the wall, documenting the damage, she felt sick. Thankfully, he gave her privacy as she leaned her palm against the stones and retched.

Hours later, the cleanup had begun. Miranda walked toward the entrance of the castle, Larkin beside her.

"Miranda," a deep voice called.

Turning, she cried out, not even caring how desperate she sounded.

"Sathan!" she said, jumping into his arms. It felt so good to be held by him. Someone so strong who cared about her.

"I'll leave you two to debrief," Larkin said.

"Thank you," she said to him, disentangling herself from Sathan and feeling a bit embarrassed.

"You're welcome, Miranda. Today was a setback, but don't let it deter you. We support you."

Smiling, she grabbed Larkin's hand and squeezed, thanking him for his unwavering support.

He left them, and she turned to Sathan. "What are you doing here? How did you get in?"

"I can breach your walls, Miranda. We've been doing it for centuries."

"Right," she said, blowing out a breath with her bottom lip so that it fanned her hair. "Probably best not to remind me right now that you abducted and killed our people for centuries. It's been a long day."

"Come," he said, extending his hand to her. "Let's go inside." She grabbed on for dear life and led him to her bedchamber.

Once inside, Miranda grew nervous. It seemed so long since she had seen him, and she didn't trust her emotions after the brutal attack she'd suffered that day. Rubbing her hands on her upper arms, she shrugged. "I really messed up."

"How so?" he asked.

"I let those bastards breach my compound. Fuck," she said, angry at the world. "They killed our people and raped our women. One of the soldiers told me they raped a twelve-year-old girl. Who does that?" Unable to control her anger, she shoved everything on her dresser to the floor with one furious swipe of her arms.

Hearing the metal objects clank on the floor made her feel better somehow. Sathan gave her an unreadable look. Reaching down, he began to pick up her metal trinkets and place them back on the dresser.

"Forget it," she said, not even trying to control her irritation. "Did you come to help? You're a little too late."

Pulling her toward the bed, he urged her down and sat beside her. "I came for you. We heard of the attack too late. Latimus and I led a battalion of two hundred here, but by then, all the Deamons were dead. Why didn't you call me?" Pain swam in his eyes.

"I don't know," she said, shaking her head. "It just all happened so fast, and then, I was fighting, and Larkin threw a rifle in my hands...I couldn't think. I just fought."

Sathan inhaled a deep breath, holding her hand in his lap. His thumb rubbed gently back and forth over her skin, comforting her.

"I won't leave you vulnerable again. We need to station troops here. I know you want to give your people time to accept us, but after today's events, that can't happen. We have to start acclimating our people to yours."

She regarded him as she pondered. "I agree," she said finally.

"No argument?" His dark eyebrows lifted in surprise.

"None," she said, shaking her head. "I want your army's protection."

"Good." He clenched her hand. "Let's talk details. Where will the soldiers stay?"

They discussed logistics for the next thirty minutes, deciding that Sathan would station two hundred troops at the compound. They would bunk in the abandoned hospital that sat three hundred yards from the main house. It had been neglected after the Awakening, when Marsias had implemented his suicide decree, and the people had realized that abducted soldiers would never return to be nursed back to health. Miranda would assign a staff of laborers to the building to quickly restore the running water and utilities and to complete repairs.

Once everything had been decided, Miranda stood. "Sorry, but I need to brush my teeth and take a quick shower to wash all the blood off. I blew chunks by the wall, and I feel disgusting. I have a balcony, although it's not as nice as yours. You can wait there if you like." She gestured to the double glass doors beside her bed. Nodding, he stepped outside, giving her privacy.

Undressing, she brushed her teeth and then climbed into the shower, hoping to wash away the evil of the day. Her people deserved better than this. She had let them down immensely. Intense pain shot though her body, and she began to cry. Long, sobbing wails that forced her to crumble into a tiny ball on the floor of her bathtub, water streaming over her. In that moment, she didn't care if she drowned. Clutching her knees to her chest, she buried her face in them and shook with the agony of her cries.

She didn't feel the draft of air when he opened the shower door, too lost to her suffering. She only noticed him when he sat behind her, unfazed by the water, and hugged her back to his chest. The heat of his skin enveloped every inch of her shaking body.

Beefy arms held her, offering her silent support. He wrapped his legs around her, enclosing her inside his massive frame, giving her strength.

There, under the spray of the shower, he comforted her in her greatest moment of need. They rocked together, silent, until her tears subsided. Soft lips grazed the back of her neck, and she squeezed his forearms, thanking him wordlessly since her throat was raw.

Disengaging from her, he stood and led her out, turning off the shower and handing her one of the towels that lay on the nearby rack. He took the other and dried himself. They were both naked, no barriers left between them. She averted her eyes, embarrassed that he had seen her so vulnerable.

When she was dry, he pulled her by the hand and urged her into bed. Turning off her bedside lamp, he climbed in. In the darkness, he soothed her, and she fell asleep with her head on his chest, comforted by his embrace.

* * * *

Sathan felt her jolt awake on his chest. He had let her sleep, his own body unable to relax, infuriated that the Deamons had succeeded at such a targeted attack on her people.

"Sathan?" she asked groggily.

"I really hope you're not trying to decipher whose chest you're waking up on. Is there someone else I should know about?"

Lifting her head, she scowled at him. "Asks the man who has the fiancée at home." She really was cranky when she woke up.

"Betrothed. And I'm getting pretty tired of rehashing that, if you don't mind."

Sighing, she dropped her head back onto his chest. "I don't want to be queen anymore. It sucks." He knew she was attempting a joke because thinking about the Slayers who'd perished was too much to bear.

"Seeing war and death close up is horrible. When my parents were killed, my mother's blood was spattered from my face down to my shoes," he said, absently stroking her silky hair. "It happened right in front of me. I still remember the disappointment in my mother's eyes. Because I didn't save her." He swallowed, hating that memory more than any other.

Lifting her head again, she propped the side of her face on her hand, her elbow resting on his chest. "She wasn't disappointed that you didn't save her," Miranda said, compassion swimming in the depths of her leaf-green gaze. "She was heartbroken, knowing that would be the last image you would remember of her."

"How do you know?" he asked, running his fingers through her hair.

"Because I know." She shifted her body over his, slowly, seductively. Placing her hands on his face, one on each side, she straddled him. "I missed you." She gave him a gentle kiss. "I wasn't gonna tell you, but who knows if we'll survive tomorrow? So, there it is."

He felt encompassed by her, enthralled by her beauty. There wasn't one bone in her body that wasn't genuine and pure. It led to bouts of passion and anger, but he'd take a thousand of those outbursts for the handful of small moments when she looked at him as she was now.

Whispering her name, he slid higher underneath her, bringing his engorged shaft to her wetness. Pushing herself down his chest, anchoring on his biceps with her fists, she slid over him, sheathing him inside her innermost place.

Exhaling deeply, he moved under her. Rising up, she lifted her hands, fanning her hair out behind her as she began to ride him. Every fantasy he'd ever had paled in comparison to watching his Slayer moan, open-mouthed, as she gyrated over him.

Moving her hands down, she grabbed her breasts, squeezing them as she held his gaze. Groaning, she pinched her nipples, panting as she increased her pace.

With a growl, he grabbed her hips, helping her move up and down on his shaft. Determined to let her stay in control, he urged her on with silken words of passion.

She cried out with pleasure and moved her hand to where they were joined, rubbing her tiny nub. It was the hottest thing he'd ever seen. "You're so beautiful," he said, moving her on top of his hips. "By the goddess, you feel so good."

Convulsions began to rock her body, and he pushed into her faster, deeper. Unable to control his wail, he thrust into her, emptying himself as his body shook.

Spent, she collapsed on top of him.

Circling her with his arms, he held her to his chest. She fit there so perfectly. Fuck. She was becoming an addiction that he was increasingly afraid he couldn't control. Holding her, he waited for their breath to settle back to normal.

An hour later, they showered together, and he reveled at the softness of her skin as he ran the soapy cloth over it. Afterward, they dressed and headed downstairs. Arriving at the large foyer, she turned to face him.

"How will you get home?" she asked.

"Latimus will pick me up outside the wall in the Hummer. I'll be sending the troops to you tonight. Takel can help them get acclimated since he already knows the compound."

She nodded, looking down at his chest.

"You want to ask me something," he said.

She tilted her head back so she could see him fully. "What are we doing, Sathan? This can't keep happening. We're rulers of two different species. We can't produce heirs. We have no future."

"Our future is in negotiating peace. We do that by getting along. We seem to get along best when I'm fucking you, so we must be on the right track."

"Asshole," she said, scowling.

"See?" he asked. "We're already fighting. Maybe I should take you to bed so you'll be nice to me."

"Quiet," she said, looking around. "Someone might hear."

He regarded her, two red splotches of embarrassment glowing on her cheeks. "I understand your question. I just don't have an answer. Let's agree that we don't have to decide anything right now. Take it day by day, week by week. Eventually, I'm sure you'll get tired of me."

"I'm already tired of you," she snapped, turning to open one of the massive front doors. "Get out."

Smiling at how quickly she became angry, he shuffled out the door. Behind him, she called his name. He turned toward her. The sun was about to rise, and her eyes glowed in the waning light of dawn. "Thank you."

"I'm always here for you, Miranda." And then, he left her.

A few minutes later, he breached the wall and climbed into the Hummer, not addressing his brother behind the wheel. "You're creating a problem that we don't need, Sathan."

"Just drive." He didn't want to discuss his trysts with Miranda with his brother.

Latimus started the car and began the trek back to Astaria.

"She's the fucking Slayer queen and stubborn as hell. This will lead to disaster."

"I know what I'm doing," Sathan said, unable to hide his defensive tone.

"Don't fuck this up. If you do, I'll cut off your dick myself."

Shaking his head, he refused to honor that with a response. His brother really was a huge jackass. They drove the rest of the way in silence.

Chapter 28

Rage vibrated through every pore of Darkrip's muscular body. His father had attacked Uteria without his knowledge. Without his council. It could only mean that the Dark Lord was losing trust in him, and that was something he'd worked too hard to let happen.

He must regain his father's confidence if his plan was going to succeed. As strong as Miranda had become, there was no way she could defeat Crimeous without his help. To offer her that, he had to ingratiate himself to the Deamon Lord.

Gritting his teeth in resolve, he burst through the doors of his father's large chamber, opening them with is mind. He slammed the doors behind him, making sure the sound would echo loudly.

"Well, well. If it isn't the prodigal son. You seem upset, Darkrip." Crimeous' tone was antagonizing as he sat in his leather chair, thin fingers steepled in front of his face.

"You attacked Uteria without telling me. Of course, I'm pissed. I would've liked to have been part of the raid. I haven't tortured or killed in weeks. Why did you deny me?"

The Dark Lord's beady eyes formed into slits. "I felt it best to ensure a surprise attack. I fear that you have become emotionally involved with the Slayer princess."

Darkrip scoffed. "She is nothing to me. A nuisance. I will kill her myself if you command."

Crimeous remained silent, studying him.

"I only wish to help you conquer the land of the immortals, Father," he said. Vomit burned in his throat as he called the creature by the name he swore he never would. But these were desperate times. He must employ every method possible to regain his trust.

The Deamon stood, a look of pleasure crossing his hideous face. "You have finally called me 'Father.' It is a welcome sign. I wonder if your motivations are pure."

"My motivation is to kill the other immortals so that you can reign over all the kingdoms. If I have not made that clear, then I have failed. If you no longer trust me, then banish me, for I will never cease fighting for you." Revulsion ran through him at the words.

Crimeous slowly walked from behind his desk to stand in front of him. Straightening, Darkrip firmly stood his ground.

"She has aligned with the Vampyres. Sathan marches two hundred soldiers there as we speak."

"I could attack them as they march," he offered.

"No," the Deamon said, shaking his head. "Let her regain her footing and begin to feel strong again. Her confidence will be her downfall."

"As you wish."

"I want you to continue visiting her, gaining her trust. I will be ready for her. After she is dead, I will march on Uteria with her head on a spike. It will be a glorious day."

Darkrip nodded and pinned his gaze to those dark, dead eyes. "Do not leave me out of your plans again. I won't be so forgiving next time."

Crimeous laughed, dark and hateful. "Your threat is noted, although weak. I have kept you alive all these years because you are my blood, and a certain...fondness for you runs through me. Don't mistake that for anything else. If I decide to end your life, I won't feel one ounce of pain. Tread lightly, Darkrip."

"I will work on the Slayer princess," he said, repugnance bubbling in his gut. "I will not fail."

Pivoting, he stalked from the chamber.

* * * *

Sathan and Latimus returned to the compound as the night warred with impending dawn. Latimus parked the Hummer in the barracks, and they entered through the back doorway. His brother muttered something about needing a drink and stalked down the hallway toward the kitchen.

Sathan entered his office chamber, startled to see Lila staring absently out the window by his large mahogany desk.

"Lila," he said, coming to stand behind her. "Are you okay?"

Her slim, pale fingers closed the shade so that they wouldn't burn from the rays that would soon shine through.

"How is the Slayer princess?"

Alarm ran through him at her soft, dejected tone. "She is understandably upset. Many of her people died last night. But she's strong. She will recover."

Blond curls moved up and down as she nodded absently. "You have grown fond of her."

Sathan studied her back, unsure of what course to take. She didn't seem angry. Instead, there was a sense of sadness in the hunch of her shoulders.

"Lila," he said, "I'm sorry. I don't want to hurt you."

Turning, she gazed up at him with those violet eyes. He had always thought them so pretty, so unique. She really was a beautiful woman. Why he had never felt attraction toward her was puzzling.

"Can I speak frankly?"

"Always," he said, clasping her hand and pulling her to the conference table. He nudged her into the chair usually reserved for his brother and sat at his usual seat at the head of the table. Grasping both of her hands, he pulled them on top of the table and squeezed, giving her support as she contemplated her words.

"I have felt so lucky to be your betrothed. For ten centuries, we have been inexorably tied together. You have brought me into your council and into your family. For that, I am eternally grateful."

"Your council is valuable to me, Lila. It is I who is lucky to have you."

Pink lips formed a ghost of a smile, the light not reaching her eyes. "Although we are betrothed, I think it is time that we are honest with each other. I love and respect you as my king, but I think we both can admit that this is not a love match."

Sathan inhaled, looking at their joined hands. "Lila, it's not you—"

A tiny laugh burst from her lips, and his gaze lifted back to hers.

"What?"

"Are you going to give me the 'it's not you, it's me' speech? Because I think that's beneath both of us."

"You're right," he said, squeezing her hands. Needing space, he stood and ran a hand through his thick hair. "I don't know what to say. I truly care for you and want to honor our betrothal. I have never wished to bond for love. My duty is to have heirs, and I would be honored for them to share your blood."

Smiling faintly, she began toying with her long hair. It was an absent gesture she performed when restless. "It sounds so formal. Bloodlines and heirs. Don't you want more?"

"I want what's best for my people. That means bonding with you."

As her fingers toyed, she chewed on her lip. "I don't think it does. A bonding cannot last on mutual respect alone. Eventually, we all crave something more. Don't we?"

"I don't," he said firmly.

Standing, she seemed to float toward him. "I saw you with her. So passionate, so...*raw*. I never understood that it could be like that. You deserve to feel that every day. I won't deny you that."

Shit. He felt like an absolute jerk. "You saw us in the hallway, by my mother's portrait."

"Yes," she said. "It was...consuming."

"I don't have the luxury of feeling passion. Any chance of that disappeared the day my parents were murdered."

Compassion filled her gaze. "You have been so strong. For all of us. Such a mighty leader. It is time I show strength for you." Lifting her hand to cup his cheek, she said, "I want you to summon Etherya and ask her blessing to end our betrothal."

"No," he said, shaking his head against her hand. "You are to be queen, and I won't deny you that."

"I don't want to be a queen of an ivory castle, imprisoned in a loveless bonding. I thought I could for so many centuries. But then, I saw you with her, and it...unlocked something inside of me. I tried to push it away, but it's there. Gnawing at me. I wonder if someone might look at me that way one day. Probably not," she said, lowering her head to look at his chest, "but perhaps."

Sathan felt a jolt of awareness. He realized that he had never even thought she might have feelings for another man. What a conceited ass he was. He lifted her chin with his fingers, reclaiming her gaze. "Is there someone else? I should've asked long ago. I'm sorry I didn't."

"No," she said, but an expression of longing crossed her beautiful features. "There was someone I might have felt something for...but he didn't feel the same about me. And that's okay. It wasn't meant to be."

"Whoever he is, I find it hard to believe that he didn't want you. You're the most beautiful woman in the kingdom."

"Says the man who has fallen for a Slayer," she said, without malice or judgement.

"Miranda and I are...complicated. We have no future since we cannot produce heirs. Although I care for her, I would not jeopardize our kingdom's prosperity for her."

"You have always been a noble ruler, putting your people before yourself. But I would be careful to postulate that you know the future. Others have done so at their peril. Our future can be what we make it, if we have the courage to try."

"I can't change biology."

"There is always a way, if we choose to see it. My father taught me that before he passed. He was always able to see a solution for even the most difficult situation."

"He was our most esteemed diplomat. You must miss him terribly."

A small sigh escaped her lips. "I do. I think that the best way for me to honor his memory is to become a great diplomat, as he was." Lowering her hand from his face, she placed it on his chest. "I thought I wanted to be queen. It's all I've trained for my whole life. When I saw you with the Slayer, I was devastated."

"Lila," he said, cupping her soft cheek. "I'm so sorry—"

"Wait," she said, her palm applying pressure to his chest. "I was devastated because it was the first time I ever entertained that I might not be queen. It was jolting and confusing, and I was thrown off-balance. But as the days have worn on, I see that there could be another option for me. I could become the kingdom's diplomat, as my father was, and honor my duty that way. And that is what I wish to do."

Tilting her head back further, she looked directly into him, resolved. "I want you to summon Etherya and ask her to end the betrothal. After that, I will take my seat in your council as the Kingdom Secretary Diplomat. It was the title my father held, and it is the one I wish to hold. Peace with the Slayers is close, and I want to be the one who implements it. The trains are a massive project, and you'll need me to travel to the compounds to ensure proper adoption. I would like this to be my new role. If you agree, of course."

Sathan deliberated, his eyes darting over her flawless features. If it was what she truly wanted, he could not deny her. "I would be doing this for you, Lila. You understand this, right? I would still bond with a Vampyre when I am ready to produce heirs. This is independent of the Slayer. Is it what you really want?"

"Yes."

"Then, I will summon the goddess," he said, lowering to place a soft kiss on her forehead. "You deserve to have the life you want."

"And so do you," she said, smiling up at him. "You will find a way to love your Slayer. I know you will."

He let that one go, not wanting to discuss love. She didn't seem to understand that duty would always trump love in his world.

They gave each other a hug, and she bid him good night. When he was alone, he found himself staring at the shuttered window. Somewhere far away, as the sun was rising, his Slayer was working to rebuild her kingdom. Thousands of years of hate and tradition were being stripped away and rebuilt in a matter of weeks and months. The ground seemed to be shifting under his feet. The instability was disconcerting.

He had been betrothed to Lila his entire life. And yet, the whirlwind that was Miranda had consumed him. He owed it to Lila to end their betrothal.

Tomorrow, he would summon the goddess.

* * * *

On the other side of the castle, Latimus sat upon his bed. Drinking Jack straight from the bottle, he allowed himself to seethe in his anger.

Earlier, he had driven Sathan home, frustrated that his usually intelligent brother had become consumed with fucking a Slayer. Even if she was the most beautiful Slayer in the land, he saw the danger that came with his brother's obsession.

After securing the barracks, he had rummaged around in the kitchen, unimpressed with the Slayer blood, cold chicken and pasta in the fridge. Instead, he pulled the bottle of Jack off the shelf. Deciding that he would stay in the main house for the night, he went off in search of Arderin. His little sister always seemed to be able to pull him from his foul moods, and the one he was in now was epic.

As he had passed Sathan's office chamber, the door was slightly ajar, and he heard Lila's voice. Quietly, he stepped to observe them through the opening. Sathan was cradling her face, his gaze reverent, as she palmed his chest. Latimus' heart clutched in pain as his brother lowered to give her a gentle kiss on her forehead.

Fucking bastard. He had always accepted that Sathan was the better man. The better brother. The better king. That he deserved Lila because he wasn't filled with the darkness and rage that seemed to consume Latimus.

A twisted sense of honor caused him to grit his teeth at the image before him. How could his brother treat Lila this way? Fucking the Slayer princess and then returning to clutch her in his arms? He felt a wave of disappointment at Sathan's actions, compounded by the surge of jealousy that he always experienced when he saw them together.

He had never begrudged Sathan his betrothal. After all, he was king, and he wanted heirs. He was a noble man, certainly more noble than Latimus, and he deserved the woman who was most precious in the realm.

Latimus had never even allowed himself to think he, the closed-off, war-hungry brother, was good enough for her. But he would be damned if he let his brother treat her like shit. She deserved better.

He'd stalked to his room on the basement floor, the one he kept for when he didn't feel like venturing to his cabin on the outskirts of the compound. Sitting on his bed, he let the Jack dull the anger.

Tomorrow, he would confront his brother. He, the man who had been horrid to Lila her whole life, would defend her honor. The irony was overwhelming. With a humorless laugh, he drowned the rest of the bottle.

* * * *

A world away, Kenden sat in his hotel room, working on his notes. He was nothing if not thorough, and he felt it imperative that he document his findings accurately.

Several firm knocks sounded on his door.

"I didn't order any room service," he yelled.

The knocks repeated. Frustrated, he yanked open the door, anxious to tell the bus boy he had the wrong room.

Olive green eyes stared up at him.

"I think it's time we had a little talk."

He studied the woman, her hair the color of fire, the skin of her face slightly freckled. She seemed to sizzle with an unidentifiable energy that unnerved him. Rare, as he was usually unshakable, even in the midst of great unrest.

Why this woman, several inches shorter and with a slight frame, would faze him was beyond his comprehension.

Opening the door wider, she breezed past him.

As he closed the door, she walked to the desk in his room. Her fingers traveled over his open notebook, the pictures he had taken of her, his tiny, fragmented notes.

Gazing toward him, her perfectly-plucked, auburn-colored eyebrow arched. "Someone's been busy."

Walking over, he quickly covered his work, stuffing his notes in the notebook and closing it away from her view. "It took me centuries to find you. I figured I'd be thorough."

Her red lips curved into a sexy smile, and he felt an unwanted jolt of desire. This woman was trained in seduction. He could see it on her. Smell it. She would use it to destroy anyone she deemed a threat. "Now that you've found me, what will you do with me?" Lifting her red-nailed index finger, she traced the tip down his neck.

She gasped as he grabbed her wrist, yanking her hand away. Clutching, he held her firm. "I'm not someone you can seduce, so don't waste your time."

A nasty rage filled her grass-green eyes, and she tried to pull her hand away. "Let me go, or I'll slit your throat right here."

"Now, there's the real Evangeline. It's nice to meet you."

With a grunt, she pulled her wrist from his grasp. "It's Evie," she said, running her hand through her thick, shoulder-length hair. "And don't even begin to think that I won't kill you, Slayer. If I wanted to, I could snap your neck with a flick of my hand."

"But you won't," he said, trusting his gut. "Your curiosity is too strong. You're wondering why I'm here."

She shrugged, feigning indifference, but he could read her well. She was interested. "I'm always up for a new challenge. Living amongst humans has its advantages. They're so lively, what with their wine and their men always ready for a good lay. But lately, I have grown a bit bored, so I'm willing to listen." She sat on the bed, crossing her white pant-covered legs, leaning back on her hands. Her breasts threatened to swell out of her low-cut shirt. "Courtesy of a human plastic surgeon. Aren't they gorgeous?"

He scowled, furious at himself that she had noticed him eyeing her breasts.

"Times are changing quickly in the land of immortals," he said, ignoring her question. "Miranda, Valktor's heir, has freed the Blade of Pestilence and plans to march upon Crimeous. She won't stop until he's dead. She wishes for peace between all the immortals."

The woman shook her foot absently as she regarded him. "Good for her. The old Deamon is an evil bastard. I hope she slits his throat and he drowns in his own blood."

"I hope so too. But you and I both know she might not be capable."

She inhaled a sharp breath, her magnificent breasts rising and falling. "I want no part of this. I left the immortal world centuries ago. I would rather eat, drink and fuck the humans than be bogged down by the wars of Slayers, Deamons and Vampyres. If you've come to plead for my help, forget it. I'll never go back there."

Kenden regarded her. He had rarely seen someone as unemotional about war and death. "Is there no one left there that you care about? What about your brother?"

She scoffed, her head bending back, and then returned her gaze to his. "He paid our caretaker to kill me. So, no, I don't have any love for brother dearest."

"Is there anything you would consider fighting for? If Miranda fails to kill Crimeous with the Blade, it's possible you could be our only hope."

Sighing, the woman stood. She placed a hand on his face. The gesture would have been calming if it hadn't been so rehearsed, so fake. He wondered how many men she had unwittingly seduced. She was masterful at it.

"Sorry, sweetheart, but I don't do war anymore. You should be grateful. Back when I used to kill, I was merciless. I used to revel in the cries of men as their last breaths exited their convulsing bodies. I would fuck them as they died, coming as they spasmed into death. It was thrilling. An evil runs through me that you can't even begin to imagine. Be happy that I want nothing to do with your little wars. Bringing me home would mean certain death for many immortals."

His hand ensnared hers, pulling it from his face. "Then, why stop killing? If it was so pleasurable for you? Use that evil to kill Crimeous."

"An optimist?" she asked. "Wow. After all your wars, you still see the glass half-full. Take me at my word when I tell you that I have no interest in helping immortals secure peace."

Disengaging from him, she walked toward the door. Pulling it open, she turned back. "Don't follow me again. Forget you met me. If I see you again, I'll kill you." The door slammed behind her.

Kenden turned to the desk, making sure she hadn't absconded with anything important. It was all there.

With a feeling of foreboding, he prepared to return home.

Chapter 29

Miranda stood on her balcony watching the sun rise over the horizon. As yellow flirted with orange above the gentle curves of the mountains, she formulated her rebuilding plan. Once the golden orb of the sun was fully visible in the sky, she got to work.

She commanded Larkin to round up all who had lost family in the Deamon attack. Once they were gathered in the large assembly hall of the main castle, she addressed them. With firm resolve, she promised them that she wouldn't rest until Crimeous had been killed and the Deamons had been defeated. Although they were distraught, she asked for their continued support.

Many approached her afterward, and she spent several hours consoling them. Mothers who had lost children, husbands who had lost wives, sisters who had lost brothers. Although emotion swamped her, she knew she had to remain strong. She had shed her tears with Sathan last night. The time for weeping was over. The time to fight was upon them.

That night, she led Larkin and Aron to the cells that held her father's supporters. She had no wish to kill them but couldn't allow their dissidence. Addressing them in the darkness, she offered them the chance to help renovate the abandoned hospital that would house the Vampyre soldiers. They would have to wear ankle monitors while they worked and would have to live in the hospital alongside the Vampyres, but she would pay them, allowing them to support their families. It was better than rotting away in the dungeon.

The majority of the men accepted. She secretly hoped that having them work and live alongside Vampyres each day would help soften their hatred. Only time would tell.

Commanding Larkin to prepare the ankle monitors, she headed back to the royal office chamber with Aron.

"You are doing very well, Miranda. Your offer to Marsias' loyalists is smart. They will regain some dignity while living amongst their perceived enemies. Hopefully, it will work."

"I hope so too." Regarding him, she realized how lucky she was to have him as an ally. He was descended from one of the oldest Slayer families, his blood almost as pure as her own. A true aristocrat, his loyalty cemented her claim to the throne. Aron had become a great ally along with Larkin, who had shown exceptional leadership ability in Kenden's absence.

"The Vampyre troops should arrive soon. I will meet them with you at the wall, if you wish."

"Thank you, Aron. I accept." She squeezed his hand, and they began the trek to the wall.

Once there, they opened the large wooden doors. Two hundred troops stood in the open field, awaiting entry. Miranda's heart longed to see Sathan, knowing he wouldn't have come but yearning just the same. Takel greeted the troops and led them to the abandoned hospital.

Familiar with the conditions of war, the soldiers would survive without power and running water until it was restored, which Larkin informed her should take about a week. In the meantime, she ordered them to train.

Each night would be consumed with sparring and fighting, preparing for her upcoming battle with Crimeous. She also stationed thirty of the Vampyres along the wall, ensuring that her people would be protected if the Deamons attacked. Being caught unaware again was not an option.

Every few nights, Miranda would gather everyone together on the field that stretched between the main compound and the Vampyres' quarters. Under the light of the moon, her staff would prepare a large meal of barbequed meat. She invited Slayer and Vampyre to join, hoping that they would begin to form a comradery, free from the hatred of the past.

She was encouraged by what she observed. As the shared meals continued, more and more of her people attended. Eventually, she noticed her subjects warming toward the Vampyre soldiers. An offered seat at the table here, an offered drink from a bottle of wine there...a timid trust was beginning to form. Miranda was consumed with pride that her people were strong enough to slowly let go of their hatred. It was the only way they could forge forward into a world without war.

One night, as the festivities wore down, she looked up at the waning moon and realized that six weeks had passed since the Deamons had attacked. Six weeks of living in relative harmony with the Vampyre soldiers. Hopefully, it would continue, for the time to attack Crimeous grew near. In only a month's time, she would be marching into the battle of her life.

She was careful not to show fear to her people. It was important that they see her as strong. But at night, when she lay in the silent darkness, she felt so much apprehension at her upcoming battle. What if she wasn't capable of defeating the Dark Lord? What would that mean for her people? Peace with the Vampyres was close, but she would have to vanquish Crimeous' evil in order to ever give her people true harmony.

Aron's voice shook her from her thoughts. "I think the barbeque has wound down, Miranda. Perhaps you should head inside."

Smiling, she nodded. "Do I look that tired?"

He chuckled, the smile warming his handsome face. "I would never accuse my queen of looking tired."

"Good. Because I feel like I'm a million years old." Grabbing his hand, she squeezed. "See ya tomorrow."

Proceeding to the castle, she acknowledged the soldiers stationed along her path and headed to her bedchamber. Once in her room, she opened the top drawer of her dresser. Removing the towel inside, she held it to her face, inhaling deeply.

He had used it when he dried after their shower the last morning she'd seen him. Thankfully, the towel had retained a small bit of his musky scent. Like a heartsick sap, she pulled it into her nostrils, needing to have that one small part of him.

From her pocket, her phone rang.

"Speak of the devil," she said into the device, holding it to her ear with her right hand, the towel in the other.

"Were you thinking of me?" Sathan's velvet voice asked, washing over her and causing her to shiver.

"Never," she said softly.

"Liar."

She caressed the fabric of the towel with her fingers, wishing it was his skin. "I just returned from another joint dinner. My people are warming up to your soldiers. It's so wonderful to see. I think we're getting close, Sathan. Soon, we can discuss joining the compounds under one kingdom."

"Slow down, Miranda," he said, always the contemplative, patient one between the two of them. "We have eternity to forge peace. If we push too hard, it could backfire. These things must happen naturally."

She scowled into the phone, hating that he was right. "I'm just ready. I want a better life for my people."

"I know. It will come. You've done a great job already. The shared barbeques were a brilliant idea. Let it happen. I promise it will."

She sat on the bed, pulling her knees to her chest as she still held the towel, rubbing it on her cheek. "Your soldiers are awesome. I feel ready to attack Crimeous. Only a few weeks to go."

The line seemed to crackle as she waited for his response.

"I wish I could attack with you. Latimus has forbidden it, convincing me that peace would never reign if both you and I were killed in the battle. Although he's right, it's frustrating. I should be by your side, fighting with you to defeat him."

"Latimus will be with me. And Takel and Larkin and Kenden. I know he'll be home soon. Along with a hundred of my soldiers and two hundred of yours. I'll be well-protected. I won't fail. The ramifications are too vast."

"I know you won't. I have faith in my little Slayer."

"Who says I'm yours?" she asked.

"I do, you snarky little minx. You were mine every time I was inside you."

Dampness surged between her thighs, and she squeezed them together. God, she missed him.

"In your dreams, blood-sucker," she said, smiling through the phone.

His deep laugh vibrated though her. "Are you wet?" he asked silkily.

"Not discussing this with you. Now, if you're done bothering me, I have shit to do before I go to sleep."

A pause stretched between them.

"I miss you," he finally said.

Miranda's heart pounded at his words. "Thanks," she said, hating how lame she sounded. She just wasn't ready to get all touchy-feely over the phone. "I have to go. I'll call you if anything noteworthy happens."

"Okay. Good night." The phone's light died as he disconnected the call.

Dropping her phone on the bed, she lay down and clutched the towel to her, inhaling his scent once again. Goddamnit, she was screwed. She was pretty sure she'd gone and fallen in love with a fucking Vampyre. Being that this was the first time she'd ever experienced love, she had no idea what it felt like. But it probably looked something like the sad picture she made clutching a dirty, used towel to her breast. Fucking great.

With a loud, frustrated groan, she threw the towel in her hamper, determined to wash it tomorrow; resolved to stop acting like a lovelorn idiot. Entering the bathroom, she brushed her teeth and washed her face. Climbing into bed, she turned off the lamp on the nightstand and told herself to sleep.

Not even ten minutes later, she rose, pulled the towel from the hamper, and got back into bed. Cuddling it to her, she cursed herself a fool and fell asleep to his scent.

* * * *

Sathan sat on his patch of grass by the thick elm tree. It was his place of solace, where he came to think. Sitting high atop a hill about three hundred feet from the castle, it gave him comfort to look down upon his home. It was also where he always prayed to Etherya. He had pled to her for weeks now, asking her to appear to him, but to no avail.

She had appeared to him only a handful of times over the centuries. Usually when he begged to her in the darkness, asking her why she had forsaken his people to no longer walk in the sun. On the rare occasions that she did appear, she mostly spoke in riddles, vexing him.

Frustrated, he called her name, his voice loud in the quiet of night.

Before him, a bright light appeared. Standing, he waited for the vision of her to form, wiping his damp palms on his black pants. The goddess was fickle, and her moods were hard to read. She could vacillate between calm and anger in a matter of seconds. He vowed to be thoughtful as he spoke to her.

"Your prayers have been forthcoming, Sathan, son of Markdor. Why do you wrest me from my sleep?"

Her voice was shrill, shattering the peaceful quiet of the night. Her blood-red hair flowed in long curls from her scalp, almost reaching her feet. The white gown she wore glowed in the dimness.

"My goddess Etherya," he said, kneeling to her. "I am thankful for your presence."

"Rise, my king." Her beady eyes washed over him, enveloped by the white skin of her face. "You have done well, Sathan. Peace between the Slayers and Vampyres grows. My heart is slowly healing."

"I have wished for peace for centuries. I'm glad it's finally near. Hopefully, you will let us walk in the sun again soon."

Floating above the grass, she said, "Not yet, my king. There will be much pain before the sun is to shine upon you again."

"What pain? For my family? For Miranda?"

"You care about the Slayer princess. It is something I foresaw long ago. I had hoped you two would end the war. This is why I ensured that only your shared blood could free the Blade."

"You did that? I thought Valktor decreed the prophecy."

"Valktor was only a conduit. There is so much you don't know. One day, you will. For now, your fight is true and just. It is imperative that you succeed."

Sathan inhaled the fresh air of the meadow, wary to ask the favor of her. "My betrothed, Lila, wishes to end our engagement. She would like to take another path. I humbly ask you to bless the ending of our betrothal."

Silence stretched for several moments. "She is meant to be queen and bear your heirs."

"I still wish to have heirs, but I will not force her to have mine. She must be allowed to choose her own fate."

"She loves another."

"Perhaps."

The goddess reached out her hand, the image watery. A rush of air crossed his face as she stroked him. "Done. I rescind the betrothal. What else do you ask?"

He was surprised that she had capitulated so easily. The goddess's decrees were rarely that uncomplicated. It unsettled something in him.

"I plead with you to protect Miranda as she battles Crimeous. Her actions are just, and she only wants peace. That won't happen if she dies."

"And what will happen to you if she dies?"

A jolt of fear rushed through him, as it always did when he thought of Miranda perishing. "I will go on. But claiming peace will be harder. I know that is a great wish of yours. For your people to be united once again."

"Her people see me as a false prophet, forsaking my protection. Why should I help her?"

"You once loved the Slayers more than us. Give them time to come around. I will help them regain their faith in you."

The goddess floated, staring at him as he waited. "I will offer her my protection, but it won't help. She has unseen obstacles before her."

"What obstacles?" His heart pounded with dread.

"That is only for her to discover. But I will watch over her, protecting her when I can. Good night, King Sathan. Be wary."

"Wait!" he called, wanting to know more. But his yell only echoed off the nearby tree. The goddess was gone. Her words filled him with a sense of foreboding. He must see Miranda and warn her.

Jumping into the four-wheeler, he headed back to the main castle. Once there, he found Lila and informed her of the goddess's willingness to end their betrothal. As she hugged him, he wished that she would find happiness with someone who could love her fully. She truly deserved that.

Afterward he searched for Nolan, finding him in the infirmary. Arderin's head was almost connected with his as they studied something through a microscope. His sister's capacity for learning was vast, and she had a curious mind. She spent many nights with the doctor, learning all she could about medicine and science. Sathan wished that she was more interested in her role as a royal. Someone as bright as she would make a good governor or council member for one of their satellite compounds. Instead, she focused on medicine, wanting to train in the human world, frustrating him, as he felt humans were inferior and not even close to worthy of having her in their world.

"This is great, Nolan," she said, both of them unaware he was there. "If the formula works as well on live tissue as it does in the lab, it could regenerate burnt skin."

"That, it could," the doctor said, smiling at her. "It would be a huge advance forward for any burn victim."

Sathan cleared his throat. "Nolan, I need to speak with you."

They both turned to look at him. "I want you to be on call over the next several weeks. The Slayer princess will be fighting Crimeous, and if she is hurt, I want her helicoptered to you immediately."

"As you wish," Nolan said with a nod. "Just have Heden make a pager for me that can be reached at all times."

"Will do."

"I might be able to help," Arderin said. "During my capture, I met a wonderful Slayer physician named Sadie. She was very knowledgeable and could partner with Nolan to help him, if the need arises."

"And she was friendly to you?" he asked, his tone wary.

"Absolutely." Black curls bounced as she nodded furiously. "She was amazing. I consider her a friend."

"A friend who held you captive. Wow, we really need to improve your social life, sis."

She scowled at him, obviously not finding his teasing funny. "You don't understand anything. Whatever." She shifted her gaze to Nolan. "If you need me to contact her, I will. Just let me know."

Shooting Sathan a look, she left the room.

"You two were getting along so nicely," Nolan said, his amber eyebrow arched. "You blew it."

"I always seem to. I think I should leave the joking to Heden," Sathan said, running his hand through his hair. "Thanks, Nolan. I'll make sure Heden gets the pager to you."

Later, after he had instructed his brother on the pager requirements, he decided that he would head to the Slayer compound at dusk the next day. He needed to get in front of Miranda and make sure she was extra cautious. He wouldn't allow anything to happen to his little Slayer.

Chapter 30

Miranda sat at her father's desk, exhaling after a long day. It was her desk now. Running her hand over the wood, she allowed herself to mourn him for a moment. Although they had been at odds for several of the past centuries, she loved him dearly and missed him terribly.

Lifting her head, she watched Aron enter the chamber. His expression was one she had never seen. Was he nervous?

"Hi, Aron," she said, walking around so that she faced him in front of her father's desk. "Is everything okay?"

His throat bobbed up and down as he swallowed. "I hope so. I have something I need to discuss with you."

"Okay," she said, perplexed.

"Over these past weeks, I have come to see you as the true leader you are. It is magnificent to see you finally leading our people. I have always been a Valktor loyalist, and his blood runs so strongly through you."

"Thank you. I truly appreciate your support. I couldn't do this without you."

"We make a great team, don't we?" He grabbed her hand, clutching it in his.

"Absolutely. I value your council and am lucky to have it."

She noticed his free hand was shaking slightly as he reached into his pocket. Slowly pulling out a felt-covered box, he let go of her hand to palm it. She knew what was coming. Shit.

"Miranda," he said, lowering to one knee. "I know that I am not worthy of you, nor could I ever be. But I have found myself falling more deeply in love with you, day by day. You're the most amazing woman I have ever met. It would be an honor to help you run the kingdom as your husband and father of your children. I don't expect you to feel the same for me but hope that one day you will come to love me. I promise I will do everything in my power to make that happen. Miranda, will you give me the great honor of becoming my wife?"

Her heart pounded as she looked at the handsome man kneeling before her. In another lifetime, he would be a perfect husband. Smart, strong and loyal, she could see them raising a family together and ruling while her people lived in peace.

Unfortunately, there was one hiccup. She happened to be in love with another man. A Vampyre at that. Someone she had no future with. Fuck.

"Aron," she said softly.

He smiled up at her, the ring box open in his hand. Waiting. Expectant.

"Well, don't let me interrupt," said a baritone voice from the doorway.

Miranda gasped as the subject of her thoughts appeared. His hulking body obstructed the door, his face impassive.

"Sathan," she whispered.

Aron cleared his throat and stood, stuffing the ring box back in his pocket. "Well, they say there's nothing like bad timing." He gave her a slight grin, but his discomfort was clear.

"I'm sorry," she said, clutching his hand and giving it a squeeze. "Unfortunately, this isn't a good time. Can we talk about this later? I am honored at your proposal."

"Of course," he said, placing a soft kiss on her forehead. She saw Sathan stiffen in the doorway, his teeth clenching as a massive muscle corded in his neck.

Aron left the room, acknowledging the Vampyre with a nod as he exited.

Slowly, Sathan closed the door. He stared at her, his black eyes filled with murder.

As he sauntered toward her, he asked, "Why are you being proposed to by another man? And why in the *hell* does he think he has the right to put his lips anywhere on your face?"

The possessiveness of his words sent a shiver down her back. "He's one of my most trusted advisors."

Her neck craned as he came to stand fully in front of her. The air between them vibrated with his anger. "I'm trying to tell myself there's a good explanation why my woman is getting a proposal from someone else."

Her brows drew together. "Your woman? Get over yourself."

His massive hands slid through her hair, fisting it gently as he tilted her head back, jumpstarting her body's desire. She had ached to see him for so long, and any touch was bittersweet. But his jealousy was also pissing her off.

"I didn't say you could touch me." Her nostrils flared as she looked into his dark eyes.

"Whether you want to admit it or not, you're mine, Miranda. *Mine.* I can't live in a world where another man touches you."

Exasperated, she laughed bitterly. "I'm not yours or anyone's, you fucking Neanderthal. I'm my own woman, and I'll choose who I'm with and who I let touch me."

He panted as he held her, his breath warming her face. She longed to beg him to take her, to love her, but her indignation held her in check.

As his eyes searched hers, he inhaled and exhaled a deep breath. She felt him relax, if only a little.

"I don't care for him that way," she said, holding his gaze so he could see her truth. "But regardless of my feelings, I will have to marry him or some other Slayer someday to ensure an heir. We can't change that."

With a sigh, he lowered his forehead to hers, massaging her scalp as he held her hair. "I know," he said. Her body shuddered at his rich voice, his proximity. "But I find that I want you all to myself. How do I live with that?"

"I don't know," she said, encircling his thick neck with her arms. "It fucking sucks."

Lowering his mouth to hers, he gave her a blazing kiss. A flush heated her body as she mated her tongue with his, sliding, stroking, showing him how much she'd missed him.

He kissed a haphazard trail with his lips along her cheek, stopping at her ear. "I'm sorry," he whispered into the tiny crevice, making her shiver. "I wanted so badly to see you and came here to find you being proposed to by another man. I wanted to kill him."

She hugged him tight, squeezing hard. "I'm sorry too. I had no idea he was going to propose. He's a good man, Sathan. He would make a good husband. We have to be realistic about our situation."

Pulling back, he looked down at her as he held her face in his hands. "Damn it," he said, rubbing his thumbs over her cheeks. "I convinced myself I wasn't capable of feeling jealousy."

Smiling, she rubbed her hand on his chest. "I think you'd better reassess."

Breathing out a laugh, he grinned down at her.

"Why are you here?" she asked.

"I saw the goddess last night. I wanted to discuss our conversation with you. Can we go somewhere more private?"

"Like my bedchamber?"

His fangs seemed to glow as he beamed. "Definitely."

Taking his hand, she led him out of the room.

* * * *

Sathan entered the bedchamber behind her, closing the door with a soft click. Their affair was secret, his jealousy dangerous. He needed to remember that as he continued to forge peace. Although he desired her more than he had any other woman, their trysts would end when one of them bonded, and she would no longer be his. They both had a duty to fulfill, and he couldn't jeopardize that.

They walked onto the balcony. Under the stars, he told her of his conversation with Etherya, warning her of the obstacles she spoke of.

"I'm not afraid of dying," she said, the green of her eyes seeming to melt in the dimness. "If I do, then it will be for a great cause. Hopefully, you will still ensure the unification of our people in peace."

"I will, but it will be with you by my side, alive. I won't lose you in the caves. You're too important to our people." *To me*, a voice in his head said softly.

Her tiny hand snaked up his arm, bare under the sleeve of his t-shirt. "I plan to attack at the next full moon." Green eyes searched his, filled with fear and resolve.

Sathan looked to the sky, noting the waning quarter phase of the moon. She would attack in three weeks. A sliver of terror shot through him. He didn't want her exposed to danger but knew that it was the only course forward. And yet, he had tremendous faith in her. She was the strongest of them all. In heart, determination and will. If anyone could kill the Dark Lord, it was his Slayer.

"I can't wait to see you march through the streets with that bastard's head in your fist. The image will be burned in our history books. I have no doubt you will triumph."

Her pink lips curved into a sad smile. "And then, you'll marry Lila, and I'll take a husband. Our people will be at peace while we live separate lives."

"I will always care about you, Miranda. If you trust nothing else, trust that." He rubbed his finger over her silken cheek, dazed by her beauty. Wanting to pull her inside him somehow and never let go.

Clutching his hand, she pulled him into the bedchamber, leading him to the large fireplace that comprised the far wall. Grabbing the hem of his shirt, she pulled it off and tossed it to the ground. One by one, she lifted his arms, placing them outstretched on the mantle that sat above the hearth.

"Stay," she commanded softly.

The ripe flesh of her lips brushed the skin of his chest, and she began kissing little trails along his pecs. Heat consumed his body, and he moved his hands to clutch her head. Grabbing his wrists, she placed his arms back on the mantle. "Stay."

By the goddess, she was magnificent. The rim of her mouth slid along his skin, coming to stop at the tiny copper disk of his nipple. Extending her wet tongue, she licked him. He growled in approval. Closing her lips over the hardened nub, she sucked. Clinching the wood of the mantle, he struggled to let her be in control.

She moved to his other nipple, mewling as she sucked it. Slim fingers grasped his shoulders as she plunged her nails into the skin there. Exhaling deeply, he closed his eyes, the tiny pinpricks of pain making his body pulse. Moisture formed at the tip of his cock as he imagined her sucking him.

Her fingertips slid to his slacks, the muscles of his hardened eight-pack quivering under her touch. She popped the button free and slid the zipper down. Inserting her hands at his sides, she slid his pants and underwear to the floor. Lowering his gaze, he took her in. Those gorgeous eyes were shuttered as she fisted his swollen shaft, running her thumb across the wetness, spreading it over the sensitive head.

A breath hissed out of him, his body a tense mass of nerves. "Fuck, Miranda."

"Shhhhhhh..." she said, using both hands to cradle his engorged cock. "Let me love you."

Lowering to her knees, she lined her mouth up to the tip, her pink tongue bathing those plushy lips with saliva. He almost came right there.

Holding the base in one hand, she opened her mouth wide and took him in.

His head fell back as he groaned in pleasure, determined to let her control the situation. Gazing back down, his heart pounded. Never had he seen anything as sexy as his Slayer sliding her soft lips over his cock. She moaned as she picked up the pace, her hand moving in tandem with her mouth.

Unable to stop himself, he fisted his hands in her hair. She purred as he pulled slightly. She seemed to like it when he pulled her hair, and he loved the dominance he felt when he did.

His hips began to move as she bathed him. Needing more, he took command. "Move your hand. Let me fuck your mouth."

She complied, bringing her hand to rest on the back of his thigh. Grasping her hair, he jutted his hips back and forth, gazing into her eyes as she gave him all control. Those green orbs, filled with desire as he pistoned back and forth in her sultry mouth, were mesmerizing. Tilting her head back, she took him further down her throat. He lost all semblance of control.

Increasing the pace of his thrusts, he cursed through clenched teeth. Miranda took him deeper, allowing him to plunder her as if she were made to suck him dry. He felt his balls tense, knowing he was about to come.

"I need to pull out," he said.

She grasped onto the back of his thighs, holding on for dear life, clutching him to her. Her eyes told him to finish inside her.

"Miranda..." he said, pumping into her.

Tilting his head back, he screamed, overcome with the force of his orgasm. He spasmed into her mouth, his body jerking uncontrollably. Holding him inside, she lapped up all that he gave her.

It was the most erotic moment of his life.

Trembling, he lowered his head to look at her, blurry through his hazed vision. Stroking her hair, he popped himself from her mouth, her lips swollen from his thrusts. With her tongue, she lathered her bottom lip, seizing droplets of his release that sat there. Moving his thumb to her lip, he captured one of the drops and placed it in her mouth. Closing her lips around his thumb, she sucked.

By the goddess, she was glorious. Everything he had ever wanted in a lover.

Lifting her up under her arms, he brought her lips to his mouth, reveling in his taste inside her. She wrapped her legs around his waist, and he devoured her, showing her with his tongue how grateful he was for her recent loving.

"You're wearing too many clothes," he growled, pushing his hand under her shirt to feel the soft skin of her back.

She smiled against his mouth. "It was time I gave you some pleasure. You're so good at giving it to me."

"You're an animal," he said, nipping her lips. "That was amazing. Thank you."

Her cheeks turned red as she clutched her arms behind his neck.

"You're embarrassed," he said, rubbing his nose against hers.

"A little. I've never really enjoyed that before. With you, everything is different. I've never felt this way...you know, sexually, with anyone. It's overwhelming."

"For me too." He gave her a soft kiss.

Then, he lowered her and playfully slapped her behind. "Now, get out of those clothes. I need to return the favor." Biting her lip, she complied.

After pulling off the rest of his clothes, he threw her over his shoulder and carried his naked Slayer to the bed. She giggled and pounded her small fists on his back, muttering something about how he was a caveman. Laughing with her, he climbed under the covers. With finessed skill, he made sure he returned the favor.

Much later, as she was quivering beneath him, he loomed over her, ready to fill her. "Look at me, Miranda," he said softly.

Those green eyes opened, filled with emotions that he didn't dare analyze. Lacing his fingers through hers on either side of her head on the pillow, he entered her. Nudging softly, he whispered words of passion, showing her with his body how special she was to him. Her eyes glazed over as she reached her peak.

"Yes, sweetheart," he said, overcome with feeling for her.

"Sathan," she whispered, clutching his hands as he loved her.

"Let it go."

Her body shot off the bed, and he clenched his teeth as her walls convulsed around him. Throwing back his head, he came, pushing further inside her, wanting to reach her deepest place.

Afterward, he rotated their bodies so that they lay facing each other, still joined as their breath stabilized. Gazing into each other's eyes, they communicated emotions that were too raw to verbalize.

When the first hint of dawn flirted with the night sky, Sathan rose to dress, hating to leave her. Sitting beside her on the bed, he woke her.

"Sathan?" she asked softly, her hair mussed as she looked up at him from the pillow.

"We're really going to have to do something about this temporary amnesia you seem to have when you wake." Smiling, he leaned down to kiss her. "I have to go."

Tiny teeth chewed on her lip, driving him crazy. "When will I see you again?"

Stroking her hair on the pillow, he sighed. "Probably not until after you attack Crimeous. I need to leave you here to forge your path. I don't want to do anything that detracts from your purpose."

She swallowed, her throat moving up and down. "And then, I'll return home, and we'll unite the compounds."

"Yes."

"And you'll marry Lila, and I'll marry Aron, and we'll all live happily ever after."

He hadn't told her about ending his betrothal with Lila, not wanting to murk their already emotional waters. "Let's worry about all of that when the battle is over."

Her eyes filled with moisture, and he felt his heart shatter into a thousand tiny pieces in his chest. "Please, don't cry, sweetheart." With his thumb, he caught the single tear that escaped from her gorgeous eyes. "I need you to be strong. You're so close. No one could have ever accomplished what you have in such a short time. You're the most amazing person I've ever met, Miranda. It's time for you to finish what you started."

Her smile soothed his splintered heart, if only a bit. "You make me strong. I've gained so much from you. I don't want to defeat Crimeous only to lose you. How is that a victory?"

His thumb traced over her wet skin. "It will all work out, little Slayer. Trust me." Lowering down, he gave her one last kiss. "See ya," he said, his throat closing with emotion.

"See ya," she whispered.

Leaving her was the hardest thing he'd ever had to do in a thousand years. With finality, he closed the door of her bedchamber behind him.

* * * *

Miranda cried softly into her pillow, her heart breaking at her lover's goodbye. Feeling sick, she stumbled to the bathroom and proceeded to retch. With her head resting on her arm, which lay limply on the seat of the toilet, she gave a humorless laugh at the mess she'd made of her life.

Here she was, about to embark on the greatest mission of her life, in love with the Vampyre king. If someone had prophesized this a year ago, she would've thought them mad. Absolutely insane.

Forcing herself to rise, she completed the menial tasks she needed to in order to start her day. Unfortunately, destiny didn't wait for heartbroken Slayers.

Once dressed, she headed out to find Larkin.

Chapter 31

Almost two weeks later, Miranda finished a grueling training session and threw her sword to the ground. "I'm done, Larkin. No more tonight. I need a break."

"Yes, princess," he said, his eyes filled with worry.

"I'm fine," she said, reassuring him. "I just need some rest. Even I am fallible sometimes."

"Of course. I plan to train the troops for another hour. Let me know if you need me."

Nodding, she headed back to the barracks and then to the stables. Heaving Majesty's large saddle on his back, she jumped on top and caressed his silky mane. What she needed was some space. As she rode to the clearing where they had buried her mother, she admitted that she wasn't in the right frame of mind. Ever since Sathan had left her bedchamber two weeks ago, she hadn't felt the same. Not only did she miss him terribly, but she had come down with an awful bug and had been puking her guts out on a daily basis.

Sadie had informed her that a terrible flu was circulating around the compound and had given her some concoction that was supposed to help her nausea. Unfortunately, it hadn't served its purpose. Miranda knew she had to get herself healthy. She would need all her strength to fight the Dark Lord.

Once she got to her spot, she tied Majesty's reins to the tree. As he munched on the soft grass nearby, she placed her palm on the thick bark, looking up at the branches in the moonlight. Was it possible that a piece of her mother's soul was here, being that they had buried her here all those centuries ago? She longed to hold her, to ask her for help in the upcoming battle. Loneliness swept through her. Yearning for Sathan and Kenden, she cursed their distance, wanting so badly to hug them both.

"I still feel her here," came a deep voice behind her.

Joy burst in her chest as she rotated around. "Ken!" she yelled, jumping into his arms, holding him for dear life. His chuckle rumbled in her ear as he rocked her back and forth.

"I missed you so much," he said, squeezing her tightly.

"You missed *me*? I thought I was going to die without you. Why in the hell did it take you so long?" Pulling back, she punched him in the chest. "If you ever leave me for that long again, I'll burn down your fucking shed. I mean it."

His brown eyes looked down at her, filled with love. "Not my shed. It's my favorite possession."

"I fucking know it. I swear, Ken, up in flames. Just try me."

"God, I missed you," he said, scooping her up and swinging her around in a huge embrace. Placing her back on her feet, he ran his hand down her hair before it fell to his side. "How are you, Randi? I saw the texts about your father. I'm so sorry."

"I'm okay," she said, her heart filled with intense pain. "I can't believe he's dead."

Kenden sighed, shaking his head. "He never recovered after Rina was kidnapped. I should've done more to help him secure peace."

"It's not your fault," she said, taking his hand and squeezing. "Sathan wrote him letters asking to negotiate peace several centuries ago."

His brow furrowed. "That can't be true."

"I found them in his desk and burned them outside the barracks. He caused so much death, Ken. How could he have done that?"

Kenden exhaled a large breath and shook his head. "I don't know. It's so sad. His mind was crazed from losing your mother. I just don't think I ever realized the extent."

"I loved him so much, even though he never loved me back." Tears welled as she struggled to control them.

"He loved you, Randi. I know he did." His thick arms enveloped her in a warm embrace. "Don't let your grief take that away. He loved you as best he could."

Several moments later, she lifted her head. Straightening her spine, she pulled from the hug and regarded him. "Did you find Crimeous' daughter? I know you wouldn't have been gone so long unless you were successful."

Worry crept into his features, and she stiffened.

"It's bad news," she said.

"It's...*unexpected*...to say the least. I'm wondering how to tell you so that you won't be completely blindsided."

"Just tell me," she said, crossing her hands to rub the chill bumps that had formed on her upper arms.

"I found her," he said, his features glowing in the moonlight. "She lives amongst the humans and has for almost eight hundred years. But she's only part Deamon."

Miranda's eyebrows drew together. "What does that mean?"

"She's part Deamon." His gaze drilled into hers. "And part Slayer."

Disbelief coursed through her. "That's impossible. Different species can't produce children."

"So we all thought. But she's a hybrid. I met her and spoke to her. I confirmed it with my own eyes, Randi."

Miranda puffed out a breath. "Okay, well that should only want to make her want to help us more. Right?"

"There's more," he said, lifting his hands to gently grasp her upper arms.

"Okay," she said, her heart fluttering, anticipating that his next words would change her world somehow.

"She's—"

"Your sister," a strong voice said from the riverbank. Slowly, Darkrip came into view. "Sorry, Slayer," he said, giving Kenden a dry look, "but I was becoming bored with the drawn-out story."

His green gaze swung back to hers. "She's your sister, Miranda. Borne by your mother after being raped by my father."

Miranda's body pulsed, adrenaline rushing through her as she looked into the Deamon's eyes. "And you're my brother," she said, finally allowing herself to acknowledge the small shafts of recognition that had seized her during their previous meetings.

"And I'm your brother," he said, coming to stand in front of her. "Good grief, Miranda. It took you long enough."

She studied him, emotion flooding her. "You have her features. Her eyes."

"As do you. I thank the goddess every day that I look like her and not like my wretch of a father."

Miranda clutched her chest as her knees buckled, the knowledge overwhelming her. Kenden rushed to her side, comforting her.

"I'm fine," she said, waving him off. Feeling anything but. "As you might have figured out, I've already met Darkrip," she said to her cousin. "Although, I'm just figuring out our connection now." She shot him a dark look.

He shrugged. "Would you have believed me? Hi, Miranda, I'm your long-lost half-brother from the Deamon caves?"

She breathed a small laugh. "Absolutely not."

With a nod, he looked at Kenden. "Your cousin is the most infuriatingly stubborn person I've ever met. How in the hell do you put up with her?"

"It takes practice," Kenden said, lightening the mood slightly. Miranda punched him in the arm.

Rubbing it, he regarded the Deamon.

"So, you met Evie," Darkrip said.

"Yes."

Darkrip's Adam's apple bobbed up and down as he swallowed, his expression filled with what Miranda could only identify as regret.

"And she is well?"

"She lives a good life among the humans. She's still pissed about you ordering her death though."

Darkrip rubbed the back of his neck with his hand. "It was a long time ago. I was trying to rid the world of my father's blood. It was a huge mistake that I cannot ever atone for."

"She has no desire to help us. This doesn't help our cause, as she is a descendant of Valktor."

"Shit," Miranda said, fully understanding the gravity of her newly uncovered knowledge. "The prophecy says that a descendant of Valktor will kill Crimeous with the Blade. It doesn't say which one."

Kenden nodded. "So, it could be one of you, or it could be Evie."

"I wanted to befriend you, to align with you, so that I can fight alongside you to defeat my father," Darkrip said. "Together, we have a two-thirds chance at beating him."

"Does he know you're plotting against him?"

"He suspects," Darkrip said, his eyes narrowing. "Which is why we must form a plan and work together to defeat him. The full moon is a week away, and if we squander this chance, we won't get the opportunity again."

"Then, we'll work together," Kenden said. "How often can you meet with us?"

"I have erected a barrier to my thoughts. A shield that won't allow my father access. I have also erected one for Miranda."

"How did you—?"

"Details don't matter. I told you I would do what I could to ensure your success. I can meet with you all each morning while my father sleeps after his nightly torture sessions. Let's start tomorrow morning. Somewhere private, where no one will discover us."

"My shed," Kenden said. "It's private and sits well off the main part of the compound."

"Yes. I've seen images of it in your cousin's head."

Miranda swirled toward him. "You read my thoughts?"

"Relax. Just images. Small snippets that come to me when I concentrate. I need to know where your mind is at so that I can manipulate my father."

"I don't want you in my head," she said, angry at the intrusion.

"You are a very private person, Miranda. You have no reason to trust me, but I assure you, I don't invade your thoughts. In this pissant excuse for a world, we all deserve our moments of peace and solitude."

She struggled to believe him, knowing that half of him was pure evil.

"Then, we'll start at nine a.m. tomorrow. At the shed," Kenden said.

"Yes." Darkrip gave a firm nod.

Pulling Kenden away from him, she spoke softly. "Leave me with him. I need to speak with him privately."

"Do you feel safe?" he asked, worried.

"Yes," she said, speaking truthfully. She didn't understand why, but she honestly felt that Darkrip wouldn't harm her.

"Okay," he said, placing a kiss on the top of her head. "Come find me when you get back."

Nodding, she watched him retreat into the darkness.

Alone with her brother, she faced him. Approaching him gingerly, she lifted her hands, framing his face.

"You look so much like her," she said, sadness threatening to overtake her.

"Not as much as you. You're the mirror image of her. It's unnerving."

Lowering her hands, she struggled with the breadth of her questions. "How did she die? Did she suffer terribly?"

"You know I won't answer that for you. You've had enough pain in your life. At least I can let you remember her fondly, as she was before he abducted her."

Studying him, she asked, "Did you deliver the parts of her body to me each year?"

"Yes," he said. She heard a rasp in his voice. "I felt you should have some part of her to bury. I would watch you here, with your cousin," he said, gesturing around them with his hand. "It brought me some sense of peace, knowing she was getting a proper send-off to the Passage."

"You loved her."

He nodded, slight and contemplative. "The only person I have ever felt emotion for. Besides you." Lifting his hand, he placed it on her cheek. "I find it paralyzing and unwelcome. Caring about others is a sure-fire way to get yourself killed."

She smiled, her heart breaking for him. "Please, don't be afraid to care for me. I'm so happy to have found you. To have another piece of her with me. You're my blood. I won't hurt you."

Sighing, he lowered his hand from her face. "Hurt is often bestowed upon us by those we care for the most."

An image of Sathan popped into her mind, and she admitted that he spoke the truth. Gazing down at the plushy, moonlit grass, she felt a rush of sadness.

"You're in love with the Vampyre king."

"No, I'm not—"

"It's pointless to lie to me. I see everything. Notice I didn't mention it to your cousin. I told you, I won't violate your privacy."

"We have no future, so it's futile to discuss it."

"As stubborn as you are, Miranda, I'm sure you'll find a way."

"What of our sister? Evie, you said her name was? Shouldn't we find her?"

"Evangeline," Darkrip said. "She is lost to this world. I hope that you or I are able to fulfill the prophecy. If we have to count on her, we're all doomed."

"You tried to kill her?"

"Long story. For another time. Suffice to say, I am still the son of the Dark Lord. I have killed many in my time, and a dark evil lives inside me. Although I care about you, I'm extremely dangerous. You would be wise to take caution around me. I don't want to harm you."

"You won't. Your Slayer blood courses through you, making you stronger than you know. I have it too, and it has led me here. My people are on the verge of peace. I have faith in you."

"It's undeserved, but I won't waste time arguing with you. We only have another week to train, Miranda. I will make sure that you and your troops attack my father where he is most vulnerable. I'll be inside, waiting to turn against him. It is imperative that you tell no one of our plan, even Sathan."

She frowned, feeling uneasy. "I don't want to lie to him. If he discovers our connection, I have to tell him the truth."

"No," Darkrip said firmly. "My father already distrusts me. He can read people's images in their minds as I can. I have erected a barrier for us, and I'm able to do this for you because we share blood. I won't be able to do the same for Sathan. He can't know of our plan. We're too close. Telling him will jeopardize everything."

Miranda chewed her bottom lip, contemplating. She felt so sure that the man she trusted with all her heart would understand if she told him the truth. Surely, that was the right course.

"No, Miranda," Darkrip said, tilting her chin up to his with his fingers. "It will cost us everything. Trust me. When this is over, and we kill my father, you can tell him about our connection."

"Okay," she said, anxiety burning in her stomach. "I trust you. I won't tell Sathan of our plan."

"Thank you," he said, lowering to place a soft kiss on her forehead. "I'm so glad you finally know who I am. It took me almost a thousand years to tell you. I was a coward, held prisoner by fear of my father's retribution if we failed. But with you by my side, I know we will succeed." Surprising her, he drew her to him for a hug. "You're my secret weapon."

Pulling back, she smiled. At her brother. The wonder of it filled her.

"And you mine. I'll see you in the morning."

With a nod, he disappeared. Miranda climbed onto Majesty's saddle, never noticing that they were being observed from behind the darkened canopy of trees.

Chapter 32

Miranda met with Kenden and Darkrip the next morning, feeling energized by the session. Their plan was clear. Darkrip would lure his father to a vulnerable spot in the caves, one that could be accessed from above with just a small amount of TNT.

The walkway to the cave was also short. This allowed troops to enter quickly and attack while others detonated the dynamite above and entered there. The two-sided attack would hopefully lead to a quick victory of the Deamon army, isolating Miranda and Darkrip with Crimeous while they wielded the Blade.

Miranda would attempt to kill him with it first, and if unsuccessful, Darkrip would try.

After the meeting, she went to the gym and listened to Alice In Chains through her earbuds as she sparred with the punching bag. She felt healthy and strong. Ready to ensure her people's future.

Later that night, she texted Sathan.

Miranda: Feel great today. Flu is all gone. Less than a week left. We're so close.

Heading into her bathroom, she prepared for bed. Several minutes later, under the covers, she glanced at her phone. Usually, Sathan wrote her back by now. He must be busy at the compound.

Pulling the covers to her chin, she settled for talking to him in her dreams.

* * * *

The day had also been eventful for Evie.

When she'd approached the Slayer in his hotel room, she had been annoyed. She had confronted him, told him to fuck off and gone about her life.

But as the days wore on, she became increasingly filled with fury. Partly due to the evil that always coursed inside her, and partly due to the arrogance of the Slayer. How dare he attempt to upend her life? To ask for her help? She owed the immortals nothing and seethed in her contempt.

Eventually, the anger consumed her. Unable to control it, she plotted her revenge. Thriving off the fact that they underestimated her, she conspired against the Slayer and his cousin.

Her mother had always called her Miranda. It had burned her soul with a pain she could never assuage. She had always resented that the broken woman her father mercilessly raped and tortured in front of her each evening could only find it in her heart to love one of her daughters. Her father had used it against her, taunting her that she was wretched, undeserving of any emotion, much less love.

She had worked so hard to move on but seeing the Slayer had conjured up every ounce of self-hate she possessed. He would pay for unsettling her, and the cost would be high.

Armed with the knowledge he gave her, she skulked back into the land of the immortals for the first time in centuries. The air almost choked her as she inhaled the stench of the world she'd once left behind. She hated it with her entire being.

When she first spied the Slayer princess, she was taken aback. The woman was the embodiment of her mother. It was off-putting. She couldn't wait for her to meet the same fate as Rina.

Her opportunity came several nights later, as she recorded the secret meeting between Miranda, the bastard Slayer who had rousted her from her respite and her brother. Traitor. He seemed to show true remorse for trying to kill her all those centuries ago. Smiling, she reveled in his weakness. It would make him easier to defeat.

Capturing a video of them on her phone, she returned to her hiding spot to edit the footage. Finally, she had everything she needed.

Tomorrow night, she would decimate the Slayer and his cousin. They had been unwise to mess with her. Closing her eyes over her shiny new brown contacts, she reveled in her upcoming revenge.

* * * *

Sathan worked at his desk, signing off the last approvals for the trains. Anticipating that they would have peace soon, he had asked Heden to also design tracks to connect Uteria and Restia to their compounds. He felt secure in his optimism, knowing that Miranda would prevail. His tiny Slayer was intent on saving the world.

Smiling, he signed the last document and lifted his head at a commotion at the doorway. A woman was standing inside, her breathing labored.

"Can I help you?" he asked, alarms sounding in his head as he stood.

"Yes," she said, advancing toward him.

"Stop," he said, holding up his hand. "I would urge you not to come closer. You have not been vetted by my soldiers, otherwise they would have escorted you to me. Who are you?"

"I'm sorry," she said, tears escaping her eyes. He noticed that her clothes were torn, her feet bloody. "I came as soon as I could. To warn you."

Hitting a button on his desk phone, he said, "Send soldiers to my office stat. We have an intruder." Then, he turned back to the woman. "Who are you? I won't ask again."

"I'm a Deamon. One of Crimeous' harem women. He has kept me prisoner for several centuries."

"And tonight, you were able to escape?" Sathan studied her, noticing her red hair, large breasts and full lips. She seemed to be in genuine distress. When she clutched at her shirt again, he advanced toward her.

A soldier arrived, and Sathan commanded him to bring a t-shirt from Heden's nearby room. The soldier complied, and Sathan handed it to the woman.

"Thank you," she said, sniffling as she donned the shirt. The action reminded him of Miranda for some reason, all those weeks ago, when she had stuffed herself into his oversized shirt after the first time they made love.

"You are so kind. I knew that if I made it to the Vampyre king, you would protect me."

Two more soldiers appeared at the door, and he silently commanded them to keep guard.

"How did you escape?"

"While Crimeous was busy torturing another girl, I ran as fast as my legs would carry me. I was able to steal a vehicle from his son, Darkrip. I drove as far and as fast as I could."

"That's very brave," he said, still not trusting her fully. "I would like to help you, but these are dangerous times in the land of the immortals. Do you have anything that proves who you are?"

"I have something that proves I'm your ally. As I drove through the land of Slayers last night, I camped by the river on their compound. While there, I observed a secret meeting between the Slayer princess, her cousin and the Dark Lord's son."

"That's impossible. Kenden is currently on a mission in the land of humans."

"I assure you, it was him. I took video with my phone. Please," she said, holding it toward him with her shaking hand. "Look. Watch. They are plotting against you. I felt that if I came here and showed you, so that you knew of their treachery, you would protect me."

Scowling, Sathan glared at her phone. The screen showed an image of Miranda speaking to her cousin, an arrow superimposed on top. With a sense of dread, he pressed the arrow, causing the video to play.

"We could've aligned with the Deamons." Miranda said. "He set our people back hundreds of years."

"Your strength is noble," Kenden said.

"Aligning with Sathan was a huge mistake that you cannot atone for," Darkrip said.

"Does he know you're plotting against him?" Kenden asked.

"No," Miranda said.

Sathan's heart beat furiously, unable to reconcile what he was seeing.

"There's another. Scroll to the right."

Swiping, he landed on another video. As anger began to bubble underneath his skin, he pressed play.

This video only featured the Deamon Lord's son and Miranda.

"The only person I have ever felt emotion for is you," the Deamon said, bringing his hand to frame Miranda's face.

Miranda smiled up at the Deamon. "Please, don't be afraid to care for me. I'm so happy to have found you."

They looked at each other, and Miranda said, "I have faith in you. I trust you. I won't tell Sathan of our plan."

The Deamon lowered his lips to kiss her forehead and then pulled her in for a hug.

"You're my secret weapon," he said.

"And you're mine. I'll see you in the morning."

The video concluded, and Sathan clenched the phone in his hand. Knowing the footage to be impossible, he watched both of the videos again and again, ignoring the woman as she stood beside him. His body felt torn into a million shattered pieces.

Finally, after he had watched both of the videos multiple times, he couldn't deny what he had seen with his own eyes. His beloved Slayer was planning to betray him. A pain so deep and dark, further into his soul than when his parents had been gutted in front of him, took hold. Growling with rage, he threw the phone against the wall, shattering it into multiple pieces.

"Sathan?" Latimus called, finally arriving at his office. Of course, he had probably been fucking one of his Slayer whores at the edges of the compound. Rage for his brother filled his chest as well, since he had forbidden the practice of sheltering Slayer whores centuries ago.

"Where the *fuck* have you been?" he bellowed.

For the first time in his life, Latimus regarded him with a sense of unease. How fitting that his stronger, war-driven brother would finally come to be wary of him at the same time the woman who had trashed his heart had betrayed him.

"Who are you?" Latimus asked the woman, ignoring his question. "Are you a Slayer?"

"She's a Deamon," Sathan said through clenched teeth. "She has video footage of Miranda secretly plotting to betray us with her cousin and Crimeous' son."

"Betray us, how? I thought Kenden was in the land of humans."

"Well, it seems that he's back. This woman escaped from the Deamon caves several nights ago. She came upon the secret meeting as she was trying to get as far away from the caves as possible."

"That seems convenient," Latimus muttered.

Sathan turned to his desk, flattening his palms on top, trying to control his wrath. "Take her to Nolan. Have him clean her up and get her some fresh clothes. Tell him to take her blood so that we can discern her bloodline."

Latimus shuffled behind him, and the woman spoke. "Thank you, King Sathan. I will forever be grateful to you."

Turning his head, he watched as Latimus handed her to a guard, holding her by her upper arm. "You heard the king. Do as he commands."

"Yes, sir." The soldier led the woman from the room.

Once they were alone, Latimus spoke to his back. "You are not yourself, Sathan. I need you to calm down and think logically. Several days before Miranda is to attack Crimeous, a strange woman shows up on your doorstep with a video of her betraying you? It is unbelievable at best. Questionable at the least. We need to verify the video."

Sathan gestured at the wall. "They're over there. On her phone."

Latimus picked up the pieces, shaking his head. He handed them to one of the soldiers outside the door. "Get this to Heden, stat. Tell him to reassemble all videos so that we can view them. Time is of the essence."

"Yes, sir."

"Sathan," Latimus said, advancing toward him slowly, "I understand you're upset. I would be too. But you're a smart leader. Your emotion for Miranda has clouded your judgement. We need to compile all the evidence before we condemn her."

Sathan laughed, angry and stilted, and rubbed his hand over his face, clutching his chin as he shook his head. "She wrapped me around her finger so easily. How did I not see it? How could I let this happen?"

"Calm down." Latimus lifted his hand to his brother's shoulder, stiffening when he pushed it away. Sathan clutched the small golden statue of Etherya that sat on his desk.

"Don't tell me to fucking calm down. I don't know what to believe anymore. Until Heden can reconstruct the videos, and you can view them with a fresh pair of eyes, I want our soldiers pulled from her compound. I don't trust that they'll be safe there."

Latimus straightened, his discomfort visible. "I don't think that's a good idea."

"I didn't ask for your opinion!" The walls bellowed with his scream, and he wanted to grab his brother by his large neck and strangle him as he cried in agony. Hurt filled every pore of his body.

"There are many things you don't know, Sathan," his brother said, his tone unwavering. "I won't let you sabotage yourself or her."

"So, you've kept secrets from me too?" Sathan asked, his tone nasty. "Perhaps you two deserve each other. What haven't you told me, brother?"

Latimus shook his head, disappointment swimming in his ice-blue eyes. "I won't stand here and let you accuse me of betraying you. We've had our moments, but you've always been my brother. The person I trust above all others. I refuse to let you say things that will damage that bond." Turning away, Latimus began walking from the room.

"Pull the troops from the Slayer compound," Sathan yelled. "That is a direct order."

Lifting a hand to his forehead, Latimus gave an angry salute. "Yes, sir," he said through gritted teeth. Sathan understood that he really meant *fuck you*. He stalked from the room.

Alone in his office, Sathan cursed, unable to control his anger. With a loud growl, he threw the statue of Etherya through the window, causing it to shatter. Wanting to find Heden, so that he could watch the videos again, he stalked from the room.

* * * *

Miranda was training with the Vampyre troops when she saw the headlights in the distance. Calling a halt, she told Larkin to tell the men to take ten. Jogging over to the vehicle, she was surprised to see Latimus exiting from the driver's side.

"Hi," she said, smiling up at him. "I wasn't expecting you. Is Sathan with you?" She craned her neck to view the passenger side of the car.

"No," came his short reply. Grabbing her upper arm, he pulled her from the car, further into the darkness where no one would hear. "Sathan believes that you have betrayed him. That you are plotting against him."

"What?" she said, her heart starting to pound in her chest. "Why?"

"A red-haired woman showed up at the compound tonight, presenting herself as a tortured escapee of Crimeous'. She had video of you conspiring with Kenden and Darkrip. I thought Kenden was in the human world." He studied her, his face impassive.

"He just came home last night. I swear. The three of us did have a conversation out by the edges of the compound, where the river flows."

Latimus sighed and nodded. "I was hesitant to let you keep meeting with Darkrip without Sathan's knowledge. He's cunning and evil. I was worried something like this might happen."

"You knew that he came to me? That he met with me secretly?"

"Of course," he said, his arrogance showing in his shrug. "I'm the greatest war commander this planet has ever known, Miranda. Did you think I wouldn't discover that you secretly met with him? My cameras caught your entire meeting with him on the night you first met Sathan. And I know that he met with you by the lake when we traveled to free the Blade."

"But you didn't tell Sathan." Confusion swamped her. "Why?"

"Because I'm not an idiot. His connection to you is plain to the naked eye. You share the exact same green-colored eyes. It's obvious that he is your brother."

"You knew. I didn't even know until last night. But somehow, you knew."

"I knew," he said with a nod. "And I understood why he was approaching you. If you aren't the heir of Valktor's to kill Crimeous, he will need to step in."

"Yes."

"You should have told my brother that you met with him in secret. Your omission has cost us all greatly."

Regret coursed through her body, choking her. "I should have," she said, silently pleading for his understanding with her gaze. "I was just so afraid. We were forming such a close bond, and I felt that if he knew, it would be damaged somehow. Fuck, I was so stupid." She rubbed her fingers back and forth over her forehead.

"No argument there. You fucked up big time. But we don't have time to dwell on it. Your actions have set things into motion that can't be undone."

"What do you mean?" she asked, fear entering her voice.

"Sathan has commanded me to pull our troops from your compound. Being commander, I cannot disobey a direct order. However, if you attack tonight, before I arrive to pull the troops, he won't be able to stop them from marching with you."

"But you're already here."

He gritted his teeth, glaring down at her in frustration. "You're smarter than this, Miranda. I hope I haven't placed my trust in someone who can't think quickly on her feet."

"You came alone to warn me. So that you can tell Sathan you tried to pull the troops but we had already marched."

Latimus nodded, regarding her, his gaze almost angry. "Don't make me doubt my decision to help you. Take the men and march tonight. I'll be back in an hour. If our troops are still here, I'm pulling them."

"We'll be gone." Lifting to her toes, she hugged him. Stiffly, he returned the embrace, patting her back awkwardly. "Thank you," she whispered in his ear.

Disengaging from her, he scowled. "Don't make me regret this. Kick that Deamon's ass. We're counting on you."

"I will," she said, watching him start the car and drive away. Inhaling a deep breath, she ran to gather the troops.

Chapter 33

Miranda marched, Kenden by her side, under the light of the waxing gibbous moon. It wasn't full, as she had hoped, but she was grateful to Latimus for his warning, knowing that the fate of her people depended on this night.

She had updated Kenden on everything. Being the calm commander that he was, he had summoned Larkin and Takel and they had gathered the troops. Not wanting to alarm the Vampyre soldiers, Kenden informed them that they would be secretly working with Darkrip and needed to strike earlier than anticipated to ensure a surprise attack.

Miranda had also texted Darkrip, whose number she had obtained in their meeting that morning.

Miranda: Sathan thinks I betrayed him. Wants to pull troops. Attacking tonight before they can be pulled. Need your help.

Darkrip: Understood. I will get my father to the designated area in 2 hours. Stay strong. We will defeat him.

Miranda clutched the phone to her breast, hoping his words were true.

She wanted so badly to sit and contemplate how quickly Sathan had believed the story of her betrayal. Did he truly think she was capable of that level of deceit? Did he even care for her at all? Surely, caring for someone meant that you gave them the benefit of the doubt, didn't it? Her heart broke with the knowledge that he might only see her as an ally. Indifferent. Only needing her to bring his people peace.

Unable to live with that conclusion, she pushed him from her mind. If she lived beyond tonight, there would be much time to contemplate his lack of faith in her.

She, Kenden and Larkin led their soldiers—two hundred Vampyres and a hundred Slayers—to the meeting point at the Deamon caves. They had traveled most of the way in large armored vehicles that seated many, brought by the Vampyre soldiers when they arrived weeks ago. As they approached the meeting point, the soldiers disembarked from the vehicles.

Marching quietly toward the meeting point, Kenden gave his orders. The Vampyres were to travel by foot, through the short walkway that led to the center of the cave. The Slayer soldiers would attack from above, blowing the top of the cave open with TNT and lowering themselves in by cables anchored to nearby trees.

Miranda would enter the cave as the troops fought, hopefully near Crimeous so that she could strike him down. Reaching behind her, she felt the Blade, sheathed on her back. Firmly, she clutched the hilt. She was determined to slay the Deamon Lord.

Led by Larkin and Takel, the Vampyres marched toward the entrance of the cave, their footsteps so quiet for creatures so large. Miranda watched them grow smaller as they faded into the distance. Following Kenden, she climbed up the path that led to the top of the hill.

Silently, the Slayers attached their wiring to nearby trees, pulling and testing to ensure they were secure. Miranda inhaled a huge breath, trepidation rising in her chest.

"You can do this," Ken said, coming to kneel beside her as she hunkered to the ground, the cable secured at her waist. "I have every faith in you, Miranda."

"I love you, Ken," she said, fearing that this might be their last conversation.

"Stop saying goodbye," he said, clutching her wrist. "I'll see you on the other side of this battle. When you've plunged the Blade into that bastard's heart."

Loud cries sounded from afar, and she knew the Vampyres had charged the cave. Summoning all her courage, she stood and screamed, "Fuck you, asshole! I'm coming for you!"

Dynamite exploded, blowing the top off the cave. Following her men, she jumped into the opening, lowering herself inside by the cable. Howls of war sounded all around her as her eyes adjusted to the dim light of the cavern. Landing on the dirt-covered ground, she assessed her situation.

These motherfuckers were in for a good ass-whipping. Pulling her sword from her belt, she charged.

* * * *

"See here?" Heden pointed at the screen as Sathan leaned over him, unable to discern what he was pointing to. "It's been edited. Whoever did it was awesome, but I'm more awesome, so I'm able to see." He chomped on his gum, driving Sathan crazy with the smacking. Moving the mouse, he advanced the video forward and pointed again. "This one's been edited too. Someone really wanted to make it look like she was betraying you, brother."

Sathan ran a hand over his face, doubt clouding his busy mind. Why would this red-haired woman go to so much trouble to deceive him? And why was Miranda meeting with the Dark Lord's son in the first place? Questions swirled in his brain until he thought he might go mad from the churning.

"He only wished to align with her. As Valktor's grandson, he also could be the one who fulfills the prophecy."

Sathan turned at Latimus' voice coming from the doorway of the tech room. "Valktor's grandson?"

"Borne by Rina after Crimeous kidnapped her. Darkrip is Miranda's half-brother."

Sathan stared at his brother, unable to contemplate his words. "I don't understand."

"Fucking A," Latimus said, running his hand over his face. "Between you and Miranda, I can start a fucking club for dimwits. He's her *brother*, Sathan. He aligned with her to help her. The prophecy states that a descendant of Valktor will kill Crimeous. It doesn't state which descendant."

Sathan swallowed thickly, struggling to understand his brother's words. "Why didn't you tell me this earlier?"

"When you were clutching a metal object in your hand and accusing me of betraying you? Yeah, I chose to pass. You were delusional with anger. I knew there was no reaching you."

Running a hand through his hair, Sathan exhaled. "Did you pull the troops? Shit. That leaves the Slayer compound open to another attack."

"Thankfully, as the smartest brother, I figured out a solution. Miranda marches upon Crimeous as we speak."

"What?" Sathan yelled, fear for her closing his throat. "She was supposed to attack under the light of the full moon."

"I wasn't sure you would be able to calm down before the troops were pulled. You left her no option."

Cursing, Sathan began to pace. Lifting his head, he trained his angry gaze on his brother. "Was her meeting with Darkrip staged for the video?"

"No," Latimus said, shaking his head. "She's been secretly meeting with him for months. She didn't think you would understand their connection."

Clenching his jaw, Sathan contemplated what would make his beautiful Slayer distrust him so deeply. Didn't she know that if she had only come to him, he would've helped her in any way he could? His heart clenched knowing that she didn't feel she could tell him everything.

"She marches on Crimeous now?"

Latimus gave a nod.

"We have to help her."

"You can't fight with her, Sathan. We've discussed this. Putting both of your lives in danger isn't an option."

"But what if she dies?" he screamed, grabbing his brother's shirt with both fists and shaking him. "She'll think I pulled my support from her. That I didn't trust her."

"Well, you didn't," Latimus said, shrugging.

"Okay, okay," Heden said, approaching them. Gently, he disentangled Sathan's fingers from his brother's shirt. "I understand your argument, Latimus, but Sathan really fucked up. He's finally in love with a woman for the first time in his life and he wants to save her. If it was Lila, you'd feel the same way."

Sathan felt his eyes grow large as he gawked at his brother. "You have feelings for Lila?" he asked.

Latimus shoved Heden away. "Fuck you, Heden. You don't know what the hell you're talking about. I don't have feelings for anyone," he said, addressing Sathan. "And I never fucking will. Look at you. Overcome with emotion. It's pathetic."

Heden rubbed his chest where his brother had pushed him. "Just because you're a coward doesn't mean Sathan is. She's your woman, brother. Go save her. Fuck Latimus."

Sathan regarded his youngest brother. "You're right. I have to go help her." Training his gaze on Latimus, he said, "Either you're with me, or you're not."

Latimus rolled his eyes. "You two are a bunch of fucking pansies. Come on," he said to Sathan, "we'll take the copter. I'll be ready in five." Turning, he left the room.

"Thank you, Heden," Sathan said softly. "I had no idea that he had feelings for Lila."

"Only for about a thousand years. You're pretty oblivious when you want to be, bro. Now, go save your Slayer." Patting him on his shoulder, his brother urged him toward the door. "I'll watch the compound and keep an eye on the red-haired woman. Go."

Placing his hand on Heden's shoulder, he silently thanked him. And then, he ran to the copter to help Miranda defeat their enemy.

* * * *

Miranda grunted as she wielded her sword. Striking down another Deamon, she searched for Crimeous. An evil laugh sounded behind her, and she turned, ready to strike.

"Hello, Miranda," the Dark Lord said. He wore a long gray cape, flowing as he seemed to float toward her. Everything about him was gray, from his long fingers to his skin to his lips. Beady eyes drilled into her own. "I hear that you have come to kill me."

Heart beating with fear, she threw down her sword and pulled the Blade from her back. "I have," she said, clutching the hilt with both fists. "I will avenge my mother and bring my people peace. You have terrorized us for too long."

He smiled, revealing teeth that had been shaven into sharp points. "Is that so? And here I thought I was only getting started."

Giving an angry yell, she charged. Swinging the Blade at him, he seemed to dodge her blows as if they were in slow-motion. "Come on, Miranda. You can do better than that. Even your mother fought harder as I fucked her."

Bile rose in her throat as she thought of this awful creature touching her beautiful mother. With a yell, she sliced through the air.

"I'm bored with this," he said, shaking his head at her. "Darkrip, take her hostage. Perhaps we can have some fun with her before we kill her."

Her half-brother walked to stand beside his father. In that moment, she saw the evil in his eyes. Although he favored her mother, he did share features with the Deamon as they stood side-by-side. She felt a brief flash of terror that he would betray her.

Then, he lifted a Glock, aiming it at his father's head. Pulling the trigger, he shot him point-blank in the side of the face.

The Dark Lord wailed in pain, bringing his hand to cover the wound. Stunned, he looked at his son. "You would betray me?" he asked, reaching out a hand to Darkrip.

"Strike him quickly, Miranda. We don't have much time."

Lifting the Blade, she pounced, slicing Crimeous' head off his neck with one sure thrust. His body collapsed onto the floor, his severed head lying beside it. Stunned, Darkrip looked back and forth between them. "Holy shit, you did it, Miranda." Wrapping his arms around her, he hugged her tight.

Unfortunately, this obscured their view, so they didn't see the Deamon's severed head realign with his body. Blood vessels reattached and skin congealed, as if drawn together by some unseen dark force. As Miranda disengaged from her brother, Crimeous grabbed her by the ankle. "Did I miss the celebration? Too bad." Yanking, he pulled her to the floor.

Darkrip howled, lifting the gun, and proceeded to pump bullets into his father. They only seemed to make the Dark Lord grow stronger. Lifting to his full height, he grabbed his son by the throat, choking him as he lifted him off the ground.

"Your hate makes me grow stronger, son. Don't you see? I thrive on it. It will fuel me to kill you and the Slayer."

Below, Miranda grunted and swung the Blade into his calves. Crimeous howled in pain. Angrily, he kicked her in the face and then the abdomen. With a groan, she doubled over on the ground.

"You align with *her*?" his father screamed, still holding Darkrip's throat. "Over me? I could have given you unlimited power. Now, you will die no better than your mother. What a disappointment. I should've killed you centuries ago." Scowling, he squeezed his son's neck, smiling with joy as his eyes began to pop out of his head.

"Let him go," a baritone voice warned. "I won't say it again."

Crimeous' head snapped, and he smiled with malice. "Latimus. How nice to see you. Have you come to join the fun?"

Latimus pulled the trigger of the AR-15, spraying bullets into the Deamon's chest. With a loud wail, he dropped Darkrip to the floor, sputtering to reclaim his breath.

"Miranda!"

She heard the voice, so faint as it called to her. "Sathan?" she called, her voice hoarse with pain.

"I'm here," he said, rushing to her side, lifting her to him. "I'm here."

Suddenly, an eight-shooter materialized in Crimeous' thin hands. Training it on Latimus, as he still sprayed bullets from the AR-15, the Dark Lord fired. Latimus fell to the ground in a large heap.

"Shit," Sathan said, leaving Miranda so that he could tend to his brother. "Hold on, brother. Hold on." Flipping him over, he assessed the damage.

Latimus looked up at him, his blue eyes swimming in pain. Softly, he croaked, "Watch out."

Turning his head, Sathan saw the Deamon cock the eight-shooter, reloading. Darkrip, who had finally stopped gasping, grabbed Latimus' AR-15 and began to pump his father full of bullets from his position on the ground.

"Yesssssss," the Dark Lord hissed, absorbing the bullets as if they were bubbles blown to him on a sunny day. "Your hate is consuming. I feel it everywhere."

Crimeous lifted the eight-shooter, training it on Sathan.

Sathan pulled a Glock from his belt, cocking it as he aimed it at the Dark Lord.

Miranda heard the click of the eight-shooter deploying. "No!" she screamed, unwilling to watch Sathan die in front of her. Forcing her wounded body to move, she threw herself in front of the man she loved.

Gasping, she felt the pain explode everywhere. And then, her eyes closed.

"What the hell?" she heard Kenden's voice above her, a million miles away. Metal clashed and bullets exploded, but to her, the sounds were so muffled, so distant.

"Get her to the copter," she heard Kenden say. "And Latimus too. Darkrip and I will get the Blade. After that, we retreat."

Someone was carrying her, jogging with her in their arms. She felt weightless, dazed, as she floated on the air. Slowly, she became aware that someone was slapping her face. Damn it, it hurt. Struggling, she opened her eyes.

Sathan's face was over hers, contorted in pain and grief. "Miranda," he called from afar. "Hang on. I've got you."

She coughed, trying to tell him that she loved him, that she didn't betray him, but she couldn't speak. "Don't talk," he said. She felt his fingers on the skin of her battered cheek. Gathering all her strength, she lifted her hand and touched his chin.

"Didn't...betray...you," she said, unsure if he could hear her.

"I know," he said, his eyes searching hers, wet with unshed tears. "I know, sweetheart."

She tried to tell him she was sorry for everything, for keeping her meetings with Darkrip a secret, but she just couldn't keep her eyes open any longer. Giving up her struggle, she gave in to the darkness.

* * * *

Darkrip pumped his father full of bullets, hating that he seemed to grow stronger with each discharge. Noting his own fucked-up reaction to pain, he shouldn't have been surprised.

"Darkrip, we have to go," Kenden yelled behind him. "Grab the Blade."

"This Blade?" Crimeous asked, bending down to grab it and hold it high. "I don't think so. I'll just hold onto this for safekeeping. I can't have all of Valktor's bastards coming to threaten me with it."

"I hate you!" Darkrip screamed through his clenched teeth. Finally, his rifle ran out of bullets.

"I know," the Deamon Lord said, lifting his hands in triumph. "Your hate is amazing. It flows so purely through you. Stay with me. Let me train you how to use it to control others. You could be so much more."

"Fuck you," Darkrip said, spittle spraying through his teeth. In frustration, he threw the gun to the ground and charged his father, determined to die fighting him with his bare hands. His father knocked the handle of the Blade into the side of his face. As he fell, he thought of how he'd failed Miranda. He'd wanted so badly to help her. Accepting his death, he exhaled.

Strong hands grabbed his shoulders, and he wondered if his father was repositioning him before stabbing him in the chest. Unable to open his eyes, he prayed that the bastard would strike swiftly so that he didn't suffer. And then, he succumbed to unconsciousness.

Chapter 34

Latimus awoke with a gasp. Jerking his head around, he could see that he was in a hospital bed. Wires and tubes were inserted in both of his arms. With a growl, he sat up and yanked them all out.

"Hey," Arderin said, coming over and placing a hand over his. "Stop doing that. You'll only make it worse."

"How the fuck can it be worse? Am I in Nolan's infirmary?"

She nodded, and he noticed she wore a white lab coat. "You were shot with an eight-shooter but thankfully, it only grazed you on the side. Many others weren't so lucky."

Latimus cursed, running his hands over his head. "How many did we lose?"

"I don't know the exact count. Kenden would know. He's been running point."

Nodding, he threw back the covers and stood, swaying due to his wooziness. He grabbed onto the railing of the bed.

"Please, rest," his sister said, trying to push him back toward the bed. "You won't do anyone any good if you're not well."

"Fuck that," he said, pushing himself to stand again.

"Don't curse at me!" she said, her mouth forming into a pout.

"Sorry," he said, placing a kiss on her cheek. "I don't want to fight with you. But I can't be in this bed. Where is Kenden?"

"In the barracks. He set up point there."

"Thank you. Don't let Sathan give you any shit. You look good as a doctor. If you like it, keep it up." Squeezing her wrist, he walked away, warmed by her smile.

After stopping by his room to change into fresh clothes, he headed to the barracks to find the Slayer commander. The one man who had been his greatest enemy, and his greatest challenger, for almost a thousand years. Spotting him, he walked toward the tables that had been set up.

"Did you escape with the Blade?"

Kenden's brown eyes assessed him. "No. Crimeous has it."

Latimus cursed.

"What do you need me to do?"

Kenden spoke with resolve. "I need to know why we lost. How Crimeous has grown so strong. Can you interview the soldiers and compile their statements? We need to piece their accounts together before their brains muddy their memories. Perhaps we can find a clue."

He regarded the great strategist. With a nod, he extended his hands. "Give me a notebook." The Slayer placed one in his hands. "You fought well in the cave. Now that we're done destroying each other's people, I look forward to building an even greater combined army with you."

"As do I," he said, his chestnut-eyed gaze firm.

Latimus decided he was okay. Stepping from the barracks, he got to work.

* * * *

Sathan watched Nolan as he stood over Miranda, gently cleaning her wounds. Kenden had helicoptered in a Slayer doctor, and she stood on the other side of the hospital bed. Miranda lay face-down as they cleaned the eight grisly lesions on her back. The Slayer, who was badly burned on one side of her body, sniffled as she worked. Sathan couldn't blame her, as he was fighting his own emotions.

Miranda looked so small and frail, lying unconscious in the white, staid bed. Her copper skin seemed to glow against the sheets, and he longed to hold her to his chest. Nolan had urged him not to touch her, informing him that her wounds were severe.

Swallowing thickly, he watched them work.

"Does he always stand and watch you with your patients?" the Slayer physician asked, her hands working to suture one of Miranda's wounds.

"Nope," Nolan said as he pulled a needle through the flesh at Miranda's back. "But he's not usually in love with my patients. I guess that makes this a special occasion."

Wanting to strangle both of them, Sathan left the room, needing to get outside and inhale some fresh air.

About an hour later, he went back downstairs, finding Nolan as he wrote in a chart. The Slayer doctor was beside him, furiously writing with her unburnt hand. They made a serious pair indeed.

"What's the prognosis?" Sathan asked, his voice raw. He dreaded the answer.

Turning, Nolan urged him to sit down in the chair beside Miranda's bed. "I'll stand," he said, and Nolan nodded.

"Do you mind if Sadie helps me detail you on Miranda's prognosis? She is well-versed in Slayer anatomy."

"Fine," Sathan said, rubbing the back of his neck with his hand.

"Her injuries are severe, Sathan. I won't sugarcoat it. As you know, I advised against trying to save her, but you insisted, so here we are."

Sathan tried to control his scowl.

"I advised against it because her chances of recovery are poor. Probably ten to fifteen percent. Not only does she have severe trauma to her back from the eight-shooter wounds, but she has extensive head wounds and internal bleeding."

"I understand," Sathan said, his voice thick. "What can we do to increase her chances? Will transfusing her with my self-healing blood help?"

"Unfortunately not," Sadie said. "We would've had to infuse her on the battlefield for that to be effective. One must be exposed to self-healing blood or saliva within the first few minutes of severe injury. Her body is in extreme shock. The only way it will heal is if she rests. And fights. She's the strongest person I've ever known and a dear friend. If anyone can recover, she can."

"But we don't want to give you false hope," Nolan said. "All we can do is wait. She is in a medically-induced coma so that her body has a better chance of healing."

Sathan looked over at her small frame, lying face-down, tubes attached, monitors beeping. "Can she hear me if I talk to her?"

"Some patients can, and some can't," Sadie said. "When they're in a coma, it's hard to know. Personally, I don't think it could hurt. If you want to talk to her, I would encourage it."

"I agree," Nolan said.

Sathan nodded, unable to continue as emotion swelled in his chest.

"There's one more thing we need to tell you."

Sathan lifted his gaze to Nolan, indicating he should continue.

"She was pregnant, Sathan. Most likely eight weeks along. Unfortunately, we weren't able to save the baby. Sadie ran a test on the fetus. It was a hybrid. Vampyre and Slayer. The first we've ever seen."

Clutching his heart, he fell into the chair, unable to stand on his wobbly legs. "How is that possible?" Shock reverberated through every nerve in his body.

"After analyzing the DNA, we can only assume that it's because your bloodlines are so pure. Most species' wombs will reject sperm from another species, because they see it as foreign. Because your bloodlines are both so pure, her womb must have accepted the sperm, recognizing it in some way."

Sathan ran his fingers through his hair, unable to comprehend that they had conceived a child. And lost it. Fury at his stupid decisions swamped him. "Does that mean we could conceive again?"

The doctors exchanged a look. "We can't be sure, but the probability is high that if she recovers you can conceive another child. We see no reason why her body would reject your sperm if it's already accepted it once," Nolan said.

Sighing, Sathan buried his face in his hands as his elbows sat on his knees, rocking back and forth. What an idiot he was. He had pushed her here, threatening to pull his troops and forcing her to attack early. Hating himself, he tried not to drown in his despair.

"There, there," the kind Slayer said, stroking his shoulder. "It will be all right. Take some time to clean yourself up and then come back and sit with her. Hearing your voice will do her good."

Lifting his head, he thanked her, determined to follow her advice.

* * * *

In the barracks, Arderin buzzed around the semi-private makeshift rooms they had set up for triage. Waves upon waves of soldiers were being coptered in, and she rushed to assess each one. She had been training with Nolan for centuries, enthralled by the practice of medicine. It was time to put her knowledge to use.

Another soldier was brought in, badly bleeding, with large, swollen lacerations on his face. "Put him here," she said, pointing to an open bed. Once he was laid on top, she examined his face. His wounds were deep but not life-threatening, so she decided to check the rest of his body before cleaning and suturing his facial wounds. Surprise washed over her as she spotted the tops of his pointed ears. Was he a Deamon? Had the troops mistaken him for a Slayer and loaded him in with the injured? Unsure, she decided to treat him, knowing time was of the essence.

Grabbing the scissors, she cut off his shirt.

His chest didn't show any major damage, so she checked the rest of his body, cutting off his clothes as she went. When she got to his underwear, she hesitated. As a virgin, she had never seen a man's genitals. Of course, she had spied on the soldiers as they bathed in the river. Curious, she had always tried to see their naughty bits, but had never really gotten a good look.

A severe laceration ran from the man's hip under his black underwear. It needed to be cleaned. "You can't be a healer if you're scared to assess wounds in private places," she muttered to herself. Deciding that it was her Hippocratic duty to suture him, she cut off the man's underwear.

She gasped, observing his thick shaft. She understood that a man was only supposed to be erect when he was aroused. Yet this man's phallus was stiff and turgid, blood vessels threatening to pop as it strained upward, the purple head resting just beneath his navel.

Her inquisitive mind slammed into overdrive, understanding that there was no way this unconscious man could be in any state of arousal. How in the hell was he so hard? Following instinct, she grasped the shaft in her gloved hand and squeezed slightly, wondering if it would ease the swelling. No such luck.

Swallowing, she felt a wave of shame rush through her. Telling herself not to be a sicko, she cleaned the red wound that ran from his hip, stitching it up. Her hands would brush his shaft as she worked, and it would make tiny jerks as she brushed against it.

Finishing up, she couldn't deny herself one more look. Removing her gloves, she grasped him again, needing to understand why he was so erect.

"Don't stop," came a low-toned voice, pained and gritty.

Gasping, she withdrew her hands, looking at her patient. "I'm so sorry," she said, embarrassment flooding her. Lifting her hands to her cheeks, they were on fire. "I don't understand why you're erect. I...it doesn't make sense. I thought I could give you some sort of relief."

The man's deep green eyes seemed to flash with desire. "There is no relief," he said, his voice raspy. "Etherya cursed me to be this way. Because I'm the son of the Dark Lord, borne of torture and rape."

As a trained clinician, she understood how painful that curse was. Although arousal was amazing in short bursts, being in a constant state would be maddening. The body would always be in overdrive, straining for release but never achieving it.

Lifting the sheet, she placed it over his lower body, covering him. "I didn't mean to violate you. I feel...awful."

The Deamon regarded her through slitted eyelids. "I guess it makes us even for me knocking you unconscious and dumping you in the river."

"What?" she asked, confused.

"The night of your abduction. By the river."

A flash of anger jolted through her. "That was you?"

He nodded on the pillow, breaking into a coughing fit.

"I could've died," she said, her tone furious. "Why did you attack me?"

"It was the catalyst that was needed. You served your purpose."

Her nostrils flared as she studied him, his indifference infuriating. "You still have some wounds on your face, but I'll be damned if I help the man who shoved me in a river and left me to die. You fucked with the wrong Vampyre." Calling over a nurse to help stitch up the man's face, she scowled at him, giving him her best look of hate.

His deep chuckle reverberated down her spine, causing her to shiver.

"God, are you this passionate in bed?" he asked, his lips forming a cruel smile.

Disgusted, she left him in the nurse's hands and stomped off to find another patient. One who wouldn't make her insides quiver and her heart pound with fury.

Chapter 35

Sathan sat beside Miranda's bed, his hand rubbing the soft skin of her upper back, above her wounds. Nolan had instructed him to leave her uncovered so the fresh air could help her heal. His other hand held the lower part of his face, and he felt his chin quiver as he looked at her.

It was all his fault. The entire fucking dilemma. If he had only trusted her and vetted the red-haired woman to be the liar that she was. Fury surged as he anticipated questioning her later. Heden had locked her in the dungeon, and he was waiting on Latimus and Kenden so they could interrogate her together. Unashamed, he imagined strangling her. It was no less than she deserved.

And what did he deserve? How could he have doubted Miranda so quickly? He had worked so hard to calm the passionate judgement that dictated the decades after his parents' murder. Over the last several centuries, he had prided himself on his dispassionate restraint. For some reason, his little Slayer had broken through the walls of his carefully-built control.

His fingers caressed her, moving up to her hair. Softly, he stroked, hating that she still had dirt from the Deamon cave in her silky tresses. Mentally, he made a note to ask Sadie if she could wash her hair the next time she checked in on her.

He couldn't see her face. It was encompassed by the plushy pillow usually reserved for massage tables, so that the wounds on her back could heal. If he'd had access, he would've lowered down and kissed her soft lips, murmuring words of love and asking her to come back to him.

Instead, he gently stroked her, barely able to control his emotions.

"I have rarely seen you in such pain," a voice screeched behind him. "Even when your parents died."

Sathan turned to see the goddess floating at the foot of the bed. "I love her," was all he said, unable to justify the hurt any other way.

"I know. I foresaw this ages ago, although it was murky. I knew that a Vampyre and Slayer royal would come to mate and bear a warrior."

Surprise flowed through him at her words. "That prophecy wasn't in any of the Vampyre archives or Slayer soothsayer fables."

"And what are fables, if not stories that are half-truths?" she asked, curly red hair seemingly on fire as it surrounded her white robe. "Archivists and soothsayers are fallible and malicious. Many stories were changed after the Awakening. As I told you before, there is so much you don't know."

Sathan inhaled a deep breath. "Will she live, Etherya?" he asked softly.

The goddess closed her eyes, searching, and opened them to train her gaze upon him. "Unclear. She is in the Passage now, but the portal has not closed. She can return here if she chooses."

"Miranda," he said, lowering his head to speak into her ear. "Please, come back to me. If you can hear me, please, I can't do this without you. Your people are so close to having the peace you crave. Come back to me and let me help you." Unable to continue, he stroked her glossy hair.

"Keep speaking to her. I hope she chooses to return. Stay strong, son of Markdor."

Like a cloud dissolving under the rays of the sun, she vanished.

Minutes later, Latimus and Kenden stalked into the room. Kenden walked to the head of the bed and stroked Miranda's hair, his expression filled with concern.

"How is she?" Latimus asked.

"The same," Sathan said, exhausted.

"Come," Latimus said. "It's time to question the red-haired bitch."

With resolve, the three of them headed to the dungeon.

* * * *

Miranda jolted awake, shielding her eyes from the blinding light. She gasped, needing air in her lungs, and brought her hands to her throat. The choking sensation ceased slightly, and she inhaled a large breath. Panting, she pushed herself up with her arms, the appendages wobbly underneath her. As her eyes adjusted to the light, she searched her surroundings.

A root from the large tree beside her rested under her leg. Water gurgled nearby, and the grass she sat upon was plushy. She was at her mother's gravesite. How had she gotten here? She fought to remember what had happened before she slept, her mind clouded.

"Well, hello, my dear. It's been such a long time. I've missed you so."

Turning her head toward the voice, she regarded the smiling man with the vibrant green eyes. "Grandfather?" she whispered. Confusion swamped her.

"Miranda," he said, his voice so kind, as he caressed her cheek with his hand. "My goodness, you are so beautiful. Perhaps even more so than your precious mother."

Heart pounding, she studied him. She was always down for a dream about her dear old grandfather, but something seemed strange. The setting seemed plastic; fake somehow.

"I don't think this is real," she said, looking at the man she only remembered in faint memories. "How can I see you?"

His smile was warm and deep. "You are in the Passage, my dear."

"The Passage?" she asked, her head jerking back and forth to assess her surroundings. "No, I can't be." Lifting her hands, she felt her face, testing. "Am I dead?"

"You are very close, child. You have only moments to make another choice."

"Another choice?" Her brain wasn't working, and she felt woozy. "What choice?"

"You can choose to return to your world or stay here with us in the Passage. Hurry, child. The window is closing."

Fear shot through her, and she struggled to piece together the jumbled images in her mind. Sathan threatening to pull the troops. Latimus helping her. Attacking with the soldiers. Cutting Crimeous' head off only to have it reattach. She had jumped in front of Sathan to shield him from the eight-shooter...

"You are not the one who will kill Crimeous with the Blade, Miranda. I'm sorry. It is another one of my lineage who will complete the task. You fought bravely, and I promise you, the day will come when he is defeated."

Looking at him, she asked the one question that had always eluded her. "Why did you murder Markdor and Calla?"

His eyes, mirror images of her own, clouded with intense pain. "Crimeous fashioned the Blade for me and told me he would release Rina if I killed them. When I returned to claim her, I realized he had no intention of honoring his word. I fought to rescue her but lost. When I reached the Passage, Etherya pulled me out, transporting me to the Cave of the Sacred Prophecy. She had recovered the Blade and helped me forge the prophecies. Once I was finished, I was unable to live with what I had done. I threw myself into the Purges of Methesda, hoping that my descendants would have the courage and bravery to set things right."

He smiled at her, sad and reverent. "You are so much stronger than I ever was. You will bring peace to our land once again."

Her eyes filled with angry tears. "All that death. All the war. Because you wished to save Mother."

"Love is not logical, Miranda. You should know this, now that you have experienced love with your Vampyre."

"It doesn't matter. We don't have a future." Her lips tuned into a frown as she pulled at the green grass at her feet.

Her grandfather chuckled. "Know everything, do you, my dear?"

"Not everything," she muttered. "I have to go back. Even though I'm not the one who will kill Crimeous, my people need me."

"Many need you," he said, and she somehow understood that he was referring to Sathan.

"Are Mother and Father here?"

"Your mother rests in the Land of Lost Souls. Your father decided to join her when he arrived here. He chose to suffer with her for eternity rather than to live an eternity without her. As I said, love is not logical."

Miranda sighed, drawing her knees to her chest. Imagining Sathan's face in her mind, she realized that if he were lost, she would travel to the ends of the universe to be with him. Fucking love. What a cluster.

"I'm so glad I got to see you," she said, squeezing his hand and lifting herself off the ground. Wiping her hands together, she shook off the dirt. "This place isn't ready for me yet. How the hell do I get home?"

Her grandfather stood and gave her a hug. Placing a kiss on her head, he stepped back. "You'll find a way, little one. I love you, Miranda. Your brother and sister too. He is strong, but she is lost. I need you to help her find her way. Never forget that my blood unites you all." Lifting his face toward the bright light in the sky, he vanished.

Biting her lip, she looked around at the strange, plastic recreation of her mother's gravesite, trying to figure out how to return home.

* * * *

Sathan growled as he clutched the woman's fire-red hair in his hand, pulling her face toward his. "What is Crimeous planning next?" he asked, spittle flying from his gritted teeth. "I won't ask again."

The woman laughed and spat in his face. Wailing, he lifted his arm to strike her.

"Enough!" Kenden yelled, grabbing Sathan's arm before he could pulverize the woman's face. Pushing Sathan back, Kenden spoke firmly. "She is our prisoner but she is still a woman. Don't go there. You're better than that. Don't let her drag you to her level."

"But my level is so fun," she said, opening her legs at her thighs since her feet were bound together. She gyrated on the chair. "Why don't one of you boys show me how big and bad and strong you can be?" Throwing back her head, she gave an evil laugh and then licked her full red lips. "Mmmm..." she said.

"I know what you're doing, Evie." Kenden walked over to stand in front of her. "I assure you, none of us are going to beat up a female. We just want to know why you're working with Crimeous. When I saw you in France, you said you wanted nothing to do with this world."

"I didn't, you piece of shit," she said, her jaw clenched. "But you found me and threw your immortal arrogance in my face. I won't have a bunch of limp-dicked immortals telling me how to live my life and who I should fight for. No one ever gave a shit about me unless they needed something from me or wanted to rape or fuck me. And you *dared* to find me and ask for my help in your pathetic wars? Fuck you."

As Kenden regarded her, sputtering and furious, with daggers of rage in her color-concealed eyes, something shifted deep inside him. If what she said was true, if she had truly been raped and most likely repeatedly, no wonder she lashed out like a wounded animal. She had been taught that life was full of pain. How alone would he feel in a world without Miranda? Where no one claimed him or cared for him? Did she have anyone who had ever shown concern for her? She'd told him in the hotel room that there was no one she loved. A wave of pity washed over him. He had rarely seen a soul so damaged.

But she was also evil. Manipulative and cunning. He would do well to remember that, lest he succumb to his pity for her. "Are you working with Crimeous?" he asked.

"Of course not. That bastard raped me from before I could speak. I hate him more than I hate you. I didn't care to help him. I just wanted to fuck you assholes over. Maybe next time, you'll check your arrogance and leave people well enough alone."

Kenden's heart clenched at her admission. No matter how evil someone was, they didn't deserve what she had been through, especially as a child.

"I propose we let her go," he said, still looking into her eyes.

"What?" Sathan screamed behind him. "No fucking way."

"She's here by choice anyway. She could escape these binds in a second. Isn't that right, Evie?"

A cunning smile curved on her red lips. "Well, look who's smarter than they appear." Pulling the ropes at her wrists and ankles apart as if they were made of feathers, she stood. Coming within inches of Kenden, she lifted her chin to look up into his eyes. "I will leave you alone if you return the favor. Consider it a prize I'm bestowing since you figured out the depth of my true strength. Don't try to find me again. I'll give you all the gift of sparing you from my wrath if you leave me the fuck alone." Turning her head, she gazed at the Vampyres. "It's the last time I will ever show you mercy."

Before their eyes, she vanished.

"No!" Sathan yelled, rushing toward the chair. "Where did she go? How in the fuck did she just disappear?"

"Her brother can dematerialize as well," Kenden said. "Their powers are vast."

"Then, that makes him dangerous," Sathan said, anger in his voice.

"He's protective of Miranda. Let's hope that calms his...urges. Evie, on the other hand, cares for no one. I trust her when she says she'll leave us alone if we do the same. Unfortunately, if Darkrip isn't the one destined to kill Crimeous with the Blade, we'll have no choice but to contact her."

Sathan picked up the chair where their prisoner had been bound and threw it across the room.

"He is understandably upset," Latimus said, as they watched Sathan run his hand through his thick black hair, cursing loudly.

"I know," Kenden said. "I've been trying to track Evie down in the land of humans for some time. I didn't understand the depth of their feelings for each other. My cousin has been alone for so long, with me as her only confidant. Although it's strange that she fell for a Vampyre, I'm happy she found love all the same. I hope she can heal and live to experience it."

"Me too," Latimus said, surprising Kenden by placing a hand on his shoulder.

"I have to get out of this fucking dungeon," Sathan said, stalking from the room, his body tense with rage.

They watched him exit. "So, my brother tells me you've invented a weapon to kill the Deamons more effectively. I'd like to see the blueprints."

"Sure," Kenden said, nodding. "I emailed them to Heden last night. Is there a place we can pull them up on a large screen?"

"Let me show you the tech room, my friend," Latimus said, patting him on the back with his large hand. "You're gonna lose your shit. Don't tell my idiot brother I said this, but it's fucking awesome."

Chapter 36

In the several weeks that had passed since Miranda's injury, Sathan had tried to run both kingdoms effectively in her absence, hoping that they would rule together when she finally awoke. Of course, this attempt at normalcy was difficult when one's heart was shattered into a thousand disconsolate pieces.

His little Slayer still slept, underneath the castle in the private room of the infirmary. Every day, as the sun set, he would rise and tell himself that this would be the night she would awaken. He visited her many times nightly, his moods often shifting from despair to hope to anger.

Sometimes, he would plead with her, begging her to come back to him. He would promise her anything, everything. He would let her win every future argument they would ever have if she'd just wake up.

Other times, he would yell at her, telling her what a coward she was, hoping to anger her so that she sat up and fought with him. He didn't care if he pissed her off, as long as she was alive.

And then, there were the times when he would stroke her skin, lost in the grief of her absence. Hating himself for putting her in danger. Promising Etherya he'd give his life for hers if she would just let her live.

After a few weeks, the wounds had healed enough that Nolan flipped her over, allowing her to lie on her back. Most of the cords and tubes had been removed, as she was breathing on her own. Only the feeding tube still passed through her pale lips. Sathan would place salve on them when they chapped, or brush her silky hair when he visited. She looked so calm in the large hospital bed, and he wondered where she was. She certainly wasn't here with him.

In the meantime, life went on, and they settled into some semblance of a routine. Sathan refreshed the troops at the Slayer compound, making sure that two hundred Vampyres guarded them within their walls. With Crimeous still alive, they couldn't chance another Deamon attack. Larkin took command of the combat troops at Uteria so that Kenden could assume a broader role, traveling between both compounds. He wished to work with Heden and Latimus, to combine their knowledge and make both armies stronger.

Lila was declared Kingdom Secretary Diplomat in a formal ceremony that he held in the castle's large banquet room. She had beamed at him as he'd bestowed the title upon her, and he felt that he was finally doing right by her. It only took him a thousand years. During the party afterward, he caught her absently eyeing Latimus as Arderin tried to pull him onto the dance floor, his ever-present scowl never a deterrent for his willful sister. Could he have been the one she spoke of? The one she had feelings for but felt they were unrequited? Making a mental note, he vowed to speak to Heden about it. Miranda had opened his heart to love, and he wanted everyone he cared for to experience what he felt for her. It was so precious and rare.

Construction had begun on the underground tunnels that would connect high-speed railways between the four Vampyre compounds and the two Slayer compounds. Although Crimeous still lived, and the threat of the Deamons grew, Miranda had gotten her wish. Their people now lived in peace.

The majority of the Slayers banked their blood freely. Barreled shipments would show up daily at the compound, giving his people more than they would ever need. At dawn, when he came down to kiss her before heading to bed for the day, he would thank her. His people were now fed and happy, unassuaged by war with the Slayers. All due to her. She truly was their savior.

Since Darkrip had betrayed his father, he could not return to the Deamon caves. Kenden informed him that Miranda would want him to be taken care of. Sathan was wary of the Deamon, distrustful that he truly had her best interests at heart, but he trusted Kenden. The Slayer had a way about him, calm and sure, and he was the closest person to Miranda in the world. If he thought that was her wish, he would honor it.

He told Darkrip that he could stay in one of the cabins on the outskirts of the compound, a peace offering of sorts. Several of the cabins were now vacant due to Latimus' release of the Slayer whores he had kept there for centuries. He had no idea why he'd decided to return them to Uteria, hoping it was because of his feelings for Lila. Perhaps with distractions out of the way, he could fully pursue her and win her love.

Darkrip had accepted and mostly stayed to himself. At times, he would come to the compound, sniffing around the kitchen for food or sitting with them to strategize their next steps against his father. On several occasions, he had observed him watching Arderin, his gaze cold and calculating. Mentioning it to his brothers, they had committed to keeping an eye on him.

Sathan would often pass him as he left Miranda's room. It gave him hope that he seemed to care for her. As the son of the Dark Lord, he was half-evil, and Sathan had seen how lack of emotion had damaged his sister, Evie. Hopefully, he was not as far gone as she and his Slayer side would prevail. Only time would tell.

Finishing up the last of his paperwork for the night, he set the pen down and rubbed his hands over his face. By the goddess, he was tired. Deciding it was time to visit Miranda, he began his walk to the infirmary.

Hearing a commotion as he neared the room, his heart sped up its pace. Fearing something was wrong, he rushed into the room, unable to believe what he saw.

His Slayer was sitting up on the bed, struggling to pull the tube from her throat, while Nolan tried to soothe her. Unperturbed, she grabbed the cord and yanked it out, her stubbornness as evident as ever. "No more," she said, her voice only a croak, flinging the tube against the wall.

"Please, calm down, Miranda," Sadie said, rushing to her other side.

"Leave me alone," she said, pushing them both away, one with each arm, collapsing on the bed when her energy depleted.

"We're just trying to help you," Nolan said, reaching down to her. Sathan almost laughed aloud when she swatted his hand away. His Slayer was awake and as combative as ever.

"Let her breathe, guys," he said, walking into the room. "Give her some space."

Those magnificent emerald eyes widened, filled with emotion as her face lit up. "Sathan," she said, her voice hoarse.

"I need to assess her. She just yanked out her feeding tube. She could've caused internal bleeding." Nolan looked about as frustrated as Sathan had ever seen him.

Coming to stand over her, he took her hand. "Can you let them just make sure you're okay? Just for a second, Miranda, I swear. Then, we'll talk. Okay?" He rubbed the skin of her hand with his thumb as he held it to his chest.

Inhaling deeply, she nodded, gazing into him.

"Okay," she said.

Addressing both doctors, he said, "Quickly."

They both nodded and proceeded to examine her. Sathan held onto her small hand the whole time. After a minute, they were done.

"She's fine," Sadie said, smiling down at her patient. "I'm so glad you're awake, Miranda. We all missed you."

"How long was I out?" she asked, her voice starting to regain a bit of strength.

"Almost ten weeks," Nolan said. "Welcome home. Everyone missed you." Looking at Sathan, he said, "We'll leave you two to catch up."

Once they were alone, Sathan pulled the chair up beside her bed, clutching her hand to his cheek.

"Ten weeks?" she asked, exasperation in her voice. "Holy shit. I was only in the Passage for a minute."

"I can't believe you were in the Passage," Sathan said, reveling in the soft skin of her hand as he rubbed it on his cheek.

She nodded, her dark hair sliding on the pillow. "My grandfather was there." She recounted her story to him, telling him of her grandfather's admission as to why he killed the Vampyre royals.

"Wow," Sathan said, shaking his head. "Two kingdoms destroyed because of his love for Rina. Thank goodness you came along to put us back together." He smiled at her, so happy she was awake, overcome that she had finally returned to him.

"How are our people? Tell me everything."

Sathan updated her on the past few weeks, trying hard to cover everything. When he was finished, she stared at him. "So, Latimus wants to bone Lila? Huh. Never saw that one coming."

Sathan chuckled. He had missed her snarky sense of humor. "Me neither. I was completely blindsided. I would've ended the betrothal centuries ago if I'd known how he felt. I want them to find what we found. What I hope we still have." Swallowing thickly, he squeezed her hand in his. With his free hand, he cupped her cheek, soothing the soft skin there with the pad of his thumb. "I'm so sorry, Miranda. For everything. I really fucked up. Badly. I was so afraid you would die before I could tell you."

"I'm sorry too," she said, shaking her head gently on the pillow as he stroked her face. "I should've told you that I was meeting with Darkrip. It was so fucking stupid of me not to. I just wasn't sure if you'd understand. Hell, I didn't understand myself. I was trying to figure it all out, but you're so smart and composed. I should've consulted you."

"I understand why you did it. I should've never believed Evie when she came to me. As you saw when the Slayer proposed to you, I'm possessive of you. I thought you had feelings for him. I didn't realize he was your brother." Slowly, he shook his head. "I feel like such an asshole. I should've trusted you."

"You should have," she said softly, emotion swimming in her beautiful eyes. "Why didn't you?"

"Because I'm new at this, Miranda. I don't know what I'm doing. I've never felt about anyone the way I feel about you. It's frustrating and infuriating and wonderful and amazing, all at the same time. I've never been in love before, so I pretty much suck at it. I know that patience isn't your strong suit, but I need you to be patient with me. I promise I'll get it. I just need to work at it." Smiling, his heart almost burst when her lips curved into a grin. She was so gorgeous, it took his breath away.

"You love me?" she asked, blushing.

"I love you. More than you'll ever know. I don't know what I did to deserve you, but you're stuck with me. I'm never letting you go."

"What if I don't love you back?" she said, teasing him.

"Then, I'll win you over." He waggled his eyebrows at her.

Laughing, she nuzzled her cheek into his hand. "But what about heirs and duty and all that stuff? Don't we have a responsibility?"

Growing quiet, he rubbed her as he contemplated how to tell her. "Wow. You just got really serious," Miranda said. "Just tell me. If it's bad news, I can handle it."

Exhaling a breath, he squeezed her hand. "What would you say if I told you we could conceive children together?"

Her raven-colored eyebrows drew together as she studied him. "It's not possible," she said.

"Actually, it is. We made a baby together, Miranda. It was about eight weeks along when you were injured."

Wetness filled her stunning eyes as she shook her head on the pillow. "No. It's not possible."

"Because our bloodlines are so pure, your body accepted my sperm. Nolan and Sadie tested the fetus. It was a hybrid."

Tears spilled over her cheeks, and he caught some of the wetness with his thumb. "The fetus? Did it survive?"

"No, sweetheart," he said, emotion clogging his throat. "I'm so sorry."

"No. Sathan, no." She began to cry in earnest, and he felt himself shattering with pain for her. Kicking off his shoes, he climbed in the bed beside her and pulled her into him, holding her. Huge sobs wracked her body as he soothed her, telling her that he loved her, that it would be okay.

When her tears subsided, she pulled back to look at him. Their heads rested on the pillow, and he caressed the hair at her temple.

"We made a baby," she said, wonder mixing with the sadness.

"We made a baby." Stroking the soft skin of her face, he let it sink in.

After several minutes, she spoke. "I was puking my guts out almost every morning. I convinced myself I had the flu. If I had known I was pregnant, I would've been more careful."

"Don't even begin to blame yourself, Miranda. There's no way you could've known, and I don't even want you starting down that road."

She nodded, her expression dejected.

"But while we're on the subject, there's something I need to say." He lifted her chin with his fingers, gazing into her, needing her to listen. "I don't ever want you sacrificing yourself for me again. I'm furious that you threw yourself in front of me when Crimeous aimed the eight-shooter. You're too important. I won't let you sacrifice yourself for me. Ever. Do you understand?"

"Stop bossing me around, blood-sucker," she said, giving him a weak smile.

"I mean it, Miranda. I'm not joking. I won't allow you to harm yourself to save me. Our people need you too much."

Lifting her hand, she stroked his cheek. "How could I not save you? I don't want to live here without you. That would be worse than dying."

His shattered heart fluttered at her words, slowly starting to piece itself back together.

"You're so fucking stubborn. If you won't promise me, then I'll send out a royal decree sentencing you to banishment if you ever try to sacrifice yourself for me again." Grinning, he figured he was half-joking. The other half of him wanted to ensure that she never put herself in danger again. He'd almost lost her, and he would do everything in his power to cement her safety.

"Try it. I'll put out a decree that you have to officiate my wedding to Aron."

Throwing his head back, he howled with laughter. Never had a woman made him feel so good.

Pulling her closer into him, he held her tight. "You're going to marry me, you little minx. And I'm going to bond with you. We'll have two ceremonies, one on each compound, so that it's official. You're going to be my queen and you'll like it."

"Wow. So romantic. I bet you fight the women off with a stick."

Laughing, he touched his forehead to hers. "God, I fucking love you, woman."

"Well, I fucking love you too. So, I guess we're even."

Chuckling, he placed his lips over hers, kissing her softly, gently. "I was so afraid you wouldn't come back to me," he said, breathing into her.

"I'm here," she said, gently biting his lower lip and causing him to stiffen with arousal. "You can't get rid of me now."

"Thank the goddess," he said, kissing her passionately until her lips were swollen and red.

Noting how exhausted she must be, he let her fall into sleep. Placing a soft kiss on her forehead, he rose and tucked the covers around her. Leaving her to her dreams, he went to his bedchamber and succumbed to the first day of peaceful sleep he'd had in ten weeks.

Chapter 37
Three months later...

Miranda looked up at Sathan, craving solace. Although she loved her people dearly, she was ready for some alone time with her husband. "How much longer do you think we have to stay?"

"It's our bonding ceremony, Miranda," he murmured. "I'm pretty sure we have to be here until the last guest leaves."

Rolling her eyes, she said, "Annoying."

Chuckling, he grabbed her hand, lacing their fingers. They sat in the middle of a long table, observing the dance floor of the large banquet room at Astaria. Tonight, they had bonded, in the traditional ways of the Vampyre species. The previous evening, they had thrown a beautiful wedding at the Slayer compound.

In front of both their kingdoms, they had vowed to love and cherish each other for eternity.

"It'll be over soon," he said, squeezing her hand. "Remember the party we threw here after your coronation? I thought Heden was going to dance all night, but even he tired eventually."

"When he started DJ'ing after the band left, I knew we were doomed."

Sathan laughed and nodded in agreement.

She had been coronated at a midday ceremony, four weeks after waking from her coma. After discussing with Sathan and the others on their newly formed council, they felt it best to declare her queen as quickly as possible. Since she hadn't killed Crimeous, and he now had the Blade, they didn't want to leave the throne open to any usurpers that still supported Marsias.

Their combined council, consisting of Kenden, Latimus, Heden, Lila, Aron, Larkin and Darkrip, had insisted she have the coronation in the main square, under the light of the sun, so that all could see. Although she wanted Sathan there, he had understood that she must be crowned queen on her own, without Vampyre interference. It was imperative she be seen as an independent ruler and the one true Slayer Queen.

After her coronation, she had thrown a lavish party, no expense spared. She felt it was time for the Slayers to celebrate again as they rebuilt their kingdom. That night, she had laughed and danced with her people, missing Sathan but understanding the importance of a Slayer-only festivity. Asking them to align with the Vampyres in such a short time wasn't as easy for some as it was for others, and she wanted them to know that she would always consider herself a Slayer first, and a queen second.

She had danced with Aron, thanking him as he held her for his unwavering support. After their dance, he'd led her over and introduced her to a nice woman named Moira. He'd explained that they were old friends who hadn't seen each other for centuries, and his handsome face seemed to glow as he recounted stories from their youth. Miranda had laughed at his tales, encouraged that he seemed enthralled with the pretty blond. She wanted so badly for him to find happiness and hoped that perhaps he could find it with her.

A few nights later, Sathan threw a party at Astaria to celebrate. She'd had a wonderful time and had been surprised to learn that he was an excellent dancer. He'd held her and danced with her until sunrise.

It wasn't as if this evening's celebration wasn't fun as well. She'd just been through so many formal events lately and needed a break from shaking hands and kissing babies. She loved her people greatly but being ruler ate away at her precious privacy.

"Your brother is watching Arderin again. It makes me uneasy."

Miranda squeezed his hand. "I've spoken to him about her, and he insists that he won't harm her. Or anyone else for that matter. I believe him. I know it's hard for you, but I want to try to form a relationship with him. He's all I have left of Mother."

Sathan contemplated, his gaze wandering over the dance floor. "And of Crimeous."

Miranda scowled. "I don't want to fight with you. You've been so kind to him. Please, trust me."

Sathan gazed down at her. "It's not you that I'm worried about."

She shot him a look.

"Okay, I don't want to argue. But I don't understand why you and Ken insisted he be on the council."

"He has powers we could never dream of and has studied Crimeous for centuries. If you give him a chance, I think you'll see that he's a huge asset."

He lowered his head to steal a quick kiss from her lips. "I'll give him a chance for you."

"Oh, did I win an argument? What's the tally?"

"Me a thousand, you one," he said, smiling broadly.

Laughing, she stood, pulling him with her. "C'mon, Vampyre. I've got a second wind. Let's show these people how to dance."

Hours later, long after the music had faded and the celebration wore down, Sathan led her to his bedchamber. Walking up the grand staircase, she looked at the man who was now her husband. How strange, and yet how glorious. This strong, handsome, thoughtful man was hers. Gratefulness swelled in her chest.

Inside the bedchamber, he helped her remove her dress, muttering complaints about how tiny the buttons were. He scowled as she laughed at him in the reflection of the dresser mirror, his massive hands no match in the battle against the miniscule pearl buttons.

Once free from the dress, which she found beautiful but stifling, she pulled one of his t-shirts from the drawer and threw it over her head. She started pulling the pins out of her hair, wondering how many Lila had slipped in there when she styled the fancy updo. Eventually, her hair was free, and she ran her hands through the silky tresses. Sathan's gaze met hers in the mirror, full of desire as she slid her fingers through her hair. Oh, yeah. She was gonna get some good lovin' tonight. She winked at him in the reflection.

Sliding on his large slippers that sat by the bed, she headed out to the balcony, hoping to catch the last stars in the night sky before the sun rose.

A few minutes later, Sathan came up behind her, placing a soft kiss on her neck, and settled beside her at the balcony rail. The metal goblet hung over the railing, firm in his hand. Every few moments, he would take a sip, and she felt a twinge in her stomach. She decided she didn't like him drinking a random Slayer's blood. She had become quite possessive of her Vampyre, and if he was imbibing fluids, she wanted them to be hers.

She blew out a breath from her puffed cheeks. "We're married. For eternity," she said, looking up at him. "Holy shit."

He breathed a laugh. "That, we are. Scared? Forever is a long time."

"Not on your life," she said, giving him a big smile. "We did it, Sathan. After everything we've been through—my father's death, the battle with Crimeous—we did it. Our kingdoms are at peace with each other."

"You did it," he said reverently. "You had the courage to free the Blade, to defy your father and reunite our people. You are the true savior of both our kingdoms, Miranda. Your fearlessness is amazing. I'm so proud to be your bonded. You give me a strength I never had."

Eyes watery, she stayed silent, unable to speak from the lump that had formed in her throat at his beautiful words.

Turning toward him, she pulled the goblet from his hand, placing it on the railing behind her. He was shirtless with sweatpants on, reminding her of the night they had first made love. Repeating her actions from that evening, she placed her palms on his chest, rubbing him in slow concentric circles.

Moisture rushed between her thighs as his body tensed, growing hard.

He brought his hands up to cup her head, tilting it back so that she gazed into his dark eyes.

"Last time you did that, I ended up fucking you. Be careful, little minx." His sexy smile almost made her knees buckle.

Sliding her hands up his chest, she encircled his thick neck with her arms. "I have a favor to ask you."

"Anything," he said, lowering his face to hers and stealing a tender kiss from her lips.

"Since my recovery, you've been so gentle with me, treating me so carefully. And don't get me wrong, I love it. I love it when you look at me like you are now, when you're so deep inside me. It makes me feel so special."

He lowered his forehead to hers. "I love it too. Believe me."

Laughing, she pulled back slightly, wanting to look into his eyes. "But you're treating me like I'm fragile. Like I might break. I won't. I'm strong and healthy and recovered. And as much as I like the touchy-feely sappy times,"—she tightened her arms around his neck—"I need you to take me inside and fuck me. Hard. Can you do that for me?"

Her hulking Vampyre literally growled, the timbre so low and sensual, sending another rush of wetness to her core. "Goddamnit, woman, you're perfect."

Bending his knees, he picked her up, and she laughed as she wrapped her legs around his waist.

Inside, they crashed onto the bed, his enormous body covering hers. Tongues mated as he pulled the shirt over her head. Kissing a path down her neck, he placed tiny pecks on the mound of her breast, stopping to breathe over her nipple. Ever so gently, he placed his teeth on the nub, biting her on the sensitive spot.

Groaning, her hips shot up, and he lathered the tiny sting with his tongue. Pulling the sensitive peak into his mouth, he sucked while his hand found her other breast. Thick fingers pinched her nipple, causing her to writhe against him as he lavished her.

"Fuck, Miranda. Do you like that?"

"Yes," she warbled, drowning in the tiny bursts of pleasure-pain he was giving her. She moaned as he moved his mouth to her other breast, biting that nipple with his teeth and then sucking to soothe the tiny prickle of pain. His fangs seemed so white against her tan skin. She found it so sexy, knowing that she was going to ask him to pierce her with them soon.

"I need you inside me," she said, her voice almost a whine. "Please."

He murmured against her skin, shaking his head no. Licking his way down her body, he kissed her inner thighs and then brought his mouth to her core. Her body tensed, and she pulled at the comforter.

His tongue bathed her, licking her up and down, sucking her. With the tip, he flicked over and over on her tiny nub, causing her heated body to go into overdrive. She called his name, needing to come, needing him inside her.

Suddenly, he flipped her over, and she landed on her stomach. Lifting her hips, he placed her on her hands and knees. Fisting his hand in her hair, he tugged. God, she loved it when he pulled her hair.

"Stay," he said into her ear, the deep-timbered command engrossing her.

The heat of his body left her back as he stood behind her. Cupping one round globe of her ass in each hand, he spread her open. Moaning, she turned her head to look at him. He slapped her on one cheek, the sound echoing, causing her to groan. Rubbing the sting on her bottom, he said, "I told you to stay. Don't move, or I'll do it again."

Loving his dominance over her, she tested him, wiggling her rear and lowering on her elbows. His hand slammed down on her ass again and then rubbed to soothe the sting. God, she was dying. She'd never been spanked before while making love and she found it thrilling.

Leaving a hand on the stinging globe of her ass, he ran his finger down her center, shoving it inside her wetness. She clenched him, showing him she needed more. Inserting another finger, she clamped them with the muscles of her core, moving her hips back and forth, wanting so badly to come. Fisting the covers, she lowered her forehead to the bed, unable to hold it up anymore since her body was shaking so badly.

His tongue replaced his fingers, swiping her folds and then pushing inside. Feeling something snap inside her, she came, flowing wetness onto his tongue as he pulsed it in and out of her deepest place.

As the last shivers of her orgasm died out, she heard him shuffling behind her, removing his pants. And then, he was there, his hard shaft at her entrance. Cupping her shoulder with one hand, he guided himself inside and began to plunder her.

Placing both hands on her hips, he slammed into her, over and over, hammering her harder and faster than he ever had. As she moaned below him, she thought she might die from the pleasure.

"Fuck, Miranda..." he moaned, his breathing labored as he pounded his body into hers. Lowering over her, still joined, he fisted her hair and pulled her face to his. Kissing her, he began to move again, the position creating a whole new level of ecstasy for her.

"Take my vein," she said, unable to see his reaction since her eyes had rolled back in her head from the intense pleasure.

"Are you sure?"

"Yes." Grabbing the forearm he was using to support his weight, she plunged her nails into his skin. "Do it."

He growled again and began to lick her neck, preparing it for his invasion. As his hips slapped into hers, he sank his fangs into the soft skin of her neck.

Thousands of tiny bursts of pleasure rippled through her as she experienced the most sensational moment of her life. Stars exploded under her closed eyelids, the pleasure of his sucking so intense as he pummeled her from behind. Unable to think, she started to come again.

Sathan moaned against her skin, sucking her life-force from her, as her walls convulsed around his thick shaft, tireless in its pounding. Bringing his hand to cover hers, he laced their fingers, clutching her. They were connected in every possible way. She had never felt such joy. Wetness filled her eyes as he stiffened behind her.

He came violently, erupting into her as he sucked her vein. Lifting his head, he shouted as the last drops of his pleasure spurted deep inside her. He collapsed, halfway on top of her, and started licking the tiny wounds he had opened.

Miranda shivered as his tongue darted over her skin, her body a mass of open-ended nerves that she didn't even try to control. Eventually, her wound closed, and he shifted a bit so that he lay on his stomach beside her. They gazed at each other, lost in their desire.

Sathan lifted a lazy hand, placing it on her head. He absently toyed with her hair.

"I think I'm dead," she said.

"If that's death, then I'm happy to go."

She smiled, reveling in the love that swam in his eyes.

"You let me drink from you."

Lifting a hand, she stroked his face. "Because I love you. And I don't want anyone else's blood inside you. You're my Vampyre, and I want to keep it that way."

He smiled as he rubbed her hair. "Thank you. I'm so honored to have had your vein."

She laughed. "There's my formal Vampyre. Always stuck in the fourth century."

He scowled at her, and she stuck out her tongue at him. God, she loved this man. "How did I taste?"

"So fucking good. You have no idea. Your blood is so pure. It is the finest I've ever had."

"Damn straight."

"I'll be able to read your thoughts now, as long as your blood flows through me. Is that okay?" He looked worried, as if he might have violated her somehow.

"I don't have any secrets from you. I learned my lesson on that. There's nothing I wouldn't share with you, so why not have access to my thoughts and feelings? That way, you'll know when I want to strangle you. At least, you'll be prepared."

His chuckle warmed her, and he pulled her closer to him. "But I'm always right. Just admit that and you'll never need to be pissed at me."

"In your dreams, blood-sucker," she said, biting her lip as she smiled.

His hand was now on her back, rubbing softly, as they faced each other, glowing from their recent loving. Miranda felt her eyes grow heavy.

"Come on," Sathan said. Giving her butt a squeeze, he gingerly rose and lifted her from the bed into his arms.

"I love it when you manhandle me," she said, her arms around his neck. He pulled down the covers with one arm while he held her.

"Don't I know it," he said, stuffing her under the covers and then joining her, pulling her close. "I can't wait to manhandle you again in a few hours. Until then, rest up, because I'm going to fuck you even harder next time."

"Don't make promises you can't keep," she mumbled sleepily from his chest. His resonant chuckle was the last thing she heard before her eyes cemented shut.

* * * *

Sathan held her, letting her sleep so that she would be rested for their next bout of lovemaking. A wet spot had formed on his chest as she drooled on him, her mouth open as she snored. He couldn't wait to make fun of her when she woke.

Rubbing the soft skin of her upper arm as she lay curled into his chest, he contemplated all the other things he couldn't wait to share with her.

He couldn't wait to fully unite all the compounds, Slayer and Vampyre, and see peace completely restored to their kingdoms.

He couldn't wait to walk in the sun again, more confident than ever that they were on the right course to make this happen.

He couldn't wait to see Miranda full with his child, her belly round as their baby grew in her body. A jolt of love washed over him as he thought of his beautiful Slayer carrying their heir. By the goddess, he was so lucky.

Waiting for her to wake, he murmured words of love to her, stroking her in the dimness.

Although Crimeous was still alive and there were obstacles to face, the future was bright. With her by his side, he felt invincible.

This was just the beginning for the immortals of Etherya's Earth.

Please consider leaving a review on Amazon, Goodreads and/or BookBub. Indie authors survive on reviews and they are so appreciated. Your friendly neighborhood author thanks you from the bottom of her heart!

Acknowledgments

When I informed my family and friends that I was leaving my twelve-year career as a respected and high earning medical device sales rep to become a fantasy romance novelist, I expected their jaws to hit the floor. Most did, but I was also surrounded with such love and support, for which I am truly grateful.

Thanks to Judy, for storing all those Judith McNaught books in the bottom of the bookshelf in your bedroom. I know you didn't want me to read them, because they were filled with...sex!...but I snuck in and read them anyway. They were also filled with love and beautiful happy endings and made me realize how rare and special true love is. Thanks for being my favorite mom. Love you!

To Bill, Helen, Vivian, Julie, Alan, and the Presnell/Hefner/Weaver clan, thanks for being my family. We're all pretty crazy but I wouldn't want it any other way. Also, I expect each of you to buy ten copies of this book on your Kindles. You've been warned.

To the JC crew—you all know who you are. Even if you don't technically live in JC, like me, we all make up one kick-ass crew of friends and I'm lucky to have you as my extended family. If you hate the book, we can burn a copy at the next Jets tailgate. I'll bring the lighter fluid.

To the OG Western NC/Owen HS crew, whom I've been lucky enough to reconnect with over the past few years, thanks for your support. I've tried not to make the book too "porny". Let me know. (Although we all need a small bit of porn in our lives, right? ☺)

Thanks to NY Book Editors and to Natasa and Dan for letting me drive them crazy with my negotiation tactics. Megan McKeever is such a phenomenal editor and I feel so lucky to have found her. She was the first person to ever read The End of Hatred and seeing it though her eyes was special and extremely helpful.

Thanks to Susan Olinsky for the amazing book cover and map of Etherya's Earth and to Margot Connery for the website design (and for talking me off the ledge when this lifelong Yahoo user tried to set up G Suite for her author email. Yikes!).

Don't let anyone tell you that you can't follow your dreams. Peace and love!

About the Author

Rebecca Hefner grew up in Western NC and now calls the Hudson River of NYC home. In her youth, she would sneak into her mother's bedroom and raid the bookshelf, falling in love with the stories of Judith McNaught, Sandra Brown and Nora Roberts. Years later, that love of a good romance, with lots of great characters and conflicts, has extended to her other favorite authors such as JR Ward and Lisa Kleypas. Also a huge Game of Thrones and Star Wars fan, she loves an epic fantasy and a surprise twist (Luke, he IS your father).

Rebecca published her first book in November of 2018. Before that, she had an extensive twelve-year medical device sales career, where she fought to shatter the glass ceiling in a Corporate America world dominated by men. After saving up for years, she left her established career to follow the long, winding and scary path of becoming a full-time author. Due to her experience, you'll find her books filled with strong, smart heroines on a personal journey to find inner fortitude and peace while combating sexism and misogyny. She would be thrilled to hear from you anytime at rebecca@rebeccahefner.com.

Books by Rebecca Hefner

Etherya's Earth Series (Fantasy/Paranormal Romance)
Book 1: The End of Hatred
Book 2: The Elusive Sun
Book 3: The Darkness Within
Book 4: The Reluctant Savior
Book 5: The Impassioned Choice

Prevent the Past Series (Sci-Fi Time Travel Romance)
Book 1: A Paradox of Fates
Book 2: A Destiny Reborn
Book 3: A Timeline Restored

Books also available in Audiobook and eBook format!

Please Follow Rebecca on Social Media! Find her here:

www.rebeccahefner.com

Made in the USA
Monee, IL
18 September 2020